Te

Tesla: A Portrait with Masks

A NOVEL

Vladimir Pištalo

Translated from the Serbian
by Bogdan Rakić and John Jeffries

GRAYWOLF PRESS

This publication is made possible, in part, by the voters of Minnesota through a Minnesota State Arts Board Operating Support grant, thanks to a legislative appropriation from the arts and cultural heritage fund, and through a grant from the Wells Fargo Foundation Minnesota. Significant support has also been provided by Target, the McKnight Foundation, Amazon.com, and other generous contributions from foundations, corporations, and individuals. To these organizations and individuals we offer our heartfelt thanks.

A Lannan Translation Selection
Funding the translation and publication of exceptional literary works

Published by Graywolf Press
250 Third Avenue North, Suite 600
Minneapolis, Minnesota 55401

www.graywolfpress.org

Published in the United States of America

ISBN 978-1-55597-697-2

2 4 6 8 9 7 5 3 1
First Graywolf Printing, 2015

Library of Congress Control Number: 2014948533

Cover design: Scott Sorenson

Translators' Note

This translation was done after the publication of the 2008 edition (second edition) of Vladimir Pištalo's novel. As we had the pleasure of frequently discussing the novel's main points with the author, he decided to make a few minor additions to the original text in order to better accommodate it to the spirit of the English language. This is why the text of this translation differs slightly from its Serbian original. The epigraph to chapter five from *The Republic* by Plato was translated by Benjamin Jowett. The quote from *Fasti* by Ovid that appears on page 42 was translated by James G. Frazer. We want to dedicate this translation to Svetlana Rakić and Elizabeth Weiss-Jeffries.

Contents

PART I. Youth

1. Father 5
2. Mother 8
3. The Snowball 12
4. Winters 15
5. The Visors 16
6. Brother 18
7. The Horror 21
8. Let Me Go! 22
9. An Aside on Flying 24
10. The First City 25
11. Secret and Sacred 29
12. The Theologians 32
13. Life's Novices 35
14. Metamorphosis 38
15. The King of the Waltz 43
16. Lusting after the Wind 47
17. In the City of Styrian Grand Dukes 50
18. A Tract on Noses 54
19. Kisses and Voltaire 57
20. The Light 62
21. The Impossible 64
22. And the Moon Is Your Neighbor 68
23. The Duel 72
24. A Different Graz 74
25. Disappearing 77
26. All Nature Stood Still 82
27. Do You Want to See Golden Prague? . . . 85

28. The Smart Cabbage 89

29. The Decadent 93

30. The Park 97

31. Without Love 101

32. The Crossing 108

33. The Light of the Mortals 114

PART II. America

34. The Deaf Man's House 119

35. The Death of the Skeleton 127

36. Nothing 131

37. Come! 133

38. To Bite Off an Ear 136

39. "The Dangerous Classes" 139

40. The Blind Tiger 144

41. The Transformations of Athena 148

42. From the Stuttering Diary 150

43. Success 153

44. Pittsburgh 157

45. The Engineers 162

46. The Blind Say That the Eyes Stink 166

47. For Everything That Lives 169

48. The Bearded Lady 172

49. Put the Hands in Jars of Water 175

50. Through Our Sister Bodily Death 177

51. After Never 183

52. The London Miracle 186

53. Paris 189

54. The Rush 192

55. *Ba-Bam* 195

56. The Sorcerer's Apprentice 199

57. The Glare 200

58. The Midsummer's Night Dream 206

59. You Will See! 213

60. The World Expo   217
61. In a Fantasy World   221
62. On Top of the World   226
63. People from the Hat   228
64. Così fan tutte   233
65. The Ice Palace   239
66. Pulse! Pulse!   241
67. A Hole in the Gut   244
68. Even the Soul   247
69. Days of 1896   250
70. Yen-yen   255
71. The Maelstrom   260
72. The Marriage of Dušan   266
73. The War   270
74. The Astoria   273
75. We Won't   277
76. Without Soiling Them   279
77. The Gorgon's Hair   284
78. Zeus Commands the Thunderbolt   287
79. Tesla Toasts the Twentieth Century   290

PART III. The New Century

80. The Fearsome Nose   295
81. The Big Nameless   300
82. The Belt   303
83. Pygmalion   306
84. The Span of a Dog's Life   310
85. Three Quiet Miracles   314
86. Behemoth   317
87. The Crash   322
88. Sorrowfully Yours   324
89. The Sinking Ships   326
90. The Swan, the Bull, and the Shower of Gold   329
91. Coney Island   332

92.	The Shaman Dandy	337
93.	From the Diary	342
94.	I Have Three Sons	344
95.	The Night Train to Wardenclyffe	345
96.	Distant Rhythms	349
97.	The New Automaton	351
98.	They Shall Take Up Serpents	352
99.	The Light of Shanghai	357
100.	For the Souls!	361
101.	East of the Sun, West of the Moon	365
102.	On the Too-Merry Carousel of the Merciless Sunset	370
103.	Millions of Screaming Windows	372
104.	*Um-Pa-um-Pa!*	373
105.	Lipstick	375
106.	The Nose and the Parted Hair	378
107.	Choose the Best Possible Life	383
108.	But People Never	385
109.	Only Pains Hear, Only Needs See	388
110.	Did We Live the Same Life?	392
111.	I Didn't Know How . . .	394
112.	Dear Tesla	396
113.	Whenever . . .	397
114.	A Letter to the Dove	398
115.	And Then	399
116.	The Honoree	401
117.	Forgotten	408
118.	The Bride of Frankenstein	413
119.	Because There's No Money	418
120.	The Ghost Taxi	420
121.	I'm Not Afraid Anymore	425
122.	The War of the Worlds	428
123.	The Furies	435
124.	Continuity	439
125.	The Bard	443
126.	Ghosts and Pigeons	447
127.	Pain, Time, and the Importance of All Things Cease to Be	449

Tesla: A Portrait with Masks

PART I

Youth

CHAPTER 1

Father

A Beautiful Phenomenon

What is this world?

What is the purpose of existence?

Such thoughts played in Milutin Tesla's head like kittens until he settled on the ultimate, frightening question: *What is "what"?* At this point the priest's thoughts died out and he started to feel dizzy.

The human mind is pragmatic—it's basically a tool, Milutin concluded. *A saw cuts trees. One can take a bow and play music on it, but that's not what a saw's made for.*

He advised his students to stop dithering and make up their minds. "I, for example, was about to graduate from a military academy," he told them, "but I quit and became a priest."

Milutin's first parish was in Senj, the windy city mentioned in many Serbian epic songs. There he kept telling his parishioners: "So I ask a favor and advise you for your own good: Don't be uncouth— you are folks endowed with common sense. Therefore, embrace the spirit of progress, the spirit of the people. Focus on liberty, equality, and brotherhood."

The parishioners ignored their priest's efforts to enlighten them. They griped about him being sickly and, actually, ridiculous. They were of the opinion that he was guilty of his ailments and wanted to fire him. The priest answered that being around people like them would make anyone sick.

"Do you think I get anything out of being here?" Milutin Tesla asked them sarcastically. "I wouldn't be much worse off if I moved to Bessarabia."

But instead of Bessarabia, Father Milutin got transferred to the village of Smiljan in Lika. During his stay there, he never failed to mount his horse to go administer last rites to the dying, even when the winter nights glowed with wolves' eyes. After a long ride, the priest would shake the snow from his mink coat and enter the sick man's shack. He would come up to the bed, bend over the dying, and speak in a low voice: "Now you can open your heart and whisper to me what weighs you down because God hears best the whispered word." And the rough men would open up their hearts and tell the stories of their lives in ways no one had ever heard before. The priest tried in vain to forget most of what he heard.

In his house buried in the snow, Milutin Tesla spent a lot of time reading. He read about railways, the Crimean War, and the new palace built of glass in London. For a local paper, the Smiljan priest wrote an article on cholera spreading from Dalmatia to Lika "like oil over a table." He also wrote about the "countless impediments" that a champion of public education encountered in the most backward parts of the Karlovci Diocese. For the *Serbian Daily,* he reported on a "beautiful phenomenon" created by atmospheric light, which occurred right on St. Peter's Day. Milutin Tesla described it as a waterfall of sparks that appeared both distant and yet so close he could touch it with his hand. The light left blue tracers behind as it vanished over a hill. At the same time, something rumbled loudly, as if a huge tower collapsed to the ground. The echo reverberated across the southern slopes of Velebit for a long time. *God's little phenomenon* "made the stars look pale." This occurrence gave common people a lot to talk about, while a more thoughtful observer (apparently Milutin Tesla himself) felt sorry that it did not last longer—this display of God's nature ended in the blink of an eye.

The weather was sweltering just before it all happened. Afterward it rained, but the clouds dissipated in the evening: *The air was cold, the sky smiled, and the stars glowed brighter than ever; but all of a sudden, something flashed in the east and—as if three hundred torches were lit—the light stretched all the way to the west. The stars withdrew, and it appeared that all nature stood still . . .*

The Parliament of the World

It always frightened the children when their father went through a transformation. Milutin forbade his family to enter his room when he worked on his Sunday sermons. All of a sudden his angry, deep voice would resound from behind the locked door, followed by a soothing female voice, and then several incoherent shouts. Anyone listening would swear that there was more than one person in there. The sermon was theater. Djuka Tesla and her sons were scared as they listened to Milutin alter his voice and argue with himself inside the locked room. Even the girls did not dare open the door. They were afraid to find their father transformed into unknown shapes. Behind the ordinary door, which suddenly looked mysterious, the priest whispered in German, shouted in Serbian, hissed in Hungarian, and purred in Latin, while in the background someone droned in Old Church Slavonic.

What was going on in there? Was it another "beautiful phenomenon" that called for an explanation? Did this Saint Anthony from Smiljan actually converse with his temptations? Did he feel lonely? Did this secluded polyglot see himself as *the Parliament of the World?* Did he practice delivering his sermon as a play in which he was both the tragic and the comic hero, as well as the chorus?

CHAPTER 2

Mother

A Spark from Flint

While Nikola and Dane listened, their eyes shone like fireflies. The head of a skinny chicken dangled from Mother's lap as she posed riddles:

"What goes through the forest without a rustle, through the water without a splash?"

"A shadow!" said Dane, always quicker than Nikola.

"What hates water?" asked Mother.

"Cats and clocks!"

The folktales Nikola, the younger boy, liked the most were "Justice and Injustice," "What the Devil Is Scheming While Pretending He Is Good," and "The Sorcerer's Apprentice." In the last tale, the devil asked the apprentice if he has learned anything. "No, I've forgotten even what I used to know," the apprentice replied. Nikola liked these stories because in them fools and younger brothers were really important. Djuka lulled him and his sister Marica to sleep by spinning yarns:

"As he traveled all over the world disguised as a beggar, Saint Sava came to the manor of a wealthy baron who possessed enormous riches . . ."

Nikola's eyes almost closed. He hovered on the edge of sleep.

"Then Saint Sava made the sign of the cross with his staff and the baron's manor turned into a lake . . ."

Was he dreaming?

"People say that every year on that day the water gurgles as a rooster crows from the bottom of the lake . . ."

Because her mother was blind, Djuka Mandić had to start managing her parents' household at an early age. Except for the stories her mother told her, she did not have a childhood. She wove all the linen in the house and took care of the younger children. To make things worse, cholera began to spread itself over Lika like "oil over a table." While her father was off administering last rites, the disease killed their next-door neighbors. The girl herself washed and dressed the bodies of five of them.

When she got married, Djuka had to shoulder the responsibilities of another household. Milutin Tesla, following the advice of some Greek philosophers, insisted that "wherever a priest takes up a hoe, the idea of progress is dead."

Thus Djuka and the crossed-eyed servant Mane tilled the church land.

"Don't aim for where you're looking, but where you want to strike," she told Mane as he split firewood.

Mother explained to Nikola that the drone bee mated with the queen high up in the sky, and that there would be plenty of bees if the queen could escape the swallows. "The enemies of bees are swallows and hedgehogs."

Once Nikola fell and hit his forehead on a chair. Mother kissed his triangular head to make it better, caressed him, laughed, and quoted: "A strike liberates a spark from the flint, which would have otherwise despaired within it." When his stomach ached, she put her hand on his navel and started to chant softly:

Almighty God, what a great event,
When Milić the standard bearer got married . . .
He couldn't find a girl to match his beauty
A great hero, he found a fault in each of the lasses
And he was about to forsake his marriage . . .

The pain melted away and the boy felt very safe.

During the day, Djuka always wore a head scarf. Every morning, she got up two hours before anyone else. She sat in front of the kitchen stove with its door open. Nikola woke up and furtively observed her as she combed her hair. The fire glowed through the door and cracks of the stove. He spied . . . Mother turned bronze from the glow. She became something else. He watched in secret.

His mother's life was deep.

Her life was soundless, like a tree falling in the forest without anyone to hear it.

The Trees

She turned to the forest on Bogdanić Hill: "Can you hear it?"

"What?" said Nikola.

"Can you hear the trees talking to each other on Bogdanić?"

"What about?"

"The birches sigh: How long till spring comes? When are we going to take off these icy shackles? The deep-voiced pines advise: Be patient. We'll take off our icy armor in three months. The streams will gurgle and you birches will sprout new leaves."

"What else do they say?" Nikola asked.

"The birches croon: The morning star will open the sun's gate and let the god Jarilo ride through it. Thus he will speak to Mother Earth: O moist Earth, love me, be my only one, and I, the sun god, will cover you with emerald lakes and golden sandbars, with green grass and swift brooks, with birds, fruit, and flowers, red and blue. Oh! You will bear me many, many children. With their new leaves, the birches will greet the rays of the spring sun and the gurgle of waters."

Nikola listened in awe and then laughed. "That can't be true. You're making things up."

His mother told him stories about plants instead of fables. She knew the herbs and insisted that many of them contained a spirit. Elm, fir, and maple belonged to the fairies.

"Where do fairies come from?"

"They come from the *mrazovac*," Mother replied. "That's why young men would never step on this plant. I'll teach you how to recognize it, so that you'll never step on it."

"Where do fairies live?"

"I've already told you what trees they dwell in. Yew is also a fairy tree. It grows only in unspoiled places," Djuka answered.

Nikola continued with the game. "How long do they live?"

Mother shrugged. "They eat garlic seeds and live until life becomes too boring, and when this happens they quit eating and die a painless death."

Nikola was proud that Mother was so knowledgeable, as if she herself used to be a fairy. He never understood why Father frowned upon the stories about a world full of radiant spirits in which plants were just like people. At that time, Nikola did not comprehend that those stories were not just about fairies and plants but also about gods older than God.

"When there's no church around, you can pray under a fir or linden tree," Mother pointed out to Dane and Nikola.

She created the world, and then along came Father and cataloged it in books. Father wrinkled his nose at Mother's stories. He wondered how such myths could have survived in a family full of priests.

"Let it go," Milutin murmured. "Let evil go, and embrace the good. Let illness and misery go. Turn to health."

CHAPTER 3

The Snowball

On the second day of Serbian Orthodox Christmas, Nikola and his two older cousins Vinko and Nenad slipped out of their parents' sight and went deep into the forest above Smiljan.

"The snow's really beautiful!" Nikola laughed.

"Beautiful, whatever . . . It gets in my eyes," said Vinko.

Nenad snapped at snowflakes like a young dog.

They looked down at their feet. After the climb, it was hard to tell which one was the most winded.

Covered with icicles, the boulders looked like monsters. A deep silence reigned among the pines. From time to time, the wind moaned through the treetops and a heavy white burden fell off the branches. It was as if the forest were breathing.

The boys plowed deeper into the snow, and their feet became soaked. They pushed their hands against their knees to help them climb up the slope. They scrambled on a big boulder in the middle of a ravine, on top of which the wind played with drifting snow dust.

"We shouldn't go any farther if we want to get home before nightfall," Nikola announced.

The boys clutched their sides and breathed heavily. On the rock in the middle of the ravine, the two very different cousins stood on either side of Nikola, each with an arm flung over his shoulders. Vinko was a quiet and squeamish boy with bags under his eyes. He disappeared once and his parents looked for him the whole day. Finally they found him sitting huddled in the church. In Nikola's family, men usually chose a religious or a military career. It seemed as if Vinko, with his quiet demeanor and bags under his eyes, had already made his choice.

His brother, Nenad, was hardly officer or priest material. Once he hoisted a big rock above his head and slammed it down on a turtle with all his might. When the Teslas' cat had kittens, he drowned them in a bucket. When Nikola created a windmill powered by junebugs, Nenad grabbed the junebugs and ate them.

The silence in the forest got deeper. The three boys breathed as one. The bitter air stung their nostrils.

Nikola was deep in thought. Vinko took his arm off Nikola's shoulder and looked down the ravine. Nikola noticed a vein pulsating on his temple. Vinko said, "At this moment a bear is sleeping somewhere in this forest. Hamsters and badgers sleep in their dens. Bugs sleep under frozen roots. And underneath all of that lies a dormant force."

Nenad also took his arm off of Nikola's shoulders and almost choked: "I'd love . . . I'd love to be a wolf in this forest."

He threw his head back, craned his neck, and howled:

"Aaaaarrroooooo!"

When his cousins let him go, Nikola felt cold and naked.

"Let's throw snowballs down the hill," he said impatiently, "to see whose goes the farthest."

"Sure."

The snow crunched between his palms. Unlike his two cousins, he did not have gloves. While he made snowballs and threw them down the hill, his fingers grew numb. As the snowballs rolled along the slope, they gathered more snow and got bigger, but most of them grew too heavy and soon stopped.

"Look at mine," Nenad squeaked. "It's the best!"

"It's crap!" Vinko yelled. "Look at mine!"

"Yours stopped too!"

"Sure it did, it hit a stump."

Nikola's hands ached from the cold. He felt as though his palms were stripped of flesh—it was as if he packed snow with clenched, frozen bones. He shoved his hands under his armpits trying to warm them up. Finally, he put them in his pants, underneath his balls.

"Look at my snowball!" yelped Nenad.

13

"Look at mine!" shouted Vinko.

Nikola did not look. He pulled his cold hands from between his thighs. Silently, he made a snowball. He threw it like he was throwing dice. The snowball bowled down the slope, gathering snow on the way. It quickly spun. It quickly grew. It turned into a huge ball of snow that whooshed and scudded. Then it stopped whooshing—it roared, storming down the ravine.

When the monstrous, rushing snowball started to amass topsoil the boys realized that things had become serious.

"Oh God, oh God," whispered Vinko shrilly. "It's turning into an avalanche!"

The snowball turned into a natural disaster. It left a jagged trail of ruination and effortlessly brushed away a row of birches and pines at the far end of the slope. Thundering and sweeping everything before it, it disappeared from sight, moving toward the village. The entire mountain shook from the impact.

At that moment, it became apparent that one of Nikola's cousins was frightened by and the other delighted with life.

"Yee-haw!" whooped Nenad the destroyer, as if the fear physically pleased him.

While the earth shook under their feet, Vinko started to cry and plead, "O God, save us from another avalanche from up the slope . . . God, please don't let this one destroy the village down there!"

Nikola stood entranced. He also felt ecstatic from the destruction. He was intoxicated by the release of this natural force.

The little white thing he tossed down the hill with his own hand tore out boulders and swept down pines as if they were matchsticks. It moved matter and released a primal force. Nothing could stop that snowball once it started down the slope at that unique, exact angle. Nikola got goose bumps as he stood between the frightened Vinko and the enthusiastic Nenad.

"Destiny," he whispered in awe.

CHAPTER 4

Winters

God was still busy with creation in Smiljan. Villagers were as tall as giants. People's words were not dead—they were alive. Nature was primal. The smell of frost was a divine greeting.

Back then, winters were colder than those that came later. They felt more Russian or Finnish than Balkan. To Nikola it seemed that the villagers left a sparkling trail as they tromped through the snow. A snowball that hit a tree exploded into a flash of light. One evening, something odd happened with the tomcat that Niko liked to hug and wrestle. On his way to light the candles, the boy rubbed the cat and felt sparks crackling underneath his palm. He looked from left to right, following his hand. Light shimmered between his fingers and the cat's back. This was yet another "beautiful phenomenon" related to God's work.

"Would you look at that!" exclaimed Djuka.

Milutin figured out that what they saw—and there was no doubt that they all saw it—was electricity. He explained that peculiarity the best he could.

That was the first time it occurred to Nikola that Nature was like a huge cat. He wondered: who's rubbing her?

"We live in an illuminated world," whispered Milutin to his wife and son.

"What does 'illuminated' mean?" Djuka whispered back.

"Lit from within."

CHAPTER 5

The Visors

When he approaches the light his eyes will be dazzled, and he will not be able to see anything at all of what are now called realities.

Plato, *The Republic,* **book VII**
(trans. Benjamin Jowett)

"It comes out of nowhere!" little Nikola complained to his parents.

He closed his eyes, and light engulfed him. The entire world dissolved in liquid fire.

"I'm disappearing. I'm getting absorbed by light," the boy whispered.

He struggled to return to the precious world of daily existence.

"This thing has a will of its own!" he cried.

"Does it feel like it does when you turn your face toward the sun with your eyes closed?" asked Mother.

"In a way. A golden visor falls over my eyes while they're open. There's a flash and I'm floating in light."

Milutin wondered, *Could it be epilepsy?*

It turned out to be something like the Tabor Light in the Eastern Church. The light that annihilated all the laws of the universe with one swoop fell on Nikola's eyes. Seen from within, a golden hemisphere replaced his face. That illumination that shook the foundation of life and annihilated the physical world frightened Father Milutin.

This was when Dane, for the first time, took the side of his brother, who was younger by eight years.

"No. What Nikola's talking about happens to me too."

The parents felt relieved. Whatever happened to their prince could not be bad.

"Do images appear along with the flashes of light?" Dane asked his brother.

Nikola nodded.

"Don't be afraid of them," Dane said. "Let yourself go."

With teary eyes, Nikola stared at him and wailed, "But that is the scariest of all!"

CHAPTER 6

Brother

"Who's this handsome boy?" visitors asked, smiling at Dane Tesla.

They turned toward younger Nikola and said, "And who's this?"

The brothers resembled each other, but no one noticed that. Auntie Deva, who was snaggletoothed like a boar, preferred Dane. So did Luka Bogić, the red-faced hunter who sometimes pointed his gun at children and threatened to kill them. The gray-bearded Father Alagić, who snorted as he laughed, also liked Dane better.

In front of visitors, Milutin never failed to boast about Dane's intelligence.

"How many priest vestments hang on your mother's family tree?" he asked impatiently.

"Thirty-six."

"Who was the first one?"

"Tomo Mandić."

"That's my clever boy!"

When he started school, Dane never had to read a page more than once. Whatever he said was well said.

"The prince!" his relatives would say.

"Will he become a patriarch?" the sly Luka Bogić asked.

"He can be whatever he wants to be," Milutin Tesla responded soberly. "But let him become a good man."

There were no signs that Dane was bored by these performances for his father's friends, even after he reached his teens. Whenever the exquisite Danilo Trbojević, the excellent Danilo Popović, or the diligent Damjan Čučković came to visit, he recited Schiller's poems in German, including "Unter Den Linden," "Die Ideale," or "Das Lied von der Glocke."

"It's obvious he comprehends every single line," praised Čučković.

"Both comprehends and feels," added Popović, who was himself a poet.

But the real mental exercises were conducted when Milutin was alone with his son. He demanded that the boy learn texts by rote, practice rhetorical skills, and read people's minds. As a cadet in the military academy, Tesla observed his teacher, a Jesuit, get into a student's face and command, "Refute Aristotle!"

He repeated the same drill with Dane. In the voice of the former officer, he ordered, "Refute Descartes!"

Dane had new growth shadowing his upper lip. He looked out the window and began: "Descartes doubted his own existence, suspecting all visible things to be merely props that a malicious demon placed around him."

The boy paused deliberately. Then he raised his voice: "Tormented by his universal doubt, the philosopher searched for certainty. Excited and perhaps defiant, he uttered the famous sentence, 'I think, therefore I am.'" Here Dane smiled and pointed out: "The problem that tortured Descartes was nothing new. In the fourteenth century, John of Mirecourt postulated, 'If I deny or even doubt my own existence, I contradict myself. Is it possible to doubt one's existence without implicitly confirming it?' Saint Augustine foresaw Descartes's dilemma when he exclaimed, 'If I am deceived, I am!'"

Dane Tesla raised his arm and, like a matador killing a bull, concluded: "After all, Descartes was a thinker, and it does not come as a surprise that for him thinking was the source of certainty. Had he been a gardener, he would be looking for confirmation of his existence in his garden. As a musician, he would say, 'I play, therefore I am.'"

"Not bad," Milutin muttered, while his face was saying, "That's exquisite, son! That's top notch!"

And who was that big-eared boy with a triangular head, peering at his father and his brilliant brother from behind the door?

Nikola did not like to be called Niko, because in Serbian it meant "nobody"—the one who does not exist. Through the half-open door, the boy watched his brother, who was turning into a young man. Dane was as handsome as Young Joseph. How could one person be blessed with so many gifts? Who endowed them? Dane was mysterious with the mystery of youth. He felt blood rushing through his veins. Surprised by himself, he strained his ears to hear the voices in his own breathing. Nikola had to ask him three times before he got a response. Then he shrugged his shoulders and turned to leave.

"Where are you going?" Dane called him back.

"I'm going to eat."

"Why? You'll only get hungry again."

Nikola laughed. His brother remained serious. When Dane's smile eventually shone through, Nikola forgot himself and his envy. He never encountered such grace again.

If he were not around, it occurred to Nikola more than once, *what kind of world would this be? Would the sun still shine?*

Perhaps Nikola would be important in that thrilling world? Perhaps he would seem bright in that horrifying world without Dane?

CHAPTER 7

The Horror

Dane leaned over a steep flight of stairs and called the servant, Mane, who was taking care of the brandy in the cellar. Nikola ran toward his brother, reaching for him. The sound of Dane's fall merged with the dull sound of something breaking. As he lay on his back at the bottom of the stairs, Dane pointed a finger at Nikola.

Whenever he talked about that moment, Nikola spread his arms and whispered in an agitated voice, "But that wasn't true!"

Mother's heels clattered as she ran down the stairs. She slowly removed her lips from her son's temple and looked at Father.

Accusing eyes multiplied around Nikola.

Something whispered into his ear: *The horror!*

Something growled from the dark: *The horror!*

Something screamed in his mind: *The horror!*

The news spread to the neighboring houses. People started to bang on the door. The Young Joseph, the incomparable Danilo Tesla was fifteen when he died. Visitors filled the house and whispered condolences.

"The prince!" they wept over the casket.

They could not say to God, "Don't aim for where you're looking, but where you want to strike." Mane served drinks to the teary-eyed relatives.

The suit Dane was to wear at his graduation turned into his funeral suit. Andja Alagić, who lived next door, stood by Djuka as she washed her dead son's body and asked, "How can you do that?"

Djuka gave her a dark look and said, "Those who can't do this should never have been born."

CHAPTER 8

Let Me Go!

The chapel was right in the middle of Nikola's room. The open casket was next to his bed. His brother was lying in the casket. His face was the color of tapers. He looked real, and seven-year-old Nikola stretched his arm to pat him on the forehead. His hand went through Dane's face, but the face did not disappear. Nikola started to cry.

"Let me go," he whispered into his brother's ear. Dane refused to go away. "Please, let me go."

Didn't his mother always insist that it takes a peg to drive another peg out from the hole? It had happened before—someone would utter a word and the image of the physical object would appear in his head. Nikola was aware that what he saw was conjured, so he tried to protect himself with his own imagination.

He envisioned Mother's face over the face of his dead brother. When his mother—a pure soul—appeared in the room, he felt greatly relieved. She stayed there for a while and then faded out. The horrifying face from the casket replaced his mother's image. Nikola kept repeating the word *Mother* and she came again, but this time paler.

He said *Father* and the tall man with eyeglasses obediently came into his room. Then he vanished but was called back. When Father faded away, he whom Nikola feared appeared again.

It was bad. And when it was bad, you heard the music only for yourself. It was so frightening that he didn't dare to feel scared. Every night, Nikola tripped over the same vision. The phantom tormented him even during the day. This obsession made living difficult for him. He fought back. The obsession persisted. He had to persist even harder.

He projected other images over *that* image. Thus he invoked all the people he knew, including his detested aunt Deva and the menacing Luka Bogić, who was still less frightening than the dead Dane. Finally, nothing he had actually seen in his small world was left to help him confront his brother.

And the funeral scene kept coming back. Father Alagić and the entire family walking behind the hearse kept coming back. The muddy spot where the black horses balked also came back. Each night Nikola's dizziness deepened Dane's grave a little. Each night they took the casket out of the hearse. His brother was lying in the open casket with his eyes open.

"Let me go!" Nikola cried. "Please, let me go!"

CHAPTER 9

An Aside on Flying

When I take a breath in a particular way, I begin to lift off the ground. I fly up through the chimney and leave the room and my terrifying brother. I ascend toward a solitary star without wondering if I left my body behind.

I say India, and I see the Ganges and the sacred monkeys of Benares. At another time, I see boatmen pulling the oar with their leg on the lakes of Burma. And then, I see the white monkeys in the hot springs of Japan. Next, I ride on gazelles among the birds and lilacs in Chinese Turkestan.

The world is marbled with lightning and full of images. I fly above forests outlined with yellow light and dread, over mountaintops and purple seas. Cities glow underneath. I see tiny people. I see them clearly when I squint. I alight like a bird, make friends with them, and we talk for a long time.

Sometimes I fly all the way to the stars, where it's always morning and where people made of silver live. Sometimes I plunge through the blue void in between the lights of the universe or dive in the ocean depths among the glowing fish. In the middle of the night, I long to see the day, and I see it. Sometimes I see the day on my left and the night on my right. I am Alexander, the conqueror of apparitions. Now I can choose my own thoughts and steer them like Helios his chariot. I can see things that I imagine and hold them before my eyes as long as I want. I've learned how to defend myself. I've learned to cope with a wonder as vast as death.

CHAPTER 10

The First City

Milutin could not bear to live in the house where Dane died, so he turned the Smiljan parish over to Mile Ilić, gave his successor a farewell embrace, and moved with his family to Gospić. Holding his father's hand, Nikola gazed at burly town houses and whispered, "So many windows!"

Native costumes, civilian clothes, and uniforms jostled against each other in the streets. A brass band played in the square on Sundays. The noise of clattering carts was deafening. In the barbershop, retired soldiers talked about the Italian war. Coffee shop doors opened and closed. In a bar, young people crowded around a billiard table. Old domino players were sitting in another tavern. They stacked the bones, which clinked like coins and cursed "bloody Sunday."

The river Lika looked very green to Nikola. Gospić seemed huge. In Milutin's new church, innumerable candles burned for both the living and the dead. On holidays, Milutin went to visit the local Roman Catholic church.

He and the Catholic priest, Kostrenčić, stood in the churchyard holding each other's hand after the service.

"So many windows!" the boy whispered.

Since the move, Nikola listened to the pulsating noise of the streets and its distinct and muted sounds:

"I'll talk to Tomo when he gives me back my tools."

"He went to school with my late brother."

"I was sick all day yesterday. I'm not used to being sick. So I said, 'Mila, fix me a bowl of soup.'"

"Hey, buddy, we need another one for the game."

"So that guy just kept filling my glass. And you know how they blast the music over there . . ."

". . . and I had four bowls of soup."

"What I want is for you to take care of the kids, not simply let them fly around like ladybugs so you can go to the liquor store with your drunken friends."

It appeared to Nikola that people were not talking with each other but past each other.

"People are blind," Djuka told her son. "They don't see anything. They don't understand anything. Most of them, anyway."

Nikola missed life in Smiljan.

He was not the first boy in his village to figure out that it was much easier to take a pocket watch apart than to reassemble it, nor the last to try to fly with an umbrella. He buried things in the ground all the time. He spread walnuts to dry in the attic. He rode a ram and tried to ride a gander. The gander had cold crocodile eyes and nipped Nikola's navel. Spurred by a lecture titled On the Damage That Crows Do to Crops, Nikola tried to exterminate the birds but ended up getting pecked all over.

In Smiljan, Djuka poured water for Milutin to wash his face above the garden bed so that she could water her plants at the same time. In spring, trees in blossom looked like clouds. At night they resembled ghosts. The bees sang in summer. People were sitting in front of their houses in the evening cracking watermelons with their fists. There was a smell of dust. In the dark, a junebug hit Nikola right in the forehead.

In this Homeric world, Mother sang the epic song about the twins Predrag and Nenad. Father's friends looked like Menelaus and Hector.

Not all of them, however.

"Give me your hand," Father Alagić bawled at Luka Bogić.

"On one condition—I want it back," the hunter said.

His fawn-like face stared at Nikola. The boy tried to endure the hunter's leering green eyes but got frightened and lowered his head. Bogić walked through the morning fog, which came up to his knees, and was able to guess where a quail would shoot up from the ground.

He recognized the silhouette of a black grouse against the full moon. The hunter caught and ate a fly right in front of the kids. The kids cried, "That's gross!"

They did not notice that he caught the fly with one hand and ate it with the other.

A string of unicorns streamed under Nikola's pillow. Fireflies started to light up in the summer dusk. Old men stared at the new moon. They grabbed their ears, hopped on one foot, and shouted, "You—old, me—young!"

In the early afternoon, buildings in Gospić stretched their shadows like snails stretch their horns. Streets were long. Tree-lined alleys were haunted with the cooing of doves: "Who's there? You . . . you . . . you . . ."

Young men with sideburns, in long, loose jackets and light derby hats, hurried along the cobbled streets. The urchins who mimicked them knew just how to curl their lips in passing. Nikola preferred to stay indoors so he would not run into their sneers. In this new environment, he became a loner and read a lot.

"No more!" Father ordered.

"Why?"

"Because it will ruin your eyes."

At night Nikola filled the keyhole and the crack under the door with hemp fibers. He read by candlelight with candles he made. At one time, the flame was so still it looked like a drop of light, and he teased it with his finger. At another, it looked like it wanted to flutter off the wick. Delighted, the boy devoured words while his shadow grew on the wall. The book in his lap was bigger than its reader. He blew out the candle and trembled each time he thought his father was coming.

Nikola grew tired of these secret reading sessions and soon became a member of the Gospić library. With the permission of the drunken librarian, he cleaned the books on the shelves that had been buried in dust. Nikola wiped the leather covers, which smelled like dried fruit. He was so thankful for the people who wrote books, so thankful. They were his friends in the town where he had none.

"Look how much this boy hangs out in the library," the librarian griped to his wife.

She tapped her pimply brow with her index finger and whispered, "I think he's crazy."

Some other people thought the same.

In the school hall, Nikola lugged books around all the time. Once he was confronted by Mojo Medić, a chunky, dangerous-looking boy, who planted himself in front of Nikola.

"Hey, you, big ears! Are books all you care about?" he asked.

Nikola said that his childhood in Smiljan was much more dangerous than Mojo's in Gospić.

"You don't say!"

"I could've died many times," Nikola said softly.

"You don't say!"

"The first time I was still a baby. Mother put our laundry in a huge vat on the stove to soak and cook. I was crawling on the table. When I tried to stand up, I tottered and fell into the vat."

Nikola looked surprised by his own words, but he continued.

"Once, my brother locked me in a mountain chapel that's only opened once a year. And I could've drowned many times."

Mojo raised his eyebrows in disbelief.

"It's as if fate loves to bring me to the brink of death only to save me at the last moment . . ."

Surprised, Mojo said, "You're a good liar."

"I never lie," retorted Nikola.

As he laughed, Mojo's fat cheeks engulfed his eyes. "Actually, I don't think you know that you can lie."

CHAPTER 11

Secret and Sacred

Who could have imagined that Nikola and Mojo Medić, whose girth was increasing every day, would squeeze into the same desk at school and mix their blood in a blood-brother ritual? They played together during summer days, which stretched like shoreless oceans, and stayed out until their mothers' calls brought them in for dinner:

"Nikolaaaaaa!"

And a moment later:

"Muooo-Joooooo!"

"Just five more minutes!" yelled the two friends.

Buttons were very important in the life of a nine-year-old. A large button was worth four small buttons up until Adam Smith's inexorable economic principles imposed themselves on the button trade. After that, the invisible hand of market economy shifted the value of the large button into five small ones. Nikola got a kreuzer from his uncle Pavle. The number 1, the letter *A*, and the year 1859 were encircled by a thick wreath on one side. A double-headed eagle stretched its legs on the other. In Nikola's world, a kreuzer was worth four large buttons.

To Nikola, other people's homes were like different planets with totally different atmospheres. Even his relatives were of another race. Their skin and odor seemed alien.

The inner breathing of things told him that everything was alive. He was a part of and whole with the outside world. He made a world out of himself. Under a blanket, his knees turned into mountains on which he arranged tin soldiers. These mountainous knees were his stage. In the cracks and moldy patches of the ceiling, he looked for and always found human faces, eyes, noses, and mouths. His vision became blurry as passages opened in the ornamental patterns in the rug.

His soul called to him from the outside world. He was fascinated with the liveliness and transparency of running water. Water turned his hands and feet into ice. He looked at swaying trees and heard a sweet song. He was mesmerized by the motion of treetops; they swirled around and drew him in.

He and Mojo Medić were friends with Vinko and Nenad as well as the Cukić brothers. They kept their distance from the Bjelobaba boy, who was sitting in front of his house, eating dirt with a spoon.

"Look at that cretin," Mojo said.

"He doesn't know he's alive."

Mojo and Nikola shook their blackberry-stained hands. They played a game called the sting of the wasp, which was not fun because Nenad Alagić did not hit with his hand but used his foot. They whittled wooden swords that had to have a hand guard because a smashed nail stayed black for months. They shot arrows straight up in the air until they disappeared from sight and watched them come back. In winter, their sleds turned into Indian ponies. Niko called his pony Hatatitla: "That means *thunderbolt* in Apache."

They conquered the world in a series of small heroic feats. They battled a boy named Opača and his gang. Rocks zipped by their ears. Once, Nikola watched a rock grow in size until it hit him on the forehead and fell to the ground.

In spring, they played the game of *klis*, which led them far away from home. They played jacks, picking up pieces from the ground with deft movements. One time, Nikola threw a rock and killed a trout as it leapt from the stream. They explored the attic of a ruin overgrown with sumacs. They climbed trees, spied on clouds, and invented their own language.

They played hide-and-seek in summer evenings when bats started to fly. They chanted:

"Phoocy, phooey, we're not having fun, Maria Theresa took all our guns."

After that they disappeared from this world, hiding like butterflies that went back into their cocoons.

The blindfolded boy looked for them.

Mojo and Nikola shared this mystical, semidelirious childhood.

All was ritual.

All was secret and sacred.

Between two rocks, they cracked apricot pits, which tasted like almonds. They stole potatoes from home, baked them, and ate them half raw. Even cooking was a ritual. As they baked the potatoes, they talked about worlds beyond this one, animal and supernatural. A bear killed a donkey in the cemetery above the town. In India, the British were settling scores with the Thuggees, a secret sect of sworn assassins. There was an oasis in the Arctic and there was a secret world. Mummies could come to life but only under certain conditions. A dragon visited Mane Cukić's crazy aunt. Vinko Alagić's grandma had a vision of a woman in white who told her that Gospić would sink into an underground lake that was a thousand yards beneath the town.

CHAPTER 12

The Theologians

One summer in Gospić, Milutin Tesla agreed to tutor two theology students who were preparing for their exams. One of them, the stocky Oklobdžija boy, was a relation of Father Tomo Oklobdžija, who baptized Nikola long ago. Milutin sat down with the young men and told them that in his own time, under Bishop Jovanović, he had to take exams in dogmatic, polemic, moral, and pastoral theology, in history, Slavic grammar, and rhetoric and—what was that called?—oh, yes, the *Typikon* with chanting, as well as the methodology of teaching. He asked them if it was still the same. Pleased with what he heard, Milutin nodded his head and noted that it was good to combine subjects pertaining to practical and dogmatic theology. He laughed good-naturedly and explained, "In this way you will become well-rounded men."

First Milutin spoke briefly about the clash between the iconoclasts and the iconophiles in the Eastern Church. While he passionately argued how essential it was to represent or omit the human form in all three monotheistic religions, Oklobdžija stifled a yawn. The other boy, Korica, yawned openly.

It was not until their next session that Milutin Tesla was able to understand the meaning of the phrase *the patience of a saint*. Not even that virtue helped him explain the conflict between medieval nominalists and realists in the Western Church to those two blockheads. At the beginning of his lecture, Milutin humbly admitted that the philosophical disagreement he was about to discuss was similar to the proverbial dilemma of what came first—the chicken or the egg. The twelfth-century theologian Roscellinus insisted that every abstract notion was nothing but a name—*flatus vocis.*

Milutin dramatically paused before he addressed the position of the realists. Often labeled naive, the realists were medieval thinkers who maintained that general notions objectively existed in reality.

"Is that clear?" Milutin cautiously asked.

Instead of answering, young Oklobdžija stared at the ceiling. Korica, realizing that his friend was so interested in ceilings, directed his attention to the floor. Faced with their silence, Milutin girded himself as he reached the conclusion that the problem under discussion could be basically reduced to three questions: Do general notions exist as words, as logical premises, or as parts of the real world outside human thought?

His students resembled roasted lambs on a spit as they stared at him.

"The learned Abelard says," Milutin Tesla continued tirelessly, "that the universal concept of *Man* is a confusing idea, derived from many images of various people I've met in my life.

"Elsewhere," Milutin elaborated elegantly, "Abelard concedes that universal concepts exist—as logical constructs."

At this intriguing point, he paused and gave his students an inquisitive look. "But how about this question: does *man as such* exist in reality, outside our minds?"

Confronted with this subtle issue, Korica scratched himself systematically, while Oklobdžija stared at the wall as if he expected it to represent him in this affair.

Nomen est omen, Milutin Tesla thought. *I have never met such a numskull as this Korica in my life nor anyone as permanently armored against all knowledge as this Oklobdžija.*[1]

"What those general words refer to does exist in reality," Djuka Tesla interjected.

No one had noticed that she was listening to their conversation as she stood in the doorway with her hands covered in flour.

Her husband gave her a look. "How so?"

Djuka struggled with unfamiliar words.

---

1. The name Korica means *crust* in Serbian; Oklobdžija is a derivative of *armor.*

"When you think of bad people, you cover all of them and lump them together into one word, while each of them still exists as a person."

"Bravo!" Tesla was genuinely pleased. "That's exactly what Abelard says. Only particularities exist outside our minds. Unity belongs to ideas, not to real objects."

Milutin clapped his hands and turned toward the embarrassed Oklobdžija and Korica. "There you go, you sage scholars. This illiterate wife of mine has put you in your place!"

He turned toward his wife: "Nikola! Look at your mother. She's a real man. She's the sharp one."

Djuka choked up at these words. She had not cried at her son's funeral. Now she cried because she never went to school.

CHAPTER 13

Life's Novices

Who could ever imagine this!

Who could imagine that, years later, Nikola and Mojo would embark on an important journey, huddled together on a train?

Nikola wore the shoes that had been bought for Dane when he was about to start high school. His father's raised hand disappeared in the cloud of steam on the platform.

"My Niko," murmured the father to his son, who could not hear him. "You've just barely learned how to be a child, and now you're becoming a young man. When you learn how to be a young man, you'll become mature. Then you'll understand that in this life we're always novices."

"Here we go," Mojo sighed.

A child with meticulously cropped hair entered their compartment, nudged on by his parents. The newcomers raised the window to protect themselves from sparks and soot. Nikola's shoulders drooped. He and Mojo were adults now. They were supposed to discuss serious topics, which made Nikola's tongue stick to his palate from boredom. But he had to be a man. He remembered how soldiers from Lika returned home from the war in Dalmatia in 1866, so he asked Mojo if the Austrian emperor had won that campaign.

"Yes, he did," Mojo replied, ever the straight-A student. "He won at Vis as well as at Custoza."

"But then why is the emperor losing territory in Italy?"

The steam in the engine's boiler powered the merciless thundering of the wheels: *Chunkity-chunk, chunkity-chunk, chunkity-chunk.*

They were on their way to start high school in Karlovac. Nikola's heart beat in time with the wheels. The feeling of expanding space intoxicated him. As the world grew wider, he could take deeper breaths. The train roared like a dragon, curled its tail, and sped into the wide, wide world. The rails did not seem to exist but somehow materialized right in front of the locomotive.

In the compartment, the precocious boy put his head on his mother's lap and said excitedly, "Let me tell you what I dreamed about. We went for a walk and all of a sudden some dragons came out of the ground . . . What's a badger?"

"An animal," his father explained. "With teeth this big."

"Bigger than a rooster?"

"A rooster is nothing!"

Nikola and Mojo were glued to the window as they tried to catch the lay of the land.

"Look at that little house."

"The railway guard lives there," Mojo explained.

The little house, a horse tied to the fence, and the chickens in the yard flashed by and were replaced by other scenes.

"It's really foggy in these parts."

"Look at the castle."

People disembarked at stations.

"There are open seats in the compartments. We have to be considerate to one another. We simply have to," mumbled a woman standing in the corridor.

Hanging pots of geraniums swayed in the breeze in front of station buildings. Railroad men hit the car wheels with long-handled hammers and listened to the clang. Uniformed dispatchers raised their signs to signal the train's departure. The sound of their whistles pierced the mouse-gray afternoon. The train's entering and exiting tunnels resembled a game of peek-a-boo.

The engine cooed like a monstrous dove. A trail of sparks zigzagged behind it in the twilight.

Nikola felt helpless as he stared into the future that was so obscure, it resembled nothingness.

"There are no more hills," he said.

They saw the flatlands for the first time in their life. The houses were much richer than those they were used to in mountainous Lika.

"People seem to be wealthier where the soil looks like shit," Mojo concluded.

CHAPTER 14

Metamorphosis

Nikola's uncle Branković met him in Karlovac and took him to a two-story baroque building, number seventeen. In front of her husband, Nikola's aunt Kaja made the boy recite that—in addition to the famous Trbojevićes of Medak, the Milojevićes of Mogorić, the Bogdanovićes of Vrebac, and the Došens of Počitelj—the Mandićes of Gračac were among the families that had given the most Orthodox priests in all of Lika.

Then she put a finger on the boy's mouth and said, "Remember, illness comes from overeating."

Whenever his good-natured uncle threw a chicken leg into Nikola's plate, the aunt would scream: "Niki!" and her quick hand made the leg disappear. She apparently had come to the mystical conclusion that spiritual food could replace earthly fare. After dinner, Nikola pulled on the sleeve of the buxom cook, Mara.

"Will you spread some lard on a slice of bread for me?"

"I dare not cross the mistress," Mara said, sulking.

Although poorly fed, the boy's body was changing. While other children were out playing, he withdrew into the pantry and grew up unseen. As he became taller, he assumed a stooping posture. Uncle Branković had a habit of slapping him suddenly on the back and yelling, "Straighten up!"

That friendly gesture was supposed to be encouraging. The uncle liked to be asked questions and Nikola accommodated him.

"Why does Karlovac have two sirens and two anchors in its coat of arms if it's landlocked?"

"Karlovac is a true river town." Major Branković raised one eyebrow. "Not only does it straddle two rivers, the Kupa and the Korana, but in fact there are four of them altogether, if you count the Dobra and the nearby Mrežnica. Our wealth is based on barges that bring wood and grain from Posavina. Then we ship those products to the Adriatic ports from here."

Branković cleared his throat and continued: "And we'll keep doing that until they build the railroad between Zagreb and Rijeka."

Yes, in Karlovac water played an important role. Nikola stared through his aunt's window at the rain, which had been coming down for a week.

"It'll probably stop," he guessed.

"There's not a single hole left to fill," the aunt responded.

After the water withdrew, rats invaded the cellar.

Mara the cook ran into the room. "They ate everything, even the garlands of dried hot peppers."

The little wolf from Lika called the flatlands "ratlands." He learned how to kill hostile rodents with a sling. With sad eyes, the rat hunter watched the endless rain and pined for home. Back in Lika it was spring, so lamb and coarsely cut potatoes were now served in place of wintry smoked mutton with cabbage and mush. He also missed the Dutch oven buried in the ashes. He missed the Lika round cheese and bread. He missed the stubborn wind and the traditional red Lika hats that looked like poppies in the field.

He also missed his sisters, Marica, Milka, and Angelina.

"Aren't you doing well in Karlovac?" they asked him in their letters.

"I'm doing fine," Nikola answered.

He studied languages in Karlovac and discussed history with Uncle Branković.

"Please, take a look." The uncle handed Nikola books on Benvenuto Cellini, Lorenzo il Magnifico, various princes, popes, condottieri, the Sistine Chapel, and the imperfect leg of Michelangelo's *David*. The uncle's subtle suggestions did not bear fruit. After the three years of fasting at his uncle's home, Nikola associated art with hunger for the rest of his life.

In Vienna, a long time ago, the major made friends with the antique shop owner Jehuda Altarac. Branković's small art collection was the product of their long years of haggling. The major showed Nikola the Czech crystal and German brooches with images of human eyes. The paintings from his collection were metaphorical representations of the transience of life—the so-called vanities. They showed a dual "person," the left side of whose face displayed a youthful peachy smile, while a skull grinned on the right. These paintings only confirmed Nikola's belief that art represented starvation in disguise.

"She's a snake." That was what his old friend Mojo Medić called Nikola's pale-eyed aunt.

The aunt fired the buxom Mara without giving her a letter of recommendation and replaced her with the much older Ružica.

"When you bake a fish, it's done when the eye pops," the aunt instructed her.

Once she slapped that elderly cook right in front of Nikola.

"Will you spread some lard on a slice of bread for me," Nikola asked Ružica.

"I dare not cross the mistress," Ružica responded through her nose.

Kaja Branković used such words as *naturally* and *obviously*, but under her timid mask, there was a person who would not meet anyone halfway. And yet, although her frequent pauses in conversation put a lot of distance between her and her nephew, she still took care of him. Kaja Branković's salon in Karlovac resembled a white piano. It was frequented by the local pharmacist with his touchingly stupid wife. Jakob Šašel, a globetrotter, also came. The Orthodox priest Anastasijević would sometimes drop by with his two good-looking daughters. In her nasal voice, the maid would invite them to the table. At dinner, Nikola's uncle bored his guests with his stories about how a horse was shot from under him at the Battle of Solferino and how he retired just in time so that he did not have "to embarrass himself in the war against the Prussians." A gas chandelier hissed above the table. The silverware clinked in the guests' hands. The pharmacist's wife whispered to Šašel that the Solferino hero now lived in fear of his wife.

They would then recline into chairs whose backs were covered in needlepoint. Mrs. Anastasijević's hands turned the keyboard into turbulent waves.

When a German opera company visited Karlovac, they all went to see *The Magic Flute.* The uncle talked the aunt into taking Nikola as well. In the opera, Sarastro whittled a magic flute during a stormy night while lightning illuminated him. Other characters asked Papageno if he was searching for wisdom.

"No!" Papageno responded. "Food, drink, and a good night's sleep will do."

Food and drink would also have done for the starving Nikola—if he could only get enough of them. His photographs from that time show him as an awkward youth with the same hairstyle that would make Tarzan famous later on. His aunt kept an eye on him all the time.

"Why are you failing in your drawing class?" she asked him.

"Because I don't like it."

"Who do you hang around with?"

Nikola admitted that boys at high school were as raucous as crows. An exclamation point was to be put after every statement they uttered: "How can I talk with that crocodile!" "Hey, tough guy!" "You're insane!" They could not wait to graduate, throw their hats in the air, and turn their brains off.

Whom could he hang around with?

After some hesitation, he answered, "With Nikola Prica and Mojo Medić."

"I see. The fat one!" She remembered Mojo.

Nikola Tesla was able to talk about everything with Prica and Mojo. That is, almost everything. Whenever he came across some philosophical topic, their faces would fall.

"What kind of poppycock is this?" they complained.

Everything Nikola considered important was like a tree that falls in the forest, without anyone to hear it. And yet his chest swelled as he sensed his own power. He felt like an expanding balloon. Sometimes he felt weightless, and with each breath he heedlessly embraced the world. There was a wide gap between his sense of inner exhilaration and the outer wave of crippling skepticism. Like a salmon, Nikola felt he was swimming against a current of disapproval. Surrounded by derision, his only consolation was in the thought: *They will forget all of their current "ideas." I won't forget mine.*

The well-read boy remembered Ovid's words: "There is a god within us. It is when he stirs us that our bosom warms; it is his impulse that sows the seeds of inspiration."

He realized that in this world people allow us to be something but not to become something—because that unsettles them.

And yet, Nikola was changing . . .

Outwardly, it was quite obvious. He had come to Karlovac a gloomy provincial boy but was now turning into a dandy. He used to slouch but now his back was straight, thanks to the sudden correctional slaps from his uncle. In addition to German, he could also speak a little English and French. The voice with which he practiced conjugating irregular French verbs became manly. But more important was the change in his soul. At one point he felt that life was opening up for him. Surprised by these changes, he was listening to the voices in his own breathing just as Dane had done before him. He felt giddy. The sky made him tingle. The world expanded around him and mirrored his soul.

"If you stare into the looking glass for too long, you'll see the devil," scolded Kaja Branković.

Every day he carefully examined his face in the mirror. Something was spreading in his soul like oil over a table. Someone unknown was surfacing out of the other side of the mirror. That one was slowly— *pianissimo*—turning into something horrible. When that emerging phantom became more frightening than the dead brother, Nikola stepped back and gave a small scream.

CHAPTER 15

The King of the Waltz

Mojo Medić and Nikola Tesla went for a stroll along the fortress in the center of Karlovac. Above the roofs, smoke rushed toward the sky. The friends stayed close to the buildings to avoid the ice.

"We shouldn't be out when it's so slick," Tesla said rationally.

Instead of answering him, Mojo grabbed his arm and looked into his eyes.

"Outside of school, I only see you at church," he said hoarsely. "What's going on with you?"

Nikola assumed a half-inspired and half-anguished expression. He had been in love many times—with his mother's hair, with his father's library, with his brother's fame, with his nocturnal flights, with the sense of the world expanding. Now, he was in love again, but not with one of the dark-eyed Karlovac beauties. In each of them this great hero found a fault—so said the folk song. But Nikola's love of electricity was unlike any other youthful love.

The young Tesla remembered that Saint Augustine said, "Where is it? Where is the heart of the mystery?" As far as Tesla was concerned, the heart of the mystery revealed itself in the shape of a silent ball that danced in Mr. Martin Sekulić's school laboratory.

The experimental ball that Sekulić invented was covered with layers of tin foil. Once connected to the static generator, it turned into a swift, soundless spinning top, which beckoned to Nikola like light that lures a moth until he responded, "Here I am!" He wanted to worship the power that the ball made visible. If that pedagogical toy was no more than a tool of the experiment, then Nikola wanted to be an experimenter. If that was called science, Nikola wanted to be a scientist. He wanted to partake in that indescribable excitement. As the date of his graduation neared, he became more and more certain that he wanted to jump on, fly, and grow with *that*. Without hesitation, he confided in his friend.

"An inventor?" Mojo raised his eyebrows.

"Yes!" Nikola affirmed. "He who removes the blindfold from the eyes of the world."

"And how do you plan to remove it?" his friend mocked.

"Imagine, for example, if we made a ring around the equator that would freely hover in place, held by inertia and the resistance of air. Using that circular road around the earth, people could travel thousands of miles a day."

"And who would pay for that?" Mojo Medić grunted. "Come on, wake up, Nikola."

Nikola had never been more awake in his life. During that pivotal year, he became Sekulić's assistant.

"Nikola is a quick-minded creature. God's greyhound," Sekulić praised him in front of everyone.

For the first time, the word *brilliant* was used to describe him and not his late brother, Dane. His knowledge was not of the dry, academic kind. In fact, it was no knowledge at all. At night, in place of the faraway cities he envisioned as a boy, Sekulić's ball spun in front of his eyes. Nikola's thoughts danced with it.

After graduation, he refused to study theology.

"That's what my father wants, not me."

Mojo grabbed him by his arm.

"Be careful!"

On the ice, people were falling as though they were in a slapstick comedy. The two friends skated more than walked along Karlovac's cobbled streets. In front of Miller's tavern, Pavo Petrović, a red-nosed policeman, slipped and got up. Brushing his jacket too briskly, he popped a button off his fine uniform.

"Steady!"

"Good job!" the town bums hooted.

"You son of a bitch . . ." Pavo growled.

The boys tipped their hats to greet the gunsmith and painter Jakob Šašel. This friend of Nikola's uncle was a local celebrity. He had traveled in Egypt, Nubia, and Sudan and written a travelogue based on his journeys that was praised at an exhibition in Zagreb. Responding to the boys' greetings, he touched his hat. That slight gesture was enough to make him lose his balance. As he fell, he broke a vial he had bought at the pharmacy and stifled a curse. Waving off their offer of help, the globetrotter disappeared through a carriage gate.

"Shall we go on?"

"Don't be afraid," Mojo said. "Just walk with your knees bent. Also take your hands out of your pockets. That way you won't break anything if you fall."

As they walked across Wheat Market Square, Mojo sensed an aura of eccentricity and solitude engulfing his friend, and he pitied him. So he switched the topic to something more interesting than inventions. Smiling broadly, he challenged his friend with a plural noun Nikola did not want to hear: *women!* Women with milky skin! Women with fragrant hair! Women with *those* eyes! Women! Waltzing with women was a less banal topic than Nikola's preaching about science and humanity.

How could Mojo Medić explain to his sad, pathetic friend that the very marrow of his bones tingled from a mere glance from a girl? Nikola did not hear the tickling whisper of life, while a million rosebuds were opening in Mojo's ear. Now it was Mojo's turn to get inspired, and it was Nikola who felt that his friend was blind to the real secrets of life.

Mojo breathlessly told Nikola how he, together with Jovan Bijelić, Nikola Prica, Julije Bartaković, and even Djuro Amšel, took dancing lessons with Pietro Signorelli. Anyone who knew Mojo Medić from his Gospić days had to be surprised by his newly developed taste for dancing. Among Gospić's urchins, Mojo the "Teddy Bear" was remembered as a pensive, chubby kid who waddled as he walked. In high school in Rakovac, he grew taller and slimmer and started to walk straight. He began to dress up and now was delivering a lecture on waltzing to his indifferent friend Nikola Tesla!

Mojo told Nikola in confidence that in his dance class they learned not only old waltzes, such as "The Morning News" and "The Blue Danube," but also newer ones. Mr. Signorelli promised that he would shortly get the latest composition Johann Strauss announced for the current year, "The Vienna Blood." Mojo chuckled as he told of his quarrel with Jovan Bijelić over whether Strauss wore only a mustache or if he also sported sideburns like Emperor Franz Joseph. Mojo insisted his indifferent friend show some surprise that the Waltz King, under whose baton all of Europe revolved, confessed that he himself did not know how to dance.

"He doesn't know how, but I do!" beamed Mojo. "And the waltz is a simple dance. One, two, stand on your toes!"

"Isn't that a little silly?" Nikola asked.

"Maybe it is," exclaimed Mojo. "But it's fun. One, two, stand on your toes."

Nikola was surprised to see the once clumsy Mojo pirouette on the Karlovac cobblestones. Not just the body of Mojo Medić, a high school senior, danced—his thoughts danced as well. The wide world was full of whispers and promises, and above it swayed Mojo Medić, the romantic lover, the Pushkin and the Byron of our time.

"One, two, stand on your toes." As he twirled without fear, Mojo lost his balance and fell on his back. He tucked his chin to avoid hitting the back of his head against the icy road.

"Mojo!" Nikola Tesla quit frowning and showed genuine concern. Running to help, he slipped himself and was almost paralyzed by pain as he hit the ice. He rubbed his buttocks slowly to help the pain subside.

A new wave of pain made him cough. He grimaced. Mojo looked at him and puffed up his cheeks. Tesla returned the look and broke out laughing.

Nikola's laughter was contagious. The king of the waltz stretched back on the ice and convulsed with the raucous laughter of youth.

CHAPTER 16

Lusting after the Wind

It is highly unlikely that a young man,
especially he who studied at a university for several years,
will dare to follow the valorous path of the priesthood.
Milutin Tesla in a letter to the city government of Senj, 1852

Although the human mind cannot find the answers to every question, Milutin Tesla believed it was still possible to know that people dye eggs for Easter. It was also possible to know that a priest blesses the bread baked for the Patron Saint's Day and that the bride and the bridegroom, wearing crowns, walk around the table three times. He believed pondering a dilemma did not necessarily lead to the truth—the truth was revealed through a daring effort to stop dithering and declare what was and what was not.

"Father! Please listen!" Nikola pleaded, to no avail.

Milutin could not bear the inspired look on his son's face.

"Please understand," his son said, raising his voice, "that the very idea of becoming a priest horrifies me. It's like pushing a cat into the water, and I can't do that. I can't because I am who I am!"

"What does *I* mean?" His father looked at him as if he heard the word for the first time. "*We* need priests. *We* can barely make ends meet in this poverty-stricken country. *We* need men who will open minds and hearts of our people."

Milutin slid his glasses down his nose.

"This science you crave is nothing but vanity. Vanity and lusting after the wind! It's childish to flee from the censer to please your own ego."

Nikola's blood grew cool. He was barely able to protest: "Father, I'm talking but you're not listening."

"I don't have to," Milutin crowed. "There's no law that says that those who speak should be heard."

An Announcement

Ladies and gentlemen, esteemed friends:

When Nikola Tesla refused to become a priest, his father used all the means at his disposal to force him to do so. Under pressure, lacking the will to live, Nikola came down with cholera. One can die from it on the first day. Nikola suffered from vomiting and diarrhea. His nails turned blue. His sunken eyes stared out from deep, black circles. Spasms gave him chills and tore his innards apart. He alternated between burning and freezing. His voice turned hoarse. His heartbeat was barely audible.

Fever Roulette

The fever turned his room into a maelstrom.

Nikola was not in this world. He was in a narrow corridor whose walls were hung with the portraits of his ancestors. On the left—the damned priests. On the right—the damned military officers. Both rows stared at him with empty eyes.

His father sat at his feet.

The devil sat at the head of his bed.

"I'll kill him, you understand?" the devil whispered to the priest.

"That can't be," Milutin growled. "In our family, we've all been priests."

The devil's green eyes bored into Milutin's skull. "You're not listening," he said. "He won't live to see the morning."

"All my hopes . . ." A sob tore out of the depth of Milutin's bosom.

"Come to your senses, man, or he'll die."

"He's my only son." The priest started to rock back and forth, like a woman. "My Dane died. The rest are girls. Only he can continue the family tradition."

"I'll kill him," repeated the devil.

Large drops of sweat beaded on young Tesla's forehead.

"Let him go," cried the priest.

"I'll kill him."

Nikola jerked his sweaty head on the pillow. His nostrils narrowed.

"For the grace of God, leave him alone," the priest wanted to say, but he only sighed. "Let him go."

"Kill."

"Nikola, my son," Father Milutin said in such a powerful voice that the apparition on the other side of the bed faded away. "Get well, son. Just get well, and I'll let you study polytechnics. Go to Graz. Study what you want. Just get well."

"Really, Father?" Nikola's chapped lips barely opened.

"Don't you leave me too," Milutin said gazing at his son's forehead. "Go where you want. Study what you will."

At that moment Nikola opened his eyes.

The fever roulette stopped spinning.

And slowly . . . the things in the room came to a halt in their proper places.

CHAPTER 17

In the City of Styrian Grand Dukes

When Nikola ran into the university building, the outside voices became hushed. The atrium whooshed like a seashell. Students playfully skated across the marble floor. They mostly spoke in German, although one could also hear Serbian, Hungarian, and Polish.

Now I'm in a different world, a castle, the young man from Lika thought.

Nikola was able to breathe more easily in the City of Styrian Grand Dukes. For the first time in his life, he could choose the subjects he preferred. He even liked the cold room he rented on Attems Street. There was the small problem of his roommate, though. Once, Nikola bought some apples and, on the way home from school, smiled as he imagined their taste. Then he entered the room . . .

"Why are you eating my apples?" he shouted from the doorway.

"Because they're here," his roommate, Kosta Kulišić, answered, chewing.

Nikola gargled warm salt water because of his sore throat.

"You look like a bird swallowing a snake," Kulišić told him.

In the morning, when Nikola was about to wash his face, he stopped short: "Why did you use my towel?"

"Because it was clean," Kulišić responded with composure.

It was easier to laugh than fight. Kulišić, who had a broken nose and the eyes of a bear, suffered tremendous pain because of the current bloodbath near his native town of Trebinje. Whenever Kulišić put on a brave face, it seemed to Nikola that he was barely able to contain his tears. On Sundays, Graz was quiet as if inhabited only by butlers. The two roommates lingered in bed. Frost dotted their window and they could see their breath. Nikola told Kosta about his flying engine while the wind swayed their room.

"Where do you think hell's located?" Nikola suddenly asked.

"I don't know," Kosta said, "but it must be closer than we think."

Kosta could not follow most of what Nikola talked about. He also did not understand why his roommate had to get up so early on the coldest weekdays.

"How can you get up when it's still dark?" he murmured. "God hasn't created the world yet."

"It's a shame to miss a single class. They're such great professors," Nikola explained.

In Nikola's opinion, the most brilliant lecturer at the university was Doctor Allé, an expert in integral and differential equations. Allé considered stupidity a form of brazenness. At the end of each class, he looked for Nikola and asked, "Shall we?"

For an entire hour he would make him solve special problems.

"Bravo!" Allé shouted.

After these mathematical sessions, they left the building together. The student surprised his professor with a question: "Do you see these carriages on the streets of Graz?"

Allé's eyelids fluttered in assent, magnified by his spectacles.

"Many of them are mounted on springs, and their upholstery follows the fashion of the nineteenth century."

"Yes?"

"But in principle, those are still the same carriages found in Homer and the Old Testament."

"So?"

Nikola opened his bag and produced the blueprints for a flying engine powered by electricity. "Isn't it time for people to fly?" he asked.

During that first year, Nikola had no interest in the world outside the library and the lecture hall of the School of Polytechnic. He was not impressed by the region's temperate climate or the hot springs in Tobelbad, and he didn't care for the sixteenth-century watchtower. Not for the Mura. Not for its bridges. Not for the breweries. In the city known for its hatmakers and lensmakers, his only interest was in electrical engineering and books.

He pretended not to be surprised by the life of the city and its incomprehensible fashions. Ladies wore what looked like lace bibs, while gentlemen's overcoats were fastened just below the chin so that they resembled tents. In rooms, people danced to Schubert's "Graz Waltzes." Gentlemen in black and ladies in lace swirled underneath chandeliers. In those circles, Plato's *animus* and *anima* seemed to merge. Officers softened their bows with subtle smiles. People discussed the Herzegovina uprising, the recent economic crisis, Czech cuisine, and the advantages of the academic style in painting over French impressionism.

And Nikola?

Nikola was free. Until recently, he had appeared to be an imaginary character and was only now becoming real. Every day he took a walk on top of the Schlossberg, where an invincible fortress defied first the Turks and then Napoléon. He claimed to like the "electric air" of the place. Soon, Murko the tailor made him a suit and a few shirts on credit, with interest. Up until then, everyone had called him Nikola. Now they started calling him Tesla. Mr. Tesla.

Mr. Tesla spent every evening in the library. Hegel's reptilian eyes stared at him from the wall. Baroque angels fluttered under the ceiling, and it smelled like the seventeenth century. In his head, Father continued to gripe and to cast doubt on Nikola's decision.

I see that Progress is now your God, Milutin said in his son's head. *But even if progress exists, it doesn't focus on anything in particular—it enhances everything, including evil. It enhances* Homo homini lupus.

Embittered, Nikola pushed those thoughts away. He studied Voltaire to arm himself against his father. Voltaire convinced him that "the exquisite is the enemy of the good." So Mr. Tesla started working eighteen hours a day.

He passed nine exams his first year—twice the number necessary. "Your son is a first-rate star," the dean wrote to the priest in Gospić. Milutin, however, showed little enthusiasm for Nikola's success and a lot of concern for his health. Nikola dismissed his father's worries as commonsense banalities. "Knowledge—if real—leaves you breathless," he would say. "It's much more exciting than the business of living."

Warm and cold loves clashed within him. Warm love was for human beings. Cold love was for what his father called God (whom Milutin gave warm love). Nikola's cold love was focused on the fierce, flame-like power of invention. Warm love was nothing in comparison. Nothing at all. A shadow. For Nikola, the library was the place of certainty that Father Milutin had never experienced. Other students absorbed science by rote, like a poem they would later live by and recite for the rest of their lives. For his part, Tesla was truly interested in the very essence of things. In addition to physics, he devoured volume after volume of classical and philosophical works.

He read and the world expanded for him. After all, he wanted to be an inventor, and inventing meant the expansion of the world. Just before the library would close, he went out and stared into Kant's starry night. He felt that he was growing under the explosions of stars. Soon, his pointed ears would be at the same height as the city's towers. And then? Galaxies would become entangled in his hair.

And then?

CHAPTER 18

A Tract on Noses

From the lecture Nikola Tesla gave to
the Young Serbs Society on December 3, 1875

My dear colleagues, where would we be without noses?

Believe me—nowhere!

Noses connect us to the invisible world. They inform us about things healthy and unhealthy, let us know if the bed is clean or if the soup is hot, endow us with the smells of the morning and of the coming storm, and unite us with nature.

This is why noses are often compared to plants. We're all familiar with so-called bulbous, cherry, or spud noses.

Human noses are bridges between us and the animal world. You've all heard of beak, snout, or pug noses. Many unfortunate young men are called toucans, unicorns, or rhinos.

Noses also tune us in to the seasons. They bring us the aroma of the frost in February and the linden blooms in June. A whiff of roasting peppers heralds August.

The nose is a kind of tool. People wonder if you can use it as a can opener. They often compare it to a spade, ax, or adze.

It's a musical instrument similar to a trumpet, bassoon, or trombone. The nose provides a notorious sound box for snoring, which makes it unpopular with roommates.

The nose defines the timbre of the voice and therefore blesses singers and curses those who talk through it.

People sniff each other out in social situations as well. We're all familiar with the "smell of money" and the "stench of poverty."

The nose mirrors the features of Mother Earth, invoking her glorious mountain peaks as well as her deep, fathomless caverns.

The nose is a maze through which the light and the air find their way down to the darkness of the throat. It keeps us alive. Don't forget that the nose gives us breath even before it endows us with fragrances.

The topic of noses has always inspired thinkers. Pascal believed that the fate of the world wouldn't be the same if Cleopatra had had a shorter nose. Heine joked that "no matter how hard somebody sobs, he always blows his nose in the end." Voltaire insisted that people come into this world with ten fingers and a nose but without the knowledge of God.

Picking one's nose shows our eternal immaturity and unmasks our pretense of refinement.

Tycho Brahe had a nose of gold.

Just like the ear, the nose can be embellished with a ring.

My dear colleagues, we've all seen a man tugging his dog who refuses to budge until he's finished reading some smelly story left by the roadside.

The nose is a storyteller.

This supreme awakener of memories still remembers the smells of the attic and of the cellar of our parents' home.

The nose is the throne for our pince-nez.

Perfume makers from Paris and Cologne are the great friends of the human soul.

The nose gifts us the fragrances of basil, coffee, and lemon rind.

The Greeks, Jews, and other ancient peoples believed that the gods, just like us, loved the smell of barbecue. Those gods of antiquity received burnt sacrifices with their—undoubtedly beautiful—noses.

In front of inns, beggars try to satisfy their craving for food as they anxiously inhale the smell of soup, stew, and roasted meat.

Eskimos kiss with their noses.

The nose is fragile and delicate, and boys like to punch that precious thing.

"Hit him in the nose!" they yell. "His eyes will well with blood. He won't be any good after that!"

According to legend, one of Napoléon's gunners blasted the Sphinx's nose off her face because it was too perfect.

Many people are unsatisfied with their noses. Visionaries dream of being able to swap noses or even establish a nose stock exchange under the control of the East India Company, with its centers in both London and Amsterdam.

My grandfather used to say that any face with a nose is beautiful.

What works for horses, works for noses: a good horse has a thousand imperfections, while a nag has only one—it's no good.

My dear colleagues, spirited colleagues—follow your noses!

As he reached this salient conclusion, Tesla raised his chin and presented the audience with his profile.

Big-nosed Kulišić, who was sitting in the first row, turned sideways, like a parrot, in order to get a better look.

CHAPTER 19

Kisses and Voltaire

In the darkness of a baroque entryway, a young man and a girl clung to each other. The shadow of the gate was thick with cuddles and kisses. The girl unwrapped her fingers only to have them intertwined with the boy's again. Her cheek rubbed against his and that was so interesting. Their bosoms touched and that was so exciting. They could not have kissed with less passion even if the world were to end the next day, or if the young man were to leave for war. His lips brushed her lips, her cheeks, her eyes. Then the girl put her fingers across his lustful lips.

"I have to go."

"Wait," the young man said dreamily. "Just a bit more."

She tried to push him away.

"Just one more."

When their magnetic lips parted, the girl touched her brow and whispered, "I really have to . . ."

At that moment, a window on the upper floor banged open and a harsh voice spoke: "Ulrike, you little slut! Get in here!"

The girl flushed and stiffened. Frightened, she hissed, "My landlady is calling."

"You have no shame," the voice boomed from the window.

The girl looked at the young man with horror. She tore herself away, but turned back to blow him a kiss. Then she vanished into the entryway. The young man adjusted his clothes. He raised his eyes and noticed that the roofs and the chimneys on the houses stood awry. Only the moon above them remained straight. His feet felt unsteady. He smiled to himself and admitted, "I have no clue where I am."

Humming to himself, the young man lowered his eyes from the stars and saw a late passerby. It was a tall man with a sharp nose. Oblivious to the cooing couples in the gateways, the lanky fellow strode on with determination. There was no doubt that he knew what city he was in, what year it was, and who he was. If one had asked him, he would have readily responded that it was Graz, 1876, and he was . . . Then the young man from the gateway recognized him and shouted, "Hey, Tesla!"

The busy stranger turned around and a smile lit up his face: "Szigety!"

"Where have you been?" The nighttime lover caught up with Tesla.

Szigety noticed that Tesla had a sharp but classical profile. His nose was like a road sign he followed with haste. Tesla's high brow bulged between his eyes. The voice in which he responded was raspy and quiet: "I worked late, so I got all foggy inside. I took myself out for a walk, like I was a dog."

Under his arm Tesla had Voltaire's *Philosophical Dictionary,* one of the hundred volumes people said he had sworn he would read.

"I've just walked my sweetheart home." Szigety tried to suppress the triumph in his voice. "If you'll allow me, how are things for you . . . in that regard?"

"What?" Tesla asked.

"What do you mean, 'what?' Do you have a girlfriend?"

Szigety's question was in a language Tesla did not speak. His eyebrows knotted and he assumed an anguished expression. He did not respond. When the silence grew uncomfortable, Szigety raised his arms: "Oh, please, please! I didn't mean anything by it."

"No, it's all right," Tesla said kindly.

Nikola had nothing to say on that topic. While still in Karlovac, Mojo Medić chided him for avoiding girls "like the plague." In Graz, he stayed away from those *displays of God's nature* even more. Szigety was amazed by his fellow student's reaction to the mention of the most fascinating thing in the world. He decided to turn left at the next corner and leave this oddball alone with his Voltaire. At the corner, he showed his perfect teeth and remarked that he was going a different way. In order to make up for his sudden change of direction, he mumbled, "Maybe we could have breakfast at Alexander's sometime?"

"Great!" Tesla said. "Tomorrow at nine?"

Szigety was sure his hardworking classmate would not accept the invitation. As he did so, Szigety exclaimed without thinking, "No, wait a minute . . ."

"What?" Nikola responded.

Szigety pulled out his pocket watch. The hands piggybacked on the Roman "I."

"It's been Monday for a while," Szigety informed his colleague. "How much sleep do you get?"

Tesla's eyes were the color of a wild chestnut fresh from the shell. Sparks flashed in those unusual eyes and he said, "Out of twenty-four hours, I sleep four."

Late-riser Szigety cursed under his breath. "All right then," he sighed. "I'll see you at Alexander's at nine."

They both went home—Szigety to float in bliss from Ulrike's embraces and then to sleep, and Tesla to work long into the night. Finally, the latter turned off his lights as well. The night streamed on while people snored under the high roofs. Then the indigo sky paled. A rose-fingered dawn touched the roofs as the sun began to rouse the world: first the Austro-Hungarian Empire, then the city of Graz. The students Antal Szigety and Nikola Tesla arose, dressed, and—in accordance with their commitment—went to meet at Alexander's.

"Come in, please come in," the owner of the café greeted his first customers of the morning. Big Elsa's and Little Elsa's smiling faces were arrayed above identical collars and aprons. At forty, Big Elsa was more attractive than her daughter. She gazed into Szigety's eyes a bit longer than necessary. Antal and Nikola chose a table near the window, sunlit and covered with a checkered tablecloth. Little Elsa, pug-nosed like a bat, had quick movements and a broad smile on her face. In the blink of an eye, coffee cups appeared, nestled on lace napkins. Dew-beaded balls of butter curled in a silver bowl. In a basket, buns lay covered with a cloth to keep them hot. The sunlight that warmed Szigety's cheek fell on a small jar of apricot jam. The atmosphere was pleasant from the very beginning. Their conversation was spontaneous and in a half hour the young men dropped their air of formality and called each other by their first names. Amazed but still drowsy, Antal examined the impeccable Nikola. His hair was combed back, and his bony fingers placed his cup of café au lait precisely back in place.

He looks so fresh, Antal could not help thinking.

Their conversation showed Nikola to be neither rude nor arrogant, at least not in the way Antal expected him to be. Antal took the liberty of suggesting his new friend part his hair in the middle rather than to comb it back. Sure, Nikola would consider it.

Tesla had found the young man likable ever since—in the lecture hall—Szigety first smiled at him from under his blond mustache, extended his hand, and said, "Antal Szigety." What he especially appreciated was the other's ability to say the funniest thing with a straight face—just like Professor Pöschl. Whenever they wanted to emphasize a point—or, as young people commonly do, to interrupt each other—they tapped each other's shoulders. It turned out that Szigety also read Voltaire. They were anxious to show off their knowledge of the great Frenchman's ideas. It so happened that they chose contradicting quotes.

"The physician knows all mankind's weaknesses, the lawyer all its corruptions, and the priest all about its stupidity," Tesla said.

"If God didn't exist, man would have to create Him. But everything in Nature hails His existence," Szigety quoted the same Voltaire.

Continuing to smile, Tesla told Szigety that he had no recollection of such a quote by Voltaire. Breaking a bun and watching the steam rise, he admitted, "I probably don't remember such a statement because, in Voltaire, I always looked for arguments against my father, who tried to crush my soul in order to save it. If I hadn't almost died, he would've forced me to study theology."

At these words, Antal became serious and said that, on his part, he once believed he felt the "call" to become a priest.

"Why?" Tesla wondered.

"I dreamed about purity." Antal fixed him with his blue eyes. "Not only did I read religious books, I also felt a mystical unity with all that exists. I desired to address the world in words of love, like Saint Francis of Assisi in his famous hymn:

> 'Be praised, my Lord, through all Your creatures, especially through
> my lord Brother Sun . . .
> through Sister Moon and the stars . . .
> through our sister Bodily Death . . .'"

CHAPTER 20

The Light

In moments of inspiration, Nikola had a feeling that he had been struck by lightning. The uppermost branches of his nerves lit up. The glare blinded him. Light spread from his forehead downward. While this was going on—or in its aftermath—he saw what he otherwise could only imagine.

"That's the same energy!" Szigety exclaimed.

"What energy?" Nikola asked.

"The energy that binds a man and a woman together and leads to procreation," Szigety said, grinning. "The cosmic energy, if you will—the most powerful energy that people are endowed with."

Nikola raised his eyebrows.

"Let me tell you a story. When I was thirteen, I discovered that thing between my legs . . ."

Nikola raised his eyebrows even higher.

"So I started to explore it," Szigety went on unabashed, "with gentle rubbing! You know what they told us at school, that masturbation is self-mutilation, that it saps your *nervous substance*, and all that stuff. So I was afraid to push it. But one day I decided to cross the line."

"Oh!" Nikola's eyebrows wanted to hide in his hair, but could not traverse his exceptionally high brow.

"Don't get me wrong," Szigety said. "It's not important what you talk about—it's how you say it. So, one day I found myself alone at home. I undressed and stood in front of a mirror. Then I lay on my sister's bed and firmly grasped the tree of life."

Tesla looked at his friend in polite disbelief.

"I started to make those movements, you know." Szigety was so wrapped up in his story he frowned. "And all of a sudden, a light started to spread from my toes upward. Nikola, it lapped over my feet and washed up my knees. This flood of inner light spilled over my thighs and reached my loins. The first time, I got frightened and didn't go all the way, so the light receded to where it came from. It's the same. Don't you get it? The same thing."

"No," retorted Tesla. "Discovery is the greatest excitement in the world. A discovery is a kiss from God.

"Compared to that all other thrills are nothing.

"Nothing!"

CHAPTER 21

The Impossible

When Nikola first saw Jakob Pöschl, the professor of theoretical and experimental physics, he did not know if Pöschl was a man or a bear. If he was a bear, where did they catch him? How did they succeed in shaving him? Who bound him into this gray suit? Pöschl's feet would make a shoemaker despair. His hands were like shovels. The first-year student wondered how the professor could carry out his delicate experiments with such hands.

Another thing eluded Tesla. Why would Pöschl, a man of real abilities, be bragging about the three-story townhouse he acquired through marriage? Why would he talk about the Dominican mahogany desks he bought for his daughters, insisting that—without one—"intellectual work is impossible"? Why these stupidities? To Tesla it seemed that his professor craved things he did not respect and was proud of the unwanted things he already had. It appeared to him that Pöschl relied more upon his average shrewdness than upon his first-rate mind—as if he, without noticing, had lost the guiding light in his life, which Tesla was just discovering in his own.

The revolutionary year 1848 found Jakob Pöschl in the midst of the liberal demonstrations at the capital. In March of that year he was the hero Schiller and Byron envisioned. With the wind in his hair and a song on his lips, he shouted "Freedom!" and "Constitution!" As a member of the "Academic Legion," he protested against Metternich's spies and called the Archduke Ludwig a jackass in public. He envisioned himself taller than any of the Vienna church spires and imagined history following the moves of his baton. When an older relative cautioned him about the impossibility of his demands for universal voting rights, civil marriage, and the abolition of censorship, the young man responded with confidence, "We decide what's possible."

Pöschl never forgave himself for becoming so frightened on October 17, the day when Alfred Candid von Windischgrätz received the order to suppress the riots with force. Fleeing from Jelačić's soldiers—in whose ranks Nikola's uncle Branković humbly marched—he took shelter in his hometown of Graz. He was no longer the lawgiver who thundered against all the princes of this world. Now he paid attention not only to what was possible but also to what was expected. As he watched, the gains of the revolution either withered away or took root decades later. He let the social routine lead his life.

Pöschl never forgave himself, however, for betraying his youthful convictions and never completely lost all his rebellious traits from 1848. Instead of riding in a carriage, he sometimes came to the university on horseback. Like a pigeon from a conjurer's hat, something so unexpected would occasionally flow from Pöschl's mouth, his students would reel with laughter. Naturally, some of the students liked him and some did not. His wife told him, "I think those who don't like you understand you better."

Their friends insisted that his rich wife's sense of humor—just like his own—somewhat compensated for her bad temper.

"Everyone has prejudices," Pöschl told his colleague Rogner. "Some hate the Slavs. Some hate the Jews. Some hate the French. I hate the students."

A sympathetic nod did not cost Rogner much. He knew that his erratic colleague was a good teacher, capable of sudden outbursts of enthusiasm. At the beginning of Nikola's first year, with a glance around, Pöschl silenced the auditorium and promised, "Next year we'll do experiments with the Gramme dynamo. I give you my word of honor. We just ordered one from Paris."

So it was that the following year he triumphantly unpacked the dynamo with his huge hands.

"The Jacobins marked the beginning of their calendar with the French Revolution," he said. "I suggest that we mark ours with this moment—now!"

He tuned the dynamo on.

To the students' amusement, the machine crackled loudly.

"This electrical discharge can be reduced but not eliminated," the professor's voice rose above the noisy static. "The Gramme dynamo will continue to crackle as long as there's direct current and magnets have two poles."

"Why does the current have to stream only one way?" Nikola whispered to his bench colleague, Szigety.

Pöschl gave a reproachful look first to Tesla and then to Szigety. He continued in a louder voice: "As long as magnets have two poles, each affecting the current in an opposite way, we will have to use a commutator that redirects the current at the right moment."

"As long as a magnet has two poles, rather than—let's say—five," Szigety whispered to Tesla.

Józef Pliniecki, a nobleman from Krakow, raised his hand and observed, "That means both the machine and we who utilize it are limited by the direct current we are using."

His comment was as reasonable as it was superfluous.

Pöschl gave a peevish nod. At that moment, Nikola's face took on a look of horror. Something was happening to him. It looked as if he was about to sneeze. He sensed something approaching that just needed a catalyst. A more mature person would compare that feeling with an oncoming epileptic fit or an orgasm. For a moment, Tesla did not know where he was. The sphere of his forehead was bathed in light. Recovering from the powerful stress of intuition, he raised his hand and asked, "But why . . . why couldn't we get rid of the commutator altogether?"

Pöschl threw his arms up in exasperation, like a man faced with an unreasonable suggestion. "What?" he barked, lifting his eyebrows.

"Why couldn't we eliminate the commutator?" repeated Szigety in the archbishop's basso.

Pöschl ignored him as he sought out Tesla's almond-shaped eyes. His own large eyes swam in the lenses of his glasses. For a moment, the professor and his student faced each other like David and Goliath.

"Why? Let me tell you why," sputtered Pöschl with a vengeance.

He pointed out the critical importance of the commutator, which was designed by André-Marie Ampère and first manufactured by the maker of electrical instruments Hippolyte Pixii. With ease and conviction, he spoke about the dangers of alternating current and the irreplaceability of direct current. Just a moment before, Nikola had known in his gut that eliminating the commutator must be possible. Pöschl's eloquence confused him. At the same time, Nikola knew that his professor was wrong, just as he had known that his father Milutin was wrong when he wanted to send him to the seminary. Milutin was wrong because he was "only" a priest. Pöschl was only a professor.

This is not the truth, he thought. *This is just a word game.*

Tesla was not entitled to think that way. He was powerless. He was young. He did not have the right. He himself was shocked by what he felt in the depths of his soul. Pöschl smiled with malice and pity while delivering his final blow.

"Mr. Tesla may accomplish great things, but this he won't be able to do. It would be like changing a constant force that attracts—like gravity—into a rotational force."

Tesla nearly blurted out, "Well, isn't precisely gravitation the reason why the moon orbits around the earth, and the earth around the sun?"

But he bit his tongue.

Pöschl waved his gigantic hands in victorious conclusion: "That's not just difficult. That's impossible!"

"We decide what's possible!" slipped from Tesla's mouth.

Pöschl did not say a word, but his eyes grew warmer. The man who used to say, "I hate my students!" suddenly got confused. His piteous smile encompassed Tesla, Szigety, Pliniecki, and the rest of the large auditorium overflowing with youth.

CHAPTER 22

And the Moon Is Your Neighbor

After he finished his first two years of college in one and earned grades "better than the best," Nikola went back home. Both his Militärgrenze[2] scholarship and his decision to study electrical engineering were now justified. Upon his return to Gospić, his neighbor Bjelobaba wondered, *Is this the same one who went away?*

Mother cast a spell of cleanliness over the entire house. Each window, table, dresser, even the chest, was decorated with embroidery that her fingers—"nimble as fire"—had created. In Nikola's childhood, Mother used to kiss him on the head while his hair was still warm from the sun and say, "Home is your home and the moon is your neighbor." When he came back from Graz, she put her hand on his shoulder and surprised him by saying, "My Niko! You can't do small things, but you can do great things."

And yet, something was strange. Father frowned, changed the subject, and avoided looking him in the eye.

"Yes, I'm in good health." Nikola was puzzled as he answered Father's questions.

---

2. The Military Frontier (*Vojna granica* or *Vojna krajina* in Serbian), created by the Habsburgs in the sixteenth century, was a military buffer zone between the Habsburg Empire (later the Austro-Hungarian Empire) and the Ottoman Empire. Among other territories, it incorporated all the regions with the Serbian majority in present-day Croatia, including Tesla's homeland, Lika. The Military Frontier was abolished in 1881.

When he found himself alone, Nikola made a face like he was about to play the trumpet and broke into tears.

He still hasn't gotten over Dane's death, he thought. *He'll never accept me. I can't replace Dane!*

In Graz he worked eighteen hours a day to please Father. He expected joy and recognition in return. And what did he get? Nothing!

"So that's how it is," he whispered. "All right then . . ."

After long months of nervous strain, Gospić made him feel drowsy. He snuggled under the bedcovers and pulled them up to his nose. His eyelids were heavy and sweet honey bound one thought to another. The stars in the sky over Lika buzzed like hornets, but they did not bother him in his sleep. The old wind groaned in the forests that God himself had forgotten. The language of dreams seemed to be the only real language, while everyday life looked like a foggy deception.

"Hey, Nikola! Nikola!" Mother's shouted. "Nikola!"

"Who?" His hand reached out into empty space. Mist dissipated from his eyes, and he saw Mother's dark eyes and understood the plea they conveyed.

"Nikola, please wake up," she said. "Your relatives are here to see you!"

Nikola got dressed and went down to the living room, where two oil lamps shed light on the dining table. The sons of his two aunts were sitting there. He was still sleepy and saw them as if in a dream.

The posture of the first one, an officer, revealed a sense of natural pride. While they hugged each other ceremoniously, it occurred to Nikola that the currency of his cousin's dignity was not gold standard. The self-sufficient reticence of the tall, mustached man appeared to be a virtue by and in itself. His body simply radiated a natural sense of pride that was almost palpable.

The other cousin's green eyes shone from dark circles. He was a village teacher. He smiled only with one side of his face, smoked cigarettes till they burned his lips, and crowed when he laughed. His insecurity made him boastful, so he never missed an opportunity to interrupt a conversation. "You are clueless," he would say. "Let me tell you about that."

The third cousin was a chubby man with a startled demeanor. He smiled freely, with both sides of his face. He spent most of his life as a shepherd trilling after his flocks only to stun his family members when he joined the Herzegovina rebels as a volunteer in 1875. With a shocked expression, he told Nikola and his parents about the severed Serbian and Turkish heads he saw on stakes in Bosnia. He also talked about Montenegrin volunteers who used to call any man who died of natural causes a coward.

The light from the oil lamps danced over their faces.

The visitors crossed themselves and dug into the roast lamb. The proud man with the mustache was silent, and the other two became agitated when the conversation touched upon certain people.

"Mitar!" The fat volunteer made a face. "God, what an idiot! You won't find such an idiot on the moon! What do you say, scientist?" he asked Nikola in a serious voice.

"An idiot! An idiot!" the village teacher concurred.

The visitors drank red wine that stained their teeth and even sang a little as the evening progressed. The fat volunteer proved to be a good singer of Bosnian songs. He held one note for a long time. A shift of pitch would bring momentary relief, until the singer landed on another painful note.

My God, this sounds like a toothache singing! Nikola Tesla thought. *How much pain there is in all of this! Even in bragging, even in joy!*

As soon as a male child was born in the Militärgrenze, his name was entered into the ranks of a particular military unit. By birth, Nikola Tesla belonged to the First Lika Regiment, Medak Company Number 9, the same unit of the township his father belonged to by birth. As is well known, Nikola's name joined the long list of officers and priests in the family. His ancestors' duty was to secure the military border with Turkey. To be a "professional defender of Christendom" was not a particularly pleasant occupation. For centuries, brass buttons rippled on the chests of those officers, and feathers shimmered on the badges of their hats. They killed and were killed in the Austrian Empire's endless wars, and the priests glorified their deeds. But was not human goodness more important in an uncertain world than good laws in a certain one? Did not someone have to pity the blood those men shed in vain, stitch together their shattered lives, feel sorry for the selfsame heroes, know how much that heroism cost in sorrow, and make lives, regulated by soldierly imperatives, a little softer? Did not someone shed the tears the men were not allowed to shed? The women.

The women knew the high price paid for life in the world of severed heads. They knew about all the pain. The pain! They told stories in order to soften reality. The women offered stories as the bandages for wounded life. Just as their hands washed the bloody shirts, their words washed the world.

That was what Nikola was thinking about as he looked into Mother's hazelnut eyes that had grown darker with years.

After the guests had left, there was still enough food on the table to serve another supper.

Whenever a guest shut the door after him, Nikola's family would say one of two things: "He's a really good man" or "God, what an idiot." This time, Father compromised. After he saw his visitors off, he sighed. "Good people—but idiots!"

The relatives faded into the dark, like three demons whose goal was to point out to the prodigal son how things were at home. As soon as they left, Nikola started to yearn for the lecture halls of the polytechnics. After twenty-four hours, the very blue of Lake Plitvice started to lose its magic. Everything back here was tangled up in knots. One could make one's fingers bleed without being able to undo them.

The sobbing, metallic sound of dog's barking resounded outside all night. The reflection of rosy light finally started to pulsate on the wall. The student sat up in his bed and looked into the ruddy dawn.

"The maternal light," he muttered. "The maternal light."

Despite the great peace that reigned under his mother's roof, this young man with the divided heart felt a desire to leave immediately for Graz.

CHAPTER 23

The Duel

Once, a red-faced student accosted Nikola Tesla in the atrium of the Graz Polytechnic.

"Run home," he said. "Study hard so that your professors love you even more."

This student was a member of a fraternity and had a rapier scar on his face. And he was jealous. His name was Werner Lundgren, but they called him Tannhäuser, after Wagner's hero who cried for help from the hell of pleasure.

"We all know that you're good at burying your nose in a book," Lundgren told Tesla. "But can you live life to the fullest, sing a song, or raise hell?" He emphasized the words, staring mockingly into Tesla's eyes.

Tesla's animated face assumed the blank expression of his ancestors, who knew how to respond to a challenge.

"How about tonight?" he retorted. "In the Botanical Garden?"

Tannhäuser nodded.

At this point of the story, I have to gently but firmly take the reader by the arm, as we are about to step into legend.

There are several disputed points: Did Nikola Tesla and Werner Lundgren, known as Tannhäuser, really meet in the botanical garden that evening? Did the storied drinking duel actually take place? Was the table covered with clinking glasses? Did Austrian and Serbian students shout and cheer for their champion? Did the room start to distort and spin? Did the waitress run her fingers through Nikola's sweaty hair? Did Tesla's opponent and cosufferer begin to waver and dissolve in the yellow light? Did Tannhäuser collapse together with his chair, and did his young head bounce off the floor? Did Nikola, deaf to the screams of his supporters, stagger out into the transfigured night?

Did the duel change Nikola's life?

Was the duel the trigger?

CHAPTER 24

A Different Graz

The hangover opened Tesla's eyes to a different Graz. People grinned like foxes and feral cats. Carriages and brewery carts full of barrels clattered over the cobblestones. Billiard balls clacked in ale houses, and students drank to each other's health.

"Down with thirst!"

Tesla also started toasting with the merry students.

He wrote in his diary: *I should have thanked Tannhäuser for opening my eyes. If you want academics to recognize your knowledge, you have to renounce personal insight, because they don't ask the questions that you ask. Students see only what their professors tell them they will see. An opportunist won't direct his thoughts to anything that doesn't bring a reward. Why? Because the right and light of his own existence do not guide his thinking. He thinks what he is allowed to think.*

The city was lively, and so was he. In that different Graz, he turned into a different man. Before he went out for the evening, he would lick his finger and groom his eyebrows and mustache. He swaggered in an overcoat he did not know how to pay for. He borrowed more money from Murko the tailor. It was hard to tell whether a fly flew up Murko's nose or whether he tried to smile charmingly. Nikola neglected his classes and started to spend more time with Tannhäuser. His friends knew a medical student nicknamed the Doctor, and whenever they called for drinks, they shouted, "That's what the doctor ordered!" Tannhäuser clapped him on the back: "Niko is a great guy!"

On the green felt of the billiard table, Tesla envisioned geometrical figures. He deftly walked around the table, while the shots multiplied before his eyes. His back arched like a cat's. He never made an unnecessary move.

As he played, he never stopped thinking about the motor without the brushes and commutator. The solution seemed to lurk on the other side of a translucent membrane. Success was like an invisible man whose hand he could shake at any moment. In Tesla's homeland everything failed, so a successful man was considered a traitor. Success smelled like the January wind and solitude. Tesla was afraid of success, the presence of which he could almost smell. He feared success like a catastrophe. That fear may have prodded him to shout, "That's what the doctor ordered!" and to play endless games of billiards.

"Everyone likes to be forgiven for something," Szigety said, defending him.

Nikola woke up to a perfect break that scattered the balls and opened a game.

He did not play for buttons anymore, like he used to do with Mojo Medić. He played for money.

Antal Szigety came to see him at the Botanical Garden.

A slim young man with a wisp of hair across his forehead threw away a cigarette and came forward to meet him.

Szigety broke into laughter: "You look like a gigolo!"

Kosta Kulišić arrived as well, emancipated from any trace of kindness as usual.

"Don't worry, these two don't bite," Tesla told the waitress. "They are quite tame."

The friends played a game together.

"You need to know what your final shot will be as soon as you first scatter the balls," Tesla instructed Szigety, brushing the hair from his forehead.

"He's still innocent," Szigety said to Kulišić when they went out. "He just looks at you with those eyes of his."

"He's a little bit scary," Kulišić replied. "He is a scary guy."

One Saturday afternoon when nothing else was in sight, Nikola put down his cue and went over to the table where people were quietly playing cards. They offered him a seat.

"Do you want to try?"

"I'd love to."

Nikola surrendered to the game with the passion of a mathematician. His "angelic mind" tried to calculate all the possibilities held in a deck of cards. He followed the ebb and flow of luck that hovered above the checkered tablecloth. The invisible current of luck ran through the cards, so the players had to feel it. When he was winning, Tesla was elated. When he was losing, he experienced an inexplicable dizzy pleasure. With his thin mustache, neatly combed hair, and long fingers, he turned into a real gambler. He met people different from those he knew before. Drunks who staggered from the tavern like chickens with their heads cut off. Waiters who poured the first morning drink into the mouths of men whose hands shook too badly to hold a glass themselves. One of those wretches looked back at him.

"I wouldn't wish this on anyone," the man said in a mossy voice.

Outside was fog. Inside was cigarette smoke. Nikola kept gambling. Sometimes he returned the money to the sore losers. No one ever gave *him* any money back. Despite his quick intellect, the riffraff played better than he did. Fat Franz, whose double chin was as big as his head, robbed Tesla blind while telling him, "You're a good kid. Why are you hanging out with scum?"

Things got so bad that Tannhäuser, red-faced, shouted, "Come on, slow down a bit!"

"Don't shout," Nikola retorted. "I can shout louder than you."

"I can't figure him out," Szigety whispered to Kulišić.

"How can you figure him out when he can't figure himself out?" Kulišić yawned.

"Why do smart people do stupid things?" Szigety persisted.

"I don't know," Kulišić answered darkly. "I'm not smart. And I never do stupid things."

CHAPTER 25

Disappearing

Tesla did not stop.

He disappeared.

Everyone wondered where he was. His friends and relatives worried. Uncle Branković in Karlovac worried. Professors Rogner, Allé, and Pöschl worried. Big-nosed Kulišić worried. His three Mandić uncles worried. The tailor Murko, to whom Tesla owned money, worried. Some fellow students guessed that he jumped into the Mura out of desperation.

The men gossiped among themselves: "How could the son of such a father do that?"

"How could the son of such a mother do that?" the women murmured to each other.

Where did Nikola Tesla disappear to?

Kosta Kulišić unexpectedly found out when he applied for a position as a geography teacher in Maribor. Oskar Rösch, the school's owner, interviewed him for four hours. He showed him around the town and left him in Taget's tavern, across the street from the railroad station.

"I'll get in touch with you."

The young Herzegovinian surveyed the bar room and saw Tesla playing a game of piquet with some rough-looking men. Kulišić's first thought was that—missing his opportunity to jump into the Mura in Graz—his roommate was pushing his luck for a second time in Maribor.

"Tesla, my goodness!" Kulišić yelled.

"Kosta," Tesla beamed as he saw the well-known, imperious nose. "You know, we thought you drowned in the Mura."

With a smile, Tesla explained that an engineer had hired him for sixty forints a month.

"Why should I go back?" he said in a surprised voice. "I'm doing just fine where I am!"

In his head, Kulišić was already writing a letter to Tesla's father. With an agitated eye, he scanned Tesla's swaggering mustache from one end to the other. All in all, Nikola looked normal.

"I returned home reassured," Nikola's ex-roommate recalled later.

But soon after Kulišić's departure, on March 8, 1879, Oldrich Taube, a Maribor city official, signed a document regarding case number 2160. The writ, initiated by local police, ordered Nikolaus Tesla, a person without any visible means of support, to vacate Maribor for Gospić, where his father lived, in order to "find gainful employment." By March 17, the Gospić judge confirmed that Nikola Tesla had arrived at the specified destination.

Thus the fool and younger brother came back to the small town from the wide world. Just like the sorcerer's apprentice, Nikola could now say, "I haven't learned anything. I've forgotten even what I used to know."

"What do you mean, *don't?*" Father shouted at Mother. "Senile Granny Anka asks every man if he's seeing a girl. She even asks her son-in-law if he's seeing a girl. Whenever Nikola pays her a visit, she asks him the same question. And he just turns his head away."

"Please don't," Djuka whispered.

"He didn't want to become a priest . . . and why? To become a monk!"

"Easy, Milutin . . ."

The priest waved his hand at his wife. With that same hand, the one that so many people had kissed, he motioned Nikola to a chair.

"Sit down."

Mother went out so they could talk. In the kitchen, she lifted the lid from the boiling pot of cabbage the color of gold. Then she stole back to hear what they were talking about.

"My God, the way you live!" the priest said with disgust as soon as his wife left the room. "I used to say: let him drink and gamble if only he could live like a normal young man. And then I heard that you did gamble. And that you did drink."

You didn't care about my top grades, Nikola thought vengefully. *So how do you like this?*

On the icon, Saint George, their patron saint, was killing a dragon, oblivious to what he was doing.

"You're the one who lost the scholarship! You're the one who got expelled from school! You're the one who came home escorted by the police!" Father growled.

"God help me!" Djuka whispered behind the door.

"You don't care about anything. Even the great Victor Hugo has written about us Serbs. This is what he said: 'The Turks are killing off one entire nation. Where? In the heart of Europe!' And what about you? How many times have you thought about your Serbian God and your people as you consorted with gamblers over there in Graz?"

"I may not have thought about those things very much, but I certainly did more often than Victor Hugo," Nikola could not help saying.

In Gospić, Milutin criticized his son every time the young man took a breath. All his reproaches boiled down to this: he wanted a solemn promise from Nikola to quit gambling.

A mysterious, impish smile hovered on Nikola's face.

Honesty was Milutin Tesla's answer to any question that life posed. On his daily trips to the tavern, Nikola sometimes looked up at the clouds in the sky and wondered if Milutin's honesty had any effect on them.

"Rest from thy righteousness and thou shalt live peacefully for the rest of thy days." He mocked Father in the words of Abbot Pimen.

During the day, Nikola was lazy and apathetic. At night, he mounted the darkness. His heart beat one somersault forward, one somersault back. He ate little. He fed on the tavern's lights, like a moth. Gamblers thought he was a weak-willed creature and an easy mark. With their servile and ironic grins, they greeted the man who was an irreplaceable part of the gambling scene. He, however, knew that he could quit at any time. Was he not the master of the will that "unlocked" hundreds of volumes by Voltaire and cracked any mathematical problem that came his way? He occasionally decided, *I won't play again.*

Then the demon's falsetto called, "Let's go to the tavern! You'll win!"

It started with a yearning in his belly. An itching slowly spread over his body like oil over the table. *Perhaps . . . I might*—an uptight inner voice whispered. The whole world felt ticklish and irritating. He was like a man running to the bathroom, unbuttoning his pants on the way. Powerless. Passionate. Trembling. God unhooked him from the hook of his reason. God made him greed incarnate.

He gnashed his itching teeth.

The inner rhythm repeated: *I want! I want! I want!*

His obsession led him to the place where fingers spat out and received the cards. He fell on his chair. He bolted his drink down. The brandy drove a spike into his heart, burned and wormed up his stomach. He felt the heat creep across his shoulders. His shoulders fell, his thoughts grew softer. A forgotten cigarette charred the edge of the table. He sighed and a shameful sense of surrender turned into a sweet relief.

One suicidal, boring winter night he lost all his money at the Lamb in Gospić, playing with a defrocked priest and Nenad Alagić. He went home and said to his mother, "Give me more money to win back what I've lost!"

Mother did not believe people could be changed—they could only be loved. She opened a drawer and handed him all of the household's money. "Here you are. Lose it all. Get it out of yourself!"

Nikola left the house and went toward the Lamb where Alagić and the defrocked priest waited for another bout. And again he turned into a rolling rock. With each step, he tried to prevent his fall. His hands crumpled the stash of cold money. And his legs walked by themselves, carrying him along. And the force carried him. And he tried to stop it, like a brakeman yanking the lever on a train heading toward an abyss. Inertia pushed him on. Metal screeched. And Nikola stopped.

He felt like swallowing and throwing up at the same time.

"What am I doing?"

He started to sob, his steps took him in the opposite direction. They continued to echo across the Gospić cobblestones until dawn. When he returned home, he found that Mother was still up.

"Never again!" he swore, his face beaming.

But she interrupted him: "Your father had an attack!"

"What happened?" The newly reformed gambler was upset.

Djuka put her finger to her lips and made him go to bed. Then she went up to her bedroom and tenderly addressed her husband: "My poor Milutin!"

"Never pity me." He clasped her hand. "Not even on my deathbed."

CHAPTER 26

All Nature Stood Still

"My father was an honest man, but not a good one," Nikola Tesla told František Žurek in Prague.

During their last meeting, the tension between father and son ached like an old wound. It seemed their icy silence would shatter the walls of the room. Nikola sat on the sick man's bed, just like Milutin had sat on his son's bed during his bout with cholera. Father's eyes and cheeks were sunken. Milutin could barely utter what he'd planned to say: "I promised to send you to study in Graz. Now you must promise me that you will continue your studies in Prague."

When the old man was buried, Nikola was not there. They told him that the day was dark, but when they lowered the casket into the ground, the sun broke through. They told him that a lot of men and women passed for three days through their house—as was the custom— exhausting the family so much they could barely think.

The flood of visitors drowned Djuka, Milka, Angelina, and Marica in the noisy maelstrom of life—the visitors asked for brandy, quoted proverbs, made coffee, did the dishes, and gave advice. Everyone talked about the dead man. Alagić recounted a story that he once told Milutin about a man who spent a night nose to nose with a wolf and turned gray before dawn. Milutin would wave his hand, saying, "He's no man, and that's no wolf, either!"

They remembered his many-voiced arguments with himself and his incredible memory. He graduated from the School of Theology at the top of his class. The tall Milutin! He recited Schiller. He would push his glasses up on his forehead and forget that they were there. During the summer, he would not take shelter in the shade but would walk in the middle of the street. A smart man. A good man. They were all in agreement.

"And he had just turned sixty."

"So sad!"

All of that tiring bustle was fine—anything was better than emptiness and solitude. Only when they were left alone did it become unbearable.

"How did he die?" Nikola asked as soon as he arrived in Gospić.

Mother put her hand on his shoulder: "He was lying in my lap breathing heavily. He was suffering. I let him go. Milutin, I told him, Milutin! You can go now. He looked at me. He closed his eyes. He sighed his last, relieved."

It took Nikola three days before he unlocked his father's desk.

In the drawer were Father's treasures.

What was the scroll tied with red and blue string?

A letter. "Your son is a first-rate star." Good!

And this? Professor Rogner's letter in which he suggested that Father Tesla should bring his son home from school to prevent him from working himself to death.

He found a folder and untied a purple ribbon. Some old letters fell out. Father Milutin wrote to the citizens of Senj like Saint Paul wrote to the Corinthians, and saved the copies. This is what he wrote:

The man who installed the support bar for the hanging lamp on the church floor right in the middle of the painted body of Our Savior didn't do anything praiseworthy.

From his strange father, Nikola inherited the gifts for mathematics and languages as well as a phenomenal memory.

He always lived in opposition to Father. He read Voltaire to oppose him. Nikola craved the relief of tears but did not know how to start. His hand trembled. Some newspaper clippings slipped out of the folder. He sniffed a twenty-five-year-old *Serbian Daily* in which his father reported on the "beautiful phenomenon" in the sky over Lika. This time, the son felt that the description did not read like a scientific article by an amateur, published in a provincial paper. It was true poetry:

The sky smiled, and the stars glowed bright as ever; but all of a sudden, something flashed in the east. . . . The stars withdrew, and it appeared that all nature stood still.

CHAPTER 27

Do You Want to See Golden Prague?

After returning to Prague, he walked a lot. He stood by the railing of the Charles Bridge and stared into the black water. A long time ago, Rabbi Levi created the golem in this city and breathed life into the clay giant. Very few among Nikola's professors could do the same with their lectures. In the university halls, dead knowledge remained clay untouched by spirit as the professors' flat voices drained meaning from their words. Nikola learned this was not something he could talk about with his peers. He murmured to himself: "There's nothing worse than stumbling upon a prejudice people believe they don't have."

The academic bureaucracy was more complex than the hierarchy of angels in Assyrian mythology. It was as if huge insects sat on the other side of the counter. These gnats informed Nikola that due to his lack of knowledge of Greek, he could not enroll at Charles University as a full-time student. Therefore, twice a week, he attended the seminars of the famous Karel Domalíp as a part-time student. He also attended Adalbert von Waltenhofen's lectures in physics at the German School of Engineering.

Szigety's letters arrived in regular intervals. They were all the same, the only difference being that his object of adoration was named Erica at one time and Maria at another. Tesla wrote to him that he had separated the collector from the engine and affixed it to the other axle. In the letters he sent to Budapest, he repeatedly stated that a motor powered by alternating current must be possible.

In the morning, he drank coffee in the Národní Kavárna on Vodičkova Street. Wherever he went, he was followed by that other one, who was slowly becoming frightening. It seemed to him that the imposing contours of Hradčany Castle constantly hovered above him. He admired the dollhouses on Zlata Ulička, while the old Jewish cemetery with its layers of graves filled him with horror. In the evening, he went back to the Národní Kavárna for a beer.

One of the pleasant bohemians he met there was František Žurek, a former Charles University student. He started to take Tesla to concerts. Not unlike the moon, music created tides and swayed huge waves within Nikola's soul. In the Národní Kavárna, Žurek pointed out to him the composer Bedřich Smetana sitting at the next table. The man looked awful.

"They say he's crazy," the bohemian whispered.

A supporter of Pan-Slavism—with a German grandmother—Žurek became interested in Tesla after an incident in the Imperial Public Library at the Clementinum. The red-haired philosophy student was comparing the German translation of Byron with the English original when Tesla approached him. Tesla grabbed the book with a bony hand.

"Read the beginning of any Byron poem to me," he said, "and I'll finish it from memory."

The young Czech read a first line, and Tesla took it to the end. Žurek chose a poem from the back of the book. Looking him straight in the eye, Tesla finished it. He knew all of Byron by heart, so Žurek called him Manfred. "Manfred" spoke about everything in a "worldly and indifferent manner." Whatever he said was well put. Slanderers spread rumors that he played billiards to support himself. At the Národní Kavárna, Tesla picked up the cue only occasionally but then played in such a way that everyone in the café quit talking.

"A prince!" they whispered in awe.

Manfred and his new friend walked around Prague and talked like poets:

"All things in the world are interconnected just like madmen believe they are," Tesla murmured.

"Can you lose what doesn't exist?" Žurek wondered.

Žurek's goal was to show his guest every inch of the mysterious city.

Did Tesla know that here in Prague each stone could tell a story? He already knew the one about the golem? That's good. Did he know that at least one-quarter of Bohemia was destroyed during the Thirty Years' War? And did he know that tulips, before they became common in the Netherlands, adapted to the European climate here first, in the Royal Gardens, next to the Singing Fountain?

"And here"—ha, ha—"here we have something much more interesting," Žurek the chaperone continued. "In the house at Forty Charles Square—I'm going to show it to you in a second—lived Dr. Faust. The devil took him away through that chimney over there."

Tesla stared at the chimney.

Tesla's soul suffered in Prague. Sorrow suffocated him. He was restless because he could not pretend that the world was not in flames. In his dreams, his late father visited him, legless and hovering, his frock undulating like an octopus. He also dreamed of a man who, instead of having a face, had two backs, and whose voice spoke from the fissure, sounding like many rivers running together.

"Who are you?"

"I'm your brother."

"How come I've never seen you before?"

Nikola washed his face, put on his clothes, and walked until morning, pacing up and down in front of Dr. Faust's house.

Something whispered in his ear: *The horror!*

Something screamed in his mind: *The horror!*

With his wounded, burning eyes he followed the flight of the snowflakes and their shadows. He went back after ten minutes, and his footprints were already covered. He walked up and down the street three times, and each time he found his footprints covered with snow. He did not notice that it was growing light. Old ladies bustled past him, hurrying to morning Mass. Organists in churches started to play the music of God's thoughts.

"Have you heard about the tragic end of Master Hanuš, who built the astronomic clock?" Žurek went on. "Did you know that when Wenceslaus the Fourth cut out Saint John the Nepomuk's tongue in Prague, the severed tongue continued to preach? When the saint was thrown off the Charles Bridge, the bridge started to crumble and no one could fix it until an architect entered into a contract with the devil and—"

Tesla interrupted him: "It seems to me there've been a number of contracts signed with the devil in Prague."

"Quite a few, quite a few," Žurek answered with pride.

CHAPTER 28

The Smart Cabbage

Nikola's uncle Pajo Mandić came to Prague from Budapest. He looked at his nephew with his bovine eyes and informed him that the director of Edison's office in Paris was named Tivadar Puskás.

"So what?" Nikola wondered.

Colonel Mandić took a shot of Becherovka. He looked askance at his nephew—he still remembered Nikola's gambling days.

"Tivadar gave his brother Ferenc all the rights to build a telephone network in Hungary. Ferenc is my friend. He needs electrical engineers. If you want the job, it's yours."

The first man who embraced Tesla at the Budapest railway station was Antal Szigety.

He's a good-looking man, Tesla thought with some envy. Szigety's laughing eyes reminded him of the Plitvice Lakes. Antal had the body of a swimmer or a gymnast who does squats with barbells. Antal raised Tesla off the ground in a hug, then jumped and shouted, "You're too thin! We'll change that!"

On Saturdays, Tesla's rich uncle Pajo Mandić and Farkas Szigety alternated entertaining the young men. The elder Szigety was an architect who spent a long time bouncing across rutted roads and sketching examples of Hungarian rural ornaments. He found accommodations for Nikola with a female family friend.

"Is she widowed or divorced?" Tesla asked.

"She's divorced from her own mind," Antal grinned.

The salon in Tesla's new apartment was decorated with a white tiled stove in the shape of a pagoda. There were two paintings on the wall. On the landlady's portrait as a young woman, paint cracks wrinkled the green-eyed blond's face. On the other painting someone was being crowned—a foreigner could not tell whether it was Saint István or Matthias Corvinus. The ceilings were so lofty that even a tall man standing on horseback could not touch them. All the furniture suffered from elephantiasis.

As soon as the move was complete, Szigety put a potbelly-shaped bottle on the table. As Tesla smiled, Szigety announced, "It's real Tokay."

They invited the landlady to join them.

Her name was Márta Várnai, and she was the author of two children's books: *The Smart Cabbage* and *The Hedgehog's Lecture.* Her foggy Hungarian accent hung above the stream of her fluent German. In a sensible voice, she spoke about the works of Miklós Jósika, the Hungarian romantic writer, whom Mojo and Nikola enjoyed reading in Gospić. Her son recently became an army doctor serving in Sarajevo, which was almost in Nikola's homeland. In her sensible voice, Mrs. Várnai stated that Budapest—the empire's "other capital"—needed new blood.

"We need engineers like you, Mr. Tesla." She continued eagerly, "We need a new opera house, new bridges, new streets."

Márta spread her arms as if creating space for future boulevards.

The sensible voice of Mrs. Várnai said one thing, but her charm said another. It surfaced as a glint in her eye, as a ticklish lilt in her laughter. Light engulfed Tesla. Some amorphous warmth from her entire body brushed against him and Szigety, who just happened to drop by.

Szigety sighed when she left them. "Did you see that?"

"What?" Tesla asked.

"I'm not surprised she buried two husbands," Szigety whispered. "She didn't outlive them—she wore them out!"

He sorely regretted having not known her thirty years before.

"Smart cabbage, my ass. Only children can buy into that. Ha! If only I could have been a fly on the ceiling in her bedroom."

In Budapest, Antal Szigety first spoke openly about his desires. He liked for women to undress and show him the sacred places on their bodies. He liked them to walk around the room naked and with their hips reveal the same force that makes stars and planets rotate. Antal frequented brothels where girls' smiles radiated erotic fire and cunning. He told Tesla of the inner slickness of women and offered to take him to a house of ill-repute, which Tesla sensed had something to do with Dante's *Inferno*. In his friend's room, Antal left a copy of Casanova's *Memoirs*. Nikola did not read beyond the titles of the chapters, such as "A Disquieting Night," "I Fell in Love with Two Sisters and Forgot about Angela," and "The Captain Left Us in Reggio Where I Spent a Night with Henrietta."

"Casanova!" Tesla murmured. He put the book aside; his yawn was wide like the sound hole on a guitar.

Just like in Tobelbad a long time ago, he and Antal soaked in the hot springs. His friend took him to hear some really odd-looking musicians. The female singer was twice as tall as the violinist, who played with his eyes closed. The man who performed on the hammer dulcimer hit the strings with mallets wrapped in burning flax. The tamboura players broke their fingernails on the strings. Women twirled around in folk costumes embroidered with pearls. Men danced with carafes of wine on their hats. Tesla's soul responded to upbeat songs, but even more so to melancholy ones. The empire's "other capital" agreed with him, especially since he had enough money for the first time in his life. Not only did he dress well, he had completely mastered the silent language of clothes. Mrs. Várnai assisted him with her subtle advice. Tesla thanked her with a bouquet of roses into which she buried her face when she was left alone.

A lot of construction was going on in Budapest—one sharp tower tried to outgrow the other. And what sunsets they had over the city! The pink and purple sky disintegrated above the roofs. Tesla worked with the engineers who built the sixth European switchboard. Everything smelled like Big Time.

A blond conquistador's beard was always in the thick of things. Ferenc Puskás! Puskás slapped Tesla on the back like Uncle Branković used to do a long time ago. He promoted him and started to call him "sonny."

"Faster, sonny, faster!"

If someone asked, Tesla would say that *impatience* was a synonym for *genius.* He complained that the world was too slow and enjoyed cramming his days full of obligations. Day was on his right side, and night was on his left. He could not wait for dawn to break so that he could continue to work. It was so fascinating, so painfully fascinating. Tesla disappeared at work—a blind force that resembled fire was in his place. A visor fell over his eyes. In the glare, he saw an even brighter window and in it something that did not exist before. That is how he came up with his first invention.

"What did you make?" Szigety was curious.

"A telephone earpiece! I increased the number of magnets in the receiver of the telephone," Nikola responded. "And I changed their position in relation to the diaphragm."

"Does Puskás like it?"

The young man's face lit up:

"He'll use my invention in the telephone broadcast of an operatic performance in February."

During the pre-Lent Season, Erkel's opera *Hunyadi László* was performed at the National Theatre. "The whole of Budapest" simultaneously followed the production in the Vigadó Concert Hall. The quality of the broadcast was better than in Paris. In the electric light, dignitaries looked a little touched in the head.

"But where's Tesla?" Puskás asked Szigety in a disgruntled whisper.

Up until the day before, Tesla planned the broadcast with utmost enthusiasm, rushed Puskás on, and kept repeating, "Work created man. Let it destroy him too!"

Nikola had accelerated until the finest wire in his head snapped. His soul seemed to have hung by that wire. After it broke, the young man turned into a bundle of burning nerves. He was lying in bed behind heavy curtains in Mrs. Várnai's apartment. When they told him about the success of the broadcast, he did not have enough strength to smile.

CHAPTER 29

The Decadent

And when he thus had spoken, he cried with a loud voice,
"Lazarus, come forth."
John 11:43

It would be a mistake to judge Mrs. Várnai's educational background from her books for children. Tesla's landlady could recite Verlaine in French. She asked her tenant if he had read Baudelaire only to discover that he remembered just one line: "Satan, have mercy on my ultimate despair."

By that time, *Les fleurs du mal* was the same age as Tesla. A generation of poets inspired by the book had already stepped onto the scene. Poets and painters started to insist on morbid hypersensitivity, the urban cult, and life with dark circles around the eyes. European art turned into the princess and the pea. But Mrs. *Várnai* knew that none of those artists who worshiped hashish and the green spirit of absinthe were any more sensitive or decadent than Nikola Tesla.

Before the opera broadcast, Tesla rested five hours a day but slept only two. He woke up before dawn and hurried to his office. He could not decide whether to blame Budapest or fate for the deterioration of his health.

This city gets under my skin, he wrote in his diary.

"Let's go! Keep it up, sonny!" Ferenc Puskás shouted.

For his part, Tesla also egged Puskás on and increased the pace.

Then something snapped.

The whole world quivered, and Tesla with it. And yet, instead of quietly falling in sync with each other, these quivers clashed. Below the trembling, even in complete silence, a conversation went on that only the sick man could hear. Nikola broke that hallucination down into its basic components. The murmur of the universe, both distant and close, sounded like g-a-aaa-arbl-ed words. Beneath the sounds of the outside noises, these words ran on, slow and drawn out. Who was talking—God or a monster hidden behind the face of daily life?

The whistle of a distant train shook the bench he was sitting on. A clock in the third room struck like a hammer hitting an anvil. Tesla heard ants scuttling across the floor. A fly alighting on the table sent a flash under the dome of his skull. In the darkness, he could sense an object several yards away through a creepy feeling on his forehead.

"You're a bat," Szigety declared.

The vibrations of Budapest traffic, penetrating through the frame of the building, his bed, and his chair, shook the bat's entire body. Sun machine-gunned through the leaves of the houseplants and dazed him. He was grateful for the heavy drapes in Mrs. Várnai's apartment. He put rubber pads under the legs of his bed. He wanted to lie down eight stories beneath the ground. He was so tired.

"What's happening to me?" the young engineer trembled.

Doctors passed through the rooms of potted rhododendrons and smoky mirrors. Szigety showed their self-assured spectacles and goatees to the door. After a fortnight of physicians' visits, Tesla still did not feel any better. His fingers dangled as if they were about to fall off his hands. His arms dangled as if they were about to fall off his shoulders.

"How do you feel?" Szigety asked from the door.

"Like Saint Sebastian," Tesla whispered.

The arrows opened holes in Saint Sebastian's skin, while eyes started to open on Tesla's: one on the back of his head, another on his shoulder, and yet another on his stomach. Perception flayed him alive. He was all eyes and lips.

"We need your help," Szigety told Mrs. Várnai.

The landlady gave a sidelong look, full of understanding and compassion. From that moment on, she was a daily visitor to the darkened room in which she could hear the sick man rave.

"Dane, let me go! Please let me go!"

She brought in some cakes and chamomile tea sweetened with honey, and whispered, "Eat."

Nikola bared his fangs, trying to smile.

Mrs. Várnai's clasped fingers went white as she prayed for him. She longed to caress that tormented creature. Once, while he was asleep, she branded his forehead with a kiss. The young man pretended not to notice it. He gave her a furtive look and instantly regretted it. Her entire feminine soul was in her eyes.

When Lajos Várnai came to visit his mother from Sarajevo, he felt Tesla's irregular pulse and prescribed a large dose of potassium bromide.

"He's at death's door," he said and insisted on a second opinion. A distinguished specialist, Dr. Rosenzweig, came, snapped his bag shut in the end, and declared, "Medical science can't help him."

"Fuck science!" Szigety raged.

Since he had already failed to get Tesla to a brothel, the next best thing was to at least make him do some physical exercise.

"Trust me," he told Tesla as he lifted him off the bed.

Did not John the Golden Mouth say that men are just shadows of bursting soap bubbles? Nikola was cloaked in numbness and suffered from spells of deafness and nausea. In the fluid of his own fear, he pulsated like an amoeba. He walked on the streets as if they were caked in ice. In the buzzing world, he moved as if his next step would be his last.

Szigety urged him on.

"Get up. Illness comes in bulk and goes in parcels."

Szigety was the only one who believed that his friend could beat his illness. Disgusted with doctors, he said to himself, "People are blind. They don't see anything. They don't get anything. Most of them."

He forced Nikola to live. He dragged him out for a walk every day. The wind played with the powder of snow on the roofs. The smell of frost was a greeting from God. Under his breath, Nikola cursed the obnoxiously noisy city to its steeples. Whenever he passed under a bridge, he felt as if a huge weight was crushing his skull. This is why they preferred to walk in the open fields. Szigety gradually added calisthenics to their outings. Holding dumbbells, Tesla spread his arms from his hips and lifted them above his head. He felt bad, and when a person does not feel well, he hears the music only for himself. This was how he felt when it first occurred to him that he might make it. He was like a shipwreck survivor who sensed the nearness of the shore. And in the next moment, it was not a mere sensation—it was a veritable shore. He even started to believe his painful hatching was coming to an end. Something was prodding him from the other side of the membrane. The solution to the mystery was close at hand.

CHAPTER 30

The Park

As it set behind the Buda Hills, the sun lit up the frozen river, the big city, and two elegant young men taking a stroll along the graveled paths in the park. February 1882 was without snow, but frosty. One young man wore a black overcoat, buttoned all the way to the top, while the other was cloaked in a yellow camel hair coat. The hair of the man in the dark coat was black and slickly brushed back. His companion was chubby, with a fair mustache. He frowned unwillingly every so often.

Tesla was in a good mood, and he whistled a tune from Vivaldi's *Winter.* Szigety's lips were curled in a "smile of playful Eros."

"In this very park a scene from *The Memoirs of a German Lady Singer* by Wilhelmina Schröder-Devrient is set," he informed the indifferent Tesla.

Two women wearing hats with large plumes went by. They were talking about a famous violinist.

Tesla and Szigety overheard one saying, "He doesn't look like much in person, but his music is so intoxicating."

Two maids followed the women. A brunette with straight hair and a square jaw held the arm of a little blond who resembled a jelly roll.

"My teeth are bad. Whenever I eat anything sweet, I cry," the blond complained in a joyful voice. "But I still like to . . ."

A little boy dressed like a girl sat on his bottom and the maid with bad teeth yanked him up. "Come on, Herve. Don't try to be cute, please."

A high-spirited sparrow hopped across the path. With their quivering bills, tame ducks pecked at grain scattered for them in the grass.

"I've almost forgotten that all of this exists," Tesla sighed.

Szigety had also forgotten about the world.

He was thinking about Rita's lips on his!

He dreamed of spreading her thighs with his knee and—shivers ran down his spine at the thought—of her stockings making a hissing sound. Her face was dancing. Oh, Muse, help me describe the dancing of that face. Was she disgusted? Or was she melting with pleasure? Was she furious but unable to resist the force that carried the two of them away . . .

"Look!" Tesla shook him. "By God, look at the sunset!"

The young Hungarian raised his eyes and saw inky clouds behind which the golden disc drowned in crimson.

Tesla was seeing the sun off by reciting lines from Goethe's *Faust:*

The daily work being done, the glitter is going away,
Rushing to create new life on a new day.

Szigety looked around and stammered, "Look—the entire park has turned red from the sun. Everyone has become an Indian."

Tesla did not respond.

"The evergreen bushes have been trimmed into chess pieces! Look at the screaming colors!"

Again, Tesla did not respond. A golden spike flashed in each window in Budapest. The horizon was peppered with birds, and the sun was going down behind them. When the flock flew over the park, Szigety became aware that his friend was still locked in place, gazing at the sun.

"What happened?" Szigety was flustered.

Nikola stared at the flaming orb without blinking.

"Look at me," Szigety called out.

"Look at me," Tesla echoed.

Then he said, still gazing at the sun, "Watch me turn it around."

Szigety looked left and right in search of the closest bench.

"I switch it on—click!—and it turns one way. Then—another click!—it reverses its course."

This is the last thing I need, Szigety thought in desperation. Tactfully, he took Tesla by the elbow and suggested, "Let's take a little rest."

Tesla held his ground.

"I turn it off. It stops! And"—his face broke into an inspired, anguished smile—"can't you see it doesn't crackle?"

"What?"

"Well, the motor."

Szigety's face looked as if he'd grabbed a live wire.

"Wait a minute!" he shouted. "Where's your motor?"

"Right here," Tesla pointed at the space between them. "Turn it on—click! And the problem is solved!"

When talking with someone, Szigety often closed one eye. It was impossible to say whether it was out of irritation or the need to focus. So he squinted with one eye and asked, "What problem is solved?"

"The problem of my alternating current motor! Listen to how quietly it works."

Like the wind, the spirit goes wherever it wants, but we can only know it by the sound, Jesus told Nicodemus the Pharisee. An inexplicable sense of excitement engulfed Szigety as he realized that what seemed like raving was not. An old print representing Ptolemy's system, with the fixed earth surrounded by the celestial spheres, came to mind. Some rascal stuck his head through the spheres in the print and was looking out into space. Szigety felt like that rascal. He was suddenly cold.

Tesla's face was bronzed by the setting sun.

He had that inspired and tortured expression his father hated so much.

"I've solved it. Now I can die happy!"

"Please, explain it to me!"

Tesla pulled himself together and started to draw diagrams on the gravel path with his cane.

"You see," he began. "Up until now, everyone who took on this problem had used only one electric circuit. I'll use at least two. Why? Because more alternating currents in the same generator can produce magnetic fields in a number of electric spindles on the engine's stator. Each spindle has the same frequency as the others, but their electromagnetic waves are out of sync."

Szigety imagined a gentleman and a lady dancing without being able to coordinate their steps.

"Their strikes alternate," Tesla continued. "This produces the effect of adding another cylinder to the engine. Two magnetic fields perpendicular to one another add up vector-like and the resulting field spins . . ."

Abstract concepts flew from Tesla's mouth like cosmic winds that powered ethereal engines. He still drew on the gravel path with his cane. He spoke exhaling steam.

"It spins as the current changes its direction. This is how a mutable magnetic whirlpool is created, which firmly embraces the rotor. There's no need for the commutator anymore." He looked at Szigety openly. "Isn't it beautiful? Isn't it simple?"

"It is simple," affirmed Szigety.

"It will be possible to conduct electricity over long distances," Tesla exclaimed. "This motor I invented is like Aladdin's lamp. Once liberated, the genie inside will do huge favors for mankind."

Nikola's eyes were tearful as if he was about to sneeze. A spasm of wild joy ravished his bosom. Szigety pondered his words, his face colored by the setting sun. When he finally understood, a thrill shot through his legs. The wounded beast that was restrained under his skin snapped its leash. He felt jealous and did not want to listen anymore.

Your motor . . . your world . . . Szigety thought. *Pretty cosmic recitals. Aladdin's world! And what am I going to do in it?*

The west bled a most tragic crimson. The two young men stared at the middle of the path that showed the blueprint of the motor.

Warm fog floated in Nikola's brown eyes. The frost smelled like flowers. Szigety gazed at the drawing of the rotating field. Then he looked at the setting sun and overcame his selfishness like Jacob did the angel. For the first time, he grasped the importance of what his friend was telling him. Antal Szigety's eyes flashed like Tesla's, and he whispered in triumph:

"Impossible!"

CHAPTER 31

Without Love

The Budapest switchboard began to operate in the spring. There was no more work, so the young engineer packed his bags. Ferenc Puskás rubbed his happy belly and asked, "Why don't you transfer to our central office in Paris?"

"Really?" Tesla asked skeptically.

"Really," said Puskás.

Two weeks later, Tesla got off the train and sighed. *Here I am!* During the first month, he bathed in the lights of Paris like a sparrow in the dust. It seemed that the entire city was infected with an amorous fever. Love's pressure was so strong it could crush a man wearing lighter armor. Couples embraced and rubbed against each other in alleys. Lips smeared with honey could barely part. Young men and women cooed in entryways. Trembling fingers intertwined and frightened eyes asked, *Do you love me?* Love pouted and rustled from every dark lane lined with trees, from every corner of the city. Who could ignore such an intoxicating whisper? But Nikola was deaf to the tittering coming from the alleys. He rushed through Paris streets following his own nose. In brothels, judges and bankers nibbled the fat thighs of women. On sidewalks, street girls pursed their golden lips and called out with laughter, "Monsieur, what are you up to? Are you lonely tonight?"

Tesla had his own definition of love. Paris was the center of the world and the national library was the center of the center. There—with love—he read Maupassant's early short stories. With love he gazed at the buildings along Haussmann's boulevards. He looked at the mansarded houses, wondering who lived in them, and got to know the demonic bestiary carved into the cathedral. Love also led him to the opera and—believe it or not—to art exhibitions. Since his Karlovac days, Nikola had associated art with starvation. The first thing that came to mind whenever he entered a gallery was roasted chicken. And yet, he dutifully nodded his head before the framed smudges of color that Durand-Ruel made famous.

Because of his love for Paris, Nikola ignored the meagerness of his little room in the Saint-Marceau quarter, "the suburb of martyrs," which still remembered the Paris Commune. On the first of each month, the widow Jaubert, his landlady, snatched the rent from his hands. Although Tesla gave her money to buy soap, she always stashed the bar until he himself bought a new one. A couple of uncertain marital status lived next door. In the evenings, a tragic male voice echoed from their room: "You don't love me like you used to!" Across the hallway lived a grayish old woman with her husband who had suffered a stroke. She took him out for snail-paced walks.

"Good day, Monsieur Tesla." The old woman always greeted him first.

"Good day, Madame Masquart."

After a while, Tesla got to know the neighbor who screamed, "You don't love me anymore!" He was a biologist, and his name was Gaston Labasse. At one point, when they had a long conversation in the stairway, he suggested, "Why don't you come to my institute and take a look through a microscope?"

Tesla accepted and took a look. An abyss opened up under Paris. In the illuminated circle, he saw a Hobbesian world of invisible creatures. They were shaggy beasts, each one tearing apart the others.

"They're devouring each other!" Tesla exclaimed in horror and yanked his head away from the eyepieces.

After he beheld the pit of microcosm, he bought five bars of soap and washed his hands as soon as he returned home. He'd almost prefer not to go out at all, if only the city were not so fascinating. On Saint-Marcel Boulevard someone played the accordion—the poor man's organ. It seemed to him that the accordionist was the twin brother of a busker he remembered from Graz. A little farther, another street musician was on call with his sad street organ and a jolly monkey. The fire-eater next to him looked like a dragon. Still farther down the street, a magician poured water from his sleeve into his pocket. A falling leaf danced down into a beggar's hat. He tossed it out and smiled a toothless smile.

Tesla hungered—for those boulevards, the voices of famous sopranos, books . . . He wanted to learn more about the research of French electrical engineers. When he received his salary, he turned into Louis XIV. With a wad of bills in his pocket, he immediately went to the Café Anglais, where the headwaiter looked like a prime minister. Through eight entrées, he ascended to the apex of the feast—rabbit in lemon juice. Finally, he ate frozen champagne with a spoon, which helped with his digestion. The rest of the month, he dined at the Two Brothers, which was frequented by charcoal deliverers. All the patrons sat at a large table, ate the same dish—beef Burgundy—and drank wine dipped from a barrel and poured into carafes.

"How are you?" Tesla shouted into the Paris sun.

During the summer months, he swam in the Seine each morning. Then he walked to the Continental Edison Company in Paris in the Ivry-sur-Seine suburb. It took about an hour to get to work. On Sundays, he rowed to relax. Blue and black smudges shimmered on the water's surface. Exhausted from rowing, he would lie down in his boat. Bridges over the Seine blocked his view of the sky. Clouds foamed above the river.

The rains started in September. The whole of Paris put on the colors of the city's pigeons. In November, Tesla started to ride horse-drawn streetcars. The common humanity of the people crammed in the vehicle smelled like homemade soup. The brief sense of camaraderie appealed to the lonely foreigner. During his first autumn in Paris, he lived on correspondence with his old friends. He did not forget them and regularly answered Medić's and Kulišić's letters. Szigety informed him that he had broken off his engagement. Tesla sighed: what a talented engineer and what a waste of time!

Each morning at seven thirty, he ate breakfast with French and American engineers in Ivry. Edison's friend Charles Bachelor spoke with a heavy British accent, and Tesla was barely able to understand what he wanted. Bachelor's beard was so full that people were tempted to touch it.

"I work so hard I don't even have time to plan what to do tomorrow," he complained to Tesla.

Tesla shyly mentioned his motor. Bachelor stroked his well-groomed beard and said under his breath that both Edison and Werner von Siemens were against alternating current. The inventor ignored the remark with a patient smile. He had no doubt that all of them were in error, but his motor would rectify that shortly. As soon as he secured his position with the Continental Edison Company in Paris, he convinced his employer, Tivadar Puskás, to write to Szigety and offer him a job in Paris.

One day, Monsieur Pierre Raux rushed into Tesla's office and hissed, "What a disaster!"

"What happened?"

A circuit had shorted out at the opening of the railway station in Strasbourg. A wall partially collapsed right in front of Kaiser Wilhelm I.

The company did not need this kind of scandal.

In short, Tesla was dispatched to Strasbourg.

"If you can fix this mess," the winded director of the company promised, "you won't regret it."

He named a hefty sum.

Nikola took Szigety—who had just arrived from Budapest—with him to Alsace. The porter staggered behind them because the athlete Szigety had packed his dumbbells in his luggage. The friends arrived at their destination, the city embraced by waters. Here Nikola first tasted the sweet fruit of maturity. Very wealthy people accepted him as an equal.

Was that an ordinary life then?

No, our hero had never had an ordinary life. Capricious miracles shackled him forever. He could not control the onslaughts of light. Whenever the golden visor fell over his eyes, the universe made decisions for him. In Strasbourg, just like in Budapest, it was too easy for him to fall off the edge of the world. Powerful flashes pounded behind his eyelids, so he went to bed early. The frequencies and signals from the starry sky caused the branches of his nerves to fire up.

What else happened to him? Well, yes, he took command of everything, paid the engineers, and sent reports to Paris. At the end of the day, he locked his office and had a drink with Hyppolite Bauzain, the formerly French mayor of Strasbourg. With his uplifted hand, he invited Tesla to admire the Rohan Palace. The city had suffered some damage during the Franco-Prussian War, but not as much as during the religious conflicts of the seventeenth century.

"Two centuries ago people were eating each other here," Bauzain said. "What can you do? Let's go to a restaurant."

He asked his guest about the books he read. Tesla mentioned Maupassant's *A Woman's Life*. Bauzain was happy. He had already read Maupassant's story about a prostitute and a Prussian officer, which was published in a magazine.

"I'm glad you're not one of *those* engineers," Bauzain put his hands by his eyes like horse blinders.

Tesla shaded his eyes with the same gesture: "No, I'm not one of those engineers."

"What kind of name is Nikola?" Bauzain asked. "Serbian?"

He knew that Hugo wrote favorably about the Serbs during the Serbian-Turkish War. Tesla reminded him of Lamartine's poems about Serbia and Mérimée's imitations of Serbian folk songs. Bauzain preferred Balzac to Stendhal. He was especially fond of *The Wild Ass's Skin* and *The Unknown Masterpiece*. Flaubert left him cold. "You can shoot me, but he leaves me cold!" He could not believe that Tesla liked Racine more than Molière. Both of them were devoted to Voltaire.

Bauzain married late, and he adored his two children. He himself cut food into small pieces for his four-year-old son, Pierre, and was the happiest man in the world whenever his eight-month-old daughter grabbed him by the mouth.

"Look at her!" His ecstatic look bore into Tesla's face.

And yet—in his wife's presence—he reminded his guest of Robespierre's idea that all children should be separated from their parents at the age of seven or eight and raised together so as to acquire openness to new ideas. With a smile, he spoke of Saint-Simon's insistence on the "sexual minimum."

They were eating Alsatian fondue and angels tickled their palates through the taste of Gewürtztraminer. Madame Bauzain claimed that there was no flavor in the world that was not to be found in some cheese.

"Big words," Tesla said.

In reply, Madame Bauzain issued another La Rochefoucauldesque maxim: "Once you feel like closing your eyes while eating—when you wonder and sigh—those are the signs of great cuisine. The rest is nothing."

The glow of recent motherhood enhanced Madame Jeanne Bauzain's radiant beauty. She liked the softness of Tesla's eyes.

"You're single, Monsieur," she addressed him both as a coquette and a mother. "Why is that?"

"I work," Tesla responded good-naturedly and gave a cheerful wave. "I'm not wasting my time."

Jeanne brushed him off. "Without love, all time is wasted."

One day, Bauzain called Tesla aside and told him that in 1870, when the Germans came, he buried quite a few bottles of Saint-Estèphe that dated back to the time when Nikola's grandfather was a soldier in Napoléon's army.

"I recently dug them up," Bauzain said. "There's no one else I'd rather drink them with than you."

Nikola asked him if he could invite Szigety as well.

"Fine," Bauzain agreed.

Tesla threatened and warned Szigety to stay away from Madame Bauzain. They gathered around the table in an atmosphere more churchy than a church. The host brought in a bottle, holding it like a baby. He opened it and poured a round in silence. They took a sip. Tesla was the first to recover. He declared, moved, "I have never . . . Something like this . . ."

After the evening filled with laughter, the time had come for him and Szigety to go back to Paris. Bauzain promised that he would see to the education of Tesla's heart and recommended his own tailors, one from Strasbourg and another from Paris. Upon his return to Paris, the young engineer sat down in his office, adjusted the knot of his tie, and wrote a letter to his illiterate mother in Lika. In a good mood, he entered Monsieur Raux's office and said, "The job's done. What about my reward?"

This was how Tesla got to know French politeness, which is more implacable than German meticulousness. He discovered that Monsieur Raux had undergone a complete and mysterious change. All of a sudden, he became a reserved man of terse words who explained to Tesla that the reward was not his responsibility, and that Tesla should talk to Monsieur Laibl about it. In turn, Laibl explained that he should see Mr. Stone. The mustached Mr. Stone brought the circle to a close by referring him to Monsieur Raux. They were the three proverbial monkeys who declared, "See no evil, hear no evil, speak no evil."

"If only Edison knew what these European paper pushers do in his name!" Tesla complained to Bachelor.

"So why don't you transfer to our central office in New York?" Bachelor asked.

"Really?" Tesla asked.

"Really!" Bachelor nodded.

The Crossing

I have forgotten the beginning, the departure,
the journey, and the arrival.

The immortal Pierre Loti

The Fight

A dangerous face bared its teeth at Tesla. He removed it with his fist. A painful blow from a club paralyzed his shoulder. Tesla turned around, kicked sideways, and swept a sailor away. With an arm longer than a truncheon, he displaced another sailor's nose. Someone shoved him. Tesla hit the wall with the back of his head. The people around him turned into flailing rags of light and shadows.

"Break it up!" the captain shouted.

He pulled out a gun.

Bang!

The people involved in the fight on the deck froze in the void that followed the shot.

The captain shouted, "Who started this?"

The Men from Lika

"Someone in the crowd pushed me to divert my attention while someone else picked my pocket," Tesla explained. "They took everything, my ticket and my money."

"So how did you get on the boat?"

"I had a reservation under my name. No one else showed up, so they let me on."

Two burly men from Lika listened compassionately. They introduced themselves by their surnames:

"Baćić."

"Cvrkotić."

Then they put their arms around each other's shoulders and announced, "Two big shots from Lika."

The third one, a skinny sixteen-year-old, held out his hand and whispered, "Stevan Prostran."

The ship's horn blared. The harbor receded in the distance and shrank to the size of a bluish mock-up. Sea mist sprayed the passengers. They threw apple cores to the seagulls.

Tesla wiped his face. "Where're you from?" he asked Stevan.

"From Rastičevo."

The expression of Tesla's face did not change.

"Near Velika Popina," the boy explained.

"I don't know where that is," Tesla said. "But my father would." He asked the three men what they planned to do in America.

"Same as the others," Baćić and Cvrkotić said.

Stevan Prostran was the only one who looked downhearted. He told a story about some man from Lika who got off the boat in the New York harbor. As soon as he stepped on land, the man became depressed.

"He sat down and simply wouldn't get up," the boy told them, wide-eyed. "Our people helped him for a while, but later they went their own way. That man, however, died right where he sat. Maybe the same will happen to me," Prostran sighed.

"No, Stevan, it won't." His friends slapped him on the back.

Stevan shook his head in doubt.

Fear and hope whispered in his ears. What should he believe? On one hand, black coal mines and howling blast furnaces threatened to drain his life away. On the other, golden opportunities of wealth beckoned to him. The bright-eyed, skinny kid finally mustered some courage and told them about his big plans. He would stay in America five to seven years. Then he would buy some land in Lika.

"I'll let my brothers work the land," he beamed childishly. "And I'll open a tavern."

"What will you call it?"

"The American! I'm going to sit in front and read the paper all day." Prostran leafed through the imaginary paper. "People will go by and greet me: 'Good day, Master Stevo.' To some I'll respond and to some I won't."

"And why are you two going to America?" Tesla asked Baćić and Cvrkotić.

"Because our entire village has just one comb," Cvrkotić laughed humorlessly.

As they explained what made them undertake such a trip, they used the words "there isn't" in various combinations. There isn't enough for the kids. There isn't enough for the old. There's no money to pay taxes.

"Why are you going?" they asked him.

The Saturnia

It took Tesla a day to get used to his cabin. All night he was awake listening to the throb of the engines.

When their ship, ominously named the *Saturnia,* sailed out into the open sea, all the upper decks were filled with excitement. An old French woman prayed for the souls of the drowned. Mothers hung linen along the rails to dry. The ship started to rock. A child began to cry inconsolably, and the captain suggested that throwing him overboard would be the most expedient course of action.

The morning started with pouring rain. The hiss of waves muffled its sound. That day, Tesla did not go out on the deck. He was in the salon, talking to the captain. Claude Rouen invited the young engineer to lunch. The captain drank like tired people do after work and asked his guest about the possibility of using phones on ships. At dinner, a Scottish engineer insisted that in the old days traveling by sail was much nicer. The irritable wife of a banker from Lyon gave hushed advice to her ugly daughter, who looked like an ostrich. A Czech violinist, who cherished hopes of a job at the New York Opera, was there as well. He harped on spiritualism, a topic that did not interest Tesla in the least.

"There's a waterfall that divides this world from the other," the Czech explained to the ostrich girl.

At breakfast, he again talked about the photographs of spirits and dreams, and of the imprints of "hands" in beeswax.

"Have you heard of the ghost songs that the spiritualist Monsieur Jaubert, who's also the top judge in Carcassonne, collected?"

"No!" Tesla cut him off and left.

He gave up on the "educated class" and decided to spend more time among the "dangerous class," that is, with Stevan Prostran and the men from Lika.

"When I saw the ocean for the first time, it was like I had always known it," Prostran confided to Tesla on the windy deck.

Tesla was freezing on the ship because he had not brought enough warm clothes. And yet, he brought a book of his poems and the blueprints for his flying machine. Most of the people who had berths were French from Alsace. Two bright-eyed women gazed out in the distance. They were picture brides, traveling to meet their unknown husbands. Baćić twirled his mustache in their presence. Prostran gazed with frightened eyes—one minute he was delighted about his American prospects, and the next he was horrified by them. The travelers prayed to the gods of yesterday to help them tomorrow in America. A group of Basques stood guard by their bundles. There were also some Italians from Nice and even a few families of Polish Jews. "Vagabonds who throw their lives around like dice," is how Polyphemus described Odysseus and his shipmates.

How It All Started

On the third day, the rain stopped but the wind still raged. The ship rose and plunged into the waves. Many passengers were seasick. The stench in the hold was deadly. The sailors forced the people up on deck, where the wind slashed their ears. And yet, someone pulled out an accordion the size of a hand. Another man accompanied him on a comb. Tesla thought they would play a melancholy tune in which everything was lost forever before it even began. But they played a jolly one. Dancers' heels started to click on the boards. Some women began to sing in their duck-like voices. The passengers swirled in the wind. Baćić and Cvrkotić did not dance—they twirled their mustaches as they stood close to the picture-brides from Alsace. The girls lowered their eyes. The sailors grinned and busied themselves around the women. Each wild tar was a suitor for a Penelope donning a head scarf. One of them grabbed a girl from Alsace around the waist. Baćić shoved him away. More sailors with wild grins on their faces rushed to their friend's aid. It was such a pleasure to beat on helpless rabble! But this time it was different.

"Hit 'em!"

"Take that!"

An all-out fight broke out on the ship. Several noses got broken. After the incident, Captain Rouen stopped inviting Tesla to eat with him.

The Truth

With hollow gazes, the passengers gawked at the dazzling sky above and the white void in the direction of America. Something drew a crowd of caps and head scarves to the deck. After he cleared his throat by way of introduction, a gimpy Basque told them a story that belonged to all nations—the old story about truth:

> *A young man went out into the world to look for Truth. On his quest, he traveled over seven mountains and seven seas. He asked the sun, he asked the moon, and he asked the wind. He wore out three pairs of iron shoes before he found her.*
>
> *Truth was old and ugly.*
>
> *The young man stayed with Truth for three years. She taught him many, many things. So the time came for them to part. As he took his leave, Truth asked, "Would you do me a favor?"*
>
> *"Yes," the young man said.*
>
> *"When you go back among people and they inquire of me, tell them I'm young and beautiful."*

Even Maids Have Maids There

A day before they reached their destination, flocks of terns appeared.

"The seagulls are back too!" someone exclaimed.

At last they saw the harbor. Thousands of columns of smoke rose above thousands of roofs. Just before sunset, objects responded to the sunlight with their own inner light. Redbrick buildings glowed most beautifully. All the languages of Babel and the universal language of crying babies were silenced at the sight of the harbor.

All the passengers on the deck rose to their feet to see. Each pauper was an epic hero, each an Aeneas. The American wind licked their faces. The seagulls reeled above their heads.

The granite faces of Baćić and Cvrkotić, and the frightened face of Stevan Prostran, were turned toward the dark contours of Manhattan. The people of the world gazed on America—those for whom someone waited at the dock and those who had nobody there, those who would go back and those who would never return.

"Jesus, Joseph, and Mary, where are we?" a woman whispered.

The lice-infested crowd smelled like village life. They were frightened but brave. They desired what they feared.

Manhattan!

That's where Uncle Jules sleeps on a mattress and eats meat and white bread every day, like a millionaire. Nothing is the same there, Mother. Nothing is the same there, Father. People's backs break from work there. Even maids have maids there.

The saddest eyes beheld Manhattan with hope, trepidation, and helplessness: This is too big. This is destiny.

CHAPTER 33

The Light of the Mortals

During the trip, sleepless Tesla often watched the morning star open the gate of night, the rosy fingers of dawn touch the ocean, and Helios, the light of the mortals, start his daily journey in his chariot.

Tesla constantly imagined his first meeting with the divine Thomas Edison, the only man in the world who could understand him. Like a spider on a golden thread, Edison descended from the sky and the two of them engaged in endless conversations.

"Good morning!" Tesla shouted into the void above the waters.

The ocean whispered and everything in it responded. Beneath Tesla and the keel of the *Saturnia,* the "uncataloged creatures of the deep" undulated.

One day, our voyager cajoled the sea: "You proud white-capped sea, you!"

Another day he said: "You that heave and roll forever."

"You cold, fish-full sea. You inhuman sea," he cried out like Homer.

In the space between the two worlds, Tesla looked around. He grabbed the rail and stared at the line between the sky and the ocean. At times he lost his sense of self and imagined the eternal blue around him to be his soul.

With his binoculars, he scanned the watery realm they entered and, naturally, it could appear to him that . . . what? In each wave there seemed to bob the head of a lone swimmer. Sometimes the swimmer disappeared from view, only to resurface, arms stroking against the waves.

Who?

Who was following the ship? The dual circles of the binoculars merged into a single spot and framed a face. Tesla recognized him. It was Dane, his brother, who had long since drowned in the ocean of time.

Many years ago, Tesla learned how to deal with phenomena as enormous as death. He started to whisper because God hears best the whispered word.

"Let me go!" he silently and hopelessly pleaded. "Please, let me go!"

The phantom in the joined circles of the binoculars steadily gained on him. The tilt of the head and the consistency of the strokes told Tesla:

I will never leave you, my brother!

PART II

America

CHAPTER 34

The Deaf Man's House

Tesla disembarked from the boat in New York. The city itself held no interest for him. He immediately sought out Edison's laboratory through the maze of avenues and streets.

"Here we are!" He congratulated himself as he knocked on the door.

At the laboratory, people were busy constructing the gate to fairyland, the hat that makes you invisible, love potions . . .

Ah!

Cameras for thoughts, peepholes into the future, stethoscopes for internal music . . .

Ah!

It was here that the electric bulb started to flicker.

It was here that a human voice first spoke from a machine.

God's creative work continued in this lab—it was carried on through the efforts of the Inventors.

This was the navel of the world, the quiet eye of the vortex.

Out there, raucous New York growled and bilked. Edison felt at home in New York, like a fish in water. He was the fish-wizard, the fish-king!

Drowning in debt, the wizard was constantly on the move—he stalked rich clients and bribed newspapermen in Manhattan. Hemp fibers littered his sawdust-strewn floors. Engines hummed in his workshops, manufacturing parts for other engines. The corridors smelled of black oil and were always full of people. Two young men with unkempt hair—the louder one was called Connelly—got into a dispute and insisted that their boss declare the winner. In front of the door, a businessman from Astoria checked his gold watch.

"He'll see you now," the wild-haired Connelly said, acting like a secretary and pushing Tesla inside.

With the finest smile on his face and four cents in his pocket, Tesla walked through the fateful door. Who cared about Milutin Tesla? His true father—the most famous scientist in the world—awaited him behind this door! In a few moments, Edison would recognize him as a great man and a kindred soul.

A fan turned slowly on the ceiling. The office was cluttered. A likable boy with a hat on his head looked out from a silver-framed daguerreotype.

The biography of that barefaced boy read like the life of a saint. He began his career selling newspapers on trains between places named Port Huron and Detroit, and ended up selling light to the City of Light.

Under the slow fan, Tesla was like a young dog. His almond-shaped eyes gleamed. Two starched triangles protruded beneath his chin. Two thick waves of hair parted in the middle of his head. He looked like a fresh young man who wanted to leave a favorable impression. He thought, *Ah!* and then he thought, *Oh!* Then he strode across the office in two steps and handed Bachelor's letter of recommendation to Edison. The gun-slit eyes took him in one more time. At last, cordiality displaced the wary smile. With a theatrical gesture, the king of inventors dropped the letter. His face rounded up.

"If you want, you can start tomorrow."

And that was that.

Tesla was so excited he almost fainted. *This will decide everything!* he thought. *Everything!*

And he liked the first step—as Whitman would say—so much.

Radiant with hope, he strode an inch above the ground. The sky tickled him—the sky was his soul's namesake. He could not wait to wake up the next day so he could go to work. That was so fascinating, so *painfully* fascinating, like gambling, like alcohol, like . . . There must have been something about his face, some airy, happy expression, because people looked at him and smiled. He worked from 10:30 in the morning until 5:00 a.m. the next day.

During Tesla's second week at Edison's, two dynamos on a transatlantic ship, the *Oregon*, shorted out simultaneously.

"It can't be done!" The workers frowned and shrugged their shoulders.

"What do you mean it can't be done!" raged Edison.

"It can't be fixed!" the electricians repeated.

Edison fired the whole lot.

The *Oregon* was the first transatlantic ship lit by his system.

They sent Tesla. He rushed off.

His troubleshooting was based more on intuition than knowledge: This is the problem! This isn't . . . Covered in soot, he left just before dawn, looking like he'd been beaten with torches.

"Is that our Parisian! So, how was the party?" Edison greeted him outside the laboratory.

An unexpected answer hit him in the face: "I fixed the problem on the *Oregon*."

"Well done," Edison acknowledged, huskily.

Tesla smiled readily.

"It's an honor for any engineer to work for you."

Often he talked about his motor to Edison in Edison's absence. His excitement pushed the walls of the surrounding buildings away.

"In my case, that honor is even greater because I've long desired to show you my alternating current motor. Its huge advantage over direct current is that the existing power stations can only cover a one-mile radius . . ."

While the young man spun the golden yarn of his eloquence, his heart pounded.

"Imagine how many direct current power stations need to be built in New York alone!"

Connelly the grouch, who again assumed the role of secretary, leaned toward Tesla's ear and whispered, "He's hard of hearing."

The young man had to repeat what he had already said.

The narrowed eyes and disgusted smile were part of Edison's charm. In the first light of the morning, his face remained impassive. His words caught Tesla by surprise: "Ninety percent of an inventor's skill is in his ability to judge what is and what isn't possible, and this is"—he made a reassuring gesture toward Tesla. Since Tesla did not react, Edison concluded, "impossible."

"But I have already built a working model," stammered the Parisian.

Edison put on his disgusted smile again. "You know, when I started to build my first direct current power stations, I had to battle the natural gas industry. My journalists wrote, 'Gas is poisonous,' and other things like that up until I was able to open my plants. Imagine," he added, this time with a rakish smile, "if I had to oppose your competing system . . ."

Connelly and a man with a beat-up hat, called Little Benny, laughed in unison.

"Imagine if I had to pay reporters to write 'Beware of alternating current!' One gets tired of such things, you know."

Edison clapped his hands and exclaimed, "Let's just drop those . . . those fantasies. Fortunately, your system is absolutely inapplicable."

"It's not . . ."

"Inapplicable! But, look, if you can really improve direct current motors the way you've said you can, there's—there's fifty thousand dollars in it for you."

Tesla looked at him with fire in his eyes.

Edison's eyebrows were a straight line. He emitted a sour odor because he bathed once a month "whether he needed to or not." There was a rumor that his wife was going insane. There was a rumor that he managed her condition himself. There were all kinds of rumors. His slimy lips throttled his cigar. His nose resembled a vegetable. His hair was limp like grass in a drought.

Tesla stared at him—he simply could not believe it. He depended on that man so much he did not dare see him in a different light. He did not dare get angry with him.

He was hesitant to admit that this sweaty deaf man with drooping ears and dead hair disappointed him. If Edison could not understand him, who else could?

He would continue to work. He would prove his point.

He spent every day installing lightbulbs in the power plant on Pearl

Street and in the nearby Gerk Steel Mill. He stepped over springs, cartons of glass tubes, and boxes labeled with mystical names. Those were shipments of materials for their experiments from places with names like Paramaribo, Malaysia, Congo, which Tesla imagined to be colonial mirages, swarming with lemurs and parrots.

The laboratory was the entire world. For him, New York did not exist. And yet . . .

That year he got to know the New York summer heat for the first time. Financiers paid visits to the famous laboratory. John Pierpont Morgan, the Sultan of Wall Street, also came, with his top hat resembling the smokestack of a train. The millionaires in black looked like funeral home officials, and Morgan was the owner of the funeral home. Tesla saw him only from a distance and the man left a disquieting impression.

"As if someone put a sack over my head," he said to Little Benny.

As he worked on designing new arc lamps and direct current motors, Tesla met a man with a long face, cold eyes, and thin, extremely agile lips. The man smiled with effort and introduced himself: "Robert Lane."

With an air of intrigue, he handed Tesla his business card. "In case you need someone to back your lamps financially."

"No. I'm fine where I am," Tesla responded.

"I know you're fine," Lane said pointedly.

At the Gerk Steel Mill, experiments sometimes went on for twenty hours. There, with ant-like persistence, the engineers tried and tried and tried. One night, Edison locked his assistants in the laboratory. Another night he decided that they should have some fun.

"Let's go, my insomniacs," he yelled. "It's time, my insomniacs."

Like dogs released from their chains, Edison's insomniacs charged into the summer night. They first invaded a Hungarian restaurant at 65 Fifth Avenue. Its floor was strewn with pine shavings. A melancholy saw cried under the musician's bow.

"Beer! Meat! Pickles!" they shouted, scraping chair legs across the floor and shoving tables together.

"Goulash for me!"

"Me too!"

"Excuse me, what's that huge lump on your shoulders?" Tom Connelly asked old Johan, who came to wait on them.

The owner disappeared, came back, and put glasses and plates on the table.

Outside barked the golden dogs of summer.

Little Benny flashed the most charming smile that ever adorned a complete bum. He slapped Johan on the back and laughed until he choked. "I've never seen such a sullen mug on such a fine waiter!"

From the side of his mouth, Connelly told them how New York was endowed with one of the wonders of the world—the Brooklyn Bridge—just a year before Tesla "got off the ship."

"The Hanging Gardens of Babylon are no more, but our bridge still stands," the learned Edison pointed out to his assistants.

Not a week after the opening, someone shouted, "The bridge is falling!" and caused a stampede in which a dozen people were crushed to death.

"How we ran!" Connelly whistled.

The miserable, drunken musician played on his saw, his head swaying and his eyes closed.

Like a multiheaded hydra, Edison's group got up and left the restaurant. They commandeered an omnibus. With his hands deep in his pockets, Bachelor, who had recently returned from Paris, joined them.

Cracking jokes and shouting each other down, the insomniacs took a ride to the Golden Garter on Bowery. They hushed and shoved each other while a frowning German led them to their table. Sitting, they guarded their glasses of rum with their elbows. A woman with smeared makeup pushed those greasy elbows aside and sat at their table. "Hon, won't you buy me a drink?" she said.

"It's a feudal system," Benny explained. "Brothels pay policemen. Policemen pay captains. Captains pay politicians." He let out a hellish belch that singed the hair on his chest, and he swore.

"You know what Steve Grady said as he jumped off the bridge?" The green-eyed Connelly was on fire. "Going down!" He downed a shot of rum.

"Ha! Ha! Ha!"

Exaggerated, almost frightening joy reigned at the table. Their mugging stripped their words of meaning. Edison's mood always improved after a meal. That was when he hijacked conversations. As a young man, he electrified a metal urinal at a railway station and watched men shake and wet themselves while urinating.

"Ha! Ha! Ha!"

He presided over a table full of fogged spectacles and gaping jaws. It was hot in the bar.

The door was open. Outside, the lions of summer roared, and its mighty bulls bellowed down unfamiliar streets. The fragrant dust teased the soul and intoxicated the nostrils. The broken lights and the distant voices of the city turned into a painful temptation. All eyes filled with longing. Smoke rolled out into the night through the open door.

The main characteristic of the music was speed.

Everyone bolted down their drinks.

Benny lit Connelly's mustache instead of his cigar.

A red-haired woman sang with a cracked voice. From time to time she disappeared only to reemerge in a shorter skirt. Hawk-like waiters tripped over women's crinolines and charged double for everything except beer.

"What's this?" Edison asked with a huff.

"An error, sir," the sly waiter said apologetically.

The prince of electricity warned him with a shake of his finger and continued to cackle. "Mrs. Peterson asked me what kind of material burned in my lightbulb." He reddened. "So you know what I told her? Limburger cheese!"

"Ha! Ha! Ha!" The insomniacs thundered, like a chorus in an opera.

Edison did not drink, but he still crowed, tears in his eyes, drunk on other people's intoxication.

"And once I frightened a black man to see if he would turn white with fear."

Tesla grew scared because it seemed that Edison, who did not drink, was more drunk than the others.

Connelly cut in. "And do you remember that Swiss fellow, you know, the prim and proper one, the one who ate salad for breakfast? So one time he sat at our table and I pulled out a gun this big. Says I, I'm gonna rub you out!"

"So he never showed up for work again," Benny roared.

"Ha! Ha! Ha!" The insomniacs were delighted.

Right there, in the whirl of those grimacing masks, Tesla celebrated his twenty-eighth birthday. He was learning. His eyes were opening up.

The very moment Edison left for the bathroom, the insomniacs started to talk behind his back.

"He's stingy and he lies."

"You know, Benny, his folks were Tories. They were loyalists during the Revolution, you know."

"His father whipped him because he set a barn on fire," Bachelor declared in a funereal voice.

"A conductor boxed his ears because he set a railroad car on fire."

"That's how he lost his hearing," Benny asserted.

"He lost as much as it suits him." Bachelor stroked his epic beard.

"What are you talking about?" Edison asked suspiciously when he returned to the table.

"Nothing." Connelly was glad to see him. "We're talking about what a good fellow you are."

CHAPTER 35

The Death of the Skeleton

Two things worked against Tesla.

First of all, he came from Paris. The insomniacs knew that he still figured prices in francs and therefore called him a "Parisian." And when they heard that he liked opera, they started nudging each other and mocking him behind his back.

"Look at that triangular cat face! Look at those bat ears!"

Perhaps he wore ladies' undergarments?

Second of all, Tesla was not a true Parisian.

On one occasion, Edison coughed dryly and asked him if he had ever partaken of human flesh as a child.

"What do you mean?"

"Well, I can't find Smiljan, Lika, on the map of the civilized world," the prince of all inventors replied, sneering.

"You mean the same map on which Milan, Ohio, is marked in gold letters?" was Tesla's polite response.

Edison imagined fanged birds and carnivorous butterflies living in Smiljan.

In Tesla's opinion, the only problem with his birthplace was that it was crowded with Edisons—intelligent but crude men who, in order to maintain their sense of identity, refused to take baths. Edison believed only a guilty man would choose to be polite and that the people he tricked appreciated him even more for it. He reminded Tesla of Luka Bogić, who never failed to point his gun at little Nikola: Now I'm going to kill you! Later, in the tavern, Bogić and the other hunters laughed about it.

Each one in his own trance, Tesla and Edison walked past each other every day.

The newcomer from Paris reported directly to Bachelor concerning the progress he was making in improving the new motors.

At first Tesla refused to listen when the insomniacs talked about Edison's spy in the Patent Office Bureau, but he changed his mind when Connelly pointed his finger at a drunk. His name was Zenas Wilbur Fink. Edison used Fink's tips to modify other people's inventions and then patented them in his own name.

Edison's luster wore off on a daily basis.

Without generosity, what will become of this world? Tesla wondered. *It will turn into a prison . . .*

Tesla started to cut the Olympian down to human size. Edison did not mind sleeping on the floor. His hair looked like he cut it himself, with a knife, at night. But most importantly, he never bothered with anything he could not sell.

"Cunning," Tesla murmured in disappointment. "Cheap cunning . . ."

After one year to the day, the magician's apprentice completed exactly twenty-four direct current motor projects.

"I believe these will become the standard and replace the ones we have," he told Bachelor.

Unannounced, he barged into Edison's office. The ceiling fan still turned slowly. Edison leafed through a paper. His gray eyes swept over the inflammatory headlines:

Troubles with Apaches! Malcontent Commits Suicide! Corruption in Louisiana! Last Hours of Victor Hugo! Eight Victims of Fire in Tenement! Kids Thrown out Window! Death of Skeleton! Abraham Kreutz, the Brookstone Skeleton, Died Yesterday!

Without waiting for his boss to acknowledge his presence, Tesla enthusiastically announced, "All projects completed! You said fifty thousand dollars!"

"What's that?" a voice spoke behind the rustling newspaper.

Tesla was about to repeat himself when Edison threw the paper on the floor with a theatrical gesture. As soon as he looked at his boss's face, Tesla knew that he was not going to get a dime.

The fan kept turning relentlessly.

Edison, composed in an attitude of light-hearted betrayal, remarked, "Young man, you don't understand the American sense of humor."

Tesla was dumbfounded. There was nothing particularly American in this universal brazenness. While in Edison's office in Paris, he believed it was only the underlings who took advantage of him. But this . . .

The ever-present fan barely moved.

Tesla's textbook morality was no match for Edison's street smarts. Up until that moment, Tesla had performed for his boss like a ballerina—he would have gladly tiptoed on a spider's web. For a year, he looked at Edison with stars in his eyes. The magician's apprentice believed that evil came from misunderstandings. He assumed that gifted people were natural allies.

On the other hand, Edison's father had whipped his son in the middle of the public square as if he were a runaway slave, while women shied away. In the smell of the dust, the boy's soul detached itself from the body. As the whip cracked across his back, another Tom rose above the first one. The first Tom's pain turned into the other Tom's anger. Amid the stench of dust and blood, Edison vowed that he would never spare anyone from what he had to endure. You'll never get the better of me, he told the entire world. He was in a state of competition with every man, woman, and child alive. In his eyes, victory itself was always more important than its meaning. The stench of dust and blood forever lingered in his nostrils. For his own small gain, he was ready to inflict on any other man a sizable injury.

"But . . ." Tesla searched for words.

Ashes snowed down on Edison's waistcoat. His obstinate mouth gnawed at the cigar. He reminded Tesla of a dog that would not let go of a bone. His jaw was a byproduct of the evolutionary need to develop fangs capable of ripping flesh and crushing bones.

Tesla froze. "How ugly people are without the light of our sympathy," he said.

"But"—Edison belatedly interrupted—"I'm ready to raise your salary from eighteen to twenty-six dollars a week."

"There's no *but,* sir," Tesla said softly. "I'm resigning."

Edison waved him off.

Cold chills of betrayal engulfed the young man. "Unwashed filthy clown! Cur!" he murmured in Serbian.

Not knowing which way to turn, Tesla fingered Robert Lane's business card in his pocket.

Edison puffed out his cheeks. He tried to make the persons he double-crossed laugh and thus turned his betrayal into cheap comedy and tragedy into farce. It was the victims who suffered the need to apologize, as they felt that the sense of human balance was upset.

CHAPTER 36

Nothing

Tesla's "no hissing, no squinting" lightbulbs lit up the town of Rahway, New Jersey. Herds of demonic shadows were chased out of town. Under the electric lights, people sang, danced, and floated in the air.

"Congratulations!" the cold-eyed financer Robert Lane and his fat partner, Wiley, exclaimed.

"This is all good and fine," Tesla thanked them with a melodious voice and shy smile. "But when are we going to start on the real work?"

"What real work?"

Tesla's voice became serious: "Manufacturing my alternating current motor!"

Wiley and Lane gave a genial chuckle. Tesla repeated his question and for the second time was treated to the chirping of their mirth. After mentioning his motor for the third time, he received a nicely designed certificate in the mail, resembling a diploma, penned in Gothic script.

And—yes!

He could frame it.

But—no!

He could not pay bills with it.

After a day of contemplation, it dawned on him: "They squeezed me out of my own company!"

He had to vacate his house with the garden. His furniture went into storage.

He accepted a position as a draftsman, but there was no steady work.

"A week is all we have," they told him.

After that, he heard: "A couple of days, maybe."

Finally: "Nothing available."

And again: "Nothing available."

Before, Tesla lived isolated in his laboratory. In the city that was so easy to get around in, he often found himself disoriented.

A sense of amazement yawned in him:

"How fast everything moves! How huge these streets are!"

CHAPTER 37

Come!

A popular joke said anyone could stand at the corner of Broadway and Houston, shoot a gun in any direction, and not hit an honest man.

Italian women, Poles, Greeks, Jews, and Lebanese jostled between the yellow walls of the city. The only thing they had in common was their love for shouting.

Rich Upper Manhattan never had anything to do with the lower part of the city. A young man with a sketchpad occasionally ventured into these streets to draw the picturesque poor and to imagine that he was in Naples or Cairo. Here everyone shouted—the fruit seller with his cart and the policeman who shooed him away from the street corner. In the evening, the streets switched from allegro to crescendo. An Irish woman with a stumpy pipe sold apples and "George Washington" pies. A Civil War veteran peddled shoelaces. A boisterous hawker of secondhand clothes exhibited five hats on his head. Black people selling corn cried with raw throats, "White hot—right from the pot!"

Shoe shiners with impudent faces rapped on their boxes and fought for a good spot on the street corners. Poor people soused themselves in bars called blind tigers. Newspaper boys screamed, "Read all about it!"

A celebration with fireworks marked the lighting of the Statue of Liberty's torch on Bedloe Island. The slayer of Indians, General William Tecumseh Sherman, picked the site for Liberty, financed through a lottery. Liberty was first envisioned as a black woman with broken shackles. Then black Liberty transformed into white Liberty. Newspapers reported that cannon were fired and "land and sea were bathed in glory." Meanwhile, a lanky man with an unhappy face whispered the word *tenement* with disgusted reverence. He could not find an equivalent in Serbian. The word referred to huge buildings where the goal was to cram in as many poor people as possible. Water pumps and indescribable outhouses were in their courtyards.

With great effort, the rays of sun reached through wet linen on clotheslines. The Parisian wrinkled his nose: "It smells of urine here!"

After he groped his way up the dark stairwell, the new tenant entered his windowless room and was overpowered by the stench of ashes. As soon as he locked himself in, he felt a kinship to the biblical Ecclesiastes. He was tormented by the suspicion that a sage was no better than a fool, that a man was no better than an animal. The walls made of plaster and sawdust did not keep out bodily noises or marital secrets. Poor people snored, hacked,,and coughed all around him.

How fast everything is moving, Tesla repeated to himself.

He had never liked money, but now he thought about it all the time. Breakfast—four cents. Lunch—the same. And tomorrow? Tomorrow will take care of tomorrow.

With the first autumn rains he rented a bed without a partition around it for ten cents. Sleeping on the floor cost a nickel. Unshaven cheeks tore pillowcases. The so-called barracks in the basements of police stations were considered the lowest of the low. As soon as the beginner vagrant entered the "barracks," his nemesis stench assailed him and grabbed him by the throat. But outside, the demon frost awaited in ambush. The former Budapest decadent warmed himself among his stinking cosufferers. He pulled the blanket over his head to forget where he was and to fall asleep. He could not wait for the dawn so he could get out in the streets.

On a sleety, foggy morning, Tesla's worn-out shoes were slipping along Mulberry Street when a familiar face suddenly appeared before him. Stevan Prostran! His eyes were as green as a goat's. Between his rounded cheeks, his nose appeared to have shrunk a bit because the young man ate way too much at a German bakery where he worked.

Stevan was glad to see his friend. He spun around in delight: Baćić and Cvrkotić had left for Pittsburgh while he happened to stay in New York. "What about yourself?" he asked.

Tesla's voice rose to the pitch of a bird's twitter—to the very edge of a sob—and then deepened: "Fine!"

Without hesitation, Tesla's young friend from Lika put a hand on his shoulder and uttered the words Tesla would remember for the rest of his life: "Come with me! Enough for one is plenty for two."

Stevan took Tesla to his room.

It was as gloomy as an idiot's heart.

The only good thing about the room was that Nikola never dreamed of Dane there.

Whiter than a ghost, Stevan sifted flour at night. During the day, he dressed up "as an American." On Sundays, his comb whistled through his hair like the wind through sharp grass. He tilted his hat and tapped his cane against the sidewalk. In the afternoon, he went to the Bowery theaters. On stage stood two actors with pirate beards, in the flashing light of their raised stilettos. A naive kneeling beauty screamed, "No!"

As furious as the rest of the audience, Stevan Prostran loudly cursed the villain in heavily accented English as well as Serbian: "Leave the girl alone, you son of a bitch!"

Theater provided images to flash under his eyelids. The dizzy enormity of New York intoxicated Stevan. Whenever he saved some money, he bought a new hat.

"What do you think, should I get a gold tooth?" he asked Tesla.

Tesla retorted, "Out of the question!"

That autumn, which he later refused to remember, Tesla slept in Prostran's bed: the young baker used it during the day; Tesla used it at night.

It is impossible to determine the moment when Tesla's surprise turned into despair.

According to the fashion of the time, our long-suffering hero tried to "improve himself by reading" on Sundays. He went to the library, checked out *Scientific American*, and took it with him to his stinking tenement. Reading one of the issues, he was informed by the sociologist W. G. Sumner that "it was a matter of very little importance if there was a huge discrepancy between the rich and the poor in society."

"Thanks, Sumner," Tesla whispered in his stuffy room as he turned the oil lamp off. "God bless your merciful soul."

CHAPTER 38

To Bite Off an Ear

A few thugs held the wall up in the churchyard between Mott Street and Park Row.

"Who are they?" Tesla asked, frowning.

"Don't look," Stevan Prostran whispered.

"Why?" Tesla said when they were out of earshot.

"They're the Whyos," Prostran explained with bitterness. "The most dangerous gang in town. Don't talk to them—it's better that they don't know you."

Returning home, Tesla was always slightly anxious. He asked around and was told that he should avoid the Whyos. These Irish giants reminded him of the Lika giants. At the Morgue, they drank punch mixed with whiskey, hot rum, camphor, gasoline, and cocaine. They were armed with handguns, brickbats, and copper hooks for gouging eyes. Robbery was their trade, but they also sold women like cattle. They skimmed money from gambling dens and brothels, and they bribed the police. The lawyers Howe and Hummel, with a whole stock of false witnesses on their payroll, represented them.

"Why do they call themselves Whyos?" Tesla asked.

"That's how they call to each other at night—like tomcats."

"Where do they live?" Tesla would not let it go.

"Their headquarters are right here," his young friend answered, squinting as if he was looking at the sun. "Otherwise, they hang out at the Morgue on Bowery and drink. There they have their price list for beatings and murders posted."

"How much do they charge to bite off an ear?" Tesla joked.

"Fifteen bucks," Prostran's answered in earnest.

The morning was the worst part of the day. That was when his whole being started to hiss like a snake. Tesla planted his boot on it, but the sinewy serpent kept wriggling under his foot.

"Be quiet!" The desperate man tried to outhiss the voice of his own panic. "Be quiet!"

It was getting light, but the city was still hidden behind the gray drizzle. Autumn issued its order: die! Wandering aimlessly through the city, Tesla came across a group of ditch diggers. He squatted by the edge of the trench and asked them if there was any work for him. The toothless diggers grinned. Without a word, the well-dressed young man jumped into the ditch and grabbed a pick.

"C'mon, get on it!" the others jeered at him.

His whole body ached that evening. All of it.

That first Tuesday was the worst. The last blister broke on Wednesday. Its slimy liquid dried on his palm.

Dirt covered his sores.

"I've always assumed there was something guiding my life," Tesla said to himself. "Now I doubt it. Maybe there's no invisible ball of yarn rolling ahead of me to show the way. Maybe there's only nonsense and emptiness. Inertia helps me dig, but shoveling dulls my mind. I work for the City of New York, digging ditches into which Edison's cables will be laid. So I'm still working for Edison."

He talked to himself like the crazies in the streets do. And he lived against his own heart.

In Prague, and even more so in Paris, he developed a taste for opera and went whenever he could. Horrified by his own envy, Tesla lingered around the New York Metropolitan Opera. The posters announced that Wagner's *Siegfried* was to be staged. In the photograph, the tenor Max Alvary, dressed in a short robe, raised his eyes meaningfully toward the ceiling. Hunched, Tesla admired the straight postures of male and female backs. The angelic smell of cleanliness tickled his nose. The refreshing drone of the audience in the lobby sounded otherworldly. Middle-aged women flounced in their youthful dresses. The explosion of their laughter resembled the breaking of plates. The chandelier was full of embers. Smiling men in coattails talked to innocent women in low-cut dresses in the anteroom. The twenty-eight-year-old laborer observed all of it from the perspective of a temporary dog. Despair flooded his soul, spreading slowly like oil over the table. The pinging from the dwarf's smithy in the opening scene of *Siegfried* resounded in his head. Threadbare elbows, bad shoes, filthy shirt, the odor from dirty hair and sweaty armpits—that was who he was now. His clothes were like a floor mat. People in front of the theater looked at him as if he was a hair in their soup. He almost shuddered when he heard the rotund doorman shout, "Hey, you! What are you doing here?"

The worst autumn in his life was followed by the worst winter. The wind turned snow into fog. The blizzards were so bad that newspapers called them "whiteouts."

Tesla could see his breath as soon as he woke up. His clothes felt cold, as if they were wet. Blessed Stevan returned from his night shift with a joke on his tongue and warm bread in his hands. Stevan's serene face dispelled Tesla's gloom as he finished his coffee and went out to let his friend have the bed.

"All my life I've been working to serve mankind," the morose inventor complained to himself. "Is mankind the waiters who sell buckets of leftover beer? Or the wretches to whom they sell it? The Whyos drinking alcohol mixed with liquid camphor? The prostitutes whose shelf life is two years?"

He was able to piece together some sort of meaning for his life, but it dissolved in the first icy rain. Steam rose up from horses' backs in the streets. Rails disappeared in the sleet, and buildings vanished in the fog.

He soothed himself thinking of Mother's deep eyes.

CHAPTER 39

"The Dangerous Classes"

Late March in New York could hardly be called spring. The foreman, Obadiah Brown, kept his word and rehired all of his autumn workers. Brown was from the southern part of the proud state of Mississippi, where they cut their hair according to the phases of the moon and then burned it together with their nail clippings. His bushy mane hid his big ears. A cigar pulsated in the corner of his mouth. A rare good word came out of that uncouth man. "I don't like Slavs." He waved his arms around. "I don't like the Irish either. Or Jews. Or Italians, for that matter. But I can't be that way when I'm looking you in the eye, brother."

The first week after the winter thaw, Brown and his men were working on the route of the elevated train for the Bronx at Third Avenue. Carmine Roca was digging next to Tesla. The sounds of the body delighted him. He informed his cosufferers in the trench, "This morning I took such a huge shit that I remained amazed for the rest of the day."

He had a habit of unexpectedly rolling his head and then belching like a lion. When he passed gas, he announced, "I just ripped my pants!"

Someone should kill him! Tesla thought.

In the morning, Carmine snorted and declared in the trench: "Fabriccarisi la furca cu li so stissi manu." (He is digging his own grave.) After the lunch break, he raised his finger and said, "Zoccu si cumincia, si finisci." (Finish what you've started.)

When they asked him where his family was from, he responded irritably, "Adrano."

Roca knew everything, although he could barely speak English. He was here temporarily, and then . . . his own oyster boat in New Orleans, and then . . .

His nephew Giovanni Romanello worked alongside him. He could only smile at his uncle's antics as if he wanted to say, "What can you do?" The sight of the uncle tired Tesla out—the sight of the nephew relaxed him. That Italo-Byzantine native of the largest island in the Mediterranean intrigued him. The songs Giovanetto hummed betrayed two thousand and five hundred years of melancholy. Tesla wondered: What gave that Sicilian peasant such natural elegance? Was he an offspring of the Syracuse tyrant Dionysius who sold Plato into slavery?

Nikola and Giovanni obviously resembled each other—the same little smile hovered at the corner of their mouths. Using his melodious l's and r's, Giovanni loved to talk to Tesla. He pointed out that the donkey was a good animal, even beautiful, so he could not understand why people made fun of it. The donkey was a much better creature than the Marquise di San Giuliano, for whom his family members were working themselves to death. He mentioned the bloody oranges and sweet lemons of Sicily. He told Tesla how half of his native village lived in the tenement on Mott Street, and how its bustle and smells made Mott Street look like the marketplace in Catania. The only thing missing was the marble fountain.

"One of my relatives has offered me a waiter's position at the Venice," Giovanotto smiled. "The ceilings are high, cupolas and a gondola are painted on a blue wall. Wages aren't bad and the work is much easier. Hah, *vediamo!*"

Twenty-two-year-old Paddy Maloney dug alongside Tesla and Giovanni. He could spit and whistle at the same time.

Leaning against his pick, he told Tesla the story of his life. In the year of the potato famine in Ireland and the revolution in Europe, his grandfather came to America. He was from the town of Beltra, in the county of Mayo, the old province of Connaught, where the starving were green around the mouth from eating grass.

"I saw my grandfather sober only once and couldn't recognize him," Paddy told them.

He lost both his grandfather and his mother within a year.

"The dead," the young man blushed and looked up to the sky.

"They had their own time on earth and we have ours," Tesla said, trying to console him.

"Cigarette ashes were falling on me when I was a baby," Paddy concluded deadpan. "They found me in the arms of my drunken aunt. Cigarette ashes kept falling on me . . ."

His neighbors took care of him for several years. After that, a Catholic hospital for foundlings took him in and sent him on the Orphan Train to a farm in Iowa to get adopted.

"Why don't *you* get adopted!" With an obscene gesture, Paddy took his leave from the nuns. He jumped off the train and returned to New York on foot. He was a shoeshine boy. He was a newspaper boy. He hung around other shoeshine and newspaper boys. "All of these famed friendships are bullshit," he told Tesla later.

The boy floated like seaweed, moved by the ebbs and flows of Manhattan. Tesla learned about the seamy side of the city mostly from him. As a child, Paddy frequented whorehouses where small newspaper boys visited nine-year-old girls. He grew up in a maelstrom of popular impressions. He adored Stevie Brodie who jumped off the Brooklyn Bridge. He celebrated the rat terrier Jack Underhill, who killed one hundred rats in a half hour at a beer den on First Avenue and Tenth. To him, John L. Sullivan the boxer was God. Paddy remembered Sullivan's first fight in New York, when he crushed Steve Taylor in two and a half minutes. "Then he defeated Paddy Ryan, the Irishman from Ireland, in just eleven minutes." Paddy's memory was infallible.

He was on speaking terms with such important personages as Googie Corcoran and Baboon Connelly from the Whyos gang.

"He's just a show-off," the foreman grunted. "Otherwise he's a good kid—a working man."

Paddy recited the legends of the boulevard in the same way one would retell *The Odyssey*. He followed the developing saga of Tender Maggie and Lizzie the Dove, who wanted to slit each other's throats because they were both in love with the elegant pimp Danny Driscoll. Lizzie's last words were, "I'll gouge your eyes in hell!"

Paddy listened to anarchists' speeches at Tompkins Square. He was convinced that the Haymarket bombing in Chicago the previous year was organized by the Knights of Labor. He insisted the Chinese would steal white women and keep them as slaves and was glad Congress banned them from entering America.

"About time!"

Once after work, desperate Tesla let Paddy drag him to a bar that looked like a dilapidated theater, where a fierce cornet player competed with a tipsy pianist. The audience loudly applauded the singer's blue stockings. Her mouth was so big she could sing two songs at once. Paddy tried to lure Tesla into the back room, where naked girls danced the cancan. A slight ironic smile was ineffective, so Tesla had to protest: "Please don't! I really can't."

Paddy played Jewish faro at Chick Tricker's Fleabag and at McGurk's Suicide Hall. When he was drunk, he would sometimes visit the black bars and return with a black eye. The foreman called him his "little bull."

"I lived like that too," Obadiah Brown said, pointing at the scar on his eyebrow. He felt Paddy's muscles and said, "You could be a good boxer."

"Have you ever boxed?" Paddy's broad face suddenly came to life.

"I had a great uppercut." The foreman swung his arm.

In the morning, before work, Paddy would puff up his powerful chest. He loved to sing while he worked, and Giovanni subtly joined in with his own tenor. The black Portuguese Joaquim added the bass line. After the song, Nikola sometimes talked about his motor. The workers listened wordlessly and without derision.

Paddy Maloney was a fine fellow when he was sober. When he was drunk, an anger much older than himself spewed out of him. Fuckin' Limeys. Fuckin' rain. Fuckin' heroism. Fuckin' legends. Fuckin' life!

"How much sorrow is hidden underneath that anger! How much stupid sorrow!" Tesla murmured.

Once Paddy came to work hungover. He turned away and threw up a little bit on a dirt pile. As soon as he realized where he was, he looked at Giovanni and Roca with scorn: Paddy's father was born in America, while those two just got off the boat.

Paddy could not stand Roca, and Tesla understood why. The Sicilian kept blabbing about his future oyster boat. He went on talking, but his words were lost amid the sounds of work, the shovels scraping and the picks swinging.

"Spring," Roca grunted in discontent.

Paddy frowned. "What the hell are you talking about, fatso." Paddy's trouble-bent glare bored into Roca's glowing eyes. The Sicilian glanced at him briefly as he stuck out his lower lip.

"You got a problem?" Paddy had a nasty grin on his face. "Nigger!"

Roca could not match Paddy's stare and lazily stepped aside.

"I got a problem," the nephew unexpectedly said.

Giovanotto dropped his pick and straightened up. Paddy turned around quickly. Without a word, he charged forward and immediately took a step back, holding his stomach. He gagged as if he wanted to say something.

"Don't take the knife out!" Obadiah Brown jumped in. "He'll bleed to death!"

"Oh my God!" Tesla whispered.

Giovanni stood paralyzed by his decision and its consequence. He appeared calm, almost smiling. With numb feet, he plodded across the space that opened up as they led him away.

Paddy's amazed eyes took in the world around him for the last time. Then they glazed over, and the images of distant windows froze on them.

CHAPTER 40

The Blind Tiger

After the fight, Nikola and the foreman Brown ended up at a blind tiger. Brown drank rum, and Nikola drank beer. They talked about Paddy's death and Giovanni's arrest.

"It's horrible!" Nikola muttered.

"We live beneath the city," began the foreman. "My father always told me to make something of myself. And I wouldn't do it. My brother is an engineer, you know. But I didn't want to do anything. I just wandered around out West."

"Oh my God!" Nikola shook his head in disbelief.

"This whole thing stinks. It's such a fucking American misunderstanding," Brown had his eyes wide open above his third rum. "That Paddy liked to fight, but he would never use a knife. The other guy, Giovanni, is peaceful, but he would use a knife in a fight. So different rules cancel one another. The bottom drops out because of violence, and people live in hell."

In the dim light of the illegal tavern, Brown's hair turned unnaturally yellow.

The waiter took their glasses away and brought new ones. Brown touched the scar on his forehead: "I was in prison. Because of—" He laughed viciously. "Because of whatever happened. But, when you get old—you'll see for yourself—you start thinking differently."

Nikola was still in shock.

"Do you remember how they sang together?"

Usually, Obadiah Brown was a man of few words who preferred two mistakes to one explanation. Now he became talkative. Rum number five replaced beer number four.

"As a little kid I had a nanny. I was better in mathematics than my brother. Right now he sits in his office with books stacked to the ceiling. And I live like this," he pointed at his scar again. "Each Thanksgiving he invites me for turkey as big as a camel. But I don't go."

Brown's face stretched into a derisive smile. He bared his teeth, yellower than his hair, and stared at Tesla. "You told me about your motor. You think I don't understand. But I do. I went to school. That's simple—you just leave out that . . . commutator"—he grimaced as he pronounced the unusual word—"so electrical current is conveyed great distances. Which is what Edison can't do, right?"

The waiter slammed a mug of beer in front of Tesla and gently placed the rum before Brown. Brown sniffed the rum and winked at Tesla, who was amazed by the man's recall.

"You don't need any more of this crap in your life," Brown passed the verdict. "It has to stop. I'll introduce you to my brother. He can help you. Even though he can't help me."

Ragged apes in bowler hats, whose brains had been stolen by demon rum, jabbered all around them.

"We live in a chasm," Obadiah Brown made a face. "Beneath the city. At least someone should rise above it."

Brown staggered out of the bar like a headless chicken, and Tesla thought he would not remember anything the next day.

But the next week Brown showed up with his hair combed down and his ears sticking out. His yellow hair was parted in the middle, and his white scalp showed through. He told Tesla to put on some nice clothes and to follow him.

"Hey, windbag! Come with me."

For a half hour they strode along in silence toward Upper Manhattan. The walk produced magical results. Garbage disappeared as they advanced. Passersby and shop windows became dignified. Hats grew taller and collars grew furry. At the tails of their crinolines, women dragged whole draperies. At the entrance of the Western Union

Telegraph office, there was a doorman with a sash. Instead of driving them off, he smiled and ushered them inside. Alfred B. Brown was the head engineer at Western Union Telegraph.

The brothers briefly embraced at the door. It appeared that Obadiah Brown's sibling was a kind, somewhat neurotic man. He performed each move with twice as much energy as necessary. With a quick pull, he took out his spectacles and perched them on his nose. His magnified eyes met Tesla's. "I know who you are," he said. "I myself have patented a few arc lamps. I remember your lightbulbs from Rahway."

In that office everything was in its proper place, from the warm oak paneling to the stained glass in the upper part of the window. Every now and then, Brown flashed something—his spectacles, his gold fountain pen, his cigarette case. The smell of cleanliness, Brown's starched collar, the flash of his cigarette case, and especially his kind disposition were welcoming signs of Tesla's return to his own long-lost home.

Obadiah Brown spoke first, waving his hands, which were as huge as those of Professor Pöschl. Then Tesla followed with his detailed, quiet explanation, rolling out one blueprint after another. Alfred Brown was listening. At the end, he firmly shook Tesla's hand. He saw them to the door, patting his brother on the shoulder. The deal instantly brought Tesla a hotel room full of light and several suits in his closet. Brown informed him that he was welcome to work in his lab, and scheduled a meeting with the New Jersey lawyer Charles Peck in a month. (The man's "maybe," Brown growled, was worth more than other people's "yeses.") Peck was aware that the polyphase system with which Westinghouse had been experimenting was not working as expected. "However, he's also suspicious about your model," Brown warned Tesla.

The last Saturday in April brought a sudden drop in temperature and the long-awaited meeting. The starched plastrons of their shirts shone white, and Tesla felt like a swan surrounded by his own kind.

His intensifying leanness surprised all the people present at the meeting.

His squeaky new shoes paced restlessly around Brown's laboratory. Holding his breath, he had been getting ready for this for weeks. His excitement once again pushed the walls aside. A recently built model of his motor awaited their judgment.

The wrinkles on Charles Peck's brow looked like musical staves. He was a stunted, competent man. Tesla felt that he could convince such a man but not charm him. Peck glanced at his watch. "Please begin." He nodded his head with the noticeable absence of a smile.

Tesla smiled and reminded them that the Spanish queen gave Columbus ships when he made an egg stand upright on the table.

"In order to convince you, I built an iron model of the spinning egg."

Before Peck's eyes, Tesla turned the switch on and moved the iron egg from his palm into the magnetic field. The egg started to spin, making a loud metallic sound as it loped. As it spun faster, the noise ceased and the egg stood upright, locked in the electric whirlpool.

"You see!" Tesla raised his long fingers.

Peck stopped frowning. His hard eyes flashed, ready to make an immediate decision.

"Send me the blueprint by tomorrow," he commanded.

It dawned on Tesla that no doorman would ever drive him away from an affluent person's office again. The ball of golden yarn came back to life, bounced, and once more started to roll on before his feet.

CHAPTER 41

The Transformations of Athena

The turkey was enormous. Alfred Brown carved it with an anxious smile, separating the white meat from the dark. The fragrance of the newly cut flowers on the table engulfed Tesla.

The hostess handed him a glass bowl filled with cooked cranberries. "Please help yourself."

Who's missing here? Tesla wondered, putting a second spoonful of cranberries on his turkey.

An avid reader of Homer, Tesla recalled that the goddess Athena revealed herself to Odysseus by assuming various forms whenever she wanted to help him. The next day Tesla went to look for Obadiah Brown at the office of the Rapid Transit Company. The people in the office shrugged their shoulders. "He's gone!" one of them said.

Where did that old cigar chewer go?

Once again, Tesla passed by the churchyard of danger on the corner of Park Row and Mott Street and knocked on Stevan Prostran's door. The landlady handed him an envelope. In uneven characters, Prostran informed him that he lost his job and had left with a group of Montenegrins for Homestead near Pittsburgh.

Tesla looked for Paddy's grave but could not find it either. Solitude was thus forced upon him. He felt abandoned to the needle-breaking icy wind. Where had everyone suddenly disappeared to?

Through sheer willpower, he projected a dear figure before his eyes. Djuka Tesla stood in front of him, with a comb in her hand, her hair down, looking so real he could touch her.

"What is this?" her son asked her.

Was everyone's disappearance the price of fame required by some Mephistophelian contract?

What an expert you are, devil! How subtly you go about your business! How deft is your hand!

In any case, he had no time to think about the people who were close to him. Everything happened quickly, almost impersonally, as if by magic. With a smile and a tear in his eye, he slept little and worked all the time. His work energy was like a snowball that crashed down gathering more snow as it rolled. Months rang by like fire trucks. Cash registers rang. Church bells rang. The change of seasons resounded with the laughter of ever-youthful gods.

He spent his sixteen-hour day without making a single unnecessary move. The wind carried him. Days and months flew by. His hands flew as he worked. His brain waves flew following the music. Thunderbolts flashed. Sparks cracked like whips.

Days had no end.

Nights were just a blink.

CHAPTER 42

From the Stuttering Diary

May 5 was not an ordinary day. But what made it so special, if I may ask? What made it special? Antal Szigety arrived in New York!

Szigety hugged me so hard I could barely breathe. He looked strange in this environment. He's a real spark of energy. He turned a cartwheel in my half-empty lab. Then he looked around, winded and happy, like a boy who just finished a drawing of a rooster's tail. The lab smelled of paint and new wood. The tables, the chairs, the brass lamps—everything was new. "So, whose lab is this?" I asked Antal in a surprised voice. "Yours, Nikola." "It is mine!" I just couldn't believe it, so I told him how Peck gave us cigars and how we split the patent fifty-fifty.

"The Bauzains send their greetings. So do our old friends Kulišić and Tannhäuser as well as Mrs. Várnai"—Szigety almost choked— "and the Puskás brothers, and my father, and your uncle Pajo, and all your other relatives."

I told him that, after experiencing poverty, I still couldn't get enough kindness. For a whole year I couldn't work up enough authority to call a waiter or play with a dog. I would constantly say "thank you" or "you're welcome."

My eyes filled with tears.

After those words, Szigety's eyes also filled with tears.

To conceal his emotions, he asked, "Do you know what today is?"

"What?" Tesla asked with an ironic smile.

"Today's my thirty-first birthday."

Tesla leapt to his feet. "Then champagne is in order. It's a must! I'm taking you to a Hungarian restaurant."

Szigety smiled with his blond mustache. "You must be crazy!"

"They even have a hammer dulcimer!"

"Do you think I crossed the ocean so I can eat *székely* goulash?" the new arrival to New York protested.

It all ended with the ruddy-faced Hungarian and the pale-faced Serbian at the Midsummer's Night Dream roof garden restaurant eating steak.

Of that night, Tesla wrote in his diary:

Szigety's foggy accent gave off a whiff of the Old World. My un-expected success smelled like loneliness. His arrival brought a thaw. I felt my soul defrosting. "An enormous undertaking is ahead of us," I said and my voice trembled. "You must help me." I felt relaxed after such a long, long time. The wind hasn't blown everyone away. After the third bottle, we shared sudden attacks of unprovoked laughter. "Our illuminated souls, lit up with wine, can't hide the number of glasses that make us shine . . ."

At the Midsummer's Night Dream restaurant, Antal started to slur his words.

"What did you do in Paris?" Nikola asked.

As if he was waiting for a prompt, Szigety showed his beautiful teeth. It turned out that in Paris he'd frequented brothels in which smiles radiated cunning and erotic fire. There, he said, a redhead and a bru-nette rubbed their plump breasts against one another as they shared the deepest kiss.

"I'm not talking about this just for you," Szigaty raved. "I'm talking to mankind. Feel what I feel. You! You! Feel what I feel!"

"Oh yeah," Tesla mocked him, raising an eyebrow.

"Imagine a man and a woman in a baroque brothel where the cham-pagne costs twenty of your American dollars," Szigety slurred. "Their dry lips are linked in a kiss, which is a perfect fit. She's like a doe caught in a net of passion. He passes his spread fingers across her silky hips. She gives him a deep look: I'm yours!"

Szigety stared at Tesla's long, monastic fingers. A smile of playful Eros hovered upon his lips: "He's on fire. He's shaking. The flame carries him. It lifts him up. Giggling, she's melting like sugar in water . . . Furious, anxious scenes of love unfold."

"Of love?" Tesla interrupted him. "When a paid woman puts on a show of passion for you . . ."

The Hungarian poet did not hear him. "She's horrified, shocked, furious, and she keeps her eyes tightly shut with pleasure . . ."

A wry smile attacked Syigety's face like an itch.

"Enough, Szigety! Stop it!" Tesla rose from the table.

"Her eyes are closed with pleasure," the maniac continued. "Her face is dancing, she glides back and forth across his slippery stomach. She caresses her breasts . . . Love—"

"Love is fine, but work is glorious." Tesla interrupted him at last. "Go to bed, birthday boy! Great deeds await us."

CHAPTER 43

Success

Fully aware that new inventions could be worth hundreds of thousands of dollars, Tesla's patent lawyers, Duncan, Curtis, and Page, opened negotiations with investors from San Francisco and with George Westinghouse from Pittsburgh.

"Things are happening!" Charles Peck informed him with a frown.

Tesla worked at a frightening pace. He broke down his plans for the induction motor into a series of patents. The progress of his work depended on the ability of his technicians to keep up. With the jaunty yet tireless Szigety, Tesla designed spindles and constructed prototypes, so that weeks of work extended into months.

One windy April morning, a young man with warm eyes appeared at his door. It seemed that the hair he was losing from the top of his head migrated to his mustache. The balding fellow introduced himself as Thomas Commerford Martin, the vice president of the American Institute of Electrical Engineers.

"Theologians believe that God can count every hair on one's head. In my case, that's not particularly difficult," he joked at his own expense.

Martin had come to ask a question: "Would you give a lecture at our club?"

"I can't believe it!"

For years, he had yanked at the buttons and sleeves of indifferent people, trying to tell them about his motor. Now they wanted to listen to everything that deaf Edison would not hear!

"I'm too nervous to go with you," Szigety said. "You'll tell me how it went."

When an elegant landau pulled by two smart sorrels stopped in front of the laboratory at Liberty Street on May 16, 1888, Szigety jumped in anyway.

"Move over. I'm going."

Settling next to Tesla, he turned around and wrinkled his nose. His fellow passenger smelled of violets.

Szigety, more nervous than Tesla, took a sip from a silver flask.

"Antal!"

"Everyone loves to be forgiven for something," Szigety said by way of apology.

In less than twenty minutes, the bobtail horses pulled up to the gateway of the American Institute of Electrical Engineers. The entrance was fashioned from one block of ornamental brick. Brass bars kept the carpet on the stairwell in place. From the atrium, echoing hallways rayed in different directions.

"This way," Tesla was instructed.

"Good luck," Szigety whispered, melting into the audience.

Their steps echoed along the checkerboard hallway.

"Follow me," Martin mouthed near Tesla's cheek.

The wood-paneled auditorium emitted a stuffy yet pleasant odor.

Tesla was so tall that, to the audience, he appeared to be on stilts. His face tapered from his broad brow to his long chin. His hair was parted into two black wings. His wounded, mysterious eyes burned beneath his brow.

What do they expect of me? he thought with animosity. *To step dance? To juggle torches?*

He was so nervous he wanted to flee from his own body.

As a child, he often dove into the cold Korana. Now he did the same—he simply dove in and began. Electricity, he explained, is as incompressible as liquid. It is the fundamental organizational principle of the matter in which it is bound. Only a small portion of it exists in a free state. If there were an imbalance in the electrical charge, the electrical force would rule the universe because it is many times stronger than gravity.

Tesla's face assumed a half-inspired, half-martyred expression. With his uplifted nose and fluttering eyelashes he looked like a blind man.

He said electricity was the clean essence of a dirty world—or his audience thought that was what he said.

Electricity cannot be created or destroyed, and its quantity is always constant. It is like Allah—it has no smell or shape or sound, but nothing can withstand it when it manifests itself. The lightning's crack is not electricity—it is hot air because electricity remains invisible.

The lecturer opened his anguished eyes. His heightened awareness made them glow.

He spoke about the phenomena of attraction and repulsion, and to his listeners it seemed as if he were talking about love and hate. He went on about the mysterious fascination of electricity and magnetism, about their seemingly dual character, unique among natural forces. The main question we face is, can we use these forces in a practical way? There is no doubt about it!

In the audience, a group of people, including the Serb Mihailo Pupin from Columbia University, started to boo and heckle him.

"Shhhhhsh, shhhhhsh!" came from all sides.

The hecklers were silenced.

All of a sudden, everyone wanted to listen to what the deaf Edison refused to hear. Warm ectoplasm circulated between the lanky lecturer and his audience. In that moment, Tesla knew: *"I have them!"* He could not remember what he said from that point on.

Choked up with emotion, he spoke about the future long-distance transfer of electricity and the day when Niagara Falls would light up the city of New York. "Why should a big city like New York need two thousand power plants when one would be sufficient?" he asked.

The gold ball of yarn sprightly rolled along his path again. He spoke so fast that he neglected the necessity of breathing. People listened to him with an embittered sense of awe. Many members of the audience were frozen with delight. Many felt as if someone had cut off the tops of their heads. In the end, the ceiling danced from the applause.

This was finally it. This was his world.

Long-legged as a crane, the lecturer smiled amid the applause. The balding, round-eyed Martin snatched up the copy of Tesla's speech in order to publish it in his *Electrical World*.

This is an awakening! flashed in Tesla's head. *But is it mine or theirs?*

The audience—like a single being composed of many eyes and dignified mustaches—embraced him. The many-eyed creature asked, "Are you sure that the system is safe enough?" "What distance can electricity be transferred without loss?" the noisy entity uttered through a different mouth.

"Congratulations! You swept them off their feet." Antal's alcoholic breath hit him in the face.

Even Pupin smiled at him with a self-satisfied expression and shook his hand in the most cordial manner. "May I pay you a visit?" the new convert asked.

Above the heads of the crowd, Tesla looked for his manuscript as it was disappearing "straight to print." He was deafened by the applause, which lifted him above the stage and above the human race. Charles Peck materialized behind him. His wooden fingers squeezed Tesla's elbow: "I must introduce you to someone."

CHAPTER 44

Pittsburgh

"George Westinghouse," Peck announced like an archbishop intoning a prayer.

A huge, graying man spread his arms wide and the day became a holiday. His walrus mustache glistened. His eye was clear. Everything that had to be said he fitted into three sentences:

"I heard your lecture. You convinced me. I'll buy your patents."

The sun stood still.

"I don't know what to say," Tesla muttered.

"Don't say anything," said Westinghouse. "Come to Pittsburgh."

That turned out to be a wonderful visit.

A coachman in a uniform with gold buttons and a top hat met Tesla at the station and took him to Westinghouse's mansion, which he had named Solitude. It looked like a castle. A magnolia tree was shedding its petals on the front lawn. On the garden path, Tesla noticed a patinated bronze sundial. Two robins fought around this device of Chronos. Despite the great beauty of his uncle Pajo's mansion near Budapest and the few Alsatian residences he had visited, Tesla had to admit that this was the most splendid house he had ever seen. The windows, walls, and parts of the roof took on unexpected curvy and oval shapes. Squeezed in between several palm trees, a fountain gurgled in the greenhouse. Through lush greenery, a redbrick path led to the coachman's quarters above the stables, where eight horses and their companion, a little white goat, grazed on hay. A black servant with sheep-white hair was the handsomest old man Tesla had ever seen.

The guest happily turned glass doorknobs full of light and smiled at the mirrors. A marble bust of Margaret Westinghouse in a Roman matron pose supervised the corner between two windows. The sunlight poured in through French windows, which stretched from the floor to the ceiling. The parquet floors reflected golden glints like Brünnhilde's hair.

Telephones for calling servants were built into the walls. The main hall, with a circular ottoman in its center, was so skillfully painted that its white silver color gave the illusion of encrusted mother-of-pearl. A schedule of meals and activities written in calligraphy awaited Tesla in his room.

They arrived at Solitude in the afternoon at two sharp. Dinner was at seven. He had enough time to rest.

Both George and Margaret Westinghouse were exceptionally tall. Beds were fashioned to accommodate their size. As soon as Tesla reclined, some inner storm lifted him up like a paper kite. In the huge bed, he experienced several flashes. A personal security safeguard appeared to have failed within him, and he went through a series of spiritual orgasms. Quick and rhythmical, it almost resembled an epileptic fit.

Oh, what an ascension! What light!

He was still seeing the flashes beneath his eyelids when they called him down. The rustling of Margaret Westinghouse's crinoline accompanied him as he entered the dining room. The power of God's angels imperceptibly flowed through the walls. Crystal tulips shone from the chandelier. Men in coattails and women wearing low-cut dresses assumed their seats around the table. The servants' impersonal expressions still frightened Tesla. A uniformed servant stood behind each chair to pull it out and push it back again. The quiet waiters in white served:

Oysters
Artichoke cream soup
Tomato jelly with mayonnaise
Doves with peas
Glazed ham with Madeira wine

Tournedos Laguipierre
Strawberries with maraschino
Pears in brandy
Charlotte with ice cream

As soon as the last guest was served, the plates were taken away. One had to eat quickly. Westinghouse's engineers had no appetite. As is often the case with anything that is quite logical, when they learned of Tesla's solutions they exclaimed, "We knew that!"

They spoke little. They smacked their dry lips as they ate. They took their revenge on Westinghouse's new favorite by casting quick and spiteful glances at him. They called him "colleague" with some hesitation. They believed that the praises they spared him would shower back on themselves. Personal spite is most often disguised as public concern. Westinghouse's engineers were deeply concerned about the world.

"What happened to the families of those people who were snowed in during that awful blizzard back in March?" the engineer Stillwell asked Margaret Westinghouse.

Engineer Shallenberger's gravelly throat produced some raspy sounds pertaining to the World Expo that was supposed to take place in Paris the following year. "That self-same Eiffel who constructed the base for the Statue of Liberty will build the tower there as well."

"Wouldn't you like to see the Eiffel Tower bathed in lights?" Tesla asked.

"Somebody needs to work," Stillwell retorted in the voice of a Salem trial judge.

Still seeing some flashes beneath his eyelids, Tesla responded with a little ironic smile.

A row of shapely glasses trembled next to each guest's plate. They were first filled with white wine and then with red. When the glasses were empty, gloved hands took them away. Tesla had barely a chance to take a sip of some late-harvest muscatel when cognac the color of amber appeared in the glasses. The backs of the chairs in the salon groaned under the weight of the newly fattened gentlemen. A lit cigar served as an alibi for a deep sigh.

With subdued mirth in his eyes, Westinghouse recollected how he started to pump the natural gas they had discovered right beneath the city.

"His gas actually brought industry to Pittsburgh," Shallenberger, ever the sycophant, amended.

Westinghouse waved off the comment.

"He's not a ripple—the man's a wave!" Stillwell praised his boss.

"He's a fighter who never quits!" Shallenberger exclaimed.

Stillwell did not want to be upstaged at any cost. With theatrical flair, he pointed out his employer to Tesla: "This is the man who took the fun out of stopping trains."

Westinghouse's chuckle turned into a merry guffaw.

"Long ago, each car had its own brakeman," he explained to Tesla. "At a whistle, each man would start to brake as the train entered the station. Sometimes they stopped the train too early, and sometimes they passed the station and would have to back up. In both cases, passengers chased after them."

"So when this gentleman patented his brakes," Shallenberger put down his glass of cognac on the table, "those entertaining scenes came to an end."

"Ha, ha, ha!" All the guests in the jolly mansion Solitude laughed.

Before he booked his trip to Pittsburgh, Tesla asked the frowning Peck about Westinghouse. He was told that the previous year his Pittsburgh-based company's profit quadrupled and that his parents were Baltic-Russian aristocrats.

"Nothing is created without an individual," Westinghouse raised his finger before his guests. "And nothing remains without an institution."

The host did not utter an inappropriate word the whole evening. He signaled to the butler to place a bottle of cognac on a low table. He poured some and confided to Tesla, "My entire life was linked to the railroads. I met my wife on a train. The idea for my first invention came to me on a train."

The huge host invoked the time after the Civil War, when railroads crisscrossed the country. People shot bison from the train. They used their hides for wall coverings. The owners of railroads bought senators like sacks of potatoes. Senators who "stayed bought" were considered honest. Poets glorified the howl and the sharp whistle of the engine as it penetrated the most magnificent landscapes in the world.

The silver on Westinghouse's temples highlighted the deep red of his face. "A practical man is a man with a vision," he explained. "Without a vision, he's not practical—he's pedestrian."

His enthusiasm was boyish. He loved a good fight. He moved his chair closer to Tesla's: "They said I was a bully at school. I didn't stay long in college. I'm not an academic type. I'm good at something else: I like to roll up my sleeves and convince people. That's what I want to do with your motor."

With his broad chest and clear eyes, this gigantic aristocrat greatly appealed to Tesla. Whenever Westinghouse left the room, the light became dim, and when he returned everything seemed to expand.

"I always knew it was possible," he said at the end of the evening. "I suggest we prove it together."

Ever since he had met Westinghouse, the young inventor had a nauseating and thrilling premonition. In his large bed at Solitude, he wrestled with his oncoming success like Jacob with the angel. Success was a living creature, huge but invisible, which slept in his room at night and breathed close to him during the day. Success smelled of the February wind and enormous solitude.

CHAPTER 45

The Engineers

The evil suppress virtue much more than the good admire it.
Don Quixote

The face of the newly arrived Hungarian electrical engineer lit the mirrors in Pittsburgh. He was always excited and jovial, so everyone liked him.

"With your full cheeks and your light eyes, you remind me of a lynx," Westinghouse laughed.

Westinghouse called him Anthony and asked him to elaborate on the discovery he witnessed in the park in Budapest. Szigety preferred Mrs. Westinghouse to anyone else.

"Did you see her cleavage?" he whispered into Tesla's large ear. "I wouldn't mind curling up in there like a hamster and hibernating for the winter."

Tesla rolled his eyes and introduced him to Westinghouse's engineers.

"These guys don't like you, my friend," Antal told him right after the meeting.

"Why?" Tesla was taken aback.

"They envy you because you don't envy anybody," Szigety responded. "They also believe that you have it in for them as much as they have it in for you."

Tesla recalled his father's words that *the truth is never adverse to an intelligent and honest man.* Under the influence of his arrogant naïveté, Nikola believed people would appreciate that he was in the right and they were in the wrong, which would help them lift the burden of error from their minds. The brief pauses the engineers used when talking to Tesla put him "in his place."

Oliver Shallenberger, the inventor of the electric meter, and his assistant Lewis Stillwell, the inventor of the amplifier similar to Tesla's reels, were the worst.

"I'll lock horns with them for you," Szigety promised Tesla.

Shallenberger's smile oozed sugary revulsion.

At home, his wife was careful not to give their child the best piece of chicken, which was reserved for her husband. Shallenberger finely cut and thoroughly chewed his white meat. After the meal, he gently hugged their little daughter, looked at the ceiling with his teary eyes, and wondered, *Why, God?*

The ambitious engineer was under the impression that fate had dealt him a rotten hand. Volcanic bitterness, furious impotence, and aggressive fear alternated in his chest. *He* was the former prodigy. *He* had worked on the alternating current motor for years: Why don't the journalists ask *him* about the events in China? Why doesn't his little daughter—after she's finished gnawing on her chicken wing—feel proud of her father?

Lewis Stillwell rarely bothered to ponder such questions. His nose was shapely, his eyes were a mixture of steel and champagne. The handsome, cold man did not care about recognition. At night, before his second shoe fell by the bed, he grimaced: The stranger doesn't know what to do with his money. If Stillwell had that kind of money, he would build a house above the Hudson. And he would build another house for his mother, and then a church. And he would have a stable full of horses, the best in Saratoga Springs.

People would know who Stillwell is!

There was a rumor among the engineers that Westinghouse had offered the stranger some sort of partnership. Apparently, the stranger was stupid enough to turn him down.

"But, if you don't mind, I will still stay in Pittsburgh," Tesla promised, "to work on adapting my motors to your system."

"This is how we will do it," Westinghouse proposed at a closed meeting. "I'm offering you five thousand in cash for sixty days, ten thousand at the end of that period if I buy your patent, three times twenty thousand in two-month intervals, two and a half dollars per watt by way of income, and two hundred shares in my company."

"God damn it!" swore Shallenberger.

"It's not going to work that way," growled Stillwell.

The war started right after the contract was signed.

The motor could not be adapted to the higher frequencies of Westinghouse's equipment, so Tesla suggested lowering them. Stillwell and Shallenberger used long rationalizations to grease their spiteful reluctance. Terms such as "the integrity of the system," "technological rationale," and "economic factor" were repeated at regular intervals.

In Pittsburgh, Tesla experienced frequent flashes behind his eyelids. Those bursts of light revealed to him things he could only helplessly ponder before. Formulas and forms floated in that liquid platinum. Tesla refused to work on what anyone else could do—he wanted to work on what only he could do. Every day, on his behalf, Szigety politely fought with the engineers.

Whenever they relaxed during dinner, Tesla began to philosophize: "In order to notice something original, one has to ignore required things. Institutions tend to promote obligatory concepts. Desirable concepts are rewarded with money and a pat on the back. Institutions train people not to focus on what is not rewarded and to never understand concepts that bring no personal gain."

Dealing with the engineers, Szigety scratched himself out of boredom and almost fainted from formalities. Nevertheless, he persevered. His explanations to Stillwell and the man's superior were miracles of inspired clarity. Shallenberger's strength fed on repetition. He kept telling the same story using the same words. Every evening, this Hungarian Pan opened a bottle of wine at the Anderson Hotel. After he poured, Szigety slapped himself on the forehead and cried, "What idiots!"

Tesla responded prophetically: "It seems that a man must forgo his cognitive abilities if he wants his social standing to be recognized. Oh, institutions!" he said, raising his voice. "Your purpose is to blind people and then to lead the blind. In you, they parade their knowledge as if knowledge is devoid of any elements of mystery. In you, they gymnastically exercise being brainwashed. In you, the work horses by the names of Stillwell and Shallenberger haul the cartloads of authority."

After the second glass, Antal felt inspired to declare, "Those two hate originality and consider it monstrous. They would want the morning paper to tell them what they already know." After the third glass, he screamed, "I have no clue how people can live like that. These are the people with perpetually wounded pride. If Shallenberger were given a choice between catching a cold and letting someone else die, he would avoid getting ill."

"What about Stillwell?" Tesla was becoming amused.

"He would envy a blind man his seeing-eye dog."

CHAPTER 46

The Blind Say That the Eyes Stink

Are not golden-winged myths in the long run much more lasting than dull rows of numbers? How can we not love legends that brush our feverish brows with their rosy wings and dress our wounds with the golden cotton of fluffy clouds?

Humankind calls on myth all the time: Deliver us from dark reality, O legend! Have mercy on us, O legend!

In the legend, Tesla turned his proud profile to the audience, raised his hands, and tore into pieces a check for a million dollars.

"You trusted me," the legend spoke through Tesla's mouth.

But in reality, George Westinghouse howled:

"Never!"

The chief of all undertakers, J. P. Morgan, bought out Edison's company and offered to buy out Westinghouse's as well.

"Never!" Westinghouse bellowed, like a dying brontosaurus.

After this outburst, he formed a partnership with a few small manufacturers. The sky above Pittsburgh grew dark. The investors became nervous. With their fingernails, they underscored the item of the contract that specified Tesla was entitled to receive two and a half dollars per watt. They repeated:

"Get rid of this!"

When Tesla opened the door, Westinghouse looked like a tuxedoed armoire rocked off balance. The frowning giant stared into the wind that swept the last snowflakes past the window. "The big gorilla sent his barking monkeys to buy my company," he said, sighing.

Two bluish little horns sprang from Tesla's temples. He did not listen to what his visitor was telling him. He listened to the marrow of Westinghouse's bones. Between his nose and his mouth, he caught a taste of the man's soul.

"I have no choice," Westinghouse broke down. "Please, give up your dividends."

Tesla was still a fresh young man who wanted to be liked. His eyes radiated warmth and attention. His hair was divided into two wings down the middle of his head. The whiteness of his shirt could have made Westinghouse snow-blind.

The inventor craved success with every fiber of his being and prepared himself for it. Yet he felt debilitating fear from the enormity of the approaching success he was preparing for. Everything worked against him: endless delays, ill-willed engineers, pirate competitors.

"Fine," Tesla sighed, and swapped money for fame.

From that point on, Westinghouse turned into a surging wave again. He pressured the engineers who had been stalling the project for more than a year.

All the available equipment had to be modified to fit the detested motor. Shallenberger and Stillwell closed their ears. Something had to be done. This was when the young engineer Benjamin Lamey came on the historical scene, squinting like a groundhog on Groundhog Day. He looked sleepy all the time, even when he was hunting. Westinghouse put him in charge of bringing the motor to the equipment, like Muhammad to the mountain. The good-natured Lamey simply embraced Tesla's old suggestions about adapting the system to the motor that worked at sixty cycles.

"It's out of the question." Shallenberger reddened and left the meeting.

"Wait a minute." Stillwell took hold of his shoulder in the echoing hallway. "There's something to this." The two of them whispered to each other like two scorpions kissing under a rock. Stillwell spoke with excitement; his superior's face lit up. From Shallenberger's hocus-pocus grin glimmered something truly sweet, almost sincere. "You think so?" he asked.

"Of course," Stillwell responded.

"You think so?" Shallenberger repeated, moved.

Whispering, Stillwell explained that this time the idea was not coming from Tesla, which made it a new idea. They could accept it, give all the credit to Lamey, and thus shut out the intruder, who was packing his bags to return to New York anyway. They would be as persistent as crickets. In Tesla's absence, their constant chirping would make the story true.

While a maid was putting his starched shirts in his trunk, Tesla threw documents in his bag while humming incessantly. In Pittsburgh, he had been battling the engineers for a year, like Siegfried fighting the evil dwarves.

"From flowers, a spider only gathers spite—while a bee gathers honey in her flight," he mused.

"The blind say that the eyes stink," Szigety quipped.

The maid pressed down on the lid of the stuffed trunk with her whole weight.

"Are you positive you don't want to stay at Westinghouse's?" Szigety asked.

"Don't those bureaucratic dirtbags know that what they say isn't true?" Tesla said as he closed his bag with a vengeance.

Szigety shrugged. "Didn't Goethe say that even slanderers should be taken seriously because it's impossible for people not to believe what they desire with all their hearts?"

CHAPTER 47

For Everything That Lives

The law of competition, which is sometimes hard on an individual,
is the best for the human race,
as it enables the survival of the fittest in every field.
Andrew Carnegie

He pushed his way through the crowd of porters with dust on their shoulders and took a seat on the train. Two sisters with large noses and their similarly endowed mother were sitting across from him. Laughter bubbled through Tesla's nostrils like champagne as he remembered the words from a lecture he gave as a student: "My dear colleagues, spirited colleagues—follow your noses!" He hid his smile inside a newspaper. Then he pulled his nose out of the paper and anxiously looked at the sky: It was going to rain! He had Stevan Prostran's letter in his pocket. Looking at the address written in a workman's hand on brown paper moved him.

He got off the train at nearby Homestead.

So that was where Blake's dark, satanic mills were—the workshops of the divine blacksmith, the crippled Vulcan!

A whistle sounded from afar. The factory bellowed and breathed fire like a dragon. The *fallahs* hurried to build pyramids. The air was sour from the smoke.

For twelve hours without a break, they fed the smelters with ore. Held captive inside the furnace, the sun flailed its fiery tentacles through the door. The heat singed smelters' eyebrows.

That was where people with crippled tongues lived and shared their broken memories. Tesla walked by sooty smiles. In the workers' hovels, Slovakian women sang the most melancholy songs. In front of the huts, old Serbian and Croatian women talked of aches and pains.

"How are you?" asked one.

"Bad," the other drawled.

A morning drunkard expressed strong emotions in an unknown language. Workers in muddy boots, broad shouldered, with large mustaches, told stories about a Pole who kicked a skunk.

"It was a big mistake." They all laughed.

"Hey Gramps, have you ever been young?" they teased an old man.

"If I could only have your head, kid," he replied, "so I could sleep soundly for three days."

There was a rumor about the coming strike.

Shoulders swaying above his thin waist, Tesla approached the mustached men.

"Excuse me, do you know Stevan Prostran?"

"Sure." The workers were surprised that the gentleman spoke their language. They immediately posed a mute question with their eyes: Being so great and successful, do you disown us who are so poor and wretched?

No, I don't.

They told him that Stevan had recently moved to Rankin, where they paid more—fourteen cents an hour.

"You'll wear out three pairs of iron shoes getting there," the men laughed. "You'll need to take the ferry to Keating, but it's not running today."

He was looking for his Stevan, but his Stevan was not to be found.

At times like this, it appeared to Tesla that he was surrounded by ghosts who vanished one after the other.

"Ooooo, lassie!" someone sang with a drawl under the sour sky.

The cold wind brought refrains:

"Don't look back . . ."

"Forget me . . ."

He walked along the train tracks toward the station, inhaling the lukewarm smell of machine grease. As he went, he heard a worker, obviously from Serbia proper, who talked to an old woman about someone who had died in the C smelter explosion.

"The poor soul . . . He was a good man, married to that Mara. His father, Radovan, was also a good man. Those were good people. Be well, Granny."

The simple words saddened Tesla.

He felt very sorry . . . for people and small children . . .

For everything that lives . . .

CHAPTER 48

The Bearded Lady

Edison's eyes were slits in a bunker. With a disgusted smile on his face, he inquired, "So what are their weak spots?"

"Their system may pose some danger," Bachelor muttered, ironing his beard with his palm.

Edison pointed his index finger:

"Their system is deadly. They will release demons into our houses."

Edison's hair looked like frostbitten grass. His nose resembled a pickled beet. His fingers danced over the surface of the table.

"This isn't anything new. This is how we fought the gas companies. Go call Joe Gamshoe. Sam Emew as well."

Bachelor rubbed the magic lamp. Staring with dark, shifty eyes, Gamshoe and Emew sauntered up and cried, "What's your wish, Master?"

The relentless mouth gnawed at the cigar. The ashes fell on Edison's suit. His fingers still drummed the table. "I'm concerned about Westinghouse!" the inventor barked, narrowing his eyes. "The man will never quit!"

They called Westinghouse a "human wave" for a good reason. He tirelessly bribed politicians and businessmen. He gave interviews. He sent his agents and salesmen all over America. He had already sold his alternating current system to a coal mine in Colorado.

As dangerous as an underground stream, Edison plotted with Gamshoe and Emew. He was the first to believe the ideas he tried to sell others. In various newspapers, he raised hell against the "electric murderers."

At Edison's ruthless orders, circus tents sprang up all across the state of New York and all of the Midwest.

"Let the show begin!"

In Peoria, Illinois, a frightened dog yelped on the stage. A menacing assistant attached wires to the dog and connected them to an apparatus. Hunched down, he squeezed the animal's neck and fastened the electrodes.

"Let the dog go, man!" an onlooker shouted.

With a Cheshire Cat's grin, the demonstrator resembled one of those "professors" who peddled snake oil in small Kansas towns.

The horrified-looking professor yelled at the top of his lungs as if they were children, or deaf. "Ladies and gentlemen, esteemed colleagues! Mr. Westinghouse of Pittsburgh wants to bring a new kind of electricity into your homes. Where your women play with your kids, he wants to install so-called alternating current. I know what you'll say! You'll say"—the snake-oil salesman produced a good-natured smile—"we already have safe direct current, generously bestowed on us by Mr. Edison."

Those present only knew about sooty oil lamps and flickering candles. Still, they nodded their heads in agreement.

The professor's theatrical grimaces and gestures were just as important as his words.

"Westinghouse tells us," he continued with the trembling chin of a tragic hero, "that his kind of electricity is easy to transport long distances. Anything that easy can't be good. Is that electricity safe? Is it safe?" The speaker surprised himself with his own question. "We'll see in a second!"

At the Mad Hatter's signal, a curtain lifted and revealed Tesla's frightening coils.

The dog, bound by leather straps, whined at the sight.

"Igor, please!" the professor commanded in his operatic voice.

Smiling slyly, the hunchback Igor checked the wires attached to the dog and winked at the bearded lady.

"Pull the lever!"

The bearded lady pulled the lever.

Hissing and sparking merged with the dog's pitiful wails. To the audience, it seemed that all was smoke and the smell of burning flesh. The professor bent over the carcass of the short-lived animal and announced, "It was *Westinghoused!*"

Rouge glowed on the cheeks of the hunchback Igor, the grinning professor, and the bearded lady as they blinked their rounded eyes. They laughed maliciously, held each other's hands, and bowed before the audience.

CHAPTER 49

Put the Hands in Jars of Water

The night before the event, anyone interested in the Kemmler case could not sleep peacefully. The prison guard Durston reported that all those in attendance were nervous without exception.

Someone tried to talk, but his voice failed him. The ominous sound of footsteps echoed in the stone corridor.

The Mad Hatter, Igor, and the bearded lady were not present in the death chamber.

William Kemmler, the grocer who butchered his wife in Buffalo, came in. He was composed.

"Gentlemen," he said, "I wish you luck . . . I just want to say that much of what has been said about me isn't true. I'm bad enough. It's cruel to make me worse than I am."

He sat on the electric chair without hesitation, as if he wanted to rest. They made him stand up again and cut a hole in his clothes at the base of his spine so that the electrical lead could be attached to his skin.

"Do it right," he said.

The guards attached the electrical leads to his head. The doomed man looked hideous under the leather straps that partly covered his face.

"Is it ready?" he asked.

No one answered.

Kemmler lifted his eyes to catch a ray of sunshine that danced into the chamber of death.

"Good-bye, William!" the prison guard Durston said. There was a click. The man in the chair rose to his feet. Every single muscle in his body was stretched to the limit. Had he not been strapped to the chair, the electrical shock would have thrown him across the room. They pulled the lever back. Everyone felt relieved. And then they looked at Kemmler in horror.

"Merciful God, he's still alive," Durston realized.

"Turn the electricity back on," someone else gasped.

"Kill him, for God's sake! Let's finish this . . ."

Kemmler's chest kept rising and falling.

Dr. Spitzka commanded: "Electricity, again!"

There was another click, like before, and the body of the doomed man in the chair stiffened again. However, this time the dynamo failed to work properly. Loud electrical cracks were heard. Blood appeared on the wretch's face. Kemmler was sweating blood. As the horror peaked, they noticed that the hair and flesh around the electrodes were singed and roasted. The stench was unbearable.

I Only Skimmed Over

"I only skimmed over the report on Kemmler's execution," commented Edison. "That was not a pleasant read."

"It's a known fact that some thirty or forty people have died due to electric shock. . . . In my opinion, it was a mistake to put doctors in charge. To begin with, Kemmler's hair wasn't a good conductor; additionally, I don't believe the crown of the head is the best place to attach the electrodes. . . . There's much more water in the arms, and the flesh is soft, which makes them the most obvious choice. . . . Therefore, it's much better to put the hands in jars of water."

New York Times, **August 6, 1890**

CHAPTER 50

Through Our Sister Bodily Death

Like Lightning I come, and like the Wind I go,
In Paradise you'll meet me happy again, I know.

Ferdowsi

Lately, life had become repetitive to Szigety –it tasted like a honey-comb that had lost its sweetness. In addition to his gloomy assistant Gano Dunn, Szigety hired the Hungarian Koloman Czitó because the man spoke his language. Szigety lived in a fine apartment next to Gramercy Park. His landlord was a spoiled drunk who beat his wife.

"If you need someone to take care of," Szigety said, annoyed by the woman's timid attitude, "you'd better take care of yourself first."

"Sir, why don't you take care of *yourself?*" she replied, trembling.

For some time, Szigety had quit doing squats with barbells. His honey-colored hair was sweaty and his skin was oily. He grew burly and, being stocky, seemed shorter. His natural outbursts of joy became less frequent. He complained of migraines: "If you only knew how it flashes through my head!"

Tesla did not hear him. Kemmler's death shook the very foundations of his world.

"I'm bad enough," the electrocuted man kept repeating in a windy voice. "It's cruel to make me worse than I am."

"Progress is your God," Milutin Tesla's voice outshouted Kemmler's complaints. "But Progress doesn't discriminate—it advances evil as well."

Nikola was doubly shocked because it appeared that Father was

177

correct. He remembered Uncle Branković's vanities. For the first time in Nikola's life, Progress showed him the putrid side of its face.

Edison killed. With Tesla's hand.

"Prometheus sacrificed so much only for Nero to get hold of his fire," Tesla raved.

But all of that was just his "personal life." As usual, he had no time for reflection.

Kemmler's wretched phantom moaned once more and finally left Tesla's dreams. Resorting to sheer willpower, our hero donned his professional blinders again. In collaboration with the soft-eyed Martin, he wrote the story of his life; he also finished patents for Westinghouse as well as two new types of iridescent lamps.

The force propelled Tesla on, tirelessly.

Antal lagged behind. Yet each time an envious thought entered his head, the Hungarian returned it like an unopened letter to wherever such thoughts came from.

He had aural hallucinations of Hungarian being spoken in the streets. He started to frequent the restaurant with the hammer dulcimer that he had initially found boring. Budapest became a mythic city. There, violins twittered like birds, and the upright bass thudded like a huge animal. There, peasant carts, colorful like gingerbread houses, rolled on in the shadows of streetcars.

But . . . But . . . But . . . To go back would be a defeat. So what now?

Nothing but laughter, nothing
But dust, nothing but nothing,
There's no reason why everything is happening.

Leaves buried his quiet neighborhood near Gramercy Park. The green and yellow smudges combined into a mosaic. He started to see his nice apartment as a trap. In it, he hummed beautiful suicidal songs. In it, he devoted himself to the practice of hara-kiri by self-pity.

"Everyone likes to be forgiven for something," he said, his blond mustache curled in a smile.

To Tesla, work equaled rest. Szigety needed a lot of rest after work— the rest, which, in fact, was tiresome, since he overindulged in it. During the day, he and Tesla discussed the relationship between the structure of ether, electricity, matter, and light.

In the evening, inertia sank its claws into Antal Szigety, emptied him and started living in his place. Aphrodite sent him the goddess Atë, who made his heart seasick and full of black madness. He tried to restrain the fury that raged inside his body. A satyr's smile started to form on his lips. Debauchery was his duty. He was in the power of tidal forces. God reshaped him into an incarnation of greed and slipped him off the hook of reason. Like Tannhäuser long ago, Szigety rushed helplessly toward the hell of pleasure. Whenever he entered a brothel, took off his jacket, and felt a woman run her fingers through his hair, he released a deep sigh.

This shameful capitulation became sweet relief.

He was still enthralled by the inner slickness of women. The girls, who had known all meridian of dicks, assured him that his was special. The laughter of whores was like the crackling of thorns under a cauldron. Szigety brought a top hat full of roses for his girl Nellie. He passed his palm over her cheeks and mouth. He gave her his finger to suck. He drowned in her tits and silk. He wrinkled her unsqueezable feminine roundness and waited for the orgasm to place him in the center of the world.

Szigety became a devotee of the naked cancan to which the late Paddy Maloney tried to drag Tesla. Soon after returning from Pittsburgh, he became an expert on New York brothels, both the well appointed and the cheap.

Garters. Lacy gossamer lingerie. Nestling. Legs in stockings on his shoulders. Eruptions of white. The curvature of loins enfolding his fingers. Trembling roundness. Tightness. Penetrating and banging. Embracing the mounds. Possessing. Lascivious weasels. Gyrating sluts. Spasms to the last ounce of strength. Smooching and goosing. Smacking and licking, pinching and biting. Pounding the peg home and squeezing. Recoiling and submitting, dissolving in affluence and sensuality. Innings and outings. Grinding. Passionate howling. Swallowing and cooing. Giving and breaking and panting.

It helped him survive.

Before, Antal had resorted to hot baths, shadowboxing, and hiking in order to counter his lewd lifestyle. Tesla asked him why he did not work out anymore, and he came up with some feeble anti-American excuses: "There's no nature in this place."

"How can that be?" Tesla was annoyed. "There's more nature here than anywhere else in the world. Just get out of New York."

Szigety did not go anywhere.

When he opened a bottle of Tokay with Tesla, he became faint-hearted. He closed his eyes to see how far he could slide on his drunkenness. Finally he said, "I've bluffed away my life."

"No, you haven't," his friend reassured him. "You've simply matured without realizing it."

It appeared that Antal's body revolted against something his soul refused to acknowledge.

Tesla warned him in the same manner he himself had been warned during his gambling days in Graz: "Slow down."

That spring, Westinghouse readied himself for the final showdown with Edison. He pressured the creator of his alternating current motor. "Nikola, you must counter their circus performances with a scientific performance of your own."

Nikola himself was aware of this. He raised his chin, took a deep breath, and saw the golden path. He decided to do what no one had ever done before. He was going to refute Edison's claim that "alternating current kills" by letting the maelstrom of that same force pass through his own body.

"Do you think I'll survive?" he asked Szigety.

The expression in Szigety's blue eyes went from innocent to absent-minded to almost dangerous. Finally, he smiled. "You? Yes. *You* will."

A woman rang his room from the hotel lobby and woke him up. As soon as he went down, she hit him with a cloud of her perfume. She singed him with her burning eyes.

"Please, Mr. Tesla, come with me."

"Who are you?"

"It's urgent." She did not seem to have heard his question.

He entered that kind of place for the first time in his life. Two naked whores played with a balloon, batting it with their noses and then their toes. The interior of the house was mainly white. It smelled of perfume, of lazy femininity, and of fake luxury. The prostitutes who glided around in their lingerie looked like beautiful monsters to Tesla. Their sly eyes were dull. One of them said, "He's up there."

Tesla ran upstairs.

It was not Antal. It was a doll.

A very young girl wearing heavy mascara was sitting next to that doll. Tesla and the doctor asked her to leave.

"How?" Tesla asked.

"We still don't know," the bald doctor sighed.

"Cocaine overdose," the beautiful monster said without moving.

They tactfully agreed that the body be transferred from the brothel on Twenty-Ninth Street to a hospital, and that the official report mention Szigety's apartment as the location of his death.

They also suspected murder.

Tesla was nervous waiting for the results.

"A burst aneurysm," the doctor told him after the autopsy. "Nothing could have been done. It is better that he didn't know about it."

"Did he suspect something was wrong?" Tesla asked as he remembered his friend's moods.

"No," the doctor said. Then he changed his mind. "There are more things in heaven and earth than are dreamt of . . ."

In Budapest, Szigety forced Tesla to live, but here Tesla hadn't known how to return the favor. He went to the dead man's apartment to pack his belongings and ship them to his family. He hissed like a snake and puffed up his cheeks. Szigety's shoes were on the pillow, a knife and a piece of smoked sausage were on a pair of ironed underwear. Tesla whistled—he had never seen such a mess. A lithograph of a ruddy-faced Franciscan monk offering a burning heart to the Virgin hung above the bed. Next to the bed were a German translation of a book by Dostoyevsky and a tattered volume of Saint Augustine's *Confessions*.

In this room, Antal awoke bound in sweaty bedsheets. Here he suffered from hangovers and tried to kick a moth. Here he felt the coldness of coins scattered under his bare feet. Here he rolled his eyes, which were the color of the Plitvice Lakes, and wondered how to pay his bills. Every morning, this Pan's ecstasy turned into Pan's panic.

"Everyone likes to be forgiven for something," he used to say.

Fame accelerated Tesla's life to an awful pace, and an invisible hand snatched away those he loved. Obadiah Brown, Paddy, Prostran, Szigety were taken by the wind. People receded into the distance, their faces turning into masks. Due to the speed, their forms became elongated and merged into one another. Success smelled like a tempest.

He sat under the helmet of tightly combed hair, as pale as a lotus flower, his fingers locked together. What used to be a source of warmth changed into an icy pit. He felt powerless as he stared into the foggy future, which resembled nothingness.

"Destiny," he whispered, horrified.

His larynx hurt.

The octopus of sentimentality wrapped him in its wet embrace and started to throttle him with its many tentacles. He gasped and dried his eyes with the first thing at hand—a pair of clean socks.

"Antal, Antal," he whispered.

His nose narrowed, and he asked in full honesty, "Am I crying for the dead or for myself?"

Szigety's blue eyes and the sweetness of his smile always cheered Tesla up. They shared fits of senseless laughter so often, swaying like poplars in the wind.

"You see, I can make you laugh about anything, anytime," Szigety bragged, catching his breath.

And that same lewd Antal wanted to be a priest. He wanted to address the world with words of love, like Saint Francis of Assisi:

Be praised, my Lord, through all Your creatures, especially through
    my lord Brother Sun . . .
Be praised, my Lord, through Sister Moon and the stars . . .
Be praised, my Lord, through our sister Bodily Death . . .

CHAPTER 51

After Never

Around us, everything spins,
everything moves—everywhere is energy.
Nikola Tesla, May 1891

The great day came.

Wearing shoes with thick cork soles, his six-foot-six frame looked eerily elongated onstage. The auditorium was enlivened by the faces of young and old electrical engineers. Both friends and enemies were there.

"Of all the forms of natural, omnipresent, and measureless energy, which constantly changes, moves, and brings the universe to life like a soul," Tesla lectured, fingers dancing, "perhaps the most fascinating are magnetism and electricity."

At that point, he raised his voice: "The explanation of these fascinating dual phenomena lies in the infinitesimal world, in its molecules and atoms which spin in their orbits, much like celestial bodies."

The listeners imagined minuscule galaxies revolving in their thighs, eyes, hearts.

"There's no doubt that we can directly make use of this energy and, from limitless resources, create light, which"—he paused as his gaze moved from one face to another—"can be transmitted wirelessly."

The great scientific presentation was intended to counter Edison's circus shows. With a wave of his hand, Tesla signaled his assistant, Gano Dunn.

There was a *click*, just like the one heard in the execution chamber.

The auditorium darkened.

The scientist Tesla vanished.

A lonely actor appeared within a shaft of white.

In the sharp light, his white tuxedo looked starched. The actor seemed sad and lonely. Every wrinkle on his face was visible.

On the desk in front of the actor there were several apparatuses, which, for the majority of the spectators, were mere "somethings" because they did not know their purpose. Next to the polyphase induction motor was a vertical wheel, a silver ball, and a few other more or less scary-looking devices.

The blue darkness began to hum. Two arcs of light leapt and crackled above the engine. The coil discharged a web of brilliant threads. The gorgon's hair became entangled around the ball. Electricity buzzed and popped. Behind Tesla, a Faraday cage swallowed the flying sparks.

The audience watched with a mixture of religious humility and circus-like amazement.

Gano Dunn was as grave as a matador. At Tesla's signal, he raised the frequency. The bright whip cracked between God's finger and Adam's. The lightning bolts grew longer. With his small mustache and his appallingly slick hair, Tesla straightened his back like a bullfighter before the kill. Without warning, he stretched his hand toward the machine. At that moment, the electrical cyclone puffed up his body. The lightbulb he held blinked three times and lit. Cries came from the audience:

"Look, Amelia! He's on fire!"

"Electricity is running through his body."

With his hair standing on end, the actor walked among the audience for fifteen minutes and turned lightbulbs and vacuum tubes on with a touch. He demonstrated that any lamp within the electrical field in the auditorium would work without being plugged in.

Then he returned to the stage.

The man with horns of blue light spoke from the podium like a singer hitting a high note.

"Even though a single electrical shock can be fatal, it is a paradox that the exposure to amplified voltage can be perfectly safe." He had allowed a much stronger voltage to run through his body than the one that killed Kemmler.

The applause boomed like thunder. In the loud clapping, he hovered above the stage again. When he alighted, the world was changed.

After the performance, gasping reporters wanted to know how much voltage his body endured.

"You really weren't in any danger?"

"When was it that you first dared to touch an exposed wire?"

"Were you *that* sure about your calculations? Did you try it out on an animal?"

"Only on myself," responded Tesla. "I tried it only on myself."

CHAPTER 52

The London Miracle

A Letter to Mojo Medić

Paris [smudge—smudge] 1892

My dear King of the Waltz,

I apologize for not responding sooner. So many things have happened. Fame hit me in the face like heat from a smelter. After the success I had with my New York lecture, I received invitations to speak in London and Paris. And so:

I am on my way, my fairy,
May God be with me tomorrow,
My weeping, tears, and my sorrow,
If you only knew, my fairy,
I am on my way . . .

I packed quickly. Hiergesell, my glass blower, made various types of tubes for me.

The best part of any journey is its end.

London was so gray that everything looked as if it were cut from the same cloth. The magic fog was suffocating precious lights. Even the fabric of people's clothing looked like solid fog. Golden floods swallowed the Parliament building in Turner's paintings. I spent a lot of time staring at William Morris's wallpaper and eating underdone mutton.

My friend Westinghouse warned me that the English were full of blind prejudices, which their sense of humor softened on the outside and hardened on the inside. (The way he warned me brought anxiety to the traveler's heart. He used words such as *coldness, unbearable conceit,* and even *abhorring arrogance.*) My experiences have been different. Entirely different. In February, I delivered a lecture to the London Royal Society. You know that a thousand volts are fatal. At the Royal Society, I allowed two hundred thousand volts to pass through my body and didn't even feel a thing. A spark stung me only at the very beginning, and even that can be avoided. Such current doesn't kill. Such current, my dear Mojo, oscillates a few million times per second. Our human nerves aren't sensitive enough to feel it . . .

On the stage, I lit lamps with a touch and extinguished them with a wave. In my lecture, I expressed a conviction that—just like the lamps—motors can be operated from long distances, with no direct connection to an energy source.

My dear Mojo, I tried not to bother you with my complaints when I used to sleep in homeless shelters where the poor shred pillowcases to pieces with their sharp stubble. Now I'm trying to spare you from my bragging. However, this is such a success.

A great success.

A world success.

High society attended my London lecture—Sir William Crookes, Lord Kelvin, Sir Oliver Lodge, Sir William Preece. According to the press, I kept them enchanted for two full hours.

I'm a supporter of the honorable tradition of English eccentricity. I have never felt so much among my own ilk as in London. Major newspapers and especially illustrated journals published pictures from my lecture. They usually show me amid a maelstrom of electrical sparks. One caption reads: "Mr. Tesla is playing with lightning and thunderbolts."

Lord Rayleigh impressed me with his sideburns. He told me that I have a special gift for invention, and that I should focus on one great thing. Sir William Preece looked strange to me. He reminded me of Murko the tailor from Graz. Namely,

I wasn't sure whether a fly had flown up his nose, or whether he was trying to smile charmingly. After we talked, I started to think about transferring voices and images wirelessly. That's telepathy, Mojo—with a little mechanical help.

William Crookes wanted to use electricity to eliminate the nagging drizzle that harasses the island.

I also spent some time with Lord Kelvin, the sage with a high brow and drooping eyelids, who believes that the phenomena pertaining to electricity and life are identical.

Eventually, Professor Dewar sat me down in Faraday's personal armchair, poured me some whiskey from Faraday's personal bottle, and asked me to give one more lecture. I agreed, sensing the friendliness of the old armchair. The culmination of my visit to England was my acceptance into the London Academy of Sciences.

After many exciting adventures on the island, I crossed the windy channel. For a few weeks now, I've been resting at the Hotel de la Paix in Paris. I've met Prince Albert of Belgium and sold the rights to my patents to the Germans. So many things are going on that my pen is too slow to catch up with them. My intention is to go to Lika after Paris. Consider this letter an introduction to a lengthy conversation.

Cordially yours
(no signature)

P.S.—My colleague d'Arsonval is taking me around Paris and is trying to corrupt me.

CHAPTER 53

Paris

"I won't!"

"You will!" d'Arsonval said.

The two scientists were standing in front of one of Lautrec's posters, which was washed out from the rain. The profile of a skinny man in a top hat stood out in the foreground. In a circle of male and female silhouettes behind him, a blond stuck her leg out from the rose of her skirts.

"You will!" d'Arsonval insisted and dragged Tesla into the Moulin Rouge.

The host nodded to the waiter, and a table with a flower and a bottle of wine in a silver cylinder materialized in front of them.

"Oho-ho . . . ," the host sighed.

The orchestra played at a frantic pace. Glasses tinkled. Tesla concluded that this was a place in which provincial bankers mingled with metropolitan actresses among throngs of witty young men.

Prince Albert of Belgium was late. His table also materialized next to the stage. The prince waved his hand to d'Arsonval and the famous Tesla, inviting them to join tables. Tesla had already given too many interviews. So many that . . .

"I've read . . . We'll talk . . ." The prince shouted over the music.

"God is the only one left for you to meet here," d'Arsonval whispered hoarsely.

The beauty of a few of the women was almost impossible to bear. And yet, at the sight of their jewelry, Tesla felt as if he tasted blood in his mouth. Blushing faces bloomed on well-dressed bodies. People tapped the table surfaces with their opera glasses and fingers. Some crazy guests embarked on a competition of who could shout and scream the loudest.

"Encore!"

"This is the music of paroxysm," Tesla concluded rationally.

What, in the middle of the wildest merriment, happened to the soul? What happened to the soul, which swims through the dissolving thickness and darkness beneath consciousness? What happened to the soul that is a deep-sea fish?

He suddenly noticed that he was sweating. Somewhere, something was wrong. Right now . . .

The speed in which he lived turned his friends into acquaintances, and acquaintances into . . . ghosts. He wondered if anyone would remain real.

It suddenly crossed his mind: *Where's the biblical hell? Where?*

An unnerving apprehension dyed everything green and turned the dancers, who already looked grotesque, into demons.

The musical avalanche was falling on pale Tesla and grinning d'Arsonval. The girls screamed! La Goulue (the "glutton") danced with her elastic partner. The dancers lifted their legs, kicked them out, and then dropped to the floor in splits.

D'Arsonval was beaming. He raised his handsome head with a cropped mustache and a beard the shape of a swallow's tail.

Tesla watched the show like a cat given salad to eat.

"This is cacophony." He frowned. "This has no head or tail to it."

"Well, what do you have to say?" his colleague asked him after they had left.

"Wonderful," Tesla noted with a straight face, and, with an apology, asked his new friend to take him to the Hotel de la Paix.

The city lights filtered through his eyelashes. And yet, the cold crawled up his spine and some metallic taste alarmed his palate. He somehow managed to say good-bye to d'Arsonval and stepped under the glass half shell above the hotel entrance.

"Monsieur Tesla," a eunuch's voice echoed in the lobby.

"Yes?"

A boy as pink as a rabbit's nose looked at him with his gray eyes and handed him a cable:

Djuka on deathbed. Come immediately.
Uncle Pavle.

CHAPTER 54

The Rush

The race with death began. He discovered that his mind became an insufferable player piano. Like a man plagued by a hangover who feels that the stench of alcohol had saturated his soul, Tesla felt that the rhythm of the cancan permeated his.

The thrumming train echoed that rhythm. His hands shook. His chest was a drum, and his heart pounded in his throat so hard it drowned out the sound of the wheels. The wheels rattled through the smoke. The speed stretched the line of the woods, and the woods merged into one another. Vienna, which he would never get to know, stayed behind the window. In Ljubljana, Nikola's anxiety turned into pain. The zinc taste in his mouth was even worse than the suffering. It resembled an epileptic fit. Everything had sped up since he had met Westinghouse. His success was like the frost; it came with the deep solitude. Uncle Pajo met him in Zagreb. Pajo Mandić had a habit of yelling "Hey!" at people as if waking them up. Burly, with graying hair, he turned his sheep-like eyes to Nikola.

"Hey, what's wrong with you?" he asked.

"I feel like someone's squeezing my stomach with pliers," Nikola moaned.

With the infernal cancan still ringing in his head, he transferred from train to coach. His apprehension grew. She could not die if he got there. He would grab her arms and drag her back to his side, across the edge of death.

"How's Mother?" he asked his uncle.

"The way she has to be."

Gospić was a city but smelled like a village. An old man was lighting the lamps along Tesla's street.

A storm was brewing, and everything turned green. Curtains of rain fell and white shards crackled on the pavement. The wet horses pulled up in front of his house. The old house looked shrunken, but it still radiated light.

"Maternal light," Nikola murmured. "Mother's light."

From rooms lit by electricity, he came back to oil lamps.

"Home is your home, and the moon is your neighbor."

He had not changed. He simply did not know how to return.

Theirs was a city house, but—probably due to the handwoven rugs—it still had the faint smell of sheep. For ten years, that world had not existed for him. He felt everything to be unreal, but, at the same time, only this was real. His long-gone world returned. Everything became magical and profound. It hurt frightfully. Then the noose of reality expanded. Things became ordinary again because that was how they had to be.

It seemed to him that the power of vision was more intense at the top of the world, but the experience of life was deeper at the bottom. No, this was not Lord Kelvin's, Prince Albert's, or his colleague d'Arsonval's world. The view from here was sharper and more painful. This was the old world of comb-and-grass-blade music, turquoise lakes, round loaves of bread, stubborn winds, and Lika hats looking like poppies in the fields.

The rooms, the smells—everything struck him to the quick. On Father's icon, Saint George was still indifferently killing the dragon, whose red head was like a roasted lamb's. The fool and the younger brother returned home a famous man. His relatives blinked their brown eyes. They herded together. There was much love and kindness here. It also appeared that they felt ashamed of each other.

The whole house carefully listened to Djuka's breathing as she lay in the bedroom. Tesla was more at ease talking with his brothers-in-law than with his sisters, who wiped their eyes hunched over in the hallway. Marica approached him, looking at him with the eyes of a wary dog. He noticed that she had aged considerably.

"Hug—and forget!" He had made up his mind.

Marica treated Nikola as if he were a noble stranger. She did not know how to love him because she always felt pity toward those she loved. The way she saw love tinged the whole of human existence with sadness. Her body was a well of ancient tears, filled all the way to her eyes, which could overflow at any moment. That well was deeper than her body—it reached three hundred yards beneath the ground.

Nikola put his hand on her shoulder.

"Don't cr-cry . . ."

"Don't you cry."

He reached for the handle on Djuka's door.

"Pray to God that she recognizes you," he heard someone behind him say. "Hey!"

The heat of Mother's room overwhelmed him. He sat on the bed and took her by the hand. The hand was light. The eyes were tired. She too was waiting for him. He choked when he saw her faded eyes. She caressed his head with tiny movements.

"My Niko."

Nikola pressed the feather-like hand against his cheek and felt a deep, unparalleled calm descend on him.

The departing, fragile woman was protecting him still.

CHAPTER 55

Ba-Bam

The fairies eat garlic seeds and live until life becomes too boring,
and when this happens they quit eating and die a painless death.
Djuka Tesla

Ba-Bam!
   Baba-Baba-Ba-Bam!

The internal cancan kept playing in his head. The funeral took place at the Jasikovac Cemetery. The aspens trembled and Nikola felt nauseous.

He could not understand the words at all.

"We're like water spilled on the ground that can't return," murmured one of Djuka's brothers.

Nikola could not understand the words.

"And I will go to her but she will never come to me," another priest read.

The voices came closer, and then faded away.

"Like the wind, which goes and never returns," the prophet spoke through the mouth of his uncle, Bishop Petar.

Nikola spilled half a glass of brandy for the departed soul, and drank the rest. Instead of heat, crushed ice filled his veins. More horrible than the ice, the sting in his stomach, or standing by her grave was the thought that Djuka had been buried her whole life. Her whole life, she worked from four in the morning to eleven at night.

Because her mother was blind, Djuka hit against a closed iron door at an early age. And once she hit it, she reached an undeniable conclusion: "That's how things are."

At dawn—as if he saw her there—Djuka shook her wet fingers over the stove and the droplets hissed on the hot metal.

She placed apple peels on the stove for fragrance. Before everyone woke up, before she put on her head scarf for the day, she combed her hair. The fire shone through the door and the cracks in the stove.

Lit by the flames, Mother became something else. Mother turned bronze. Nikola watched in secret. He alone. He always wanted to redeem her. He wanted to save her. But he never found (he wept) . . . time.

It was like a tree falling in the forest without anyone to hear it.

The world pushed him away.

Life lost its center.

Mother was the only human being more important to him than his work. Now he was at the mercy of his work.

The devil's deft hand gathered all the warmth from the world, like wool. The world had been divided into the warm inner one and the cold outer one. Now they switched places.

And the truth? The truth did not stand a chance against the craving for protection. The truth was just nagging. Rules and values had no meaning before the needs of the soul. His inventions and the mankind they served became worthless. Worthless was the floating world—and he in it.

Where would warmth come from now? From his own gold flashes? From nowhere?

Nikola's feet somehow found the ground. The world was expanding before it blacked out. He swallowed air as he sobbed.

Rustling swallowed him.

"And I'm not in this world anymore, but they are in this world, while I'm walking toward you."

Ba-Bam.

Yes, the aspens trembled and he felt nauseated. He stiffened his knees to avoid slipping. Vertigo deepened the grave. With an irresistible spinning force, Djuka's death dragged him into the grave as well.

Bam-Bam.

He paused in front of the headstone he had erected for Father.

Gospić Priest, Protojerej Milutin Tesla 1819–April 17, 1879. His Grateful Son Nikola, 1889.

Father used to say, "Will clay tell the potter: You have no hands! Can He be blind who created the eye?" Father believed that honesty was the answer to all the questions in life, convinced that even the clouds in the sky judged how honest he was.

The grateful son was still angry at the man who, in an attempt to save the boy's soul, trampled on it.

His feet went numb. Yes. His feet somehow found the ground.

What goes through the forest without a rustle, through the water without a splash? A shadow.

He did not know how they got home. Each window, each table, each chest of drawers, even each box, was covered by the embroidery she made with her fingers, "nimble as flames." She kissed his hair, warm from the sun, "to make it better." The house smelled like her. His sisters clattered trays as they served. The relatives raised their glasses remembering the deceased:

She believed you can't change people—you can only love them.

She believed a man can pray under a linden tree.

Thirty-six priest vestments hung on her family tree.

She could tie three knots in an eyelash.

She knew herbs and could heal animals.

She cried only because she never went to school.

Nikola Tesla woke up with the question, "Who am I?" It was like a corset burst open. Milky whiteness flooded his memory. His mind emptied itself. A glance into a mirror's shard crushed him: *Look, a wisp of my hair has turned white.*

Even before, he had complained of forgetfulness.

His job was a combination of mining ore and playing roulette. In New York, he worked sixteen hours a day with all the deepest energies of his soul. It was too late when he discovered that those Muses-demons cannot be ordered around without retribution.

He wondered, "What is love?" just as Pontius Pilate wondered, "What is truth?" He could not explain anything to himself, so he let his baffling thoughts and events run around like skittish cows.

"Has the high voltage erased his memory?" one sister asked the other softly.

"Or pain?"

"Has he gone mad?"

To have such a brother was both a blessing and a curse.

For a few weeks, Nikola rested in the enormous silence of the Gomirje Monastery garden. He did not pay attention to the cypress trees or the novices who kissed the candles before they lit them. The monastery yard was under the spell of the muffled cooing of the doves.

With unfocused gaze, he fought against the demonic whiteness of his memory. A long time before, that same Nikola had been able to fend off the sight of Dane's funeral with the sheer power of his will. Now he used his willpower to remember. It felt like moving the entire world from one place to another. The wretch searched for names in the labyrinth and put the recovered notions back onto the shelf of his mind:

Socrates was a philosopher. Phidias was a sculptor. Bucephalus was a horse.

Intoxicating and stifling images kept flying back, like soot, like gold leaves, like musical notes.

CHAPTER 56

The Sorcerer's Apprentice

In Nikola's dream, intoxicating, stifling images kept flying back, like soot, like gold leaves, like musical notes:

Nikola turned into a pigeon.

Edison turned into a fox, pounced on the pigeon, and started to choke it while the feathers flew around.

Tesla turned into a terrier and started to throttle the fox.

The fox turned into a hurricane of claws. The lynx jumped at the dog and made it all bloody.

The dog turned into a lion and grabbed the lynx by the throat.

The lynx turned into a dragon and started to tear the lion apart.

The lion turned into pearly grains of rice that scattered across the floor.

The dragon turned into a rooster that pecked at the grains and ate all but one, which rolled under the bed.

From this grain, Tesla turned into a tomcat that glowed.

The tomcat dashed from under the bed, grabbed the rooster by the throat, and snapped its neck.

CHAPTER 57

The Glare

Nikola was astonished that his acquaintances in Zagreb did not notice the state he was in. He expected someone to grab him by the shoulders, shake him, and say, "Hey, what's wrong with you?"

That did not happen.

Naturally, the cadence of speech was different than in Paris. The faces were his countrymen's faces. And yet, people glided by him politely and superficially.

"People are blind. They don't see anything. They don't understand anything. Most of them, anyway," his late mother had once taught him.

Most likely, his hosts expected that their famous guest must be strange by definition.

"People are blind," Nikola concluded, resigned to hide the state he was in.

As scatterbrained as falling snowflakes, in Zagreb he gave a lecture on his London lecture. After the talk, he spent a half hour in the bathroom trying to compose himself. Once an official delegation had to wait for him while he handed out money to beggars in front of the Stone Gate.

"How do you know they won't just drink it?" one of the delegates asked him.

"Let them."

In addition to Mayor Armuš and other dignitaries, he met the people who worked on the city's renovation, Herman Bole and Iso

Kršnjavi. The latter had a somewhat shorter beard than Bachelor and walked a dappled Great Dane with a tail that looked like a truncheon. The cathedral had had scaffolding around it ever since the earthquake. As elsewhere, journalists would not leave him alone.

"Yes, I feel extremely comfortable among my countryman," Nikola smiled.

His relatives in Lika told him about the deteriorating relationship between Serbs and Croats. He, however, remembered Milutin Tesla and the Catholic priest Kostrenčić holding hands in front of the church. He promised to help his countrymen build the future power plant free of charge. He suggested that they use the alternating current system, which had made such a breakthrough in America that even Edison had to give up. With all sincerity, he added that if they ran into any problems, they could contact him and ask for free advice. His stubborn countrymen did not listen to him, but they still sang his praises in the newspapers.

On Tuesday morning, the third day of his stay in Zagreb, the laughing, joyful representatives of the Serbian University Youth swarmed into the lobby of the Austrian Emperor Hotel, where he lodged. Their great compatriot confided in them: "It takes the same amount of energy to make a real discovery as to fake that you know what you are doing in life."

The students left crestfallen. They suffered from the infinite longings of youth. Above those longings, the inventor's raised index finger burned like Archangel Gabriel's fiery sword. Using Tesla's gloomy voice, the archangel warned them, "Beware of women like hot coals."

Yet again, the rails' glare stretched toward where the eye could not reach. Swift clouds dashed across the sky above the Pannonian Plain.

What was the difference between French and Hungarian clouds? Was there such a thing as national clouds?

The flatlands tired his eyes.

Did Mother's death widen the gap between him and people a little more? Did he become a balloon that was ascending to the sky?

Vineyards were drinking the darkness that people would turn into wine. The familiar view of Budapest woke him up. That was where, many years before, two young men had been engaged in a milk-drinking contest that Szigety won by downing thirty-nine bottles. Coaches made of gingerbread moved along new boulevards. This was the great recapitulation of his life. He could not wait to see what color his soul would paint the well-known landscape.

"What's wrong with you?" Mrs. Várnai asked upon seeing him.

"Nothing."

Mrs. Várnai was not a blind traveler through life. Her eyes did not fail to notice pain.

Tesla looked around the familiar apartment. The dusty curtains. The perplexing mirrors. The plants suffering from elephantiasis. In the painting in the sitting room, Matthias Corvinus was being crowned with as much enthusiasm as before. White brushstrokes created the impression of welling tears in the eyes of the moved spectators.

Fighting forgetfulness, the young man asked for permission to crack the door of "his room." Instantly, the room turned into his heart's resonator. "I almost died in this bed."

Yes, in that same bed his soul experienced the suffering rivaling the agonies of medieval mystics. He had been so tired that he wanted to lie down eight stories beneath the ground. His landlady once kissed him there in secret. He shivered and the world shivered with him, but their shivers were out of phase and would not harmonize.

The painful return of memories was a good sign.

"I read about you in Paris newspapers." Mrs. Várnai spoke slowly, as if delivering a lesson. She was proud of him and deeply moved in her quiet way. Her son was now a physician in Poszony. "Yes, he comes," she said. "He comes . . . whenever he has time."

The skin on her neck had already started to droop. But her eyes were alive. Her eyes were young. Her eyes were like the rails' glare flashing toward infinity.

"They started construction of the parliament building while I was still here. When are they going to finish it?" Nikola asked, smiling.

"Never." Mrs. Várnai sighed, putting the coffee cup down.

He drove out into the fragrant evening—ah, an evening of lamps hidden in treetops. Tivador Puskás took him to the best fish paprikash in the world.

Tesla laughed. "I'm living backward."

"It's good that you're here," Puskás toasted him in his hoarse voice. "It's really good that you're here."

Paganini jammed the violin underneath his double chin, and the highest string trilled like a bird. Melancholy music changed, became unstoppable. A dancer balancing a carafe of wine on his hat slapped his boots.

Tesla felt like a man who had died, then was risen, and now was walking around the place he used to live.

The next morning, he took a walk in the park. The fever led him toward the spot where he had experienced the epiphany that united him with Szigety.

The May rain first became visible on the water, and then it softly kissed the leaves. The park became fragrant. With the speed of a piano player, the circles replaced one another on the surface of the pond. The rain fell on the ducks swimming around. Overwhelmed with emotions, Tesla took shelter in a gazebo. He looked on, and someone else looked on next to him. Memories, tinged with nostalgia, brought Szigety's voice: "How are you, friend?"

On Sunday, he sat silently with Szigety's parents, whom he gave their son's ring and watch. In between, he took a long time washing his face in the bathroom. Long ago, Farkas Szigety had told them about the heart motif, so common in Hungarian folk art. He had also told them to be careful about doing favors: "Never offer a favor—but it's a sin to refuse one."

Long ago, the old architect used to sit still while he listened and became animated when he talked. Now, he barely opened his mouth. Even though he did not feel like it, Nikola did most of the talking.

It was he who had invited his friend to come. It was he who had taken him to America.

"I'm so sorry," he wanted to tell the old man. "Please, forgive me."

No one blamed him for anything.

He gave them the watch, the ring, and the money. "Thank you," said Szigety's parents.

At twilight, someone placed his dirty hand on Tesla's soul. The paw of dark melancholy felt his diaphragm to see what it was made of.

Through a tunnel made of sycamores, a coachman brought him to his uncle's mansion in Pomaz near Budapest.

The men from Lika bragged how their country gave birth to the two greatest inventors in the world: Nikola Tesla, the engineer, and Pajo Mandić, who invented a way to marry the richest Serbian bride in all of Hungary. It took two hours for a train to pass through the Pomaz estate of Mandić's father-in-law, Petar Lupa.

The aging military officer Pavle Mandić complained that his bones ached. The doctor insisted that it was gout, but Pavle did not believe him. The former beauty Milina, who now had dark circles around her eyes, scolded her husband: "You were a typical uncouth officer, and that you will remain until you die. No matter how many times I explain anything to you, you do it your own way."

The uncle puffed his cheeks and defended himself: "In addition to the famous Trbojevićes of Medak, the Milojevićes of Mogorić, the Bogdanovićes of Vrebac, and the Došens of Počitelj, the Mandićes of Gračac are one of the most prominent families in Lika."

To Nikola, he proudly pointed out the tunnel of treetops lining the mansion's driveway: "You can't go wrong with sycamores. They would make the moon more beautiful if you planted them there."

Hiccuping after the second bottle, Pavle told Nikola about their relatives. Uncle Petar became a bishop and pledged allegiance to the emperor. How's old Uncle Branković? He's still hanging on. See that "vanity" on the wall? He gave me that.

Are Marica's and Angelina's marriages happy? Bah.

At one point, apparently, a moment of change came, but it did not say: *Hey, I'm the moment of change,* because change never announces itself.

"Nikola has changed," the aunt told the uncle.

Nikola felt offended when they said that he had changed as well as when they said that he had not changed at all.

In Pavle Mandić's house, wine helped Tesla keep dark thoughts away. He stayed till the wee hours of the morning, alone, in the oak-paneled salon. More than once, he slept the night on the sofa. For two months, he never dreamed of Dane. Instead, Szigety visited him in his dreams to tell him about his brothel adventures in heaven. Tesla embraced him. "Antal, imagine—they told me you died."

Another Serbian Youth delegation found Tesla in Pomaz. Laughing, they swarmed into the baroque mansion. They became serious in Tesla's presence. A young man with long hair stepped forward adjusting his tie. Then he blushed and forgot all etiquette. "Would you make us all very happy and come to Belgrade?"

CHAPTER 58

The Midsummer's Night Dream

"I'm telling you, I waited and waited and waited for him," Mojo Medić began.

"First he wrote to me from London. So I went to Gospić to see him. They said: He's sick. Then, out of the blue, I got this cable from Budapest: 'I'll be in Belgrade, why don't you come?' I decided to go on the spur of the moment and thus came to Belgrade by boat from Zemun. I knew he was in the Imperial Hotel.

"So I went there myself.

"I knew his whereabouts all the time because he was the talk of Belgrade. While I was killing time taking streetcar rides, he was being decorated by King Aleksandar.

"The month of July endlessly stretched over Belgrade's tree-lined streets and one-story houses. Young rascals made faces and hitched free rides hanging on to the streetcar. The conductor drove them away with his whip. I looked down the long street, wondering if the people at its far end were still living in the last century. Most citizens of Belgrade well remembered the day the Turks left the city. The older ones could even recall Granny Višnja and Master Jevrem after whom they named streets.

"While the infant Serbian king praised Nikola's 'ideally enunciated' Serbian, I was eating lunch in the shadows of linden trees on Skadarlija Street. On the wall of the tavern somebody wrote, 'Woe to him who believes.' Across the street, a lad was hacking a roasted lamb on a tree stump. A sleepy Gypsy tuned his violin and started to rasp a Romanian folk tune.

"'Get lost,' a waiter yelled.

"'You're one ornery gentleman.' The Gypsy stopped playing, but didn't leave.

"Then a kinky-haired poet started to bother me. He offered to shake hands: 'I'm the Muses' favorite and the master of the sonnet.' He was so glad, he said, to see a Serb from the Austrian-Hungarian lands. How d'you like Belgrade? These institutions—he pointed at the row of taverns—are our true academy. Some of them you can see here, but there are others too. Brimming with pride, the golden-tongued bard began to recite:

At the Matchstick, the Golden Pit,
the Astronomy Tower,
the Peacock, the Moonshine, the Pigeon,
the Gardeners' Petka, Žmurko's, Pete the Horse Trader's,
the White Lamb, the Jewish Tavern,
At the Black Eagle, at the Seven Krauts,
Who Owned This House—Whose House Will It Be?
The Merry Mansion, the White Cat, Nine Coachmen . . .

"But his tone implied:

Racine, Cervantes, Goethe . . .
Goya, Vermeer, Da Vinci,
Beethoven, Vivaldi, Mozart . . .

"I bought him a drink to get rid of him.

"While they introduced Nikola to the king's regents, I was at the Belgrade farmers' market, eavesdropping on the fragments of a forgotten song dating back to the Great Migration of Peoples. I studied the expressions of surprise on the faces of the lions carved on the Terazije Fountain. Sweating, I felt flies crawling underneath my hair. While Nikola examined various collections at the University of

Belgrade, I was in a store, not bigger than a brick closet, whose owner, a Serbian of Jewish faith, Moša Avram Maca, sold me an umbrella to protect me from the sun. In the afternoon, while two-story buildings started to sprout shadows like snails sprout their horns, Nikola lectured to Belgrade students on the glowing streets and illuminated nights of the future.

"'I'm trying to inspire you,' he told them openly, 'because I didn't have anyone to inspire me when I was a student.'

"The students shouted: 'Long may you live!'

"While the students listened to him, I read about him in the newspapers. From the printed page, a strange great man peered at me, not the boy with whom I spent my entire childhood. The excitement of meeting him overwhelmed me. They wrote that he was 'a first-rate star' and 'a Serbian genius.' They wrote that his eyelids were rarely wide open because he lived in his own waking dream. With a slow smile, they said, he woke up to the reality that amused him. I was much less amused with that reality since it was an extremely hot July day, and I was running from one piece of shade to another.

"The mayor and some university professors took Nikola to Kalemegdan Park. A military band was playing. While Tesla was intoxicated with the view of the Sava and the Danube, I covered my face with a newspaper and took a nap. The heat eased some. I opened my hotel room window. In its frame, the raspberry-color fire was dying out in the sky above the Bežanija Hill. The wind from the Sava smelled like freshness. I heard a woman singing. The surface of the river shimmered. I went out for a walk and heard the whole city talk about him.

"'He has remained one of us,' someone whispered.

"They said that, in his speech at the university, Nikola pointed out that his successes did not personally belong to him but to the whole of the Serbian nation.

"'The nation, my ass.' I was mad. 'Has the nation invented the alternating current motor? Has the nation discovered the wireless transfer of power?'

"Through the open door of the Dardanells spread the aroma that the ancient Greeks and Jews fed to the gods. The smell of barbecue lured me in. I ran into a boy with closely cropped hair who carried a mug of beer outside. He fell and spilled the beer. I tossed a silver coin on a table. It fluttered like a butterfly, and the boy snapped it between his thumb and forefinger.

"A picture of a man with burning eyes hung inside. *Mr. Sava Savanović* was written in old-style calligraphy under it. On another photograph, a group of people in fur hats posed by a killed tyrannosaurus. The inscription said, 'Georgiu Jonel—Djordje Janković, Negotin, 1889.'

"A troupe of amateur actors performed the play *The Nine Jugović Brothers*. Ruddy-faced lads recited under their shining plumes. In the meantime, two poets got into a fight about who was to die first: 'I'll come up with a great eulogy for you!' They outshouted each other.

"Across the tables, the 'master of the sonnet' whom I met at Skadarlija waved at me. The place was full, so a certain bald gentleman invited me to join him at his table.

"'And—you would like?' the waiter asked me. Taking me under his wing, the green-eyed bald man ordered for me: 'Bring the gentleman something substantial.'

"Giving up on Kant's smoke and mirrors, the waiter brought me a foot-long steak.

"'That's good! That's good!' the bald gentleman said. He offered me his hand and introduced himself as Bandi Fornoski, the Serbian vice-consul in Bucharest. The learned diplomat relayed to me that the *Standard*, the newspaper of the British conservative party, suggested that Serbia be divided between Austria and Bulgaria. Did I know about that? No, I didn't. I added: 'I don't even know who Sava Savanović is.'

"'He's a very famous man,' Fornoski responded.

"'Was he a poet?' I hazarded a guess.

"Fornoski raised his hand. 'A poet he was not. He was engaged in activities of a different sort.'

"'So what was he?'

"'He was a vampire,' the vice-consul responded in a sweet voice.

"While smoke probably turned into cats and cats turned into smoke out in the street, Fornoski—in his peculiar southern accent—told me about the tin mines he and his young friend, Prince Vibescu, opened in Romania.

"'That's easy money,' he concluded and grinned like a panther.

"'Nice,' I said.

"Many people waited for a table to open. Fornoski had barely taken his leave when a waiter grabbed the wooden back of his chair. 'You don't need this chair?'

"At that very moment, the Belgrade mayor was hosting a dinner in Tesla's honor at the Weifert Brewery. The poet Laza Kostić was sitting at the high table stunned as if he had been just saved from a shipwreck. There were too many poets, bardic blowhards, and other hot-air windbags. The old Jovan Jovanović Zmaj recited verses dedicated to our guest:

Was it the very essence—I don't know,
Or were our feelings glorified,
But as soon as we learned you were coming,
We all felt electrified.

"The old poet's chin was trembling. The tall American stooped and kissed his hand. Everyone was crying. And while they were drowning in tears, I scratched out of boredom sitting in my chair at the tavern. I parted the curtains and saw that it started to drizzle.

"'What's the time?' I asked the waiter.

"'Twelve-thirty,' answered the boy through his nose.

"The rain ticktocked like a thousand clocks.

"Finally, I heard the clatter of the carriage and some voices. A group of people came in. He stood with his back to me as he was taking his leave of the mustached Andra Mitrović. (I remembered all their names as if they were my relatives.) I got up at the moment when he turned around. He came up to me. He smelled of violets. He kissed me. 'How are you, my king of the waltz?'

"I was trying to see if America had changed him.

"Always energetic, always forlorn!

"'How did you get so thin?' I was worried.

"'And how did you get even bigger?'

"I rubbed my belly without taking my eyes off him. His almond-shaped eyes became softer and moister. I expressed my condolences.

He shuddered and waved his hand. I told him that I taught high school, that our old teacher Milan Sekulić, who created the electrical ball, had died, and that all our friends—Jovan Bijelić, Nikola Prica, and even Djuro Amšel—got jobs and got married. Then I sighed: 'I was bored to death today.'

"'I wasn't,' he responded, and we both burst into laughter.

"'What kind of person is our King Aleksandar?' I wanted to know.

"'Chinless.'

"'Anything else?'

"'Plump.'

"We went out for a walk. The smell of dust after the rain tickled our nostrils. Deep in conversation, we swam through the fragrances of the summer night. Instead of the king, he insisted on telling me about Jovan Jovanović Zmaj. He most appreciated the poet's innocence. His whole family had died, he said. And yet, his eyes were meek, as if his 'soul spoke through them.'

"Sleep was out of the question. He told me—what did he say? Oh, he wanted to translate Zmaj into English but didn't know anyone who could help him with the translation.

"I asked him if he remembered Nenad and Vinko Alagić.

'Of course,' he said. 'They're my relatives.'

"'Nenad killed Vinko over the family inheritance,' I informed him. 'Then he spent years in prison. Later, gendarmes cornered him and his gang under the Biokovo Mountain and wounded him in the stomach. He died a painful death in a cave, like a wolf.'

"'Oh my!' Nikola moaned.

"We gave up on the news and talked about the old days.

"I remembered how Djuka and Milutin were different in character. Once they spread the wheat to dry. A cow came by and ate half. Djuka was so mad she almost died. Milutin consoled her: 'Let it go, Djuka. Our cow ate our wheat.'

"'I have completely forgotten about that one!' Nikola was surprised.

"We laughed as we remembered Djuka, which is the only appropriate way to remember the deceased.

"*Do you remember* was the refrain we often used that fragrant Belgrade night.

"'Yes, I remember now!' It came back suddenly to Nikola, and he beamed, adding, 'But do *you* remember . . .'

"We reminisced about how he was being starved at his aunt's house in Karlovac and about Strauss's waltzes. We talked as the night rolled on.

"'Look at the shards of the sky.' I pointed my finger. 'Someone shattered all the stars.'

"It rarely happens that a middle-aged, stocky man like myself laughs a loud laugh of youth.

"The sky reddened above the cathedral. The streetlamps were extinguished. We were still talking. Surrounded by people wearing tall and low hats, white head scarves, and high fur hats, we crossed the white Sava on a boat. Leaning drunkenly on the unneeded umbrella, I raised my chin. Birds sang in the willows along the banks. The world was waking up. It smelled like silt and rising humidity. Fishermen were in their places. The bobbers splashed on the surface. The early morning seagulls followed our wake. Without having slept a wink that night, we parted at the Zemun rail station.

"'How long has it been since we saw each other last?' He sighed and squeezed my hand.

"I returned the squeeze and said:

"'Time doesn't exist!'"

CHAPTER 59

You Will See!

Whenever the ship fell from the ridge of a wave into the trough, it looked as if the water might swamp the smokestacks and extinguish the fires in the boilers. In place of a prayer, Nikola kept repeating the words of Tiresias to Odysseus: "A fair wind and the honey lights of home are all you seek."

The center of his world had been in Gospić, at Mother's home. Now, his world did not have a center.

And his home was Manhattan.

The moment Tesla put his foot on American soil, Westinghouse and his assistant Gano Dunn sandwiched him.

"For God's sake, where've you been? There's so much going on here!"

Westinghouse slapped him on the shoulder with a folded newspaper: "Read."

No man in our time has with one stroke achieved such a universal scientific reputation as this gifted electrical engineer.

"It's your trip they're writing about," Westinghouse exclaimed in his bright tenor.

Dunn laughed. "Did they bring the blind and the crippled for you to touch while you were over there in Europe?" he asked.

"There's one more thing," Westinghouse shouted over the ships' horns. "Edison's General Electric is switching over to alternating current. They're hiring engineers to redesign your motor so they can get their own patents."

With a capricious, wild grimace, Tesla tried to conceal his joy. "Really?" His voice was distorted.

"I'm not done yet," Westinghouse bellowed amid the noises of the harbor. "You know who's going to build the electrical plant at Niagara Falls?"

"What?" Tesla cupped his ear with his hand.

"Not *what*," Westinghouse shouted into his large ear, "but *who!*"

"So *who?*" Tesla yelled back.

"Us!"

"Naturally, General Electric carved out a piece of the pie for themselves." The talkative Gano Dunn crooked his mouth. "That has to be. Pierpont Morgan is backing them."

Westinghouse's eyes had a boyish gleam. "That's it, Nikola! It's over. We won."

Tesla turned into a tomcat. The tomcat dashed under the bed, grabbed the rooster by the throat, and snapped its neck.

"I'd like to get some rest now," Nikola sighed.

"There's no time for rest," Westinghouse whispered and ground his teeth. "Never!" Then he added: "Let Gano take your luggage to the Hotel Gerlach. We'll celebrate at Sherry's."

All of a sudden, the screeching of streetcars in the city of Walt Whitman appeared to be part of a great song. When Tesla first came to America, he felt the country was lagging a hundred years behind Europe. Westinghouse's news now gave him the impression that it was leading by seven-league-boot steps. He, Nikola Tesla, was part of Whitman's poem. He noiselessly ran before the change, like a blind figurehead on the prow of a ship.

When a uniformed doorman closed the door of Sherry's behind them, Nikola felt like a mouse that had crawled into the soundboard of a piano. Silence deepened like a yawn. There was an atmosphere of calming security. The discreet aromas of roasted meat and side dishes were more intriguing than the smell of flowers on the tables. The mirrors emitted tempestuous reflections. The silverware gleamed amid the starched napkin tiaras. Ice chinked in silver buckets and sparkled in glasses.

A galaxy of waiters quickly surrounded the famous arrival from Europe.

"This way, please. This way!"

In the partitioned area of the restaurant, a group of men with straight backs and heroic gray hair practiced putting on their friendliest smiles.

"The bankers!" Westinghouse whispered to him. "Our new investors."

Near the head of the table, Tesla noticed a few faces straight out of the herbarium, the grandchildren of the Anglo-Dutch elite dating back to the city's beginnings.

With an absentminded smile, Nikki Vanderbilt presided over the meeting. The warm-eyed Martin, Tesla's biographer, was the most glad to see him. A man with lively eyes, gray hair, and black eyebrows was sitting next to Westinghouse.

Westinghouse introduced him:

"Hiram Maxim, the inventor of the machine gun."

He turned to Tesla:

"Hiram hates priests."

He turned to Maxim:

"Nikola is a longtime admirer of Voltaire."

The two inventors exchanged smiles while the headwaiter droned on about fifty different oyster dishes. Each guest picked one dish, but they all ordered champagne together. Frosty images on the bottles and silver dragons on the pitchers drew Tesla's attention. White-gloved hands served them food and drink. Silent waiters brought trays arranged with red pliers, lobster tails, and crab cakes topped with swirls of mayonnaise. They served candied lotus flowers for dessert. Nikola was different from the man he was when he came to America long ago. He had turned into a lotus-eater. Futuristic New York was an ideal place for amnesia.

"To Niagara!" Tesla raised his glass.

"To Niagara!" Westinghouse echoed. He inflated his bull-like chest, stroked his mustache, and added, "Although . . . there's something more important to celebrate."

"What's that?"

Westinghouse assumed a comically serious expression. "Now you must speed things up, Nikola. Borrow a machine gun from Hiram and threaten your assistants. Put the screws to your glass blowers."

Tesla looked at him with mute amazement.

"Leave the presentation to me," Westinghouse addressed Tesla, but he looked at the investors. "Create a show that will shock scientists and enchant the public. President Cleveland has invited members of the Spanish and Portuguese royal families to the most spectacular event of the modern times."

"What in the world . . ."

"Nikola, we got commissioned."

"What for?" Tesla asked.

"We'll light up the World's Columbian Exposition in Chicago."

Only the angelically absentminded Vanderbilt, with his granite chin and white sideburns, could get away with inquiring, "What exposition?"

George Westinghouse looked each of them in the eye. His fierce smile broke out like a geyser. "You will see!"

CHAPTER 60

The World Expo

President Cleveland, sporting a double chin and a heavy mustache, turned the "key to the future."

"Ah!" millions sighed in relief.

The lake mirrored the images of the palaces. Gondolas skated across the rippling water. The wind undulated the plumes of the fountains. At the exposition, the historian Frederick Jackson Turner announced that the continent was finally settled. At the conference of the world's religions, Swami Vivekananda lectured about the illusion of personality within the eternity of time. The Duke of Veragua, one of Columbus's descendants, took in the spectacle with dreamy satisfaction. The Maharaja of Kapurthala exhibited his spectacular mustache—the sight of which made twenty women faint. Princess Eulalia of Spain took Harun al-Rashid walks across Chicago and even smoked in public. The Ferris wheel, propelled by sighs, rotated on the largest axle in the world.

"What's the meaning of this dream of beauty?" Henry Adams, the writer, whispered.

The masses rolled in through the gates on the Midway. Ladies sweated underneath their corsets. Those sweating ladies had traveled a long way from their boring farms where the howling wind and sputtering oil lamps kept them company. For the first time in their lives, in the World of Light they could see Eastman's camera, Benz's automobile, Krupp's cannons, the zipper, chewing gum, and the electric kitchen. While they sighed wistfully, their children dragged them toward a Venus de Milo sculpted in chocolate. Shrill voices resounded everywhere.

"Let's see the lion tamer!"

"Let's go to the Lapland and the Algerian villages!"

"Let's go to Buffalo Bill's circus!"

"Let's take a balloon ride!"

"Let's do it all!"

Freckled kids with upturned noses saw the Statue of Liberty made of salt and other products of useless ingenuity, such as a locomotive made of silk and a drawbridge made of soap. At the Kansas Pavilion, a herd of buffalo made of wheat lolled about. At the Agricultural Pavilion, there was a map of America made out of pickles, and a monstrous cheese that weighed a ton.

"Would you like a piece of the monster cheese?" George Westinghouse asked Nikola Tesla.

"I can't wait!" the inventor laughed. Our hero was in a champagne mood. "You know what this is?" He grew excited. "This is a rite of passage. In Europe, they still imagine that America is full of wild Indians and buffalo. America has come of age."

"Our light casts a new light on America." Westinghouse acknowledged his words with slow pride.

MacMonnies's fountain and the exhibition palaces lined with lightbulbs were the work of Tesla and Westinghouse. Their lights used more electricity than the city of Chicago.

They raised their batons, and hundreds of thousands of bulbs responded with mute music.

In the midst of this glare—the glare they created—Tesla remembered the gold stripe that burned under the door and the candles he made as a child so that he could read in secret. And now? He was a ray that shimmered among other rays, trying to make his way through people who did not exist.

That season, purple, turquoise, and violet dresses were in fashion. Someone had to light them up! Someone had to light up Don Quixote made of plums! The Venus de Milo made of chocolate and Princess Eulalia—all of that had to be lit up.

An ideal city rose next to the "city of broad shoulders," of slaughter-houses and sooty factories. The real city was grotesquely fierce and dingy. The other one was dazzlingly white. The first was dangerous; the second was safe. Untouched by the spectacle of triumphant modernity, twenty thousand unemployed were on strike in the first one. In the second one, visitors were moved to tears.

"Thank God my miserable life isn't the measure of all things," people from Kansas whispered. "Thank God something like this is possible!"

On the roof of the Electricity Pavilion, a spotlight rotated as if asking: "What? What? What?"

In a blue watercolor, the painter Childe Hassam immortalized Westinghouse and Tesla's small kingdom.

A fifty-foot-tall kiosk rose in the middle of the Electricity Pavilion: Westinghouse Electric & Manufacturing Co. Tesla Polyphase Systems. Glass neon signs burned coldly and pointedly on it. With its blue glimmer, the name of the Serbian poet Zmaj stood out among them. The signs crackled, and the explosions of tiny thunderbolts could be heard all over the building. Only the members of the International Electrical Congress and their wives were admitted to Tesla's lecture—if they had passes.

Tesla shook hands with the dignitaries Westinghouse introduced to him. His biographer, Martin, presented a man with full lips, a small nose, and almond-shaped eyes: "This is our guest who came from India for the conference of world's religions. Swami Vivekananda!" Tesla dove into the stranger's extraordinary eyes.

"It would be good for us to talk," Vivekananda simply said.

Tesla's smile was fierce. "I'd love to!"

Westinghouse coughed impatiently.

The kiosk buzzed with excitement. On a velvet-topped table, Columbus's egg spun in an electric whirlpool. Smaller balls revolved around bigger ones like planets around suns. Not even other electrical engineers knew what exactly those apparatuses were. Our cartographer of the unknown was engaged in the magical act of naming things.

In that magnificent exhibition, he presented oscillators so small they could fit in one's hat. He also presented a radio wave transmitter the purpose of which no one could figure out.

At his lecture, Tesla appeared in a white smoking jacket. He stood in front of his audience while that other one whose hair was slowly rising stood next to him. Tesla's black hair was parted in the middle. His ears stood out. His tired eyes were the color of the sky before a storm.

The reader should become concerned about him because he looked so ill, he had to excuse himself. "Mr. Westinghouse invited many electrical engineers to give this lecture, but when the time came I was the only healthy one."

His shoulders were hunched in the beginning but straightened up as he went on. Yet again, he described electricity as an all-permeating substance that connects rough matter. That substance—which Lord Kelvin nearly equated with God—had broad and safe practical uses. Tesla described the heating of iron bars and the melting of lead within the electromagnetic field. He touched upon the possibility that electricity rejuvenates and heals.

Tesla's assistant, Gano Dunn, did not listen to the lecture. He was waiting for a sign.

Tesla waved his hand.

The kiosk drowned in darkness.

In the dark, the same thunderbolts cracked that Giambattista Vico believed had intimated the first notions of God to humans. Tesla's coil turned into the burning bush, wrapped in flames that did not consume. With soft pings, lightbulbs and glass tubes lit up by themselves. But the climax came when the man in the smoking jacket let two hundred thousand volts run through his body. Not only did he allow them to pass through him, he turned into a cyclone of electricity. People retreated in horror when his hair stood up on end.

"Oh my goodness . . ." a voice gasped.

Tesla's face would have become disfigured with triumph had he not had control over himself. Exhaustion turned into exaltation. With his crooked smile and bluish horns of Moses, the scientist turned left and right in the widening circle. No one tried to touch him. His body and clothes continued to emit a succession of fine haloes.

"What's the meaning of this dream of beauty?" a female voice asked.

CHAPTER 61

In a Fantasy World

Thomas Commerford Martin introduced Tesla to a woman with a wisp of gray hair and a man with a Roman nose. They rubbed their eyes as they had just emerged from the dark.

The curls and waves of the stranger's mustache flowed into his beard. He raised his nose a bit and looked at Tesla through his pince-nez.

"Robert Underwood Johnson," he repeated, stressing each word as if Martin had failed to introduce him.

One look from his lady companion turned many a man's knees into jelly. The flash of her necklace was as stunning as her bosom. Her nose held a mysterious air of confidence. Her eyes were cruel and bright.

"Katharine Johnson," she said.

Her sudden laughter made the entire Pavilion of Electricity spin. Still laughing, she addressed Martin: "Why don't you ever bring Mr. Tesla over?"

"I will. I promise." Martin bowed.

Three weeks later, Katharine accepted an astonishing bouquet of roses from Tesla, who gingerly encircled it with both hands. At first glance, her face appeared classically serene, calm, more angular than oval. Her untamable hair gave away her nervous temper. So did her eyes. Her smile turned the air around her body into sweet liquor.

A wicker basket in the corner of the dining room was filled with wine corks. The dinner, inspired by Tuscan recipes, pleasantly surprised both Tesla and Martin. Johnson, the Italophile, believed that Apennine cooking equaled the French despite its occasional inconsistencies. He suggested he should write a guide to Italian restaurants for connoisseurs only.

"You're a man ahead of your time," proclaimed his guests as their faces became ruddy.

A pleasant rosy current circulated through the rooms and hallways. At sixteen, Robert and Katharine's daughter, Agnes, was already a beauty. Little Owen was "a knee-high bundle of energy." They had a black Labrador on which little Owen rode. The dog pounded its head hard against the table but continued to wag its tail as if nothing happened.

"His name is Richard Higginson the First." Robert pointed out the dog offhandedly.

They also had a white cat called Saint Ives. Saint Ives constantly stalked something invisible.

"Cats tend to live in a fantasy world," Katharine observed, with a smile that hinted at something else.

During the lively conversation, Nikola and Robert started to interrupt each other. Martin smiled with satisfaction. Robert was amazed at how much poetry Nikola knew by heart.

"Art shouldn't be separated from life"—he put his wineglass away and almost choked with approval—"as something too precious for everyday use."

"That's exactly the kind of poet Jovan Jovanović Zmaj is," Nikola exclaimed. He regretted that Robert could not read Zmaj's poems. "They haven't been translated . . ."

Robert could not stop talking about poetry. "Facts themselves won't do," he shouted. "They become irresistible only when they are slapped with the flame of poetry."

Robert Underwood Johnson was generally considered to be a poet and an editor. Tesla soon understood that he was a magician. He knew everyone in New York and resembled an adult Tom Sawyer. He was a close friend of Mark Twain.

"Why didn't Mark Twain come to the exposition?" Tesla asked.

"Actually, he did," Johnson answered. "But . . ."

As soon as he arrived in Chicago, the humorist fell sick and spent ten days in his hotel bed. Other than holding a thermometer in his mouth, he did nothing but cough, so he failed to make the exhibition.

He did not go on the fifty-cent around-the-world tour. He did not view the drawbridge made of soap. He did not write about the Main Canal, over which the Statue of the Republic, "Big Mary" with gilded shoulders, raised her hands in blessing. He did not see two hundred feathers trembling on Standing Bear's headdress as the chief rode on Ferris's wheel. He did not take the measure of the frightening cannons in the Krupp Pavilion. He did not elbow his way through a throng of police officers who were soothing lost children and the farmers who were ordering bratwurst on Fishermen's Island. He did not catch the sight of the fleet of fifty electric gondolas floating along the canals. He did not see the New America that, thrilled by change, denied the fear of change. He did not witness Tesla and Westinghouse conduct a galaxy of lightbulbs.

"And he did not see you as you transformed into a fountain of sparks on the stage," Johnson concluded.

The warm-eyed Martin added that Twain also missed "Little Egypt," the belly dancer who swayed her hips on the "streets of Cairo." Then he angrily put down his glass of cognac: "I want to ask you something else. Why didn't Westinghouse sue Edison for pirating your motor?"

Tesla stared at Martin with his bright, impish eyes. "If I told you that, I'd have to kill you," he warned.

"Why?" the fearless Martin repeated.

"Because he himself pirated Edison's lightbulb."

When they stopped laughing, they remembered the Saint Paul of Hinduism, Swami Vivekananda.

"Do you know what Hiram Maxim said about him?" Tesla asked. "The man, he said, is a living example of an 'unsaved soul' who knows more about philosophy and religion than all American preachers and missionaries put together."

"I hear that he'll move to New York to lecture."

"I'll go and hear him," Martin promised.

"That exhibition was a visual treatise, the largest gathering since the destruction of the Tower of Babel," Katharine said and then yawned. "The entire town was a . . . sequin. One felt like whistling and blinking one's eyes in wonder while eating cotton candy."

Martin smiled dutifully.

Robert, however, disagreed; the World Exposition was a truly marvelous event, yet it felt empty compared to Chicago's real problems. "Did you know that crowds of homeless people moved into the abandoned palaces of the City of the Future after the closing of the fair?"

In a word—they got tangled up in conversation. Martin was already taking his leave, but the reason they came had not been mentioned at all.

"What about you?" he asked Tesla.

"I'm not in a hurry." Tesla shrugged.

Robert and he stayed on. They discovered that—when they were both boys—their fathers used to travel through rural areas. One was a doctor, the other a priest. Robert still remembered the underdone meat he was served in Indiana farmhouses for breakfast.

"I had to break the ice in the washbasin so I could wash my face."

Tesla related how the bushes in Lika were black with June bugs. The branches broke under their weight. Robert became interested. Tesla discovered that his new friend combined a good temper with a love of anecdotes. His did not divorce a serious take on life from laughter.

That laughing man successfully pushed through the international copyright law, suggested to his friend John Muir that Yosemite should be made a national park, supported suffragettes, and edited the magazine *Century* with both good taste and authority. Robert was General Grant's acquaintance and publisher. He knew the former President Harrison and was on intimate terms with the rising political star Theodore Roosevelt.

"Come sit here!" Robert told Tesla and threw a pinecone into the fireplace. It soon turned into a burning rose. The house was lavishly decorated, with Arabic incrustations. Refinement taken to a sick degree determined the shade of the wallpaper. The Bordeaux color of the room was enlivened by the blotches of two Tiffany lamps, which resembled twin jellyfish. A gold and silver clock with suns and moons ticked in its walnut case. No one knows how many glasses of wine they emptied and how many pipes of tobacco ash Johnson knocked into the fireplace that evening. Katharine was as beautiful as Venice. She swirled her skirts above her knees and settled at the piano. Glasses tinkled in the cupboard. The Labrador stood on his hind legs, and

Robert waltzed with him. "Ah!" he sighed, falling back into the arm-chair in a paroxysm of dramatic exhaustion. When he found himself alone, Richard Higginson I got in a fight with a hissing radiator.

"My dog constantly quarrels with something, like Luther with the devil," Robert said. "He barks at the doorbell, the rain, the thunder."

When a nearby clock tower sounded midnight, the Labrador barked at it. But when it laconically struck one o'clock, the dog looked sad and dumb.

"You look gorgeous when you yawn," Johnson said to his wife.

"I'm going to bed," Katharine said. "Bye-bye."

Blue-eyed like a husky, she smiled, looking Tesla in the eye: "We'll become friends."

"You think so?"

All coquetry fell from her beautiful face. The woman responded, "I know so."

CHAPTER 62

On Top of the World

Tesla's European tour and the World Expo made him famous.

In *Electrical Review,* the warm-eyed Martin was the first to ever use the magic word: "Prometheus!"

At Delmonico's, they served him flaming dishes and desserts with sparklers.

Suddenly, everyone remembered him. His old friends started to write to him—the widow Bauzain from Strasbourg, his ailing uncle Branković, and even Tannhäuser, who invited him to his wedding in Vienna.

From a starving lad with bangs—in the picture from his Varaždin days—Nikola turned into a man on top of the world. His autograph became ornate. The motion of his hand became nervous and commanding. If a fly landed on his tablecloth, he demanded that the table be set again.

Lady Astor's salon could accommodate only the Four Hundred. Tesla was one of them. In that limited space, the musicians played a sequence of numbers: a march, a quadrille, a waltz, a polka, a galop, and a couple of circular dances for each quadrille. The march was usually played before dinner. Tesla had two pairs of gloves—he wore one before dinner and the other after dinner. He attended these events but did not dance. "I waltz with my head, not with my legs," he explained.

He also said this: "Rather than waiting for some king to knight you, who may be a fool or a villain, you should knight yourself."

Tesla bragged about being the best-dressed man on Fifth Avenue.

He tapped his cane against the top of his shoe and declared, "When it comes to clothes, people judge a man according to his own judgment, which is revealed through his appearance."

The dandy did not wash his gloves and starched collars—he threw them away. A master shoemaker provided an endless supply of high-laced shoes. Monograms embellished each item in his wardrobe. Jackets flattered his greyhound-like figure. Each Monday, he bought a new tie in a Stendhalian combination of red and black.

Of late, he had been living on top of the world. In fact, he lived above the top—in the joy of discovery. He walked on water and danced his mental waltz. His elfish ears touched heaven. Stars revolved in his hair. The walls and frames that provided worldly limitations disappeared in moments of creation. He was an ancient Roman in triumph. Dane's ghost stood behind his back and whispered, "Remember that you are human."

CHAPTER 63

People from the Hat

An average American loves his family.
If he has some love left, he spends it on Mark Twain.
Thomas Edison

Robert Underwood Johnson repeatedly removed his magician's top hat for Tesla's benefit. Famous people kept springing out of it, removing their own hats in turn. First he introduced him to Antonín Dvořák. The two men remembered—or pretended to remember—their meeting in the National café in Prague.

At the *Century*'s office, Tesla encountered a young man with bright eyes. He wore a warm yet catlike smile. His mustache was heavy. His brow was high. His extremely black eyebrows bristled in an attempt to replace his vanishing hair. His nose was straight and thin. His eyes were bright and blue. Bowing like an officer, he said:

"Rudyard Kipling."

Tesla complimented *The Phantom Rickshaw*. Married to an American, Kipling badmouthed Chicago and brazenly slandered New York's Lower East Side: *disgusting endless streets, horrible people who talk through their noses, more barbaric than Hottentots.*

The following Saturday, Robert invited Tesla to Delmonico's and promised, "You'll love him! A flaming red head! Completely red—even the mustache."

"A Renaissance man!" Katharine added ironically.

"Benvenuto Cellini." Martin was enthusiastic.

When Tesla's new acquaintance blushed, blood flooded not only his face but also his hair.

"The lucky fellow," people used to say. "That devil was born under a lucky star."

The red blotches on the cheeks were not a gift of health but a sign of tuberculosis. Stanford White!

"They say that he is the devil," Katharine explained.

"They say I'm the devil," the architect humbly affirmed.

"I'll tell you a story they recite in Bosnia," Tesla said in response to White's smile:

> *A man met a stranger.*
> *The stranger was good looking, smart, and witty.*
> *"Who are you?" the man asked.*
> *"I'm the devil!"*
> *"Impossible," the man exclaimed. "The devil is ugly and dumb."*
> *The stranger answered with a delicate smile, "You've been listening to gossips."*

"Do you have any more wonders in your Ali Baba's cave?" Katharine asked as they returned from dinner at the Van Alens'.

"Why don't you drop by the cave?" Tesla asked.

"We'll bring some friends," Katharine muttered.

"Please do!"

One rainy day that smelled like a halved cantaloupe, a coach clopped up in front of Tesla's laboratory on South Fifth Avenue. A straight figure of a man with bushy eyebrows stood out among the group of arrivals. Millions of those who had never seen him knew who he was—the writer who kept his word that he never smoked while he slept.

Mark Twain!

"You don't say!" his eyes challenged Tesla even before he said anything. The expression on his face constantly changed in between his stormy eyebrows and good-natured mustache. When he addressed Tesla, a smile hovered around that mustache. "Robert says you work a lot."

"If you don't count thinking," Tesla answered, "I'm the laziest man in the world."

"Don't argue with me, young man," Twain interrupted him hoarsely. "I'm the laziest. My whole life, I've been conscientiously avoiding work. If I've accomplished anything at all, it's not because of work but because of play."

One of Twain's eyebrows was raised and shaggy and the other was brushed down. Tesla listened to his slightly growling, almost stuttering voice, ideal for telling stories.

"Thank God," Nikola sighed to himself, "that, among all the horse thieves and the envious, an occasional witty sage like Twain walks in this world."

Tesla believed that humorists were smarter than philosophers and confessed to Twain that his early stories helped him get back on his feet when he had cholera as a young man. Like many other writers, Twain sometimes suspected that what he did was—nothing. Tesla's words did away with his theatrical grumpiness and filled his eyes with tears.

In the midst of the Gilded Age, everyone got richer except the man who gave the age its name. Wherever he went during the day, people smirked and said, "Make us laugh!"

But at night, the wise clown, sleepless, paced around his room. "Like most people, I'm not quite myself at night," he confessed to his friends.

Johnson whispered to Tesla, "You know, he invested all his money in a worthless printing system." That black hole devoured all of Twain's income and the even more substantial dowry of his wife, Livy. He was so deep in debt he contemplated selling his Hartford house with its multiple chimneys and gables with gingerbread ornamentation, whose soul mirrored the writer's soul.

"You immigrated to America and I'm emigrating from America," Twain confided in Tesla. "Maybe you could provide some electrotherapeutic machines I would sell to rich old women in Europe. Fifty-fifty?"

"Sure," Tesla agreed.

The smiling inventor introduced Twain and his friends to his world of black machines surrounded with shimmering light.

"Do you know what the hell this is?" Twain asked Johnson in a cracked whisper.

"To a degree," Johnson responded.

"Listen here!" Tesla announced, as straight as Virgil. "We're not in hell yet, but we're on our way. Per me si va ne la città dolente. A very disturbing experience for the superstitious."

The air was so electrified it felt like they moved through cobwebs. The visitors expected phantom hands to appear in the room at any moment and brush their faces.

Tesla kept explaining:

"Some of the apparatuses here create vibrations the intensity of which has never been achieved before. When I harmonize my oscillators with the frequency of the earth, I will be able to wirelessly conduct not only energy but messages as well."

"And what is this?" Twain asked.

Tesla did not hear his question. "The life of all energy—from the sun to the human heart—is a matter of pulsations and vibrations at certain frequencies."

While his long fingers pointed out one nameless object after another, Tesla's clear, ringing voice rapidly fired the words *this* and *that* at his listeners: "This is an oscillator that can demolish the Brooklyn Bridge. That is a lamp that lights up by itself. This is the 'shadowgraphic' machine. That is the genie that lives in my coil."

He pulled a lever, and a fifteen-foot electrical discharge stuck its tongue out across the room. At its sound, his guests hunched. They shrank even more when tiny thunderbolts started to make friendly crackling noises all around them. "These are my minor genies," Tesla said.

His guests reluctantly straightened up.

"This is just a more spectacular version of what constantly flows through us and the world."

"This is us," Twain laughed hoarsely, his black eyes becoming brighter and brighter.

While the thunderbolts snipped around the room, Tesla suggested his friends step on the platform that held the oscillating mattresses. The old writer with quivering gray hair and bright eyes was the first to do it. Surrounded by the flashes, he stood upright like a rooster. Then he said, "This is excellent."

"Watch your . . ." Tesla wanted to warn him, but it was too late.

The humorist discovered that the vibrations momentarily stimulated the function of his bowels, and he had to rush to the bathroom. They all laughed when Twain came back with a very unusual expression on his face. They had a drink, floating in the amoeboid blue light.

"To our photographs!" the visitors exclaimed.

"To our photographs," Tesla toasted them.

Using his lighting tubes, Tesla took their pictures. The big-nosed Joseph Jefferson and the chiseled-faced Marion Crawford were the first to be eternalized in that elfish environment. Then Tesla photographed Katharine's wispy hair and her alarmed eyes. Finally, Twain's drooping mustache was captured in the picture. Twain had a glowing unplugged lightbulb in his hand.

Those were phosphorescent photographs, the first ever made. A wall calendar called this windy day April 26, 1894.

CHAPTER 64

Così fan tutte

Sitting by the open fire, the two of us feel pleasantly dull.
And yet, two is too small a number—it takes at least three to make it lively,
especially when it snows outside . . .

From Katharine Johnson's letter to Nikola Tesla

Nikola Tesla smiled as he looked at the floor. Robert Underwood Johnson raised his nose toward the ceiling as he looked for a rhyme. The photographs of his parents, Nimrod and Katharine, looked at them without understanding from the mantelpiece. The father's hairstyle was characteristic of the 1850s, and we have to call it foolish. The mother was considered a woman of great beauty, which the picture did not support.

These two model rhyme makers decided to translate Jovan Jovanović Zmaj's poems into English. The first rhyme maker provided the literal meaning. The second rhyme maker couched the poems in elegant, somewhat hollow rhymes.

Looking for the English equivalent to the Serbian phrase *crammed together*, Tesla got up and walked to the Japanese screen. He complained, "On the outside, Serbian looks like such a tiny language, but it's so roomy on the inside."

"Never write down with your hand anything that you wouldn't like to read when you come back from the dead," Johnson advised him with a quote from *A Thousand and One Nights*.

Robert's face showed the signs of settled maturity. His contemporaries considered his Roman nose to be an indication of great energy. His handsome face started to assume the agreeable expression of a Saint Bernard. The two of them communicated through messengers three times a day. In those memos, Robert signed his name as "Luka," after Luka Filipov, the Montenegrin hero from a poem by Zmaj.

While the two of them translated Zmaj in the shadow of Robert's eloquent clock, ornamented with suns and moons, Tesla's coach was waiting outside.

"Daddyyyyy, may I ask you something?" Owen crooned. "Can we take a ride in Uncle Nick's coach?" the little manipulator asked behind his cutest smile.

The coach had rubberized wheels—a miracle of shock absorption. They put a brass heater under Agnes's and Owen's feet and covered them with Scottish plaid.

The young Johnsons felt like grown-ups as they rode along the streets lined with floating yellow and blue lights and through the deep shadows of the park.

Clippety-clop!

Agnes started to howl and Owen worried that she might turn into a werewolf.

While the children were riding in the coach, Robert spoke to Tesla about his Katharine.

At their wedding, a journalist caught her bridal bouquet. "I kissed her stomach when she was pregnant. Before I held baby Agnes in my arms, I had no idea where the center of the world was. When I first held the baby, I said to myself, 'Now I know.'"

The new father and mother got up at night together to see if Agnes was breathing.

"The way I proposed to her . . ." Robert reminisced as he widened his eyes, magnified by his pince-nez. "I took her to a cliff above the Hudson, and in that spectacular landscape I asked her if she would marry me. Just before our wedding, she got mad at me and threw her engagement ring into the fire. So I had to dig it out—with my bare hands."

Robert interrupted his story to pull back his slipper at which Richard Higginson I yanked, growling. Robert smiled a healthy smile. "Then we made up. I embraced her tightly. She sighed and said, 'When they hug, a man and a woman make a fortress in the cold universe.'" Robert paused and his eyes wandered away. "I'll never forget that."

In short, the inventor and the poet slowly developed one of those Roman-like friendships that Seneca would have praised. Whenever Tesla found himself in financial straits, Robert's check discreetly arrived. Five years his senior, Robert turned into a brother Nikola had never had—kind, not godlike and distant like Dane.

The woman who was the center of the urban galaxy at 273 Lexington Avenue was still attractive. Her hair looked as if she washed it in cognac. After a bath, she stood naked in front of the mirror, applied some cream on her face, and wiped her fingers against the dry skin of her buttocks. Yes, I'm still beautiful! Touched by tuberculosis, she sometimes sunned her throat at a sanatorium in Colorado for a few months. Like many Victorian girls, Katharine Johnson was raised by the following rules: Be pretty if you can, be witty if you must, but be proper even if it kills you.

Alas, our heroine was always in a state of excitement. Her refreshing manner—in her circle—was a mistake. Even her aunt once asked her, "Kate, are you insane?"

Robert Underwood Johnson admired his wife's "temperament." He simply smiled and let her voice her opinions. The more she pushed her ideas, the "odder" she appeared.

"Thinking has been considered bad manners since the beginning of time," her tactful husband consoled her.

Robert insisted that women understood life's limitations better than men. Katharine did not. Like her cat, Saint Ives, she constantly stalked something invisible. She was suffocating. She felt guilty because she was not completely happy. She wanted to *break through to the other side of air—uninhabited and uninhabitable.* The loss of youth tormented her. She craved something really great, and a pleasant, reasonable life was not necessarily great.

"Don't be so selfish," her sister told her.

Katharine blindly groped for something—some hidden miracle.

"Like what?" her other sister asked.

The roses Tesla brought thundered on the table.

Newspapers wrote about him. Reporters did not fail to notice Nikola's eyes, which "turned blue from thought" and his "long thumbs, which indicated great intelligence." The extremely tall, lanky man who weighed less than 150 pounds was almost pure spirit. That "spirit" appeared "almost shy" and "his suits fit him well."

In her dream, he once gave her fig blossoms, though fig blossoms do not exist. She dreamed that he touched her with his unusually long thumbs, the signs of his great intelligence. This hatched the lines:

Curiosity led to the worst kind of lewdness,
So the soul was shocked, while dreaming of purity,
To find itself fingering the celestial underwear
Which Jesus had once donned to conceal his nudity.

She dreamed of him dressed only in light.

That eel-like body! What a waste! He bathed himself all his life like he bathed the dead!

Was the torch of nubility lit in her loins?

The roses thundered on the table.

She learned that Tesla had almost drowned, lost his memory, ran from wolves, fallen into boiling water—in short, that he had always been on the verge of exhaustion and catastrophe.

"How fragile his life is!" she told Robert with tenderness.

"I'm invisible! Invisible!" she whispered like a little girl.

Because she could see him, the way no one could see her.

Tesla feared the germs that crawled along people's hands and hearts. Warm and cold love fought within him. All that human exchange and all that animal warmth were so removed from the cold flame in the heart of the world.

"He's so guileless," Katharine went on. "He's a little scary."

Katharine knew that innocence characterized mediums, those who could move between the material and spiritual worlds. She noticed that Tesla could not pass a beggar without giving him something. She marked his excruciating, insightful stare as well as his awareness, which was raised to a level of pain. She perceived the elements of boyish playfulness, extravagance, and humor within him. She saw that he enjoyed bewitching those he spoke to. But she was also the only one to realize that, as a human being, he was somehow frozen and unfinished. Horrified, in his eyes she spotted the point where electricity and ice converged. She saw a man who lived in another world as well as in this one. His spiritual yet wily smile said, "I'm here, but I'm not!"

God filled her mouth with laughter on those days—which birds often made even more joyful—when the three of them went picnicking.

The roses thundered on the table.

Tesla and the Johnsons watched as their friend Ignacy Paderewski shook his lion's mane above the torrents of Chopin. They went to the Metropolitan, sometimes in the company of the big-nosed Joseph Jefferson and sometimes with chiseled-faced Marion Crawford, and listened to the tenor and the soprano voices intertwine like flames and dry grass. "When we become one with music we have the profoundest experience of reality," Schopenhauer whispered in Katharine Johnson's ear (which could completely fit into Robert's mouth). In their box, Tesla exchanged whispers with Robert about their translations of Serbian poetry. Behind the scene, the singers hummed, practicing the lines by the wise Venetian Lorenzo da Ponte, which Mozart wrapped in a cloud of enchanting music.

Katharine stole occasional glances at Tesla. Once a week, she sent invitations to that man with the absentminded smile: "Come meet Baron Kanek . . . Helen Hunt Jackson and Senator George Hurst. Come meet Ann Morgan . . . Come!"

Why could not people live according to their values rather than according to their humiliating and obnoxious needs? Was that fair? Should she be deprived of the most generous aspect of her being? Of her ultimate self? Of sincerity? Of warmth? Why should this thirsty weakness punish her for being herself? Longing ripped her insides apart. She felt like a diver holding her breath and knowing that she would drown if—right now! Right now!—she did not surface. She felt like someone completely naked, freezing in the snow. If she did not find warmth—right now!—her heart would break from the cold. She could not endure it anymore. Treacherous tears, help a weak human being!

God, why didn't you make us self-sufficient—we are always hungry and thirsty, men craving women, women craving men!

The red curtain flew to the left and to the right. The stage swam in light and Ferrando started to sing:

My Dorabella couldn't
Do such a thing.
The Heavens made her
As faithful as she is beautiful.

Guglielmo responded to him:

My Fiordiligi
Could not betray me
As her constancy
Matches her loveliness.

CHAPTER 65

The Ice Palace

Nikola Tesla's Letter to Katharine Johnson

Peter the Great made fun of his unfortunate niece Anna of Kurland on the very day of her wedding. Soon after her wedding, she was left a widow.

Anna spent her youth far away from the capital, in the rainy Baltics. When that thin-lipped, gray-skinned woman returned to St. Petersburg as the empress, she did little to dispel her reputation as a sadist.

The expression on Tesla's face became pained. With quick strokes of his pen, he added:

Anna ordered her servants to build her a palace of ice.

I don't know whether they cut the ice from the Neva or from the Finnish lakes—Nikola Tesla admitted—but I know that it took them weeks to bring the blocks to the building site through the crystal, biting frost. Workers with pickaxes and architects with wigs swarmed around the growing walls of ice. Wind and string instruments celebrated the completion of the palace. Infernal fireworks splashed the windows and turrets in light. The cupolas, the pillars, the balustrades, the staircases, the chandeliers were made of ice. The blind statues were of ice. The rows of shining rooms were made of ice.

Nikola sighed.

*Anna ordered a servant and a court maid to marry and to
spend a night in the icy palace, on a bed of ice.*

The shadow of a smile disappeared from Tesla's face. His sneering
lips froze. His eyebrow trembled. He went on with masochistic cruelty:

In my dream, those two wore our faces.
The bed was biting. The bed stuck to our backs.
*With soft clinks, the endless glimmers of the ice palace
multiplied.*
We stared into each other's eyes and shivered.
*Did we shiver from passion? Did Death clutch us with her
diamond fingers?*
The palace seduced us with its shimmerings.
We breathed in unison.
We exhaled smoke.
The translucent furniture was made of ice.
The bed and its canopy were made of ice.
My splayed arms were blue.
Your eyes were like silver bugs.
Your hair was gray with a powder of ice.
You looked at me with a smile of ghostly joy.
We could hear the crackling of the wedding fireworks.
*"If I speak human and angelic languages, but have no love . . ."
sopranos sang.*
My hair was full of snowdust.
Outside, the strings' sad music was dying.
*I dreamed I was a servant and you a maid and that we were
spending a night on a bed of ice.*

CHAPTER 66

Pulse! Pulse!

Take my advice,
and never try to invent anything but—happiness.
Herman Melville

"I can't love any man without feeling sorry for him," Katharine said.

Where had Nikola heard those words before?

"Why?" he asked, trying to remember.

"Because he's a human being. Because he will die. Because he doesn't know what life is, just like I don't."

It was an afternoon in October when they met at the *Century* office. Robert was in a meeting with Custer's widow; he planned to publish a book about her husband. So Nikola walked Katharine to Central Park.

"What a wonderful day," she told him. "The sky is so blue that I feel completely blue inside."

They strolled through the yellow and auburn of the Indian summer. They could not help feeling the sweetness of the air and the joy of taking it in. Self-important velocipedists rode through the park. Gravel murmured and acorns crunched under their tires. Squirrels chased each other under the trees and across the merry lawns. A gust of wind splashed the path with yellow and red leaves.

"That sunlit bench is waiting for us," Katharine pointed.

Tesla addressed her with a feminine tenderness. He raised his finger. "Look at the squirrels," he said.

A squirrel made three wavy hops and then froze in front of the bench. The next moment, its tail was where its head used to be. Following at the heels of another squirrel, it shot up the tree trunk. Then they chased each other over and across thin branches, flicking their tails.

"The rhythms, the rhythms," Katharine murmured.

The whole world was threaded with sunshine. The sun was in the corner of her mouth and her eyes.

Black and blue smudges alternated on the surface of the lake. Some ducks ate with their shimmering bills by the shore. Other floated asleep.

Heraclitus's invisible flame enveloped the world. Was not Moses's burning bush just the most notable symbol of that world?

Pulse, pulse—the reflection of the sun from the lake repeated, intertwined with their eyelashes.

Bees sang to the glory of the creator of buzzing.

Bees are great buzzers.

Our mystic-scientist merged with the hypnotic repetitiveness of the sunny day.

Pulse! Pulse!

Tesla felt the whole world oscillating around him. He watched the undulations of the lake and the trees; he watched the pulsating smile on her face.

"All things, from the sun to the human heart, are but oscillations at a certain frequency," he mused on his favorite subject.

And peace? Peace was the equilibrium of different tremblings.

He knew it. She felt it too.

Katharine sat with her mouth pursed and her nose narrowed. She was focused. Her knuckles whitened on her clenched fists.

"Is there anything more beautiful than the bottomless whirlpool of these treetops in the wind?" she asked, excited.

They looked each other straight in the eye and then past each other. Finally, they fell silent. They did not know how long they were quiet. She came back first.

"Are we still in the same spot?" she asked as she brushed a non-existent speck off of her shoulder.

"We flow, we flow like water," said he.

"We flow, we flow like clouds," she responded.

The next day, he could not turn down an invitation to dinner. The children took another ride in his carriage. Little Owen stuck his tongue out at the passersby and his sister rebuked him. Tesla had not stopped in at Lexington Avenue for a long time, so their late-evening encounter turned out to be quite pleasant. Robert laughed more than Katharine. His laughter slowly became tipsy. Imagine, little Owen had already started asking logical questions: Do blind people dream in color? How come animals are on islands? After they all laughed, the three of them suddenly fell silent, and each of them gazed at something over their glasses. Then Katharine went to another room, came back, and said, "I'll read one of Robert's unpublished poems to you."

In her sonorous voice, she read brilliantly, with controlled emotion. The title was "Premonitions." To Tesla, the glow of the candles on her face was much more interesting than the poem:

> *Omens that were once but jest*
> *Now are messengers of fate;*
> *And the blessing held the best*
> *Cometh not or comes too late . . .*

CHAPTER 67

A Hole in the Gut

*The destruction of Nikola Tesla's laboratory
and all of the amazing objects it housed is much more
than a single man's loss. It's a global disaster.*
New York Sun, **March 13, 1895**

"Fire!" someone shouted into his face as soon as he opened the door.

He threw a tailcoat over his naked body and flagged down a careening cab. Sparks flew under the horse's hooves. He huddled in the carriage, which had never been washed except by rain—the thing reeked of tobacco. It was even earlier than the hour when he heard about Szigety's death. Five in the morning! The clatter of the hooves pounded into his brain. As soon as he opened the cab's door, soot mingled with his hair.

In front of him, a policeman stood with his legs apart. "Stop!"

Tesla pushed him aside and rushed up the stairs of the gutted building.

Oil and black water. Melted machinery.

He emerged, his lungs irritated.

He almost passed out.

A layer of ash and soot coated the surrounding walls.

"Burned down!" he uttered, his mouth stiff.

An old woman scratched her face. Someone died in the fire. Two stories collapsed and his machinery crashed from the fourth to the second floor.

He gaped in disbelief. It felt completely unreal—*everything* was there.

His personal museum. Papers and notes. Machines.

He had once lost his memory. Now he lost the memory embodied in things.

One of the most interesting spots in the world went up in smoke like a burned offering. This was where his guests used to have drinks floating in the amoeboid blue, waiting for the phantom hands to touch them.

All the things he worked on in that place!

Vivekananda once jokingly compared him to the many-armed Shiva.

With one arm, he worked on what would later be called X-rays. That was gone now! With another arm, he dealt with what would later become robotics. Gone! With a third arm, he endeavored to produce liquid oxygen. Gone as well. He also worked on the steam dynamo that turned steam into electricity and produced an additional therapeutic effect. That too dissolved into thin air. The iridescent lamp in its experimental phase. Destroyed. He and Koloman Czitó had already exchanged wireless messages between the laboratory and the Hotel Gerlach, thirty blocks away. They were just about to send another message from the Gerlach to a steamboat on the Hudson.

"Was the laboratory insured?" That was the first thing they asked him.

He looked at Czitó and shook his head no.

"Why?"

"Just like life, it had a value, not a price."

A rosy smile spread across the eastern sky. As the unstoppable dawn broke through, Tesla's friends found him. Their eyes were bloodshot from the smoke and lack of sleep.

Czitó contacted Tesla's biographer, Martin, who in turn informed the Johnsons.

"How did it happen?" Martin asked voicelessly.

How? In New York, tenements burned like matchsticks. People cooked glue and tanned hides in their rooms. Someone could have knocked over a lamp.

"Is it possible that there was a short circuit in the laboratory?" Martin asked.

Tesla shrugged his shoulders and said frankly, "Yes."

A short circuit was indeed possible. If so, he was indirectly responsible for the death of the family on the third floor.

Katharine Johnson touched Tesla's shoulder, at the risk of letting him see her swollen face. "Who did it?" she asked.

Among the diminishing numbers of the Whyos and the growing numbers of the Hudson Dusters, there were many who would poison horses, gouge eyes, or commit arson.

Maybe the shadows of the arsonists grew longer as they fled the scene while the rambunctious flames started to rumble and howl?

Who could have done it?

He looked at the mute scene. Crestfallen firemen packed up their gear.

The gutted ruin smoked and reeked of piss.

The outside cold world and the inside warm world traded places once again. According to a legend, the universe was made from the body parts of a slaughtered monster. Chaos is just under the surface and all things crave promiscuous embrace with each other. The cold replaced the warmth, and the center of the world once more turned into an icy pit.

Tesla felt like a man who had just gone over Niagara Falls in a barrel.

The wind sniffed him as if it did not know him.

How does one act when fate betrays him—one who has been dealt a heavy blow? He does not feel the earth under his feet. He simply puts one foot in front of the other.

Tesla had to stiffen up in order to hold his body together. If the tension in his muscles relaxed even for a minute, the hole in his gut would expand beyond his body, and he would dissolve into the bluish gray dawn.

CHAPTER 68

Even the Soul

The soul is a drunken monkey stung by a scorpion.

"I have already written to you a few times, but I haven't gotten anything back," his sister Angelina wailed from Petrovo Selo.

"Petrovo Selo," Tesla whispered. "Where in the world is that?"

"I don't even know how to start because you won't drop us a single word," Marica complained from Rijeka.

Their letters grew yellow in the drawer. The pale man with the thin mustache looked at them. All that animal warmth was so far away.

"It seems like you've vanished into the air," a worried Katharine Johnson wrote. "How have you been?"

In his trance of pain, every step took thought: Turn to the left! Now to the right! He could not do anything automatically and felt a desperate need for what did not exist anymore.

Maybe people set his laboratory on fire.

He walked through the city as if it was a mirage. He repeated Emerson's words: society always conspires against the humanity of all of its members.

"Where are you?" Katharine asked in every letter.

He crossed the Brooklyn Bridge and stared at the smoking roofs. He went to hear Vivekananda's lectures on Hinduism, the "mother of all religions," and on the Buddha's Four Noble Truths.

"Yes," Vivekananda explained in his melodious, melancholic voice. "The Buddha took his leave from his faithful charioteer Chandaka with a parable: Flocks alight on the same branch and then fly off in different directions. Clouds gather in the sky and then part. That's the destiny of all earthly things."

"Emptiness is the essence of all things," the almond-eyed sage claimed. "Suffering comes from our desire to turn the transient into the permanent. Birds sing: Everything is temporary. Everything is without essence. There's not a single person or a place we won't leave behind. Clutching at certainty keeps us in a state of mental slavery."

Tesla listened to him with purple shadows in his eyes. What he heard scared and soothed him at the same time.

Bushes and coaches shook in the wind that carried papers high above the roofs. Brooklyn banged, growled, and gloated around him. Tesla took a look through the window and was crushed by the merciless poetry of the streets.

"A person who doesn't believe in himself is an atheist." The teacher with a small, shapely nose smiled. "Faith summons our inner divinity. When a man loses faith in himself, he dies."

While elevated trains rumbled and shook the building, Vivekananda sighed with confidence. "He is great who turns his back on the world, who rejects all things, who has control over his passions, and who craves peace."

Those words were a balm to Tesla, who always had problems with other people's reality.

While the whole of New York wondered where Tesla was, he spent time with Vivekananda, which was like spending time with no one.

During their long, shoreless afternoons in Brooklyn, Tesla and Vivekananda talked in metaphors. Tesla told him things he had never told anyone—how, as he dealt with delirious joy when light flooded his forehead, the world disappeared, and God talked to him in the language of angels—that is, in forms.

The quixotic scientist and the stocky sage realized how much they had in common. Vivekananda preached a lifelong restraint of any form of sexual energy. His mother had to lock him in whenever beggars passed by their house.

"Take pity, my children, take pity on the poor, the ignorant, the oppressed . . . ," the swami told his disciples.

He could quote page after page from his favorite book, an encyclopedia, and repeat verbatim what he heard just twice.

Tesla's memory was equally disconcerting. Even the depths of their eyes were similar.

They talked within the fluctuating, fluid, inconstant world.

"There's not a single person or a place we won't leave behind," Vivekananda repeated. "One day, Mr. Tesla, you will even leave yourself behind."

Faces, mountains, and granite houses change just like clouds, only at a much slower pace.

In the never-ending weaving and unraveling of the world, everything evaporates—objects, bodies, and even that wispy star which we feel in our bosom.

Even the soul.

CHAPTER 69

Days of 1896

But this isn't the whole story—that would not be fair.
Constantine Cavafy, "Days of 1896"

"Have you seen him recently?" Stanford White asked the Johnsons.

"No."

"I left a message at the hotel," the round-eyed Martin sighed.

"And?"

"Nothing."

The assistants George Scherff and Czitó crossed their arms and declared that they had no clue.

The whole city wondered: "Where is he?"

Nikola felt like he was underwater or behind a looking glass. He felt like a man with a wig made of rain.

Where was he?

A Girl

A girl in a skirt made of her grandma's curtain fed her doll on Mulberry Street. When she finished, she put her doll aside and, sitting in front of her tenement, stared at the street split by a shadow.

Her father knew Hasidic blessings for lightning, the scent of a flower, and a new dress. At yeshiva, he spent his time with an ornery Lithuanian. As soon as they met each other, they started to quarrel—if not about Maimonides, then about Rabbi Nachman.

"A man can glow with divine light!" her father shouted. "A man can be a great prophet."

"But a man can never be God," the Lithuanian yelled.

There were some cabbage pierogi, rye bread, and herring on the table. The food was enough for three but was meant for five. It was much too little, selfish Father. Much too little, quarrelsome Father!

"It may be little"—her father spread his arms helplessly—"but when I read my Torah, I forget about everything and our miserable room turns into a palace."

Her mother complained that her older children did not respect her because she could not speak English. As if English was so complicated. The blue soap bubbles sister Becca blew lingered and played in the air. Aimless joy rose in the bosom of the girl we have chosen to be our heroine.

The inner courtyard reeked ecstatically.

The girl, whose name was Miriam, covered herself at night with a piece of carpet.

A moldy smudge spread across the ceiling like a rather nice dybbuk.

The thoughtful girl wondered at the open gate of life. Would she work at Weiss's sugar factory when she grew up? Would she get married? Would something good ever happen in her life?

At that moment, a shiny coach pulled up in front of the entrance. A sorrowful-looking man turned his head around. The gorgeous horse snorted.

"Would you like to go for a ride?" the man asked.

The girl said what no girl should say: "I would."

"What's your name?"

"Miriam Ganz."

"All right, Maria," the gentleman sighed.

Everything was so natural.

The gentleman looked around. Vivekananda's words rang in his ears: "Take pity, my children, take pity on the poor, the ignorant, the oppressed . . ."

He felt pity for himself. On this street Stevan Prostran held out his hand and said, "Come. Where there's enough for one, there's plenty for two." Here he and the young baker shared the same bed, in a room without windows.

Since he came to America, he had eaten a sack of salt. And where was he now? Like the Devil's Apprentice, he could say, "I haven't learned anything. I've forgotten even what I used to know."

He told the coachman to take them to Upper Manhattan.

Miriam did not feel the cold. She proudly looked from her elevated position. Lo and behold: that was a position that suited her perfectly well in life! First she thought: Oh, if only Becca and Saul and Kevin could see me! Then she concluded that this was something:

"For me alone!"

"Can we go any faster?" Cinderella asked from her pumpkin coach.

"Sure we can!"

Sunlight blinded them from a side street. The wind swirled the dust into the color of saffron.

Clippety-clop!

Women wearing white head scarves disappeared from the streets. There were fewer people, they somehow fell silent, and the streets became actually passable. Top hats replaced flat caps. The glorious ghetto banners—laundry on the lines—stayed behind. So long, noisy neighbors! I never cared for you. So long, kids! You're not good enough for me. Piles of rubbish became less frequent. Miriam looked with her huge scared eyes and wondered, "Mr. Sorrowful, who are you?"

His complexion was pale and yellowish, similar to hers, as were his eyes—except much sadder. He looked like her "second father." Or maybe more like her uncle? All people, no matter how poor, deserve to have a rich uncle. Isn't that so?

"What do you think, Mr. Sorrowful?"

Every dog needs to lick its wounds and move on—Mother's words comforted Tesla.

Miriam could smell the odor of her calico dress and her armpits together with a new scent—the scent of the world. She was surprised with herself and listened to her own breathing. Just like Mojo Medić long ago, she heard the ticklish whisper of life. A million rosebuds opened in her ear.

They crossed the border of the known world and found themselves in the uptown, where she had never been before.

Volcanic joy erupted from her bosom. She saw the city, which she had never before seen. On a granite building, flags streamed in the wind. Sculptures with calm faces oversaw the snowflakes dancing in the sunshine. Ha! Snow and sun met in the November air. That was a small miracle in the grand miracle of the city. Shop windows were inscribed in gold. Coaches waited in front of chocolate shops and jewelry stores. Everything was clean. Her companion did not pay any attention to the streets.

Miriam looked at the gentleman's frozen face with understanding and decided, *I'll be joyful for you.*

On rich streets, women were wrapped in feathery fur. Their manicured hands were too precious to get exposed. They hid them in muffs. Even children wore fur. The vapor of people's breath was visible in the sun. She looked furtively at the gentleman. What was the color of his soul? Blue?

The blue-souled man pinched himself to keep from crying. His throat tightened. He opened his mouth to relieve the strain. God never burdens men more than they can bear. That was what he hoped. The pain. He saw elongated lightning in his laboratory. The pain. He saw Twain's long drooping mustache photographed above a lightbulb. After each thought, like a *stop* in a telegram: the pain. He was cold. He rode through the streets, herding a legion of bad dreams before him. A little sleep at night, a few bites of food during the day—those were his victories.

"There I was able to do . . ."

He lived Frankenstein-like days stitched together from dead fragments of sorrow. His soul was full of scorpions and barbed wire. And yet, in each of Tesla's gloomy days that came after the fire, there was at least one gold sting, a momentary burst of wild joy like this one. Otherwise, he felt slightly deranged and suffered from a distorted view of everything around him.

His troubles persisted. He had to persevere even more. He thought: *I've been alive for the last ten minutes. I've been alive for the last half hour.*

That helped.

The girl and the magician did not talk. Miriam-Maria looked over Central Park and the lake in silence. She witnessed the first glimmers of streetlights coming on in the park. She squinted and the lamplight became a tangle of spikes. Then the coachman turned the horse back.

Clippety-clop!

They returned from heaven by the same road.

The streets became rougher.

The sorrowful gentleman looked down his nose, which followed the straight line of his forehead; he listened to the clop of the hooves. He remembered the old synagogue and the Jewish cemetery in Prague: the layers of graves on top of other graves. Once again, they found themselves in the world of porcelain foreheads, melancholic eyes, bearded fiddlers, dybbuks, balalaikas, Socialist newspapers, Dostoyevsky, diminutives, and Yiddish chants. Oy vey! In the world of flying tzadiks and holy quarrels!

The piles of trash that Miriam had completely forgotten about reappeared on the cobblestone streets. A pigeon that a coach ran over turned into a feathery smudge. White water trickled over the sidewalks. The gray walls behind which Smerdyakov killed old Karamazov and Raskolnikov killed the moneylender were back in view. People were again yelling at each other at the top of their lungs. Some kind of tinware was sold on the corner. People with their rolled-up sleeves flashed their powerful forearms. In silence, a group of men with flat caps and dusty shoulders dragged a classical sculpture out of an art studio. Like a captured animal, it had a rope around its neck. A hen ran across the street. An Italian kid rushed after it.

Only then did she remember her home. Chopped liver, chicken fat, and bread on the table. Enough for three but meant for five. It's too little, sad Father. Too little, obnoxious Father.

The gentleman dropped her off in front of her house.

His name? She never learned it.

The gentleman took his hat off and tapped the coachman with it on the back. Maria stood at the same spot as in the beginning of the story. But nothing was the same anymore. The joy that poured from her bosom remained in the outer world. The cheerful dusk dissipated into thousands of songs: around her curls, the dusk whispered in voices of ghosts and men.

CHAPTER 70

Yen-yen

"Tesla! Finally!"

The new laboratory was completed. There were no fireworks. And yet, the news got around. Johnson was among the first to drop by. With great authority, he put on his pince-nez and looked at Tesla.

"What's going on?" he exhaled as he threw his gloves into his hat.

"Well . . ." Tesla sighed.

Last Tuesday, in the Palm Room at the Waldorf Astoria (where old women spoke in unusually low voices), he had met with Edward Dean Adams. The powerful man with a horseshoe of wrinkles on his forehead suggested they start a company with five hundred thousand dollars in capital. "It would exclusively deal with your research," Adams emphasized in a growling voice and knocked on the table.

"You turned it down?" Johnson could not believe his ears.

"I have a poor tolerance for anything institutionalized," Tesla explained. "I would die in there."

A strand of hair fell across Tesla's forehead. For a moment, the billiard player and gambler from Maribor and Graz was resurrected in him.

Unlike Rodin's *The Thinker*, Robert Underwood Johnson did not believe one had to frown in order to contemplate—or even be serious, for that matter. But now he frowned to avoid saying anything.

"Universities don't sell knowledge," Tesla explained. "What they sell is status disguised as knowledge. Institutions legitimize the right of mediocre minds to be boring. I can't breathe surrounded by empty frowns. I don't want to! You know for certain that creativity without play is . . ."

Robert did not say anything—it was useless to insist on giving advice to someone who considered you boring.

"... either a fraud or a mistake."

"Listen to me," the jittery pragmatist exploded. "The Wall Street sultan J. P. Morgan is behind Adams! You'd be backed by enormous might."

"Ideas come in a trickle when I work for money, but they gush forward like Niagara when I'm free."

"Free from the limitations of common sense?" Johnson asked. He took off his pince-nez with great composure. "You turned the money down. Have you read anything about Marconi?"

"Marconi is a lost sheep in a forest."

Johnson straightened his back. "That lost sheep now works with Lloyd's of London, one of the so-called institutions that you despise so much."

"But," Tesla added, "they don't know what frequency they're using. They don't understand the role the earth has in conveying messages."

"But they are trying . . ." Robert smacked his pince-nez against the table.

"Listen," Tesla said impatiently. "Thousands witnessed my wireless experiments in Saint Louis. I examined Marconi's patent. The signals are said to be in hertz. They are not. He's using my system."

Tesla remained a lifelong hostage to irresponsible wonder. The universe made decisions for him. And yet, he had two tiny antennae on his temples. Whenever they started to quiver, he sensed danger. The wave of hostility had not completely crested as yet, but he was already able to smell suspicion—the embryo of anxiety.

Johnson checked his eyeglasses to see if he had scratched the lenses. He blew on them, tested them with his fingernail, and then wiped them with the pad of his thumb.

"Sticking your head in the sand like an ostrich will finish you," he continued with more restraint. "Edison is ready to team up with Marconi. Mihajlo Pupin is on board too. Then Carl Hering from *Electric World*. Reginald Fessenden. Lewis Stillwell, Charles Steinmetz, Elihu Thomson."

Tesla still faced the window.

His new neighborhood, on the edge of Chinatown, was divided between noisy rum and quiet opium. Yen-yen, the hunger for opium, reigned there. Both deacons and professors of mathematics spent twenty cents a day to buy a grain of opium the size of a pea. A pale-faced man with baggy eyes once explained to him in front of his building, "A drunk will slit the throat of his own mother. An opium smoker—never!"

Johnson looked at the electricity poet's skinny shoulders and tried to figure out what the silence that surrounded him was turning into. "Don't flaunt your invincibility," he said to shatter Tesla's silent air of superiority. "That's stupid."

"I'm not as stupid"—Tesla turned around suddenly—"as you look to me."

Johnson gave a mirthless smile. He was convinced that, having turned Adams's money down, his friend made a rash and fatal mistake. Neither people nor competitors inhabited Tesla's world. He was blind to both reality and the danger of men.

Robert tried to bring him to his senses: "One should be wary of what one least fears."

Tesla looked through the window and retorted, "I can only echo Petrarch: I can't turn my mind into a commodity."

He looked at the broad street. Some Chinese called out to each other. In their mysterious world, the Chinese spoke like bells under the water. They sold sea monsters at their fish markets. They sang like mice being strangled, ate swallows' nests, opened restaurants and laundries, made paper birds, quoted Confucius: "Everything I see around me is Nothing that pretends to be Something, Emptiness that pretends to be Fullness, Dearth that pretends to be Affluence."

"It's useless to whisper to the deaf or wink at the blind," Robert concluded.

At that moment, Tesla looked at him with warmth. A softening smile started to form in a corner of his mouth. "Listen to me, Luka. This planet is packed with free energy. I'll transmit both energy and messages. All or nothing."

"But why not something?" Robert asked. "At this very moment," he continued in a tense voice, "the battle regarding the wireless transmission of messages is about to begin. That's as big as your war of currents against Edison. By the way, back then you had Westinghouse and his company behind you."

"What's the good of acting wisely if you feel bored all the time?" Tesla answered. "The wireless transmission of messages is miraculous to everyone. But I suspect that the images on one's retina—that is to say our dreams—could be recorded and transmitted by telephone. In my article for the *Electrical Review*, I hypothesized that energy possesses the qualities of both particles and matter. I'll transmit messages, images, and power that will merrily turn the flywheel on any engine anywhere in the world. I'll transmit melodies."

Still, between his delicate inner ear and his aching temples, Nikola sensed a wave of hostility. A hint of anxiety. It quivered in the air.

The journal *Public Opinion* wrote, "The facts regarding Tesla's discoveries are simple and few, while the fairy tales spun around them are extravagant and numerous."

Professor Pupin from Columbia University insisted that Tesla's inflated reputation was like an empty, echoing bucket: *"Dong! Dong! Dong!* That's precisely how it echoes," Pupin joked.

Professional journals became jittery. Tesla's colleagues—and especially his opponents—were annoyed by his propensity to live beyond his means and to take visions as if they were already completed projects.

He felt Robert's hand on his shoulder. "Remember what they told the crazy and brilliant Ludwig of Bavaria," Johnson said.

"What?" the inventor asked, removing the hand from his shoulder.

"There's no happiness outside the community of humans."

Tesla gave Robert a visionary look: "Keep this in mind, my friend—free energy!"

Tesla accompanied his words with an irresistible smile that simultaneously revealed an inspired weakness and a higher truth. The glare of that smile grew like the frequency of his oscillator. Tesla's face assumed a half-inspired, half-anguished expression that so annoyed Father. Did not Vivekananda say that the soul was a drunken monkey stung by a scorpion? In fear, Robert gazed at the luminous distances, gossamers, and fairy tales in Tesla's eyes. In addition to Tesla's irresistible charm, Robert also sensed a halo of eccentricity and solitude enveloping his friend and felt sorry for him.

There is no doubt that the reader has been worried about Tesla as well.

The smile continued to pour out. Every woman with an alcoholic husband knows that smile. It was the beatific smile of a hopeless gambler, the smile that made Tesla's mother give in.

CHAPTER 71

The Maelstrom

"Why don't you come visit me at my new laboratory?" Tesla asked.

For a moment, the red devil was confused. For no apparent reason, he was trying to straighten the brim of his white bowler hat. Then he made a quick decision and compressed his face with a frown: "It's a deal!"

The next day, in the new laboratory near Chinatown, Stanford White saw many machines he could not name. Among the flashes and pulsations, it was hard to tell what was animate and what was not. Pure spirits waited to be born from the magic coils. The coils licked each other with their white, snake-like tongues. Greek fire wrote demonic letters in the air. Touched by God's finger, things went up in flames. White inhaled the fresh electric air. He thought of the place as Tesla's blue cabaret where natural forces and bodiless spirits put on a show. It was as if the inventor were cracking his whip and taming them. The famous architect came out stunned.

"What about you—visiting me?" he stammered, barely standing on his wobbly legs.

Two weeks later, our summoner of the spirits, our Byronian mystical character, our Manfred visited the estate and its beautiful elms on Long Island. He threw his head back and looked at the sunlight filtering through the intertwining treetops. Red maple trees, full of chirping birds, livened up the park. Nikola and Stanford reclined in canvas chairs under an undulating elm. The breeze leafed through the treetop above them and—as it forgot the exact number of leaves—started to count again.

"They say that the maenads who tore Orpheus apart turned into trees," Stanford White began in a sweet voice. "As they started to grow roots, they went mad with fear."

The swirl of the treetops was fascinating.

An empty-eyed angel spewed a jet of water into a green pond. The garden, which simulated Eden, freed the two observers from all the worries of the world.

White was drinking. His burning hair was pulsating. He opened up to Tesla.

He said he hated puritans and moral reformers and insisted that they would be the end of him. With suppressed revulsion, he talked about his mother's favorite soprano, Jenny Lind, who refused to sing in France and Italy for "moral reasons."

"I'm a good father," he confided to Tesla. "But since I have no virtues, I accredit that solely to my instincts."

He introduced his good-looking son and his two ruthlessly ambitious daughters to Tesla. Their mother supervised their piano practices and Latin declensions. Betsy White was a straight-backed woman who was tired of her own impeccability. Her English face was a cross between a frog and a fairy. She possessed both intelligence and wit, but her real food was etiquette. Daily doses of humor and truth were spices too strong for her. She wore a constant smile on her handsome face, so it was impossible to tell when she was sick or tired or angry. Was the cruel wrinkle at the corner of her mouth a sign of defiance or of self-scorn? She never let on that she knew what everyone else in the city knew.

When she was alone, reality dissolved in her rosy prayers. "May he love me!" she prayed with passion. "May he love only me!"

Katharine Johnson touched Betsy White's back once and recoiled: how tense you are! The back that bore so many worries at times became stiff, and Betsy had to turn to a masseuse for healing.

Her husband dragged a flaming sixteenth-century shadow behind him.

"Benvenuto Cellini."

"The devil," they said.

Stanford White transported Venetian palaces to America. He acquired furniture, carpets, and tapestries for the American kings of steel and coal for whom Tesla's friend Stevan Prostran worked like a dog. In addition to the Long Island estate, he had one apartment on Gramercy Park, another on Garden Tower Suite, and yet another one on West Fifty-Fifth Street. White piled up books, bronze statues, paintings, and nude sculptures. Despite the envious talk, those were all originals. Behind the electric door that opened with a push of a button, mute greyhounds barked from Florentine tapestries.

White's red hair burned. He had a somewhat wooden way of speaking, his mustache twirling up like two little flames. He often finished his sentences with "and so . . ."

"Yes, the Brooklyn Bridge marked the beginning of the heroic age of New York," White said. "Yes, the tenements have been regulated, at least on paper. A minimum of oxygen should be provided to the windowless sections of the buildings. The air shafts in the middle are mandatory, although in a few months they turn into dumps and pigeon graveyards. Yes, there are fire prevention procedures, but people in tenements bind books, tan hides, and make hats. Yes, architecture inspired by Turkish, Russian, and Japanese influences is in vogue these days. It's true that I started with neo-Romantic Richardson and then admired Sullivan's ornamentation, but I still stick to Renaissance ideals. And so . . ."

White designed the Niagara dam draped in its gigantic curtains of foam. That was when he said to Tesla, "I'd love to do something else with you after Niagara."

For months, they only crossed paths briefly since both of them were busy. "Next week!" they kept saying.

When Sarah Bernhardt came to New York with her play *Izéil*, Johnson invited her for dinner. On that occasion, Tesla introduced White to Swami Vivekananda. "So you are introducing the devil to the angel?" White grinned.

"Next week, for sure!"

A few months went by.

Finally in August, they spent a weekend in Newport, Rhode Island. The coastline with sails looked like an impressionist painting. Castles competed for grandeur with one another. Marble shone in the middle of the lawn. Peacocks cautiously treaded across the grass. Swallows in tailcoats alighted under the eaves of the millionaire's mansion. Waves broke against black rocks in front of the Breakers.

"Seven million," Stanford White whispered out of the corner of his mouth, pretending to look at the ocean. "This pleasure cost Vanderbilt seven million dollars."

They observed the sunset from a wicker shelter in front of the house. At seven o'clock, a butler—as stiff as a Venetian doge—entreated them to come in. Two griffons bellowed at an urn adorned with some kind of wild cabbage in the hallway. White and Tesla changed at leisure. With their glowing plastrons, they descended under the painted sky in the atrium. Giant bronze candelabras with sixteen milky lamps hung there. The stairway was modeled on the one in the Paris Opera.

Rosy Numidian and green Italian marble decorated the walls. The fireplace in the library, which resembled Juliet's balcony, was brought over from a sixteenth-century French castle. The giant hearth oozed a chill. Boring old bronze statuettes despaired on the tables. Obsessive symmetry characterized the rooms, which were saturated with a delicate scent from an enormous quantity of flowers.

"I always used to eat before I got hungry," White confessed to Tesla. "I'm skinny because of tuberculosis."

The villa was built according to how the French from the Age of Empire imagined Renaissance style. Vanderbilt also had a famous French cook. The cook triumphantly closed his eyes and personally brought in the tray of veal.

Mmmmmm . . .

The Frenchman boasted that his country had a cheese for every day of the year, so he offered a certain number of them for the host and his guests to judge. Nikola remembered Madame Bauzain's words from Strasbourg: "When you feel like closing your eyes during a meal—that's great cuisine. The rest is nothing."

After dinner, they had a drink in the music room, in front of a blue fireplace made of Campagna marble. A labyrinth of mirrors that faced one another multiplied the ceiling lamps. At one time, three orchestras played in this summerhouse.

That evening, the famous villa was quiet.

Cornelius Vanderbilt II had recovered slowly from a stroke and spoke little. With his sideburns like dandelion fluff and his stony beard, he looked quietly deranged to Tesla. His brother William Kissam came on horseback from a nearby "summer hut" called Marblehouse, on which he had spent eleven million. They had brought electricity to the hut, he said, although that was a passing fad, ha, ha, ha. His hardheaded Alva stayed at the Chinese pavilion so that she could see the ocean. William Kissam's smile looked like a yawn, and he constantly turned the conversation to the *Defender*'s success at the American Cup.

"No, no, try one of these!" he insisted. The tips of the Cuban cigars began to glow. A sharp but delightful odor spread throughout the room. Smoke swirled around and lifted them like a magic carpet. There was the sound of bongos. Monkeys and birds started to chatter. A wistful guitar was heard. The pungent smell was a lure that drew them deeper into the labyrinth. Waves broke along sea baths for slaves in Havana. William Kissam pointed out that he enjoyed Havana more than Paris.

At the Breakers, Tesla slept on a short but beautiful Empire bed on which Napoléon's Josephine once spent a night. He felt anxious. To his surprise, he did not dream of Dane. He dreamed of the Maharaja of Kapurthala's mustache. In his dream, women looked at the mustache, lifted their hands to their brows, and fainted. Crickets went wild around midnight. Like the silver treetops, their songs spiraled higher and higher until they finally touched the starry constellations.

Tesla and Stanford met again the following Saturday, and the one after, and yet another one after that.

Unlike poor Szigety, White knew New York intimately. A number of chorus girls surrounded him at all times. Rumor had it that Carmensita stripped for him and that Little Egypt bared her indefatigable hips in his presence.

Stanford called himself "a philosopher of love" and "a tamer of women's hearts." Tears never entered that equation. He believed that the focus of a seducer's heart is never within himself, and that women found this attractive. When he spoke about women, he became enthusiastically stupid. His hair flamed brightly. He leaned in too close, and Tesla could smell whiskey on his breath.

"Seduction is mesmerizing," he confided in Tesla like Szigety had done long ago. "Love is electric. If I could add up all my orgasms, that would be like experiencing a thunderbolt. There would be nothing left of me. And so . . ."

"Isn't that a bit too much?" Tesla smiled his distant smile.

"Too much? Those words are meaningless," the redhead flared. "In the Gospel according to Luke, the Pharisees accused Christ of eating and drinking too much."

One Saturday in December 1897, when it was already dark by four o'clock, White took Tesla to Jimmy Breese's studio on West Sixteenth Street. The door handle was so audaciously twisted. Tesla readily grabbed it.

Breese wore a satyr mask made of silver. A servant played the double pipe. On the wall, three personified premonitions raised their hands toward the faint sunset. The columns were surrounded with gold mosaic tiles, like those in Monreale Cathedral in Palermo. The ceiling was built in the shape of a tear. Winded waiters from Delmonico's brought in a twenty-course dinner. All the guests ate with ivy wreaths around their heads.

"People have done weirder things to feel like something was happening," White whispered to Tesla.

The gentlemen judged the bare legs of the dancers. Over White's cigarette, smoke spelled out a signature in Arabic script. His lips moved without his knowing it. The orchestra of blind musicians sounded like a hurricane. They served a enormous "Jack Horner" pie. Like golden smoke, a cloud of canaries burst from the pie. Among the birds, Botticelli's nymph rose. Fair locks cascaded over her pear-like breasts. Those present at the birth of Venus dropped their jaws. The wreathed guests checked the holy sites on her body—her perfect waist, her mighty hips, her black triangle. The black triangle turned first into a Secession octopus and then transformed into a maelstrom and darkened the room, blinding the observers.

"Aaaaah!" the men groaned.

Tesla did not even blink.

White smiled. He tried to explain to the people around the table: "He's not from this planet."

CHAPTER 72

The Marriage of Dušan

All of New York wanted to see him married. To whom? To all of them? To Anna Morgan, the daughter of the sultan of Wall Street—among others—the tall girl with sharp knees. The slim inventor received countless invitations.

"Come and meet Miss Winslow. She can't believe I know you."

"Come and meet Miss Amasha Casner."

"Come to dinner. Miss Flora Dodge will be there as well as Margaret Merrington . . ."

He would come in, with his furtive gait, floppy-eared and grinning. He saw the ladies as a tangle of soft smiles, lace parasols, innocent low-cut dresses, provocative glances, swan-like necks, flounces, orchids and magnolias in their laps. They supposed they were, they knew they were as irresistible as Niagara. And yet . . .

All those games of neighing masculinity and meowing femininity bored him. Whenever someone mentioned *that* topic, Tesla's ironic mind heard the tense, resounding voice of a *guslar*—the singer of Serbian epic songs—chanting the lines from *The Marriage of Emperor Dušan:*

When will the emperor come to fetch his bride,
What season of the year will it be,
How many wedding guests will he bring . . .

The inventor gave a melodramatic answer to *those* questions: "Science is my only fiancée."

Whatever his sexuality potentially targeted, he did not desire to realize it. Scientific discovery was the highest degree of excitement there was—it was a kiss from God. In his laboratory, Tesla's personality faded away and a blind force, like fire, took its place. Compared to that, all other forms of excitement were nothing.

People did not believe it.

"That's my *higher love*," he added.

People winked, whispered, and reproached him. "If I speak in the tongues of men and of angels but do not have love, I am only a noisy gong or a clanging cymbal," they said.

The eyebrows of the eternal bridegroom lifted toward the ceiling with the tobacco smoke. People could not let it go—they kept asking *those questions* over and over.

He put on a show for the newspapermen: "At times, it seems to me that my celibacy is too much of a sacrifice for my work." Then he suddenly changed his story and patiently answered their questions. "Do I believe in marriage? For an artist—yes! For a writer—yes! But for an inventor—no. His is too intense a nature, with so much in it of a wild, passionate quality."

De Quincey wrote about the abyss of divine joy that yawned within him. Tesla suffered his deliriums of joy in solitude. For years, he lived in a state of almost uninterrupted bliss. Under his stiff collar, he felt passion strong enough to move mountains.

"Ever since a snowball I threw in my childhood caused an avalanche, I've been engaged to a force that, in an instant, changes the meaning of everything," he whispered in his stiff collar. "In comparison, all human institutions are just trifles."

He could not stand to look at jewelry. He would vomit if he had to touch a woman's hair. He refused "to join forces" with Edward Dean Adams, with institutions, with members of the fairer sex. In general, he refused to bow to the human condition and human criteria.

"Don't Achilles and Prince Marko stand apart from the community of humans?" he asked Stanford White. A Pullman car with encrusted ornaments on the walls was taking them to Niagara Falls. Lightning flickered outside.

"Look!" Tesla exclaimed as he touched the windowpane with his index finger. In a field, some cows frolicked before the storm and began jumping around like dogs. Stanford didn't hear him. "Send me a different waiter. Remove this clown-face!" he yelled.

White's red hair flamed. His relentless hand kept pouring. He reminded Tesla that Zeus enjoyed making love to Hercules's mother so much that he stopped the constellations from revolving a few times. Like ancient Assyrians, White believed that the sun god was the one who impregnated all women while men were just the tool. Like Zeus, he wanted to be a swan, a bull, and the shower of gold.

"Don't worry," the drunken architect mumbled. "I'll make love for you."

That's all well and good, Tesla thought. *But where does that restless watery look in your eyes come from?*

White dozed off and dreamed of embracing necks and waists. It grew dark. A fire burned somewhere in the field, and bright sparks shot into the sky. The train roared like a dragon, curled its tail, and sped into the wide, wide world. And yet again—like a long time ago— the rails did not seem to exist but somehow materialized right in front of the locomotive.

In the morning in Buffalo, the inventor felt stiff while his architect felt hungover.

A solemn crowd stood dwarfed by Tesla's turbines. From the ceremonial speeches, Tesla realized that everything had changed since Kemmler's execution. In the American mind, alternating current had transformed from the devil to an angel.

Nikola Tesla delivered a conventional speech. Halfway through, his blood turned cold. All of a sudden, he felt jealous of the dead peasant boy and guilty of the blessings he snatched for himself. Dane never married. He would not marry either. He barely kept himself from saying, "I'm bad enough. It's cruel to make me worse."

After the official speeches, the mayor grabbed Tesla and White by their arms and suggested they embark on the tour boat *Lady of the Mist* and get closer to the monstrous waterfall from below. Screaming at the top of his lungs, the mayor whispered to Tesla that most American newlyweds came here on their honeymoon. Tesla was truly excited. He stared at the rustling curtain until he forgot what he was looking at.

"This is bigger than anything else. This is destiny."

Rainbows arched everywhere in the enveloping mist. Silky water flashed right on the edge before it fell over. Falling, it turned white. Then it became a cloud. The wind blew the cloud upward and spread coolness. Despite their raincoats, Tesla's, White's, and the mayor's faces were wet. *This* moved his turbines. It reminded him once more of how that small snowball, thrown with a casual movement of his hand, tore out boulders and swept down pines as if they were matchsticks, became pure force, and grew as huge as destiny. The feeling of greatness and the deafening roar completely permeated him.

Indians sacrificed maidens to these curtains made of foam.

Only this boundless coolness finally rejuvenated him and washed the soot of the burned laboratory from his soul. His eyes were full of tears while his soul merged with the unleashed natural force. Yes, the inventor's nature was wild and passionate. The waterfall completely outshouted him. Tesla's lips moved silently. At his secret wedding with the measureless force, he softly repeated:

"I do."

CHAPTER 73

The War

It started with an explosion.

"War with Spain!" paperboys screamed.

Hearst's newspapers were selling the war. The war was selling the newspapers.

Cheeks flushed. Fingers twirled mustaches. People tossed their straw hats into the air. Like children, people were thrilled by the upcoming slaughter. Theodore Roosevelt bared his teeth beneath his walrus mustache and gathered his Rough Riders.

"Everyone talks about the Philippines," satirists smirked, "although until recently they didn't know if it's a country or canned goods."

On the wave of the war fever, backed by the music of John Philip Sousa—*ta, ta, ta, dum, dum, ta, ta, ta, ta*—the Electrical Exhibition had its gala opening at Madison Square Garden. Stanford White organized the special event ("and so . . . ," he concluded at the end of his short speech). With his customary peevishness, Garret Hobart, the vice president of the United States, opened the event.

It started with an explosion: Marconi's assistant Thomas Edison Jr. blew up the warehouse where he kept their surplus fireworks.

"Didn't I tell you that they don't know how to adjust frequencies." Tesla tried to suppress the triumph in his voice.

Then he stood in front of the audience under the amazing clouds of May. All around him was a wall of bowler hats and blinding collars. Gentlemen fended off all the dilemmas with their ties. They were all brothers in mustaches. A gaggle of hygienic old women was there as well. Some of them blinked innocently. Some cleared their throats with dissatisfaction. Two bright-eyed ladies, corseted like wasps, looked at him from under their enormous hovering hats. All faces glowed with bloodthirsty curiosity.

A faint smile started to form at the corner of Tesla's mouth. His smiling eyes gave the impression of heightened alertness. His long thumb—the sign of great intelligence—clutched a chrome box with a wire sticking out of it.

The thumb pressed a button.

The boat in the central pond started to move.

It did what it had to do.

Just like him.

Tesla stopped it with a push of the button.

With his wireless commands, he turned on the boat's lights from a distance.

He "asked the boat some questions" and the remote-controlled vessel responded with its moves.

Ah!

Another thing without a name appeared in the world.

The first robot!

The people refused to believe their eyes.

"What do you call this?" children asked their parents, turning their heads away from the pond.

"Teleautomaton."

Across the boundaries of expectation, the audience's perception, so to speak, tumbled into a void.

That was the fall of the tree in the forest with no one to hear.

Katharine Johnson put her lips against her husband's hairy ear and whispered bitterly:

"No one saw it!"

Born

Tesla left Madison Square Garden under the foaming clouds of May.

How is it possible they didn't see it? he wondered as he strolled aimlessly around Lower West Manhattan.

271

"No law says that those who speak must be heard," Milutin Tesla repeated in his ear.

The criminals he used to know, the terrifying Whyos, had all been killed or arrested. The Hudson Dusters, fierce cocaine addicts, replaced them on the corners of Greenwich Village. The Dusters were friends with city bohemians. Both groups knew of Tesla. Leaning against his long finger, he watched them with quiet irony from the pages of newspapers.

"Look at 'im," one of them remarked as the long-legged scientist passed by. "Like a bizarre animal."

"He looks kind of down. I'd like to give 'im some cocaine," the other grinned.

"Good luck with that, buddy," another one said. "He was born on cocaine."

CHAPTER 74

The Astoria

In June, Tesla was invited once more to the town of palaces and lawns on the rocky shores of Rhode Island.

"Hail, white masts! Hail, blue sky!"

This time it was John Jacob Astor IV who invited him to Newport for sailing. Tesla arrived in front of Astor's marble summer cottage hugging the world's largest bouquet of roses. Katharine had written to remind him not to forget his real friends while rubbing shoulders with millionaires.

The coastline shimmered.

The frosted surface of the glass door seemed to melt, revealing two symmetrical peacocks.

"May the universe hold no limitations for you," Tesla greeted Astor jokingly.

"May no limitations be imposed on your universe," Astor responded in kind.

The millionaire's face came straight from a herbarium. His smile was as cold as soup in an orphanage.

"What's in those eyes—melancholy, peevishness, or simply emptiness?" The guest could not decide. He could not figure out if personality still existed at such a high level of acting a part. With his ascetic fingers, Tesla picked up Astor's book, *A Journey in Other Worlds*, from the table and complimented the author.

Astor smiled and made the mistake of asking his guest what he had been working on lately. Tesla embarked on a lengthy discourse about guided torpedoes and other teleautomatons. He spoke the way Goethe would have spoken had he somehow turned into a traveling salesman.

Tesla's wounded and flaming eyes anticipated his words: Nietzsche, Schopenhauer, Vivekananda. The life principle, apparent in the formation of crystals, is operative in people. Alternative sources of energy! The concept of parallel universes! The possibility of surviving without food in the future!

"If the earth were exposed to periodical vibrations, it would split in half, like an apple," the lanky inventor stared into Ava Astor's eyes and smiled ambiguously. "The trick is to be in phase with the world's vibrations and not to oscillate against them."

His soul intuitively licked her soul.

Ava Astor, née Shippen Willing, was considered the most beautiful woman in America. She reminded Tesla so much of Salome that he feared she might offer him John the Baptist's head on a platter. Her elongated eyes addled men with their green color and unblinking, steady gaze.

In her, Katharine Johnson saw only "an enormous quantity of arrogant emptiness." Men usually saw the narrow waist, the fierce curvature of her hips, and the balcony-like bust. "She's not a woman—she's a tiger," Stanford White mumbled.

Despite Tesla's superhuman politeness, the temptress sensed his absentmindedness. She developed an interest in him. Ava Astor looked into his eyes without blinking and asked him without smiling, "Why do they attack you in the newspapers?"

"Because my inventions threaten many established industries."

At these words, John Jacob smiled with the liveliness of a Madame Tussaud's figure. To the befuddled Tesla it seemed that Astor was saving his energy for the afterlife.

Ahem . . .

The war was the topic of all topics. Johnson introduced Tesla to the war hero Richard Hobson, whose cheeks twittering girls kissed at all public events. John Jacob let the military use his yacht the *Nourmahal* for the war.

The inventor cleared his throat and mentioned that he had also offered the military the use of his—

"What?" Ava asked.

"Guided torpedoes and wireless transmission of messages."

The millionaire became interested. "So what happened?"

"I called an official in Washington to talk about practical applications of these inventions," Tesla said. "The secretary of the navy turned my proposal down because he was afraid of 'sparks that were bound to fly everywhere.' Where did he see any sparks? Afterward, a group of officers with sideburns, the straightest backs possible, and the clearest eyes in the world came to see me. They moved to and fro in my laboratory like automatons for a couple of hours."

"So what happened?" Ava Astor asked.

"After two long hours of conversation, it became clear to me that intelligence and vision do not abide in deep voices, proud straight backs, and male beauty.

"In a word: in the war with Spain, the navy is using balloons tethered to ships with telegraph lines."

Ava Astor laughed for the first time in Tesla's presence, releasing a shrill, unpleasant sound, similar to a peacock's scream.

"That's enough to turn one's hair gray," the inventor said, laughing in agreement. "The balloons make easy targets, but the soldiers have to carry out their orders—that's all there is to it."

The days with the wind in his hair were replaced by business meetings in New York. Astor's eyes said "we'll wait" and "we'll see." Tesla realized that the millionaire—just like his former professor Pöschl—lacked a golden ball showing him direction and blindly felt his way through life. However, Astor was slowly warming up to the idea of Tesla's fluorescent lights.

"My lamps will last forever," the tireless inventor insisted, his hair sleekly brushed back. "They emit light five thousand times stronger than the ones we use now . . ."

During those conversations, Astor's blasé yet anxious stare softened a bit. "May the universe hold no limitations for you," he exclaimed at the end of their negotiations.

"May no limitations be imposed on your universe," Tesla chimed.

They signed the contract in the middle of the war's excitement. Astor became a board member of Tesla's company. Tesla received one hundred thousand dollars. The entrance to the world's most glamorous hotel materialized before him out of the blue. With a tiny shiver of pleasure, Tesla moved into the Waldorf Astoria. His room number—two hundred and seven—was divisible by three. The maid always left eighteen towels in his room. He dined at eighteen hours at a table with eighteen cloth napkins.

He lived a life divisible by three.

The wrought iron eaves above the entrance resembled a railway station. The first floor windows were covered with round double cloth awnings. Mornings smelled of fine soaps. It was so quiet that he felt he was observing things through a magnifying glass. One could skate across the marble floors.

Here at the Waldorf people came to be seen.

He lived there.

"Kisses don't last long. Culinary art does," Oscar of the Waldorf hummed as he arranged his dishes between glass pedestals topped with fruit and pyramids made of flowers.

The soundless elevator turned Tesla's stomach upside down and lifted him to the top of the castle where his rooms were. Human sight could not measure the depth of the hallways. Next to each column stood a uniformed boy with a gold-fringed hat on his head. The Ming dynasty vases were taller than those patient boys. Restrooms smelled of jasmine. Even though Stanford White did not provide all the furniture, it looked as if he did. Orchids were moved away from the windows so that the light would not hurt them.

"How are you doing in Versailles?" Johnson wanted to know.

CHAPTER 75

We Won't

A week after he moved to the Waldorf Astoria, Tesla invited his faithful assistant Scherff for a visit. With his disheveled hair, Scherff looked like a deer that had strayed into the Palm Room.

The head waiter came up holding his nose as high as a Lipizzaner stallion. He turned toward Scherff, whose outfit puzzled him.

"May I help you . . ."

The movement of Tesla's hand was quick and commanding.

The waiter did not know what to do, so he disappeared.

Scherff was somewhat squarely built. Many of those who could not remember his name called him Mr. Mustache. He kept repeating himself because he thought people did not understand what he was saying. After his eyes grew weak, he bought glasses with the ugliest frames possible.

"Are those frames made of horses' hooves?" White mocked.

Tesla defended him: "Scherff's hair is gray. His eyes are brown. But his hands and heart are made of pure gold."

With a lot of tact, Tesla insinuated to Scherff that there were fine and not-so-fine items of clothing to wear. To no avail. Just like treason, fashion was an incomprehensible concept to the honest mechanic.

Scherff loved heavy, roughly knitted sweaters. His footwear looked like it came from an army surplus store. His boots sank into the thick carpet of the Astoria up to the ankles. The good mechanic did not know whether he was in a church or a bar. He kept turning his head around in awe. He had difficulty deciding what to order. He read the menu carefully, narrowed it down to three dishes, and then started to peruse it again.

To save time, Tesla ordered Oscar's veal and a Waldorf salad for him. They split half a bottle of wine. After the meal, the honest mechanic's mood lightened.

"It seems to me," he stammered, "that now we're going to settle down in New York and get rich on lightbulbs and oscillators."

"We won't," the inventor responded.

Scherff's face collapsed.

"It seems to me . . . ," he began.

Tesla looked at him warmly and even put his hand on his shoulder:

"The laboratory on Houston Street is too small and there's always the risk of fire and spies. That's why I'll journey to the wilderness, east of the sun and west of the moon. To the place where thunderbolts crack more than anywhere else in the world.

"I'll work with millions of volts, with still unnamed phenomena.

"Without human guidance.

"Without a precedent.

"As for you, please stay here and make sure everything runs smoothly on Houston Street."

"It seems to me . . . ," the honest Scherff mumbled.

CHAPTER 76

Without Soiling Them

*The range of vapor to the southward had arisen prodigiously in
the horizon, and began to assume more distinctness of form.
I can liken it to nothing but a limitless cataract, rolling silently into the
sea from some immense and far-distant rampart in the heaven.*
Edgar Allan Poe, *The Narrative of Arthur Gordon Pym of Nantucket*

He fell asleep and woke up on the train. While riding, he experienced the greatness of this land and the way she breathed. "Europe has cathedrals. America has Holy Nature," the quiet and noble John Muir (another famous person out of Johnson's top hat) used to tell him.

Tesla passed through godforsaken towns with lanes of trees and a cat in each window, where the wheels on coaches turned backward. From those towns, the train rushed toward America's horizon.

"I'm inviting you to a monthlong adoration of Nature," Muir told him. "It won't cost you a thing except your time, and even that's nothing because most of the time you'll dwell in eternity."

During his eternal train trip, Tesla decided to accept Muir's invitation. He looked through the window and saw a multitude of black birds scattered across the mountain. He remembered the lecture titled On the Damage That Crows Do to Crops from his childhood with a smile. The whistle of the engine startled him. It spiraled up through the magnificent landscape.

"Colorado Springs!" the stationmaster announced through his nose.

"Why have you come to Colorado?" a newspaper reporter took out a notebook from the pocket of his plaid jacket.

By the reception desk of the Alta Vista Hotel, Tesla shook hands with a man of few words, the contractor Joseph Dozier. Before he became a contractor, Dozier was a common laborer. "I was buying my boss the newspaper every morning for ten years," he complained, scratching himself with fingernails suitable for woodcarving and strangling bears. "He didn't pay once. And I had six kids to support."

The man of few words agreed to build a laboratory for Tesla. Dozier raised his palms with an expression on his face as if the job was already done and forgotten.

Tesla arrived at Knob Hill together with the first workers.

"Don't the words *patience* and *pain* come from the same root in Latin?" he muttered to himself.

If asked to define what a genius was, his answer would have been—impatience. In the following months, a wooden structure grew in the middle of nowhere. A steel tower rose from the roof of a barn. A mast spiked up from the tower.

In the strangest barn in the world, Tesla and his young assistant Fritz Lowenstein shouted to each other in German.

"Faster!" Tesla yelled at Lowenstein just like Ferenc Puskás used to yell at him.

In the middle of the barn, they installed an enormous coil, nicknamed "Gorgon." They put another coil nearby, which was precisely set to the electrical vibrations of the first one. As always, Tesla's apparatuses were shipped to him in magician's crates. It seemed to Tesla that the last pieces of his equipment arrived too slowly. Finally, a pair of oxen pulling a carriage brought the transmitter that resembled a spider's web. When they assembled it, they put a sign in front of the log barn:

"Extreme danger! Keep out!"

Surprised, Dozier concluded, "We're done."

The first person Tesla thought of in his newly finished barn was John Muir. The bright-eyed Scot looked like the Irish magical imp, the leprechaun, or like an ancient Serbian elf with a beard that reached his waist. Muir went blind at a young age. When he regained his sight, he swore he would never take for granted "God's smile" reflected in nature. In the spectacular environment of Colorado Springs, Tesla saw the world through Muir's eyes. Just like at Niagara, he sank into the magnificence of nature and merged with it. Did not Saint Bernard of Clairvaux say that one can learn more from the woods than from books?

The solitude thrust upon him long ago started to agree with Tesla. Most people were too slow for him. He felt fine without them.

Not before spring would he allow himself a game of whist at the local El Paso Club.

"We live in the oddest place in the world," Jeremiah Falconer, the fat president of the club, bragged. "Many come to Colorado Springs for their health, but only bachelors"—he drew a line along the threshold of the club—"enter *here*."

There was a shadow under the learned treasurer's eyes.

The secretary with a goiter handed him a business card the size of an opera program. It bore the inscription: *John "Duck" Harris: I believe in peace, progress, and brotherhood of all the people in the world.* Below it was a picture of the smiling "Duck" with his sideburns and mouth full of large teeth. The sworn misogynist warned Tesla: "You'll see how mountain ranges and other giant things will look dwarfed in this place."

"On the contrary, people far away will seemingly acquire gigantic proportions," Falconer rasped.

"The light and the laws of optics play games with our eyes here," the treasurer added in a dull, onanistic voice.

"You'll see." Falconer put down an empty glass of claret. "Colorado Springs is a different world."

As a matter of fact, the clarity of the atmosphere intoxicated Tesla. He had never seen such light. The distant lamps at the bottom of the mountains shone as clearly as if they were just a few blocks away. Sound spread unusually far, especially high-pitched voices. As in Budapest long before, Tesla heard bells ringing in far-off towns right in his head. On Knob Hill, the squealing of wheels and people's voices from the town seemed to be right outside his door.

"I ascribe this to the high level of electricity in the air," he explained to his faithful Lowenstein. "Electricity purifies and amplifies everything."

"Can you believe that the best photographs of the snowy mountain peaks were taken in moonlight?" the learned bachelors from the El Paso Club asked him.

In moonlight, the inky shadows of the clouds rushed silently across the prairie. One evening, Tesla recognized Joseph Dozier's melancholy face from a quarter mile away.

"How are you?" Tesla took his hat off to him.

Dozier pointed his finger toward the sky: "Huh! The moon! The stars! Huh?!"

Did not Tesla's father, Milutin, once see *a waterfall of sparks that appeared both distant and yet so close he could touch it with his hand? The sparkling waterfall left blue tracers behind and "paled the stars."*

Colorado Springs was a beautiful phenomenon every day. Here more shooting stars glided across the firmament than there were wishes to make. Once he saw a star explode and bloom in the sky. "Is this the true face of the world?" Tesla shook in hope. Goose-bumpy intuition tickled the marrow of his bones.

Here he embarked on something truly cosmic and—for the first time in his life—was able to work as hard as he possibly could.

Each morning was worth waking up to. As soon as Helios moved his coach, parts of the sky would turn the color of blood. Mountaintops became furnace doors gushing out molten ore. Clouds formed and dissipated quickly. Huge masses of something resembling snow floated through the air.

One evening, he wrote in his diary:

The whiteness and cleanliness of the clouds is such that nothing, not even an angel, can touch them without soiling them.

The hovering icebergs looked so solid it was hard to believe they were made of vapor. It was impossible to distinguish the celestial mountain ranges from the real ones. Tesla wrote to Robert and Katharine that he had seen an ocean with deep green, dark blue, and black waters in the sky more than once. Green islands, shiny icebergs, sailboats, and even steamships were strewn across the ocean, and they were not less real because they were made of glittering mist. Another time he saw something like heavenly Switzerland.

John Ruskin said that he poured clouds into bottles, like his father, the wine merchant, used to do with sherry. Clouds became Tesla's exterior soul. He categorized them with love:

The red ones, the white ones, those that look like enormous nuggets of gold, the clouds that contain a bit of copper, and those blinding like the sun itself.

CHAPTER 77

The Gorgon's Hair

A glowing stinger flashed in the distance. It exposed the shining fabric of the sky, woven of lightning and metals. For a second, Fritz Lowenstein appeared in the angelic world, but another thunderbolt spiked him back into the darkness.

"Forty-eight point five seconds exactly!" Manfred noted in a ringing voice while everything around them shook, rattled, and shivered. The seismic wave he correctly anticipated almost ripped the laboratory off its foundation.

"Pssst!" Tesla hissed at Lowenstein.

The underground reverberation of the thunder disappeared and came back. As pale as a jasmine flower, with his hair sleekly brushed back, our cosmic spy listened to how *that* abated and then stirred again. Two hundred miles away, he could still hear the oscillations.

"That's important, that's very important . . . ," he whispered.

"*Bang!* Dang!" His assistant tripped over a broom at the other end of the laboratory.

"Fritz! Be quiet . . ."

Lowenstein shivered whenever he as much as brushed Tesla with his elbow. He constantly apologized, felt chilled, and hunched his shoulders around Tesla. His thinning hair looked more like down than hair. The young man's skin was as delicate as an eyelid. He saw Tesla—who considered clumsiness to be rude—as divine. Finally, when Lowenstein ignored Tesla's *pssst* too many times, his boss sent him back to New York.

"He's not good to the ones who love him," the young German complained to Scherff.

Scherff looked at him through his monstrous glasses behind which floated the eyes of a giant emotionless squid.

The man with dangerous-looking eyes, Koloman Czitó, replaced Lowenstein as Tesla's assistant. He brought a letter from the Lighthouse Board in Washington in which they informed Tesla that they would much rather sign a contract regarding wireless communication with an American than with Marconi. Tesla was already convinced that doing business with the military was like dealing with fools. He responded with demonic pride:

> Gentlemen, no matter how much I appreciate your proposition, if I want to remain true to myself, I must refuse any preferential treatment, especially if you compare me to those who follow in my footsteps. I am completely indifferent to any financial gains I could make based on such an advantage.

What was it Johnson told him? "There's no happiness outside the community of humans?" Ha!

Non serviam!

They did not call him Manfred in Prague for nothing. That same evening he proudly wrote in a letter to Johnson, "I am ready to produce effects bigger than any effects *ever* produced by a human factor."

The next morning, Manfred turned his mighty machines on for the first time. The Gorgon flamed with all of her bright hair. Tesla pumped electricity hundreds of times stronger than lightning into the ground. The ground shivered slightly. The vibrations spread over the entire planet in ever widening circles and formed a bow on the opposite end—right between the French islands of Amsterdam and Saint Paul.

The earth was a huge cat.

Now he knew who was rubbing it.

The earth purred.

The wave turned into an echo, which produced the same effect in Colorado Springs. As he kept pumping in more electricity, the resonance grew like the snowball he made in his childhood. In theory, that "electric avalanche" could destroy the planet.

Under the sublimely clear skies his mighty machinery registered three signals from Mars. On the planet Colorado Springs, Tesla flew into the depths of cosmic reverberations. Taking each breath was a miracle. He was steeped in a remorseless natural force. There was no going back—he was wedded to it. He had to deal with phenomena as big as death.

John Muir was far away. Saint Bernard of Clairvaux was dead. Who else could understand his ideas that ripened in the wilderness? Did not Mara tell the Buddha: Don't even try to announce it! And yet . . . Letters flew to New York and letters flew back from New York.

"Imagine spherical lightning that the wind blows across the nocturnal wasteland," the hermit who went wild wrote to his urban friends. "Imagine a race of spirits through the night! Such lightning that resemble tumbleweeds are naturally created here in the prairie. Something similar was released during my experiments—it snapped my mast, and damaged some of my equipment. The Gorgon's hair hissed around me, and I had to roll across the ground."

"I've had wonderful experiences here," the bandaged Tesla wrote to Johnson. "I was taming a wild cat, so I turned into a mass of bloody scratches."

He dropped the pen that wanted to embellish the story.

"The Furies!" he whispered in disgust. "The Furies!"

He grabbed the disobedient pen again. He subdued it and continued to write. "The wireless transfer of messages, images, sounds and—most importantly—energy will be possible," he promised in the letter to somebody who could not understand him. "I personally tested the transfer of energy at a distance of twenty-six miles. Trust me, Robert, with a 3000 HP pumping oscillator, I could light up a lightbulb anywhere on earth."

CHAPTER 78

Zeus Commands the Thunderbolt

Suddenly there came from heaven a sound as of a violent wind,
which filled the entire house in which they were sitting;
And there appeared to them tongues as of fire; these separated
and came to rest on the head of each of them.
They were all filled with the Holy Spirit.
The Acts of the Apostles 2:2–4

"Zeus creates lightning—people don't," Koloman Czitó murmured to himself. The assistant stood with his legs apart and furtively observed his boss. Although he was not exactly a hunchback like Igor from Edison's circus tent, the Hungarian was still somewhat stooped.

"When the gush of magnetic energy hits the Gorgon," Tesla shouted, "the coil will create an avalanche that will raise the electrical potential of the earth. Do you see? Electricity will erupt back from the ground. See?" he snarled. "Our mast will fire up thunderbolts."

"Zeus commands the thunderbolt," Czitó whimpered.

The assistant realized that Tesla was ready to risk his own life using the highest voltage ever produced. Czitó too was playing Russian roulette since he, not Tesla, operated the switch that controlled the flow of electricity from the power plant.

"When I give you the sign, pull the lever," Tesla ordered with suicidal resolve.

He found a spot from which he could see through the open roof.

"Now!"

Czitó jerked the lever. A swarm of electrical snakes covered the coil. A hissing sound spread throughout the room.

"It works," Tesla's voice thundered. "Do it again!"

The fairy's hair got entangled on the coil once more. The laboratory turned blue and started to crackle. A dull boom reported from the mast.

"I'm going to go outside and look at the mast," Tesla was merciless. "I want you to pull the lever and hold it till I say so."

Swaying on his thick rubber-soled shoes, Manfred stepped out of the barn.

"Pull the lever!"

Czitó pushed the lever and held it with his extended arm, waiting for the signal to jerk it back.

A few seconds passed. The sorcerer and his apprentice were still alive. Nothing smelled burned. Like a gold coin, a whole wondrous minute fell with a clink on the stone floor. Then came the real awakening of the Furies. Tesla crossed the point of no return as he launched into the shoreless void of a new phenomenon. Inside, the crackling of the Gorgon's hair rose to a crescendo. Outside, a single thread of lightning wriggled off the mast. Then a second one, a third, a fourth. Thunder exploded and Tesla flinched against his will. Dear Mother! Thunder exploded again. He ducked as it cracked once more. The noise from the mast sounded like a rifle, then like a cannon—and soon became even louder until it seemed as though they were in the middle of the Battle of Austerlitz. The building was a straw in a flashing whirlwind.

"The Furies," the first human thunder maker whispered vengefully. "The Furies!"

Spectral blue light appeared in the barn. A mass of live electrical hair slithered around the coils. Everything in the building spewed needles of light. A pandemonium of sounds broke free. There was a stench of sulfur. Czitó clinched his jaw and broke a tooth as he tried to suppress the trembling in his body, lest he might let go. His left arm shook so much he was not able to cross himself. In the blue shimmer that completely surrounded him, he almost expected to see the spirits of his late parents. He felt sparks popping painfully from his fingers. He felt that his blood would gush out from under his nails.

The electrical maelstrom threatened to destroy the barn.

Nikola Tesla stood outside, neatly dressed, with his laced high-top shoes and bowler hat. The skies screamed and the earth responded. A new Mephistopheles grew taller under the night sky starched by lightning. Sparks flew around the rubber soles of his shoes. The awakened earth had a message for him. The awakened earth sparked all around him.

Lightning became thicker and brighter, clearer and bluer. Sparks as big as a fist shot into the sky. Sea snakes wriggled upward, eighty, then one hundred and twenty feet above the ground. The rumbling echoed for miles. With his face alternating from black to silver, the Victorian thunder maker in his Prince Albert coat surveyed them. He *was* the light—a flashing, impersonal force.

"How long has this been going on?" Czitó trembled. "This is forbidden! A mortal shouldn't do this!"

In the blink of an eye, everything went dead.

Everything.

"Czitó, did you pull the lever?" Tesla lunged at him.

The Hungarian looked at him with his bloodshot eyes, hunched like a bull with *banderillas* sticking in his back.

"No!" he gasped.

"Call the power plant. They mustn't do this to me. They mustn't cut me off."

"What are you talking about?" a deranged voice shouted on the phone when Czitó called. "You caused a short circuit. Our generator is on fire."

CHAPTER 79

Tesla Toasts the Twentieth Century

After which time the sun's bright light will have ceased to shine,
and its life-giving heat will have ebbed away, and our own earth
will be a lump of ice, hurrying on through the eternal night...
Meanwhile, the cheering lights of science and art,
ever increasing in intensity, illuminate our path.

Nikola Tesla in the *Century* (1900)

After the silent planet of Colorado Springs, Tesla landed on clamorous Broadway.

Black engines pulled elevated trains. Tourists read *A Guide for the Perplexed.*

Dr. F. Finch Strong was trying to convince mankind that electricity made the old smarter and the stupid younger.

Ah! A new century was on its way.

Traveling troupes visited theaters in godforsaken towns, bringing a thing unheard of: a gramophone!

Audiences applauded the ghostly singers.

Freedom, Wisdom, World's Exposition, and America—everything had its own Muse and each Muse had its buxom personification.

"Laws are becoming more just," visionaries insisted. "Rulers more humane; music is becoming sweeter and books wiser and the individual heart is becoming at once more just and more gentle."

The severed heads of the Boxers hung on the walls of Hunan. Water buffalo sniffed the dead in the rice fields of the Philippines.

"Everyone feels four hundred times bigger," Tesla's friend, the railroad magnate and senator Chauncey Depew, crowed.

Did not Gargantua write Pantagruel that their time was better than all previous ones put together?

A lamp in Scofield, Utah, transformed a mine into a fiery tornado. The miners were blasted from the shaft as if fired from a cannon.

Ah! A new century was on its way.

Immigrants disembarked from sad ships and filled tenements. The next day they went to moving picture arcades to see the sixteen-second-long kiss along with a train entering a station and some women leaving a factory. All of a sudden, miracles that were thousands of miles away started to happen right before their eyes.

In towns across America, the summer was hot. Theodore Roosevelt's eyeglasses gleamed as he grinned from train windows during the election year.

Standing next to her husband, President McKinley's fragile wife, Ida, looked like a bird on the back of a buffalo.

Publications were adorned with the pictures of the independent yet melancholy Gibson Girl.

A new century was on its way.

Truth-loving illustrations withdrew from newspapers under the onslaught of lying photographs. In the *Century* article "The Problem of Increasing Human Energy," Tesla was calmly reading in Colorado Springs while—next to him—lightning flew from one coil to the other.

Tesla the thunder maker toasted a lot. He toasted the new century at the Johnsons', at Delmonico's, at the Waldorf, at Stanford White's.

A new century was on its way.

He toasted with Ava and Colonel Astor.

Ten, nine, eight, seven . . .

He toasted with the Vanderbilts. He toasted as the masks surrounded him.

A new century was on its way. *Six, five, four . . .* People anticipated it with fear and excitement. *Three, two, one . . .*

At that moving moment, Mark Twain turned his back on thundering fireworks. He extinguished his corncob pipe and declared, "To this century—I don't belong."

Purple, red, and blue stars unlocked the sky.

Willows made of light, dazzling dandelion fluff, red and white sparks, smoke and explosions multiplied above their heads.

Like the ancient Chinese, Tesla believed that fireworks wake up the gods.

But which ones?

PART III

The New Century

CHAPTER 80

The Fearsome Nose

That's not a nose! That's a monument!
Edmond Rostand

He pulled his gloves off with his teeth, shook his umbrella, and put it into the elephant's foot. He held on to the gloves and hat because it was an official visit. In a desperate whisper, he told himself:

"Don't look at the nose."

Rumor had it that Morgan lived in a building that was the Milan Cathedral on the outside and the Library of Babel on the inside. The entire manor was laughing with the glitters of the silver plates. Maids polished them, readying them for Christmas. Tesla shook the snow from the folds of his overcoat. Snow flurried outside, but inside black peacocks strutted throughout the marble hall.

Don't touch your face, the inner adviser warned him. *Blink only when necessary. Breathe slowly.*

In the fountain, black fish swirled their fins like smoke. A mosaic goddess kissed his feet in the octagonal entryway. A servant discreetly pointed him toward the salon.

When he closed the door, his shoes sank into the carpet. He felt claustrophobia and the fear of heights at the same time.

"Don't look at the nose," he pleaded with himself.

"Good day!"

The voice produced goose bumps on Tesla's right cheek and stiffened his neck.

It was the same voice that had given orders to create the first billion-dollar monopoly.

Do people know how many zeros are in a billion?

Zeros with eyeglasses, zeros with the black clerical sleeve protectors, zeros with gold teeth, zeros with workers' flat caps, zeros with police badges and Pinkerton badges—they all responded to the voice of the man with the monstrous nose: John Pierpont Morgan.

Blinking antique dealers and thin-lipped connoisseurs chose paintings, tapestries, and bronze sculptures for his collections. Tireless fingers counted J. P. Morgan's money. Morgan's deep voice quoted Ovid: "He who knows how many sheep he has is a poor man."

John Pierpont Morgan had strong eyebrows. His frown could bend a horseshoe. His cheeks were rounded, his eyes small and funny looking. He almost resembled Balzac—except for his fearsome nose.

A merry voice spoke inside Tesla's head: *Where would we be without noses? Believe me—nowhere! People sniff each other out in social situations as well. We're all familiar with the "smell of money" and the "stench of poverty."*

"Too dangerous!" the inventor flinched in horror and quickly pushed out of his mind the words he had once written in his *Tract on Noses.*

The Maharaja of Kapurthala with his smoky mustache, the English aristocrats with their narrow faces—how could they match the glory of John Pierpont Morgan?! What about that old woman who—in her sleepless bed—caressed the plaster hand of her dead Albert? Could the Russian tsar's trimmed beard equal the power of Morgan? Who cared about the sagging cheeks of the Austrian emperor compared to the volcanic, hallucinatory nose of John Pierpont Morgan?

My dear colleagues, spirited colleagues—follow your noses . . .

He struggled to extinguish those words.

Medical science referred to Morgan's condition as rhinophyma. His nose was stolen from the decaying portrait of Dorian Gray. Raspberry-like, yellow, blue, red, blooming, disfigured with moles. That nose was the focal point of any room it entered. It required courage to carry such a nose through the world. It required courage to look at it and pretend it was nothing.

"Good day!" the voice affected Tesla like novocaine.

During their first meeting, Morgan left a strange impression on Tesla: "It was as if someone pulled a sack over my head!" he later said.

Despite everything, he took a peek into the abyss and looked at the nose as if it was nothing.

They sat by a fireplace that was large enough to house an entire immigrant family. A Byzantine breviary made of carved ivory lay on the table. The wall was covered with paintings in which men were brown and women were white. A dark study of *Susanna and the Elders,* a John the Baptist who held his own haloed head in the crook of his arm, and a Flemish vanity caught Tesla's eye. A roasted pig came to mind—as it always did in an art gallery.

Morgan was like a Poseidon who never laughed—but all those around him wore eternal smiles on their faces.

Cartoonists represented him as an octopus with each tentacle squeezing an industrial branch. Responding to the efforts of reformers who wanted to regulate monopolies, he claimed that one could not unscramble scrambled eggs. In addition to steel, he controlled the new electronic industry, shipbuilding, mines, railroads, insurance, and banking.

The contrast between the lily-like whiteness of his skin and his collar, the blackness of his hair and his suit, and that alarming redness was frightening. His nose glowed like Mount Etna. It thundered.

Is the whole room going to erupt? His visitor was frightened.

And—just imagine—that gloomy gorilla with his phantasmagorical nose once wanted to abandon everything for love . . .

A host of young bankers with extraordinary physical beauty—whom they called "Morgan's Cherubs"—worked for him. Many of those greedy idealists died from overwork.

Morgan's bride was so feeble that he had to support her during the wedding ceremony . . .

That gigantic antiquary had a collection of ancient coins, jewels, tapestries, engravings, paintings, books, original manuscripts, statues. Mark Twain called Morgan's treasure trove a collection of the permanent in the transitory. Tesla, however, thought that its monetary value was its sole organizing principle.

"People save up their whole lives," he pondered as he observed a painting by Sebastiano del Piombo. "But they can't save what's most important—life itself."

He took her to Algiers for her health. Then she died. He went back and took over his father's bank.

The atmosphere in the room was oppressive, as if the Angel of Death kept a continual vigil by the fireplace.

Morgan had read Tesla's article "The Problem of Increasing Human Energy" in the *Century*. He praised the piece and then said with his habitual directness, "Describe your system."

Tesla screamed inside: *Don't look at the nose.*

"My device enables the transfer of sound and images to any distance," the inventor responded softly. "Without wires. With complete privacy."

"What about Marconi's system?"

"He uses instruments others have designed, but they're set at the wrong frequencies," Tesla explained in a pleasant voice. "The smallest atmospheric change interferes with his transmissions."

Don't look into the abyss, he cried in desperation.

A spark of madness flashed in Morgan's eyes. His spy network was better than those in most countries. Yes, this man was controversial and they attacked him in the newspapers.

And yet . . .

Without uttering a word, Morgan waved to Tesla to continue.

"You should be the first to support this enterprise that will greatly benefit mankind."

The bony fingers of anxiety clutched Tesla's throat. Once again he felt that the Angel of Death was in the room.

With an eloquence that seemed to flow independently from him, Tesla explained that, in addition to the wireless transmission of messages, his system made possible the production and manipulation of hundreds of thousands of horsepower, which enabled the instruments to work at any point on earth regardless of the distance from the transmitter.

"Go on," Morgan said in his narcotic bass.

Tesla intuitively tried to lick Morgan's soul, but found only a void. The Buddhists were right as far as Morgan was concerned.

Tesla felt as if he were asleep. He bit his lip but did not feel it. Morgan's deep, drawling voice numbed his consciousness. The spark of insanity burned in the gorilla's tiny eyes! He and Morgan began negotiations in the spacious hall. The space narrowed—one wall was at the back of Tesla's head while another was in front of his nose. Terror enveloped him whenever he fell silent.

"The one in possession of these patents," he pointed out to Morgan in a voice not his own, "will be in a much stronger position legally than those who own the rights to my energy transfer system and alternating current motors."

The taciturn financier blew out smoke. "How much time do you need?" he asked.

"Eight months."

Silence deepened an octave.

Morgan said, finally, "Will you please send the financial estimate to my office."

The mosaic goddess kissed Tesla's feet as he left.

CHAPTER 81

The Big Nameless

Stanford White was chained to his drafting table. In several weeks, he completed the blueprints for the International Telegraph Center with its central tower from which the underground energy would be pumped all over the world.

"In terms of structure, it's the same as the Brooklyn Bridge," he explained. "The main difference is that it's a tower."

The thundering barn in Colorado was a toy compared to the tower: It would be built in the middle of a park; it would have the power of two Niagaras; Tesla would use it to send his stormy messages into the chaos of the stars. White penciled the tower in an exemplary futuristic town, with homes, shops, and public buildings that could accommodate two and a half thousand people.

"Airships and dirigibles will fly above the streets." Tesla rejoiced like a child.

They bought the land on Long Island in Shoreham, Suffolk County, some sixty miles from Manhattan. The construction of the roof was offered to the American Bridge Company, while McKim, Mead, and White was contracted to build the rest. The project was supposed to give an answer to . . .

"To everything." Tesla rejoiced.

The plot was cleared by July.

"The Wardenclyffe Project will be the greatest enterprise of its kind in the world!"

The local paper *Port Jefferson Echo* animatedly explained that the building of the tower was a visible sign of the clash between Tesla and Marconi.

And yet!

In the so called real world, the financier E. H. Harriman secretly bought half of Morgan's Northern Pacific Company.

Morgan thundered—and the whole world turned a summersault.

"Buy it back at any price!"

Like elevators, shares started to rush up and down.

On May 9, Northern Pacific shares jumped from a hundred and fifty to one thousand dollars. Other shares sank. In the first year of the century in which the individual heart was becoming at once more just and more gentle and music was becoming sweeter, many investors lost everything they had.

The war between the corporations cast a gigantic shadow not only on the stock market but on Tesla's enterprise as well.

"Come quickly!" the redheaded White yelled into the phone.

They had known each other for almost two decades by now.

Both of them believed that they were beyond human laws and norms.

"At the Waldorf," Tesla hissed.

"No. In my office."

The office was in the building White designed. Tesla listened to the neurotic White sigh as he put the papers on his desk in order. He reminded Tesla of a male version of Rossetti's *Beata Beatrix*. The room was large and empty; the drafting tables with green lamps on them faced the windows. Above them was Leonardo's *Uomo Vitruviano*. One mask from Oceania also grinned from the wall. How did it get here? Whenever the sun shone through, the surrounding buildings responded with their own internal light. White's hair flared at each "strike" of the sun. He still complained that old hags in love with their priests would be the end of him. Since Wilde had published his famous book, some people called White Dorian Gray. He looked incredibly well for his age.

When they asked him if the person who drank as much as he did was an alcoholic, he answered, "Of course!"

"It doesn't apply to you. You're something else," Tesla appeased him in his Sunday best voice.

And so . . .

White gazed into the distance with his snotty eyes.

"This is my colleague McKim," he somehow found the strength to say.

McKim had a likable bold rosy head and thin, animated eyebrows. He liked to play tennis and to fish, and fishermen do not talk much. He spoke so little that his own voice surprised him. His frowning eyebrows made Tesla confront the numbers for the first time.

Before he signed the papers, Morgan wanted to get Tesla's other patents as collateral. He concluded the negotiations having obtained control of two new industries—wireless transfer and Tesla's iridescent light.

"You have both your arms and legs bound by that contract," McKim explained.

In return, Tesla had not only his key patents and a system better than Marconi's but the backing of the greatest financial power in America as well.

Here McKim raised his voice in caution. "Your plans were based on the assumption that Morgan will quickly hand you the money, and that the market will be stable!"

"I see," Tesla admitted. "Morgan is slow to pay. And it's impossible to buy anything on credit these days."

"The crisis cut your one hundred and fifty thousand dollars in half," McKim explained rudely. "You know what that means."

Just like Jacob with his angel, Tesla wrestled with his own megalomania.

Factories and stores vanished in a blink of an eye.

There remained the question whether to build one or more towers.

"Wait a minute." Stanford White grew serious. "Even the building of a tower—only one tower—will be much more expensive than we thought."

"Let the airships and dirigibles fend for themselves!" McKim thundered.

CHAPTER 82

The Belt

At six o'clock on a rainy Tuesday afternoon, in the first year of the new century, a pair of amber eyes, a hundred golden freckles, and a curl of blond hair surfaced in front of Tesla.

"I'm Stevan Prostran," the boy introduced himself.

To Tesla, he looked like Huckleberry Finn. He constantly squinted as if he were looking at the sun. His hat had two holes for ears because a horse used to wear it.

"Stevan's son," he added.

"He's been waiting for the last three hours," the receptionist at the Astoria's desk said.

Tesla intuitively licked the boy's soul. The soul was brazen, unreal yet present. It touched Tesla with a thousand tiny paws. It flashed and then grew dark, so that only a small space remained. For that boy anything was possible, yet something gnawed at him inside . . . It was fear. Tesla backed off.

The boy was around thirteen.

"Stevan's son!"

He had always wanted to find Stevan, who told him "Come!" in the worst year of his life, who brought freshly baked bread in the morning, who saw the ocean for the first time in his life and instantly *knew it*. Tesla had looked for Stevan in Homestead where the air was acidic from smoke.

"Tell me about your father." Tesla moved closer to the sofa, and the boy smelled violets.

The boy pulled his sleeves over his fingernails. He spoke with the corner of his mouth as he told his story. For a time, Stevan Prostran worked for the Chicago meat industry. Afterward, he went back to coal mining in Pennsylvania.

"What was life like?"

"Ugly, by God."

From Wilmerding, Pennsylvania, Stevan moved to Saint Louis. There he married a widow. She had kids, her own and her late husband's.

"Then Pop met some Montenegrins," Stevan informed Tesla dispassionately. "We went to Utah. He worked in a mine."

Tesla raised a long finger. A silent waiter from the Waldorf appeared.

"A sandwich and fruit juice," the famous man whispered.

"You heard of the explosion in Scofield, Utah, dintcha?" the boy asked, unaware of the subtleties of Serbian grammar.

"I have," Tesla nodded.

"Train full of coffins arrived in town. Pop got shot out of the mineshaft, so at least we had a body to bury. Some barber turned priest buried him in a Catholic graveyard."

As if he were on the deck of the *Saturnia,* on which they both had arrived in America, Stevan's fair-haired countenance appeared right before Tesla's eyes. The salty wind tried to blow Stevan's hair away. Fear whispered in one ear and hope in the other. One moment he was thrilled with his future in America, and the next he was horrified.

"In the mine, Pop got all hunched up," the young Prostran said in a flat voice. "He became a hunchback. We had no idea how to put him in the coffin like that. The barkeep Baćić came up with the idea to use a belt across his chest to straighten him out. We had the vigil in the bar. Two young fellas with sooty faces almost started singin' one of our songs at the bar . . ."

A man from Bosnia got up and raised his glass: "To your health, Stevan!"

At that moment, Stevan jerked in the coffin and sat up.

Knocking chairs everywhere, men and women trampled each other trying to get away. They gathered again in front of the bar. There was the smell of the desert. The barkeep cracked the door and took a peek.

The young Stevan told the story about his father as if he did not understand what he was talking about.

"What's he doing?" the people asked.

"He's just sitting there."

Mom wailed loudly: "Alas, what has he done to me!"

Across the concrete circle embedded with silver quarters in the middle of the bar, the barkeep cautiously approached the deceased.

"Be careful, Mijo," his wife called out.

Everyone heard when he sighed with relief.

"C'mon, people, get over here."

Tesla came to his senses, rubbed his eyes, and asked Stevan, "What happened?"

"The belt snapped!"

The belt that held him down in the coffin broke, and he—who had spent his entire life hunched over—sat up straight for the last time.

"Pop rebelled only after he died. Then he straightened up, but it was too late."

The boy continued as if he were talking about someone else's life: "And so Pop got killed and Mom remarried a widower with kids. That fella used to come home late at night. Mom told him everything I did wrong that day, and he'd wake me up to beat me.

"My late pop bragged about knowing you," the boy ended his story. "And how you came over on the same boat. Our people talked about you wherever we went. And so . . ."

The boy told Tesla that he only came to say hello, but it was obvious that he had nothing in the world except his clenched teeth.

"Of course," Tesla answered the unspoken question.

He arranged with Scherff for the boy to sleep at his place and to later help him in the laboratory. From that day on, Tesla's friends noticed his "Serbian servant" following him on his way to Wardenclyffe.

CHAPTER 83

Pygmalion

Tesla did not live at Wardenclyffe—in the beginning, there was no place to sleep—but he visited every day. He boarded the Long Island train. He shared his compartment with Ali Baba's magic basket that Oscar of the Waldorf filled and Stevan Prostran emptied.

It was hard to tell if Tesla's young companion complained of or bragged about the fact that he had worked hard even as a little child.

"Look," he boasted, "I can put out a cigarette on the palm of my hand. Want me to show you?"

"I want you to quit smoking," Pygmalion answered. "And I want you to find something to read."

Stevan Prostran obediently rustled open some pages. The first movement of the newspaper's piece was *allegro:*

The President Shot at Fair in Buffalo! Wounded in Chest and Stomach! One Bullet Taken Out, Other Not Found! Leon Czolgosz Anarchist, Assassin from Cleveland!

The second one was *adagio:*

The President Peacefully at Rest! He Will Recover, Doctors Say! Assassin's Confession! Attack Planned for Three Days!

It ended with a *crescendo:*

President's Health Sinking Today! Mrs. McKinley's Condition Alarming! Mr. Roosevelt Is President!

"Theodore Roosevelt is now the president," Tesla repeated to the boy as Long Island's light-blue bays sparkled beyond the train's windows. "He says that black worry rarely sits on the shoulder of the person who rides fast enough. His house is over there. And look, there's White's family estate. Here's Port Jefferson, we're getting closer."

Stanford White's chauffeur met the big Prospero and the little Caliban at the station and took them to Wardenclyffe in an open steam locomobile.

"Ah, what a blue sky! What a sun!" the driver exclaimed, gripping the wheel firmly with his enormous hands.

The car swayed and the travelers bounced. Above them, the blue sky whirled around with a white hole above Shoreham. After the endless potato fields, they saw the sight that brought joy to their eyes—Wardenclyffe.

The steel tower with its mushroom-like top was to be eighteen stories tall, half the size of the original design.

"Nevertheless," Tesla told his assistants Scherff and Czitó, "with the additional underground rooms, the tower will stay proportional to my original plan."

The construction began. That was the only important thing. Let's go!

Despite all the rush, Tesla still found the time to pose for Dickinson Eli's camera. "Get better looking," Eli commanded him. In the picture, Tesla supported his head with a long index finger; crow's feet showed at the corners of his eyes.

Eli also took a picture of Stevan Prostran. Fear of being photographed and joy of being alive collided on his freckled face.

Tesla ordered his photographer to take a picture of every machine and tube in Wardenclyffe.

"This is the place from which we will wirelessly transmit energy for cars and ships," he explained to the mocking Prostran. "By way of artificial lightning, we will produce rain and illuminate the firmament like an electric bulb."

Who cared if that was not exactly what was written on some piece of paper?! In moments of invention, walls and frames disappeared. With the gold visor over his eyes, in the joy of discovery, he could not pay attention to trivialities such as the fact that his project did not coincide with the contract he signed with one well-mannered gorilla who happened to own barely 10 percent of the world's capital.

"Watch out!" Johnson yelled. "Morgan never forgives—"

Tesla cut him off. "Sure. We'll also add the apparatus for the universal measurement of time and interplanetary communications. We'll eliminate not only cables but newspapers as well, as they will become obsolete. How can newspapers survive if everyone possesses a cheap machine to print their own news?"

Whom Do You Believe?

To the next-door neighbor De Witt Bailey, the tower appeared to rise straight out of his nightmares.

For Tesla, however, the tower was his Crystal, his Universe, his Cabaret with Spirits. It was an Eiffel Tower with an all-seeing eye. A place for examining the borderline between a life awake and a dream. A funnel that focused underground energies. In the tower, Tesla stood between the devil and an angel, like Pico della Mirandola's man. In this scientific-futuristic wonder—with its wells reaching into the core of the earth and its tower rushing toward the heavens—Stevan Prostran was supposed to be raised.

Stevan frowned habitually. Tesla tapped him on his forehead: "That will cause wrinkles."

Tesla's friends sometimes called Stevan a boy and sometimes a young man, and he acted accordingly. Most of the time, he listened to Pygmalion's pontifications with an "I'm being bullied" expression on his face. Sometimes he would give Tesla a serious look and ask him, "Are you my father now?"

Stevan also wrinkled his freckled nose and showered him with questions:

"Where's hell?"

"Why did God create a bad man?"

"Who do you love?" he asked. "Who do you trust?"

"That question is inadequately phrased."

"If you don't trust anyone, you trust the devil."

Tesla eyed him with a look of heightened awareness. What could he read on the boy's face? The eyes too far apart. The teeth too far apart. A wrinkled nose. A foolish and elated smile. Was he maturing inside? Did signs of some new wisdom or cunning appear on that face?

"The world doesn't need the unloved, right?"

Stevan kept asking.

And he also asked, "Are you my father now?"

CHAPTER 84

The Span of a Dog's Life

Stevan ran on the nearby Southampton beach and scattered the dignified seagulls. On the sand, they resembled stodgy bank clerks. In the air, they turned into something sacred.

With a splash, he ran into the ocean. The Atlantic waves were so cold his foot cramped.

Tesla and Robert Underwood Johnson watched him from the shore. Johnson's thick mustache flowed into his beard. The throne for his pince-nez was swollen. The hair on his cheeks was still black, but it turned white around his mouth. His beard had thickened and looked frightening. Our once-handsome poet looked somewhat like a grieving lion.

"Everything is still the same at 273 Lexington Avenue," Robert said. "Nora the maid still sprinkles water on the laundry with her fingers, and steam rises above the iron. Katharine hides a silver dollar under the rug: if it's still there—Nora didn't clean properly; if it's gone—she's not trustworthy! Now, Richard Higginson II barks at the clock. You know, Luka, we've known each other for the span of a dog's life."

Robert's eyes were often red because he was allergic to cats. He kept them anyway because Kate loved them.

"The big change is that my Owen got married. Except for you and me, the only boy around us now is your Stevan."

Tesla met Owen when he was a spoiled brat who loved to ride in his carriage. Owen Johnson became an athlete who complained about his tennis elbow, and a philosopher prone to tiresome definitions. He had already published a novel titled *Arrows of the Almighty*. He was handsome, but had a slight deviation to the nose. The one-time boy had every hair in place. His cobalt eyes peered from behind rimless glasses. Not even his own wife had ever seen him unshaven. Tesla had to admit that all of that was a little disappointing. Impeccability was all right. And yet, did not life offer greater opportunities than being merely well groomed?

The dizzying fans of the Atlantic light shone through the clouds, hurt the eyes, and opened up horizons.

The waves crashed.

And crashed. And crashed. And crashed.

Robert wore an exquisite gray suit. He undid his tie and took off his collar. He felt the wind on his neck. Then he took off his shoes.

Their hands behind their backs, they walked along a section of the beach lapped by waves.

Whoooooosh! Whoooooosh!

"Would it be possible to send a message from Wardenclyffe to Morgan's yacht, the *Corsair*?" Robert outshouted the waves and Stevan's cries.

"Sure," Tesla responded indifferently.

The waves drew back. The wet shadow of the ocean followed them.

Robert looked at his old friend with the eyes of a wounded stag. He pleaded in a voice of a cursed soul: "Then do it. Forget about everything else and send him a message before Marconi does. I've told you this before, and I'll tell you again."

Tesla's big ear registered what Robert said, but his obsessions determined which words he would hear. To him—like to Socrates—his own *daimon* kept repeating something else. Perhaps it was vanity and lusting after the wind? Perhaps his obstinacy, necessary for contradicting the entire world this long, was turning against him? He did not follow what his reason dictated—it was his soul that made those profound decisions.

Tesla surveyed the sharp grasses at the edge of the dunes in the incredible glare of the sunlight.

"Don Quixote is a monster," it dawned on Robert. "Any personal trait that swallows up all other traits is demonic. What remains from Don Quixote's reason is the fragments of his potential life."

What was it that Johnson told Tesla? That one could combine haste with self-respect. That contractual obligations and other social games were worthy of the mind that would bring about the biggest spontaneous manifestation of energy on earth.

The wind caressed the tall grass.

Stevan took him by the hand. His nose wrinkled: "Are you my father now?"

"No," retorted Tesla.

For the last few years, Tesla had been writing down each dream in which Dane appeared. Relieved, he noticed that sometimes there were six-month periods between them. He had no competitors anymore, dead or alive. Dangerous "others" did not exist. Time did not exist. He was at the center of the world, and Marconi was plotting on its gray outskirts.

"Are you telling me that I should be afraid?" Tesla became irritated.

Unused to anger, Johnson frowned. "What you do at Wardenclyffe violates your contract with Morgan. He only wants a small tower for transferring stock market reports." Johnson's eyes became larger behind his glasses till they nearly shouted, *Remember the blooming nose! Remember the stinger in his tiny black eyes! Remember how you grew numb from his mossy whisper! Remember Morgan, Nikola!*

"Beware," Robert muttered to himself. "Your feeling of superiority is one-dimensional, and it impoverishes life!"

"What was that?"

"Beware!" Robert repeated aloud. "Morgan never forgives."

La-de-da. What was a contract compared to . . .

Robert was horrified. A halo of eccentricity and solitude surrounded his friend. He realized that—for this lotus-eater—people did not exist.

"Are you aware of the number of ships that already use Marconi's wireless system?" he continued with a constricted throat. "More than seventy! Mostly in his two homelands—Britain and Italy! The rest belong to the great shipping lines—the Cunard Line and the North American Lloyd."

Little Stevan did not stop yelling. He let the waves completely wash him out on the shore. Then he rushed back into the eternal ocean. He enjoyed being pulled out and then pushed back on the sand where he crawled in the rustling arabesques of foam.

The dizzying Atlantic light intoxicated Tesla.

Robert spoke in his tortured, cultivated voice. "Marconi's transmitters have been installed at Poldhu in England and at Crookhaven in Ireland."

Trying to wake the sleepwalker in love was to no avail. Oh, the reader should become worried about him!

The wind blew. Robert talked reasonably and tediously. Tesla remained silent. The eternal ocean rustled. Neckless seagulls waddled around the sand, as important as the Cunard Line officials. Tesla looked toward the ocean's horizon with his Olympian eyes.

The boy Prostran shot out of the cold waves, shivered, and hugged himself. With motionless wings, the seagulls flew at various floors of the wind. Stevan shook his feet. The withdrawing waves and the changing color of the sand delighted him. Directly from the light above, a seagull dove and snatched a sandwich from the basket they left on a rock.

"Ha!" Stevan shouted with joy and pointed his finger at the sky.

Hugging his bony ribs, he then came up to Tesla and grabbed him by the hand. "Are you my father now?"

CHAPTER 85

Three Quiet Miracles

Stevan smoked cigarettes and walked on his hands around Wardenclyffe. Then he came up to Tesla and said, "This is what girls sing in Rastičevo: 'America, may you lose all of your money; because of you, a widower is now my honey.'"

"Go read something!" Pygmalion said.

The boy threw a quick glance at him. Bored but obedient, he spread out a newspaper:

Dutch Queen Quarrels with Husband. Circe Feeds Sailors Her Herbs of Evil. Race Riots in New York: Two Men Slashed with Knives. Odysseus's Return to Ithaca Causes Bloodbath. Italian Government Insists on Italians' Rights in America. In Luxor, Alexander Declared Amon's Son. Desperate Turkish Troops in Albania with No Pay for Months.

"Don't read that rubbish." Stevan's unlikely adopted father frowned. "Read this."

Stevan was handed Plato's *Symposium*. He took it with him to the dark corners of the laboratory where he smoked in secret.

"The professors claim that Socrates said that we should be good and brush our teeth," Stevan murmured. "I don't think he meant that . . ."

At times, it seemed to Tesla that it was impossible to make Stevan respect anything. Besides the gourmet meals prepared by Oscar of the Waldorf, Stevan loved fried potatoes. The Serbian Huckleberry Finn swore to stay *forever wild* like an American national park.

Meanwhile, a Shakespearean tempest wiped out Marconi's station in England. In November, the same happened to the one in Ireland.

"This is a respite," Robert wired him. "You need to hurry!"

Stevan Prostran Jr. was ecstatic when he learned that Stanford White had become a member of the same auto club as President Roosevelt. *Dark worry rarely sits on the shoulder of the driver who drives fast enough.* With his glowing red hair, White raced to Wardenclyffe in his new electric two-seater.

"It would glow like a lamp, if only I fixed it up a bit more," he bragged.

Stevan caressed the car.

"White has tasted bread from many an oven," he said with admiration. The ailing priapus hoped to cut his debt in half by selling the artifacts from his collection at an auction. White paced around the room, smoked nervously, and inquired about everything. Night fell. With his burning cigarette tip, he drew red circles in the darkness. Then he abruptly took his leave. The tires squealed on the gravel. A sparkling cigarette butt bounced down the night road behind him.

Meanwhile . . .

"Marconi decided to try using a less powerful but much sturdier tower in England," Scherff informed Tesla. "He will install the receivers in balloons."

The obedient Stevan read Plato.

"The Sophists do not crave knowledge but power," he murmured. "However, they are curious and smart in spite of the power they crave, so their longing to know the Truth prods at them."

The more Stevan read, the more he thought that Tesla—like Socrates—preferred mankind to people.

The Johnsons invited Tesla to Bar Harbor in Maine and to their place for Thanksgiving. He turned them down and signed the note: "The distant Nikola."

In *The Symposium*, Alcibiades spoke with his ancient mouth: *Know that beauty, wealth, and honor—which many people crave—don't mean anything to Socrates. He despises them and the people who possess them. People mean nothing to him.*

Oh, yes, Marconi and his assistants finally raised the receiving antenna. On Friday, December 13, when the atmospheric conditions settled after a hail storm, they received three dots for the letter *S*.

"So what?" Tesla put his hands on his hips.

At that moment, the mustached assistant stepped on the scene again.

The eyeglass frames out of horses' hooves! The boots from a military surplus store! The hands and the heart of pure gold: Scherff!

Scherff's unblinking brown eyes peered through monstrously thick lenses. The eyes focused on the Ideal. Scherff had never been sick. Had never complained. Tesla believed that he had two disassembled watches in his left pocket. He would not be surprised if a cockroach jumped out of his right one.

Scherff!

Hunched over. His feet wide apart. His body square.

His honesty and his clumsiness, his awkward love for truth could not handle the current situation.

Marconi received the three dots for the letter *S*.

"Mother of God!" Scherff gasped under his breath.

The mustached Scherff walked around the yard raising his arms. He put them down and raised them again, like a Jew in front of the Wailing Wall. Then he spat. "Three quiet signals! Those three signals will pull down our steel tower."

"So what?" Tesla repeated defiantly.

As soon as Marconi overtook Tesla, an orgy of derision ensued. Entire opera houses mocked Tesla in singsongy fashion—the Berlin Opera, the Opéra de Paris, and La Scala in Milan.

Pygmalion neglected Stevan Prostran, so the boy put Plato's *Symposium* aside and started to read newspapers again:

Society against Animal Cruelty Protests Greased Pig Contest. Child Dies from Rabies. British Bankers Hopeful. Man Delivers Toast, Drops Dead. Deceased Exhumed for Photo.

CHAPTER 86

Behemoth

As a child, he was always afraid when Father went through *a transformation.*

It had never occurred to him that one day he would build a tower that would be his place of transformation. The tower was his personal theatrical stage on which faceless powers played assumed personalities. Under the high-voltage shower, Tesla himself turned into a faceless power. He changed into a bright whirlpool. He became a parliament of the world on the site at which various voices intermingled. He prepared to send them out into the ether.

By the end of the following year, the tower grew to two hundred feet.

At that point, the money *really* ran out.

Don Quixote sold the surrounding property for the round sum of thirty-five thousand dollars.

Not even that was enough.

It was when George Scherff put his heavy fists down on Tesla's desk and sighed. "Now we have to manufacture oscillators and develop fluorescent lamps," he said.

"But—"

"We have to!"

A few months later, Tesla tapped Scherff on the shoulder and declared in an embarrassed voice, "We've saved enough to hire workers and complete the construction of the cupola."

The shouts of laborers, deaf from riveting, yet again awoke the inhabitants of provincial Port Jefferson.

"Hold this!"

"Look out, Jack, or you'll cut my finger off!"

With pride, Tesla surveyed the completion of his "steel crown," which weighed fifty tons. The purpose of the mushroom-like cupola was to store electricity and transmit it through the air—or to the depths of the earth.

To the depths of the earth?

Yes, because the construction reached ten stories below the surface. There was a whole system of catacombs under the tower.

The humming of the hellish energies electrified the tower's roots and summoned the pale dead. On top of the vertiginous underground stairs, Dante and Virgil waited for Tesla impatiently.

At the top was the All-Seeing Eye designed by Odilon Redon.

The wind played around Wardenclyffe like a mad flutist. Nikola ascended the mosque-like stairways. The wind hissed through the steel rafters. The depths called to the depths. Looking at his legs, Tesla climbed up to the cupola. The white-blue ocean, white whales, and electrical clouds came into view. Tesla's thoughts changed floors, and the air played a fugue like an organ. The purpose of this endless steel hallucination was to help him discover new continents. From up here, he stole a glance at his thoughts in the afterlife.

At night, he looked across the sea toward New Haven and the constellations above it. With a unbidden shiver, the lonely man despaired because the stars and the dynamo were still not connected.

The devil elevated him to this high promontory, showed him all the nations of the world, and said, This all could be yours. Just serve me.

And he responded, "No!"

To escape the temptation, at Wardenclyffe he disinfected himself with high-voltage current, and the bright whirlpool lifted him. The light started to rise from his toes upward. It splashed over his feet and reached above his knees. The flood of inner light engulfed his thighs and rose to his hips. After such an experience, Nikola slept under the All-Seeing Eye of his cupola with sad abandonment. He dreamed he was Saint Sebastian. Instead of the wounds, eyes opened all over his body. The mystic scientist turned into an eye within the great eye of Wardenclyffe.

"Are you going to bring the golem to life in here?" White asked him in a whisper once they descended the spiral staircase.

Prince Henry of Prussia, the emperor's brother, followed them through the chromed corridors. The prince looked somewhat like his cousin, the Russian tsar. Wardenclyffe was made of iron, but it was woven out of Tesla's dreams. All around there were numerous coils, something that looked like metal mummy sarcophagi, fragile and shimmering lightbulbs . . . The rooms and control panels were warped by the dream. They climbed to the cupola with the view of the ocean. Then they went down to the ground floor, nibbled on Oscar of the Waldorf's hors d'oeuvres, and talked in the echoing space.

Then the prince left.

The waiter left.

White left.

In the silence that replaced the lively conversation, a realization struck Tesla: There was no more land to sell!

That night, he wandered around the ghostly tower, suffering from a headache and insomnia, like Milutin Tesla a long time before. In the dark, he ran into Stevan Prostran, who was watching over the building. The boy quickly put out a cigarette and asked him, "Why don't you sleep?"

"I never sleep."

When he finally fell asleep, Tesla did not dream of Dane; instead, he sank into some cosmic nightmares. First, there was nothing but Chaos floating in Chaos and One Thing breathing by its own power. The Lord *paid attention* and saw that it was not Chaos at all—it was the World.

After that dream, the sense of being powerless left him.

He still had his tower.

The tower was his cosmic crutch. With its help, our shaman hovered in the blue of the sky or dove into the fires of the underworld. He called out, pulling the chrome levers. Something rumbled, responded to his calls. Something alive reached out to him from the other side, calling, *"Brrr-r-roummmmm!"*

There was no more money.

"It's hopeless. All of this has been stillborn," Tesla murmured.

The forces of the earth and sky brought his monster to life. Explosions disturbed the tar-pitch night. The building quivered and quivered.

And the darkness merged with the quivering. The creator of the stillborn tower sensed enormous danger. He slept with a lion. He ate with a wolf. From her box, Pandora released all the evils—as well as hope. Tesla wrote desperate letters to Morgan. He tortured himself like people in love do: Just one more . . . one more letter explaining, and he will understand.

But power is not obliged to understand. Misunderstanding is one of the ways in which it manifests itself.

I'm sorry, I'm not ready to invest at this time, Morgan wrote back. *I've never let any human being disappoint me as long as you have.*

Lucretius believed that the sun had to be ignited daily. Upon receiving Morgan's letter, Nikola Tesla learned how difficult it was to reignite the sun. The city fell silent to hear the weeping of the man who wanted to give advice to Yahweh. The man who wanted to turn the gorgeous sun into his obedient slave was sitting on the toilet at three o'clock in the morning, leaning against his sharp knees, his nose buried into a wet towel.

O World—in you, only weaknesses understand, only pains hear, only needs see.

Our shivering, skinny Cosmos realized that he was much smaller than the world. For the first time, he was convinced that life was disgusting, coated in slime, and that people were trash.

Brilliant furrows once again creased the sky above Tesla's tower. Master Eckhart once complained that he had never heard God speak—he had only heard him clearing his throat. No real thunder was heard around Wardenclyffe—the thunder just cleared its throat. The heavens were ruled by Ishtar-Inanna, the goddess of passionate feeling in nature and strife. The world was marbled with lightning and filled with images.

Would Tesla's missile-like tower launch and shoot off into the lighted firmament?

"Brrr-r-roummmmm! I'm coming!"

If this dream was to be ruined, he would be left without dreams.

Stevan covered the mirrors to prevent the thunder from killing him. Yes, the world fell silent to hear the weeping of the man who had this itch to give God a piece of advice. Stevan's desperate adopted father roared like a waterfall and banged on the control panel with his fist.

He had no one to borrow from. This was the end.

On the third night, the sky above Wardenclyffe spat out one branch, then another, and yet another. In the newly created light, everything became delightfully clear. The world appeared starched and silvery. Instead of ivy, Wardenclyffe was overgrown with lightning. As in the Psalms of David, the foundation of the world was laid bare, hit with the breath from God's nostrils. Finally, multiple reverberations sounded, and the silver rain started to dance across the ledges.

The impoverished inventor pulled one lever and turned into the first human god of thunder.

He pulled another one and turned into a giver of rain.

The creditors—woken by the explosions of the maddened electric snakes—came the next day.

CHAPTER 87

The Crash

A pair of lips approached Morgan's ear—they belonged to the stock market wizard Bernard Baruch. The lips smacked and whispered, "That man is crazy. He wants to give free electricity to everyone. We can't put a meter on it."

"Is that so?" Morgan grunted.

Baruch sent his secretary to the library to read through Tesla's interviews. There the secretary flashed his glasses, wiped them occasionally, and coughed. He discovered that even ten years back—Baruch underlined the paragraph with his fingernail for Morgan to see—Tesla stated in the *Sunday World*, "With the transmission of electricity through the ground, all monopolies that depend on power lines will end."

In the afternoon, Morgan had a meeting with a bishop of the Episcopal Church. Then a group of engineers came to review the estimates for the building of the New York subway system.

He dined at the apartment of an up-and-coming ballerina, Miss Evelyn Penny.

He just dined and went home.

"See how quickly a day goes by," Morgan whispered, and his voice peeled off a corner of the lily-patterned wallpaper.

The whole day was spent.

The only thing that remained to be done was the last unavoidable pleasure.

Each night after midnight the grouch played a game of solitaire.

The jack of hearts suddenly opened the second row on the left.

"Aha!" Morgan exclaimed, causing a large ficus leaf to fall off the plant.

The jack of hearts sealed Tesla's fate.

Tesla was hiding behind dark drapes holding his stomach, where the fragments of his life gathered. He remembered the story from the Gospel according to Luke about a man who was building a tower without counting the cost, so people ridiculed him. The last day of May was a Saturday. The creditors appeared at Wardenclyffe and dragged out heavy machinery. All the workers were let go except Scherff, Prostran, and a guard.

No, there was no more money.

He negotiated with the well-groomed, cold-eyed Frick, the fighting dog of Carnegie Steel. A spark of interest was quickly snuffed out from Frick's eyes. Then Tesla met with Harriman, who looked like a leopard, with the mummified Rockefeller, and with the diamond collector Thomas Fortune Ryan.

"It was just different versions of the same story," Tesla complained to the Johnsons. "It always started well. One after another, the financiers came to, like sleepwalkers. First their smiles disappeared, and then they followed."

"There's only one explanation," Katharine Johnson said when the gloomy Tesla took them out for dinner at Delmonico's.

"What is it?"

"That Morgan is obstructing you personally."

Morgan could block any deal by simply pausing while he spoke or lifting those black eyebrows of his. Any deal Morgan walked away from no one else would touch.

Tesla fell silent. "If that's true, do you know what it means?"

Katharine paused and her nose narrowed.

Tesla sighed:

"The crash."

CHAPTER 88

Sorrowfully Yours

January 14, 1904

Dear Mr. Morgan:

You wish me success. It is in your hands, how can you wish it?

I could not report on yacht races or signal to incoming ships. I could not build up my business gradually like a greengrocer.

We start on a proposition, everything duly calculated; it is financially frail. You engage impossible operations, you make me pay double, yes, make me wait ten months for machinery. On top of that you produce a panic. When, after putting in all I could scrape together, I came to show you that I have done the best that could be done, you fire me out like an office boy and roar so that you are heard six blocks away. Not a cent; it is spread all over town. I am discredited, the laughingstock of my enemies.

January 22, 1904

Are you going to leave me in a hole?

April 2, 1904

Mr. Morgan, for a year now there has not been a single night that my pillow has stayed dry from tears.

Have you ever read the Book of Job?

If you replace Job's body with my mind, you will have all my sufferings accurately described.

October 17, 1904

You're not a Christian at all, you're a fanatic . . .

February 17, 1905

Let me tell you once more. I have perfected the greatest invention of all time. This is the long-sought stone of the philosophers. I need but to complete the plant I have constructed and in one bound, humanity will advance centuries.

There is more power in the wings of a butterfly than in the teeth of a tiger. I am the only man on this earth today who has a peculiar knowledge and ability to achieve this wonder and another one may not come in a hundred years!

Mr. Morgan, maybe you simply do not care. People are like insects to you.

Sorrowfully yours,
N. Tesla

CHAPTER 89

The Sinking Ships

Stanford White promised that he would arrange for Stevan Prostran's education "through some religious old lady."

Tesla was shocked. "He knows a religious old lady?"

"So long, Father!" he heard as they parted.

"Good-bye, Stevan."

The boy left, smoking and humming off-key to himself:

"I'm building a tower, and I have no stone, oh, my tower is built of my tears . . ."

Tesla looked at the back of the boy's head. When he returned to the Waldorf Astoria, he waited for Eliphaz the Temanite, Bildad the Shuhite, and Zophar the Naamathite to come and visit him.

The friends of Job.

Instead, the sorrowful Stanford White paid him a visit. The burning bush smoldered on his head. Acting tranquil, White tried to keep his body from shaking.

"How's life?" Tesla asked him.

"I drink from the cup of life." White was inconsolable. "And I pluck the bloom of pleasure."

His common sense made him eat; the lack thereof made him drink. The need for the first drink arrived earlier and earlier.

"Aaaaaai," Stanford White howled inside.

His face was calm, but his stupid soul . . . The annoying soul. The weak soul. The soul wailed the same tune:

"If I had sold that, my debt would've been cut in half."

"Only two weeks before the auction." New York gossips jauntily interrupted one another.

"The fire in Stanford White's warehouse."

"Tapestries, sculptures, and paintings burned up."

"Uninsured treasures worth three hundred thousand dollars went up in smoke."

"If I had sold that, my debt would've been . . . would've been cut in half," Stanford White sputtered.

Tesla remembered well the time his laboratory burned down. He was not able to sleep for a few nights. (Mornings were the worst.) He tried to console the architect, but without noticing, he returned to the painful subject of Wardenclyffe.

The grand project, woven from blood, heart, and dreams, was dying before his eyes.

New York had already started to reach for the sky. New Yorkers were turning into the surveyors above the clouds, similar to birds and angels. People discussed the poetry of skyscrapers.

Our two friends were like babies who cried because one was hungry and the other was cold.

With the patience of a saint, the sorrow-stricken White listened to Tesla's laments, which were supposed to be condolences. He sat stiffly. His face was red as if sunburnt. His blue eyes bulged out. The expression he had on his face could not hide how annoying it was to be right after the fact.

"We all told you," he uttered, "to accept Edward Dean Adams's offer. If you'd taken it, you'd now have all the money you need to complete Wardenclyffe."

A deep crease was cut between Tesla's eyebrows.

"I'll shut up!" the red devil White promised gloomily and emptied his drink with his eyes closed. "Nothing happens the way I want it to," he concluded as he put the glass back on the table.

Even after the fire in his warehouse, Stanford White continued to live in his little pleasure hell. Once so luxurious and comfortable, his personal hell continued to shrink. His lover, young Evelyn Nesbit, married the Pittsburgh millionaire Harry Thaw.

During the time of their happiness, he used to tell her, "Let's make love in such a way that, when someone stumbles upon this spot a hundred years from now, they can feel the vibrations and shiver."

Thus he used to speak to her. Now his cravings for her were ripping his guts apart. The cheated cheater was shocked by his sweetheart's behavior.

"Evelyn," he wondered. "You've always had so much style, Evelyn. And now, at the end—all of a sudden—you've lost it!?"

"It doesn't matter," she responded with her heart-shaped mouth. "It's over."

He replied, "You're wrong. It matters the most now."

Tesla listened to him out of a sense of duty. In truth, romantic problems—caused by a lack of self-restraint—were nonsense to him.

"Stop thinking of her," Tesla advised his friend.

"Ha," the redhead smiled bitterly. "I think only of her."

Did what they had had together mean so little to her? Did she deny everything so quickly and let it go, without a fight, without an effort?

During endless afternoons—many, many afternoons—Evelyn knelt with her eyes raised and her arms stretched as if in prayer. Between her hands, wet with some slippery substance, she manipulated White's manhood.

With a pickpocket's skill, Evelyn emptied his fly, and he emptied her bra. Their tongues touched. She gasped for breath in the whirlpool of his hands.

Hidden underneath her dress, like a photographer, he bit her perfectly molded butt. He loved to punish each transgression of her femininity. His pelvis hammered her bulging rump back on the bed. He wished his eternally pulsating member could search through her bottomless, dark softness until the end of time. Her black triangle turned into a maelstrom and dimmed his vision.

How could she?

How could he not think of her?

The worst thing was that the jealous Thaw, her new husband, hired Pinkerton's men to keep an eye on White day in and day out. White murmured, "The Furies whisper above my head."

CHAPTER 90

The Swan, the Bull, and the Shower of Gold

Then all of New York heard the news.

With a crooked smile, squeezing a pearl-handled revolver, Harry Thaw entered the penthouse restaurant at Madison Square Garden. Full of echoes, the New York night smelled like beer and sweat.

The poor slept on the roofs of the Lower East Side. In rings, boxers beat each other with gloveless fists for fifty rounds. Driven by the shadow in his mind, Thaw squinted and sweated lemony sweat.

Everything began to spin. The Madison Square Garden restaurant turned into a maelstrom.

Starched tables, crystal, silverware, and people merged into one milky smudge. The drone of people's voices was unbearable and had to be stopped. Thaw politely removed a waiter who stood in his way. Tesla's friend, the symbolist poet George Sylvester Viereck, was sitting with White. Thaw ignored Viereck. He rushed up to White and fired into his flaming hair.

The shot deafened the entire city.

The flash wiped out human faces.

The drone stopped.

Smiling as if a surgeon was sewing his lip, Thaw left the restaurant. White's head fell to the table and broke a plate. His red hair was dyed with blood. Amid screams and the rattle of dropped silverware, deafened by the explosion and the shock, the architect grabbed the starched tablecloth as he fell.

Newspapers wrote about the oppressive humidity in the penthouse restaurant on that night, about the terror ladies experienced, about the pearl handle of Thaw's revolver. They wrote about White's scandalous life.

"My Benvenuto Cellini," Tesla broke into tears when he heard the news. Then he said under his breath, "Millionaires are murdering artists." Our hero was alone in this opinion.

Just as he broke the plate with his forehead in his death throes, Stanford White fell straight onto the front pages of New York newspapers. Just like the recent assassination at the Serbian court, his tragedy turned into a street farce. It was not long before Edison's nickelodeons started showing a film about him *urbi et orbi.* The urchins in the audience snorted and laughed.

The New York elite swirled in a carnival of hypocrisy.

Society showed understanding for the imbalance and jealousy of the murderer. Somehow it did not matter that Thaw's own life was no better than White's. The New York socialites who once loved White made a mental about-face and acted disgusted by his life, though his vices were not unique.

"Old hags in love with their priests will be the death of me," the ailing priapus had often whispered to his friends.

On their part, the hypocrites whispered that the deceased was a red Pan who hopped through life following the road sign of his member. White's "moral irresponsibility" somehow spilled over into his business dealings. There was a rumor that the remains of his famous Renaissance collection contained many forgeries. Only a few people risked being seen at his funeral. Even Katharine Johnson failed to attend.

Tesla was among some dozen people who stood by the grave in the warm rain on the first day in July. The priest's murmur mingled with the murmur of rain against the umbrellas.

Shovelfuls of dirt started to thud against the coffin.

Tesla heard White's words: "Erotica is a kind of energy or mystery that one wants to merge with."

More dirt thudded against the coffin.

"I love when a woman first shows me the sacred places on her body," White spoke.

The thud of dirt.

Despite her ailing back, his wife, Betsy, stood straight. His children were there, as well as some servants, an unknown girl who was weeping, and a couple of journalists who looked like hyenas. Wardenclyffe, the project of the century, failed. Its life-celebrating architect had been murdered.

"If I could add up all my orgasms and experience them at one time, there would be nothing left of me!" Nikola heard Stanford's voice. "Like Zeus, I always wanted to be the swan, the bull, and the shower of gold."

The coldness and warmth switched places again.

The dirt thudded and thudded and thudded.

That night, in Tesla's dream, Satan laughed loudly, crucified on the cross.

Tesla was holding his friend by the hand, but the maelstrom snatched Stanford away and carried him into the cold of the universe.

That was terribly unjust.

He had lost everybody he cared for.

Stevan was absent. Tesla did not respond to Robert and Katharine's wires.

The last time they were all together . . .

Were they happy then?

CHAPTER 91

Coney Island

"Let's go to Coney Island!" Stevan Prostran exclaimed back then.

The purple flags of memory flapped like thunder.

So they went.

There were Robert and Katharine, Mrs. Merrington, White with his wife and his son, Lawrence, Tesla and Stevan.

What did they see in the paradise for the poor?

They saw minstrels and ventriloquists, the dog-faced boy, the most tattooed man in the world, the strong man with red cheeks, living skeletons trembling from emaciation, and the skull of Christ.

They saw the chess-playing machine. Midgets. Fire eaters. Female opium eaters. Wax figures. Learned phrenologists. Automatons. Lady Mephistopheles and the Palace of Illusions.

"Ah! The Palace of Illusions!" Katharine Johnson almost fainted.

Mrs. Johnson and Mrs. White briefly spoke with the woman who became a snake with a human head because her family was cursed.

"What do you eat?" they asked her.

The snake woman fluttered her eyes with a very sincere expression and responded, "Butterflies."

A red balloon that escaped someone's hand rose in the wind above the tents, above Coney Island, above the ocean.

"This reminds me of the World Expo in Chicago," Mrs. Merrington hissed in her champagne whisper.

Tesla could see it all in his memory.

"This"—White overheard Mrs. Johnson saying—"this is called the orgiastic escape from respectability."

White checked her out with a quick lady-killer's eye.

"Mark her words," he warned Tesla. "They're always a bit deeper than Robert's."

White was the only one who could see Katharine—the invisible.

Katharine conventionally despised him as a whoremonger. "He believes," she said, irritated, "that the devil will protect him just because he takes the devil's side."

On that day long ago—surrounded by clowns on stilts, children who licked cotton candy, and the furious music of organ grinders—Stanford White became melancholy.

"Human yearning," he murmured, "is the eternal sheep for shearing."

All of this Tesla saw clearly in his memory. He saw White's flaming hair and his twirled mustache.

On that day, three full years ago . . .

He thought everyone was rather unhappy.

Later on, they looked joyous, happy, and even young to him.

All around them, the sacred people of the world laughed merrily over half-eaten fried dough and hotdogs. People screamed on the roller coaster, bought brightly colored trinkets, and viewed Brooklyn from the wheel similar to Ferris's. Katharine exclaimed, "Hey, how do you like it?"

He saw her in his memory.

He saw himself, contemplating the stinger in his soul.

It was about that time that a journalist asked him why he did not build his tower on Coney Island instead of Wardenclyffe.

At least it was fun here. A magician poured water from his hat into his sleeve and pocket. A boy with his nose stuck in the creases of the accordion was starting the same tune over and over again. Amid competing melodies—like long ago in Belgrade—he could again hear the fragments of the forgotten song from the times of the Great Migration of Peoples.

"Everyone has the right to look at his watch and proclaim the end of Divine Creation," Tesla declared. "As far as I'm concerned, it's still going on."

Just like him, Italian women in white blouses, pug-nosed Russian girls, and the Hassids also believed in miracles. All the newspapers and the advertisements of the world took aim at their holy innocence.

"He's better looking, and she's more humane," he heard Katharine whispering crisply into Mrs. Merrington's lace collar.

Betsy White had the most beautiful blue dress, perfect bearing, full and pale lips.

Whenever she looked at her husband, Betsy's eyes filled with stars. When Prince Henry of Prussia visited New York, who was there to meet him? Stanford! How witty he was! Look, he just said that—together with Washington and Jefferson—Barnum and Bailey should be included among the Founding Fathers!

Our hero could see all of that.

"Tell your cook to roast a goose as long as possible," he heard Katharine Johnson's words. "If the recipe calls for three hours, roast it for five. I have no clue why they made us eat stringy goose when we were children. Ha, ha."

Were they happy?

The gray-haired girl Katharine Johnson stole furtive looks at him.

Katharine's perfect bun with a hole in its middle excited Robert. He made a mute confession to her: "I know you blame me for failing to guess the things you'd never tell me about."

They were happy.

Lawrence White watched the wooden horses sail toward the future while the music played.

Stevan watched the creamy foam on Lawrence's ice cream.

The glittering future of the marry-go-round was circular.

The wind blew a newspaper into Tesla's face. He lifted it from his nose and read the headline: *Serbian King and Queen Assassinated.*

Katharine noticed the change in his mood: "What happened?"

"A group of officers," he managed to whisper, "members of the Black Hand . . . stabbed the king and the queen to death in Belgrade and threw their bodies out the window. Her being with child had increased her popularity. She received cradles from all over Serbia. It turned out that it was only a hysterical pregnancy."

"So that's the reason?" Mrs. White was disgusted.

Tesla sighed. "In addition to not having an heir, King Alexander had a habit of nullifying the Constitution at midnight. He was an autocratic Austrophile and therefore unpopular."

"He had been in love with her ever since he was a child," little Stevan said.

Were they happy?

They?

Anyone?

"She shielded him with her body," Tesla muttered.

The king was the boy with whom he had spent a May morning in Belgrade ten years before. Tesla remembered the yellow light he had experienced as he entered the Old Court Building. The apricot brandy he was offered had given that light its flavor. On the Long Island beach, he had the same flavor in his mouth again.

"Poor man."

Did the news report real events, or was the paper printed in Coney Island?

Concerned, Tesla kept buying newspapers for a few days after the assassination. Finally, in the *New York Times* editorial of June 24, 1903, he found a reasonable and comprehensive explanation of what had happened in Serbia:

Undoubtedly there is something in the Slavic nature which predisposes those of Slav blood to throw open a window and in a liberal spirit and with a large gesture invite an enemy to become an angel without further preparation of a flying machine.

Tesla lifted his eyebrows:

As the bold Briton knocks his enemy down with his fists, as the Southern Frenchman lays his foe prostrate with a scientific kick of the savate, *as the Italian uses his knife and the German the handy beer mug, so the Bohemian and the Serbian "chuck" his enemy out of the window.*

That day, Tesla opened the newspaper in his laboratory and put it down on a table in Coney Island.

He had a problem expressing the emotion he had experienced.

The *New York Times* became Reality and the rest of the world became Coney Island.

"Come closer!" newsboys shamelessly screamed in front of the circus tent of the world. In it, officers who looked like Sicilian dummies killed King Arlecchino and Queen Colombina. They horrified the ambassadors from the Embassy of Giants and the Embassy of Dwarfs. With sonorous sighs, the clowns on stilts shed tears over the event. Hyperbolic drums announced the murder to the rest of the world. The drummers advertised and advertised and advertised—the tragic miracle of life.

CHAPTER 92

The Shaman Dandy

A mysterious visitor arrived in Worcester, Massachusetts, the town where they manufactured barbed wire "as light as the air and as strong as whiskey." Above his rounded shoulders, the Stranger carried one of the most important heads of the twentieth century.

It was 1909. The president of the United States of America was a voluminous man with beautiful eyes by the name of William Howard Taft.

Have we already mentioned that the visitor was tightly squeezed between his two companions? A hint of a boyish smile repeatedly appeared beneath the large nose of one of them. The eyes of the other companion were hidden behind the glare of his glasses.

"We bring enlightenment," the youthful-looking Ferenczi started to sing.

"No, we bring the plague," the rough voice of the Stranger cut him short.

The visitor insisted that his topic would not be about dreams.

"People wouldn't take it seriously."

Important, gentle-looking faces came to the lecture. The Sage from Concord had taught them to look for reality under the surface of the world. Emerson's admirers were prepared to listen to the Stranger.

The visitor looked at them with his bitter eyes and—in a somewhat snarling voice—started to produce a string of rational statements about the "irrational aspects of our being." He spoke without notes, without preparation. He told them that dreams were simply a different form of thinking. Culture and repression were like the chicken and the egg. Culture depended on repressive acts of previous generations, and each new generation retained the culture by going through the same repressions. The power of neurosis was rooted in sexuality. The psychoanalytical treatment for this was based on the search for the trauma that, as a rule, took place before puberty.

The Stranger publicly admitted that at first he believed his work was an ordinary contribution to science until he realized that he was one of those who *disturbed the sleep of the world.* Silence was the response to his lectures, and the circle of emptiness formed around him. He became a foreigner to his hometown of Vienna. Every now and then, at professional conferences, someone declared psychoanalysis dead.

Quoting Mark Twain, he said, "The news regarding my death has been greatly exaggerated."

What happened after the lecture?

Questions rained down on him: "Is psychoanalysis immoral?"

Freud responded with a counterquestion: "Is nature immoral?"

"What about the conscious part of our being?"

"The ego often plays the absurd role of the circus clown who—with his gestures—is trying to show the spectators that he's in command of everything that's going on in the ring. However, only the youngest ones believe him."

"Would you say that there's no forgiveness or love in your world?" a voice asked.

"Do you promote free love and reject all restrictions?" asked another.

"I'm a married man," Freud responded.

When it was all over, the aged William James—who founded the Department of Psychology of Gods at Harvard—approached him. James buried his bill-like nose into his handkerchief, blew it, and said that the future of psychology was most likely to be aligned to Freud's research.

The visitor's eyes watered when he was awarded an honorary doctorate.

"Like a waking dream."

Squinting, he carefully examined the young man who interviewed him.

"No, I have never seriously thought about becoming a writer. However, I thank you for appreciating my literary gift."

Tesla's friend George Sylvester Viereck spread his thick lips in a smile and asked, "Why did you mention that the freedom of thought is more limited than we believed? That maybe there is no freedom at all?"

The visitor lowered his eyes and said, "Because probably there is none."

"Have you ever thought about emigrating to America?"

"Yes, as a young and impoverished doctor."

With a flashy mechanical pencil, Viereck scribbled down the answers on a pad of graph paper.

"The whole world is nothing but an enormous game of blindman's bluff disguised as a state of awareness," he translated Freud's ideas into poetic language. "People are sleepers dragged behind paper kites. The libido is a horse harnessed to our cravings. Neurosis often is the result of a compromise. Its symptoms jump from one object to another, leading the psychoanalytical beaters away from the cause. In the hypocrisy of daily existence our soul refuses to haggle—it sticks to its own truth and consequently suffers."

"What has the magician from Vienna seen in America?"

"Manhattan." Viereck scribbled down the answers. "Coney Island, Central Park, Chinatown, the Jewish quarters in the Lower East Side. *The Count of Monte Cristo* at the movie theater."

"Has anything bothered you?" Viereck grinned.

Freud paused. He was used to being the person with a notebook. He cleared his throat and responded, "I was fasting for a day due to the rich American food."

He failed to mention that he organized his Vienna group of followers like a castle under siege. That was why open doors in America—both entryways and bathroom doors—greatly disturbed him.

When they got a little bit tired, the poet abruptly asked the magician if he had heard about his friend Nikola Tesla.

Freud frowned because his cigar was going out.

"The Austrian whose fingers emit lightning," he answered as he reached for the matches. "I remember the time French and British newspapers elevated him to stardom."

He blew out smoke and looked at Viereck. He had heard that the boy with the elongated head and frog-like mouth was not just a journalist but also a symbolist poet, the author of a vampire novel. They called him "the new Poe" and "the American Oscar Wilde." He had also heard about Viereck's connections with the German royal family. Viereck was an out-of-wedlock grandson of Wilhelm I and thus an illegitimate kaiser.

The youthful, balding doctor came to the door for a second.

"Ferenczi has a funny smile," Viereck commented.

They were reclining in leather armchairs in the dusky library of Clark University. The armchairs smelled like dry apricots. In the bluish smoke, the atmosphere in the room resembled a spiritualist séance. The afternoon buzzed around them.

Before he interviewed Freud, Viereck did an informal interview with Katharine Johnson.

She told him about Tesla's childhood dreams of flying, his ability to project images through objects, his fragility and great vitality, the transforming illness that was followed by his famous epiphany in the Budapest park.

Freud took the last puffs from his Dominican cigar.

Hmmm, all that appeared to be a metamorphic experience like coming out of a cocoon and the shamanic ecstasy described by Mihailovsky and other Russian scientists.

Wait a minute, what was it that Jung had told him?

Out of habit, he reached for his notebook.

The semidivine state of the heightened intensity of personality, the ability to mesmerize people and change laws. A refusal to hold a conventional job—such individuals were either kings or paupers.

A man like that was not necessarily a part of a religious community. He *was* a religion. Among the Buriats and in the Altai Mountains region, the role of lightning was an important factor in the process of such a man's selection as shaman. If his soul flew westward, he turned into a black shaman. If it flew eastward, he turned into a white one.

Everything fit. No one could acquire such a gift and its dualistic good and evil nature by choice. Had to be sickly as a child or right before the initiation. Epilepsy-like symptoms and the experience of traumatic ecstasy. *Deep dreams.* Dying and returning. Flights across the sky or under the ground on the epic quest in search of the knowledge essential for the survival of the tribe. Permanent hypersensitivity. Flashes.

"Shaman!" Freud scribbled down in his lined-paper notebook. "A Victorian shaman!"

It's getting quite interesting now, Viereck thought.

Tesla's unofficial biographer could not restrain himself anymore. He told the story and now could ask the main question he actually had for Freud. "I have to ask you one thing: Was the theft of his father's blessing more brutal than the biblical Jacob's?" he finally uttered. "Did he kill his brother?"

"That's obvious," Freud exclaimed.

With a glimmer of bitterness in the corner of his eye, he explained that . . .

. . . .
. . . .
. . . .

CHAPTER 93

From the Diary

The terrain was rough, the time was wintry and dark,
the heart was vain and sly, the eyes were burdened with sleep,
the body was clayey and sad, the hands were muddy and weak.
Old Serbian Manuscripts and Inscriptions, 1535

When they told me that Marconi was awarded the Nobel Prize, I stared at the floor for a long time. I felt stripped of glory, like Achilles or Milton's Satan. Someone else's voice resounded in my mind:

"Rage was the song of Achilles. What will be yours?"

"The man puts in my coil some kind of a gap. So he received the Nobel Prize . . ." I responded. "I couldn't prevent it."

After a while, I pulled myself together and spoke in a softer voice: "Like the wind, the spirit goes wherever it wants, but we can only judge it by the sound."

Something happened to me a week after Marconi received the award. We were in the opera. The chorus from Aida *was singing:* "Heavenly spirit, descend on us, give us glory . . ."

The world became granular and started to rustle. I wiped my forehead with the back of my hand.

The opera house went through a metamorphosis. The singer who played Radamès looked at me with deeper and darker eyes.

"Let me go!" I told him.

The voices echoed in the boxes and ladies' décolletés. They were not singing on the stage—instead, ventriloquists were singing from the audience. The ladies' and gentlemen's eyes became identical. Katharine, Robert, and George Sylvester Viereck joined the raccoon parade.

I could not follow the abrupt changes of mood in Verdi's opera anymore.

I thought I had thrown him off, like a horse its rider.

I rose very, very slowly.

I excused myself. I went out.

The marble staircase glittered like sugar. As I was leaving, they mocked me with a stinging tune. Had Radamès and Aida already started to sing their hymn to death, seen as an ideal and eternal love?

"From the darkness of our bosoms, our bird-souls fly away into the everlasting day . . ."

An usher in uniform watched me go with very clever eyes.

Skulking and stumbling, I left the opera house. Coachmen and scalpers followed me with the same eyes.

I waved down a taxi. The taxi driver kept turning the steering wheel, which stuck out between his legs like a round coffee table. I paid him, and he gave me a look.

He gave me a look.

The eyes of a cat glowed from atop a garbage can next to the laboratory door. The next moment, those eyes were not bright—they were brown.

The cat gave me a look.

The secretary, who was staying late, said hello and looked at me . . .

She gave me a look.

Yes.

With the same eyes that the rest of the world looked at me.

My throat constricted.

Ghostly. Anguished. Warm. Deep.

The eyes of my dead brother, Dane.

CHAPTER 94

I Have Three Sons

Medak
March 21, 1910

Dear Brother,

Let me briefly tell you how I live. My Jovo became a priest here in Lika, and we live in Medak now. I have three sons: Petar, Uroš, and Nikola.

It's been a long time since we wrote to each other. That's really strange because we're brother and sister. I'm not blaming you for anything, as I know how you live, and my sisterly heart plainly tells me that we're still brother and sister like we once were when we lived together.

Your sister,

Angelina

CHAPTER 95

The Night Train to Wardenclyffe

At night, Nikola's dead brother often sat by the bed and placed his hand on Nikola's forehead.

"Nikola!" he called out to the man whom others had for years called Mr. Tesla. "Nikola!"

Tears poured down Nikola's drawn face and into his ears. He wanted to scream, but knew that doing so would not get him out of his own skin. During the day, he waited for the night to come, while at night he waited for the dawn. A moralist, just like his father before him, he could not understand people. He did not need anything from them except the tribute of their admiration. His emotional development froze in his childhood, and he engaged in quarrels with the imaginary mankind that peopled his solitude.

After midnight, Tesla headed for the slumbering colossal hall of Grand Central Station. That station was once Cornelius Vanderbilt's "court." The massive bronze chandeliers reminded Tesla of the ones at Breakers Villa. He climbed the marble staircase that overlooked the deserted passenger arena. There was an orb in the middle of it. Four clocks ticked on the orb. The enormous windows were partitioned with supple wrought iron bars. In the relief on the wall he made out winged wheels—the symbols of the railway. Constellations of stars connected by gold lines were painted inside the green cupola. His solitary footsteps resounded in the empty hall beneath the gods. Following the echo of his steps and thoughts, Tesla went through the station, which looked like Piranesi's small town, and came to the "tunnel" with parked trains.

He caught the night train to Wardenclyffe.

The elevated train rumbled two stories above the ground.

The inquisitive traveler stared at other people's windows. Like a moth, he peeped into lit-up rooms from the darkness.

In one room, a hairy man with curlers on his chest soundlessly shouted into the distorted face of a woman.

In another room, a ballerina hooked her thumbs against her collar bones. A pirouette transformed her into a white smudge.

In a third room, Saint Jerome hugged the lion.

In a fourth room, a matador posed frozen in silence. Confronting him, a black bull pawed the parquet with his hoof.

On the wall of the last room hung bloody Prometheus with the eagles perched on his belly.

Rows of golden windows . . .

Ah, the rows of golden windows whipped through deserted streets.

When the windows trickled away, Tesla became bored.

Then he opened a newspaper.

The newspaper was the *New York Sun.*

Flying through sleeping New York two stories above the ground, he was reading *Little Nemo in Slumberland.*

At the beginning of each new episode of that magic comic book, Little Nemo found himself in King Morpheus's kingdom.

That was familiar, so familiar.

Once upon a time, Nikola was a boy and light caught him by surprise in his bed. Then, from the golden light in the heart of the world, images started to flow out. He was flying among the exploding stars and deep-sea fish. On his left was day and on his right was night. He saw countries and cities. He saw town squares and people who spoke different languages. He saw the sacred monkeys of Benares. He flew from Samarkand to Japan. Nikola hovered above the world, directing his flight from a spot within his bosom. He wanted to return to his bed in the room in Lika, but the bed stayed a thousand miles behind him. There was no returning for the floating spirit.

Drawn away. Drawn away.

All of that happened again when—on the night train to Wardenclyffe—Nikola Tesla, Little Nemo, and the Princess of Slumberland found themselves in the emperor Jack Frost's ice palace. The clocks and shadows were frozen. They went across an endless polished floor, full of skating harlequins. The huge Emperor Frost towered above them with a sharp halo made of icicles. Emperor Frost resembled J. P. Morgan. Mister Frozen Face looked at his watch, which was frozen. Time was frozen. He told visitors: Emperor Jack Frost is here. He is a cold-mannered gentleman. Don't shake hands. His grip is terrible.

"You'll see that this is the most beautiful place in all of Slumberland," the courtier Icicle explained.

Palm trees looked like icy explosions.

Furniture was made of ice. Rooms were made of ice. Chandeliers were made of ice.

The Ice Palace glittered all around them with multiple soft tinkles. Courtier Icicle warned: "Since the ice caught fire and the palace almost burned to the ground, smoking isn't allowed here."

In a hall too large for an eye to take in, thousands of Snowmen destroyed each other with snowballs.

They were drawn away. Drawn away.

The train pulled up.

Little Nemo always ended his flights bundled up in the bedcovers on the floor next to his bed.

Tesla threw the newspaper away.

He transferred from the train to a car.

He arrived in Wardenclyffe.

He relaxed in his ice palace, beneath his steel crown that was eaten by rust.

There, at the place of cold fire, he felt safe. He completely undressed in silence. His sharp shoulder blades were where his wings used to be. He stood under the apparatus and turned the switch on.

Light rose upward from his toes. It splashed his calves and washed up over his knees. The flood of inner light was . . .

Oh, to cleanse oneself from dirty others . . .

This bright cyclone now replaced his inner flashes.

In the world of dollars and cents, he had an enormous need to occasionally submerge himself into sacred. A bright hurricane of high voltage went through his heart. The clean essence of the world disinfected the world's filth. Was the cyclone he used to disinfect himself the same wind that blew people from his life?

Tesla's frozen, eruptive soul relaxed. Bathed in the cold fire he fell into a lethargic sleep.

CHAPTER 96

Distant Rhythms

Man is the sum of outside influences. Our desires are the desires of others. Man doesn't become anything because he isn't anything.

Mark Twain

After the collapse of his life's work, the Wardenclyffe project, Nikola Tesla shielded himself with the warmth that radiated from his belly, his being, his heart, his chakras, with the ball of golden yarn that unraveled in front of him and showed him the way.

"You don't need anyone—such an inhumane creature that you are," Katharine Johnson scolded him.

"Remember, I warned you," people told him.

"When times are bad, you hear the music only for you," he whispered to himself.

Confronted with the possibility of defeat, the creator of the automaton for the first time started to reflect on the ancient question regarding free will. With those philosophical speculations, he hid the truth of his defeat, which was not his truth.

The Buddhists believe that the soul does not exist and that the world is a succession of momentary flashes.

Things became clearer in the nonexistent soul of the philosopher Nikola Tesla: from the central source that Aristotle called *entelechy*, people not only received energy but also ideas that rang in their heads like a streetcar at the stop.

His father argued with himself in multiple voices behind the closed door.

White was obsessed with sacred points on the female body.

Distant pulsations brought Dane's image into his dreams.

All features of individuality were rented like carnival masks.

People vibrated within the intervibrations of the world.

Sorrows!

Passions!

Infatuations!

The distant, oscillating rhythms brought all of these into people's minds and hearts.

On the streets of New York, seductive machines smiled wryly, machines delivered charismatic speeches, melancholic machines gazed from the windows into the silver lining of the rain. Humans were not automatons in the whirlpool of dead forces. Machines made of flesh were parts of the world that were interconnected and alive as a whole. People themselves noticed the rhythm of ebb and flow in nature. There was no doubt that they perceived the succession of fashions in dress as well as other fashions—in their heads.

And everyone was invited to a dance.

So, hypnotized crowds swayed.

The succulent and terrifying faces of "the vanities" grinned.

Although the swinging orchestras did not play.

Nor were military bands in parks.

CHAPTER 97

The New Automaton

And he had a new laboratory. Old Scherff in his terrifying sweaters worked in it. And hunched Czitó with his raccoon eyes. And we have almost forgotten: within the great pulsations of the world, yet another automaton pulsed into Tesla's life.

It was his new secretary.

CHAPTER 98

They Shall Take Up Serpents

Tara Tiernstein was just blossoming into a young woman when they brought snakes into the church. Pastor Hensley wore a martyred frown as he noted that no evil can befall him who labors in the name of the Lord.

"My brethren, do not doubt," with a beneficent smile, the pastor raised his voice, "that through faith, the sons and daughters of Adam can overcome Original Sin."

After these words, Pastor Hensley took a rattlesnake out of a sack. Deep wrinkles cut his cheeks off from his mouth while he read from the Gospel according to Mark: "They shall take up serpents; and if they drink any deadly thing, it shall not hurt them."

The church smelled of fresh wood. Jaws clenched. The viper wriggled from hand to hand along the pews. A red-haired girl handed it to Tara. Death slithered through her hands, and she offered it to a pregnant blond next to her. She left the church holding her chin high. At home, before Sunday lunch, she received everyone's congratulations.

"Soup is ready," Aunt Pam called out.

"I'll bring it!" Tara jumped up.

A crash rang out from the kitchen. They found her convulsing in a puddle of soup.

The epileptic fit never happened again.

"We'll see." Purple-faced and gray-haired Doctor Martinson frowned.

That cold sensation was on Tara's hands as she traveled first to Cleveland, Tennessee, and then to her uncle, who was a doctor in

New York. There she completed a typing course and found a room on Riverside Drive, close to Grant's Tomb. The dark monument frightened her, even more so after she gave up praying. She checked out one book a week from the library on Forty-Second Street.

New York fired her up like a sultry sigh. She talked too loud. She loved to blow noisy kisses. With her few friends, she went to Coney Island, to minstrel shows, to the Bowery theaters, to the penny arcades.

She loved to buy brightly colored dresses and wore them while she was looking for work. Eventually, she was hired as a secretary at a private laboratory. She wrote to her sister that she worked on the twentieth floor of the Metropolitan Building, right under the famous clock.

"My boss is middle-aged but young looking. Very cultured," she bragged to her sister.

Her strange boss came in right at the stroke of noon. He insisted that Tara buy three pounds of rapeseed, hemp seed, and bird food every day and that she meet him by the door and take his hat, cane, and gloves. The office curtains had to be drawn. Thus the room acquired an evening feel.

"Open the curtains!" he ordered only when a storm rolled in.

Then a *hatatitla*—which means "lightning" in Apache—flashed in all three windows. The panes rattled. Thor, Perun, and Zeus shook the sheets made of blue light. Her mysterious boss opened the windows, and it smelled of danger and freshness.

He observed the sparkling arcs as they appeared in regular intervals above the roofs. Using his fingers, he measured the length, distance, and power of each thunderbolt. The lightning purified his nerves.

One hand he held against his heart and the other between his legs. He gasped.

Sitting on the sofa, he grumbled with the storm. He loudly preached to the open windows. He felt fortune's spurs in his sides. His voice merged with the voice of God. He triumphantly joined in a duet with the heavenly guffaw. He cheered the flashes in unknown languages. He sang with them.

"I have created more powerful bolts!" he yelled.

Then the sound of rain became stronger. Its bright multiple jets again danced on the windowsill.

Once he opened a telegram, started to cry, and went out of the room. Tara tiptoed up to the piece of paper, picked it up, and read:

Mark Twain left with Halley's Comet. He came with the comet and has left with the comet.
Yours,
Robert

When she got her first paycheck, the modern girl Tara Tiernstein treated herself to dinner at Hammerstein's Roof Garden. What else could a single girl do who was becoming a spinster?

Food shielded her from the big city.

Tara tried to calculate how many hands were in the city. Millions of them waved to someone, grabbed jewelry, grabbed the hands of fiancés. All those hands were able to snatch something out of life. Hers were empty.

Under gaslight in her kitchen, Tara guarded her plate of food with her elbows. She squeezed bread into hard, rubber-like balls and shoved them into her mouth. Her gut howled like Scylla: feed me! Her hands turned into pistons and moved on their own.

Abstract notions can assume various shapes, especially the shapes of our cravings. She craved the truth and spiritual improvement.

Lord, from the time you threw us out of the Garden, we have constantly hungered and thirsted—men for women and women for men. Why do you do this to us? Why do you send us the itch that is pain?

Even after she had heard in the office that her boss could not stand fat women, Tara continued to fantasize about him. From a distance, she stroked his hair, the back of his head, his pale lips. Oh Lord, why do you do this to me? She dreamed about the snakes from Locust Valley in Tennessee. She wished her bed would squeal in her place.

She grew out of her flowery dresses.

She liked to stay alone in the office late in the evening. She opened a newspaper and read about what John Jacob Astor and his son Vincent felt when they got lost on the open sea. She used the forbidden private restroom, where Mr. Tesla went whenever someone unexpectedly shook his hand. The bar of soap sloshed between her palms. He avoided the contaminated others. He used to say that he was protecting himself against the germs that devour each other in the invisible world beneath the world. The germs he talked about were probably people.

Tara Tiernstein started buying the special black underwear that "those" girls wore. Her stockings swished whenever she crossed her legs.

Well?

Miss—he always addressed her that way. He never used her real name.

He described the bladeless turbine to her, which would produce ten horsepower per pound.

She understood him.

She was feeding off of him, her breadwinner.

The smile of playful Eros altered her face. He deserved to be loved.

He gave her daily bread. The bread she squeezed and shoved into her mouth.

One Friday evening, she stayed late to type his letter to the superintendent of New York public schools, Mr. Maxwell:

"We will include fifty mentally retarded schoolchildren in our study," her deft fingers typed. "Electricity has the potential to raise the intelligence level of mankind and to even cure the insane."

The windows of the Metropolitan Tower were wide open. The dogs of summer barked. The month of June was fragrant. The only thing that was heard in the whole building was the chatter of her typewriter. She had been suffering from sudden fits of hunger lately. That was why she carried bread in her purse. Alone in the laboratory, Tara sat astride the corner of her desk. On the table, right under her chin she opened Carlyle's book *On Heroes, Hero-Worship, and the Heroic in History*, which her boss was reading. She pulled out slices of bread. Her hands moved like pistons. She squeezed bread and shoved it into her mouth. Faraway pulsations determined her individuality. She ate out of horror. She had no control over her state.

"Miss!" a shocked voice exclaimed.

"Mr. Tesla!" she screamed.

Nikola Tesla approached Tara. His restraint was palpable. "What

you do to yourself . . . such a lack of self-control . . . I simply cannot con-
done such behavior."

His tie made of ice gleamed before her blurry eyes.

"Of course, that's not my business, but . . ."

Her gaze sank powerfully into his. She cried out, "Mr. Tesla!"

He stood before her, tall, with his chiseled features, in his armor
made of ice.

"I will pay you next week's wages, but you don't need to come in
Monday."

She had no one except him in this city. Her whole body jerked forward from the waist, while her head jerked backward. Foam gushed
from her mouth. The man looked at the floor so that he did not have to
look at her. From some distant center of the universe, tremors shook
this woman. Her ample breasts flopped out, revealing a rash between
them. Her eyes were pure helplessness. Her empty hand clawed at the
air and grabbed the spot where her dress was buttoned together. The
buttons flew all over the office.

CHAPTER 99

The Light of Shanghai

Three months after Tesla let her go, Miss Tara Tiernstein found a job at the Light of Shanghai, a missionary organization that saved souls in China. She was not the same girl who used to blow loud kisses on Bowery Street and draw catcalls from young men with her brightly colored dresses: "Hey baby!"

She practiced restraint on each and every bite she took. She made a long face as she drank tea without sugar. The rumbling of her stomach before she went to bed was a sign that she spent her day well.

Every morning Miss Tara Tiernstein swam through rivers of unknown people. During the day, she observed New York—which was no longer hers—from the tall balcony of the redbrick Light of Shanghai building. Swirls of black smoke flew over the gray smoke like scarves over coats. The tops of buildings disappeared in the clouds. Omnibuses bellowed like whales. Passersby slept as they hurried along. People blankly stared at each other like ants.

In the newspaper, Tara Tiernstein found and circled a few evening courses. It took three sessions of the course titled John Locke and Charles Darwin—the Quiet Revolutionaries before she realized that she had no interest in it.

She suddenly realized that reason was not her home. She realized that reason was nobody's home. She realized that the question "Whom do you love?" is never asked there. She realized that the whole city was a bottomless pit.

Confused, she asked herself, "Where's the soul? Where has the soul gone to in the city?"

On her wall, the young man covered in blood spread his arms in a gesture of wonder. Henchmen prevented the embrace he offered the world. The bloody man was the sole nourisher of Tara's heart.

"Why are you tempting me?" she asked him.

Whenever she did not think about Christ, she thought about the Mother of God and her pilgrimage through hell. The Virgin was kneeling in the midst of hell and prayed to her son to have mercy on the souls of the damned.

Tara lived peacefully and did not bother anyone. But Mr. Tesla came to her at night and touched her with his long, unusually cold fingers, extended with veins of electricity. He suddenly handed her a stiff snake, which turned into a blue thunderbolt. The Laocoön snake squeezed Tara in its lusty embrace.

She did not look for anything. She did not bother anyone.

In her office, while she counted copies of the Bible bound for Shanghai, something moved up her spine and lifted her hair. She knew who was behind it. She dreamed of him. He conspired with Martians who had horns. He resembled a frozen cat. Two tiny thunderbolts protruded from his helmet-like, combed back hair. How come she did not recognize him earlier?

She started to feel scared.

Really scared.

At any hour, he would touch her thighs with blue cold fire.

She went to visit her uncle in Brooklyn and stole the revolver from his desk. She hugged the heavy purse against her breast.

She still doubted: *"Why are you tempting me?"*

Then Pastor Hensley's words spoke in her ear: "No evil can befall him who labors in the name of the Lord . . . Through faith, the sons and daughters of Adam overcome Original Sin and tame the symbol of the Evil One."

She set off toward the library where—as punctual as a clock—he fed pigeons.

The wind roughly swirled horses' manes. The wind whipped her hair across her face. Despite her thin little jacket, Tara was not cold. Everything was clear to her. To herself, she repeated the words from the Gospel according to Luke: "Behold, I give unto you power to tread on serpents and scorpions, and over all the power of the enemy: and nothing shall by any means hurt you."

Her fear was replaced by resolve. She heard the music of all beings. The wind gleamed like diamond powder. He called to her through the sounds of car horns and brakes, the rumble and drone of the subway: "Taaaa-raaa!"

Meanwhile, in the Palm Room at the Waldorf Astoria, Tesla was taking his leave of Westinghouse, whom he had not seen for years. Westinghouse still looked like a swaying cupboard squeezed into a topcoat. Tesla serenely looked into his friendly fish eyes and told him, "Yesterday the French Supreme Court judge, Bonjean, ruled in my favor against Marconi."

"Congratulations!"

Westinghouse, whom people considered a crashing wave rather than a human being, had been ebbing for a long time. His mustache was completely white, his gaze still clear. He apologized to Tesla because his company's legal department had sued him for unpaid debts.

"They also signed me off," he mumbled apologetically.

He wanted to know what was going on in the Balkans. "Could you explain that war to me?"

"Serbia, Greece, and Bulgaria joined forces in order to drive Turkey out of the Balkans," Tesla responded.

"You know, Mr. Westinghouse, it's not all that pleasant to be a 'professional defender of Christiandom.' In my family, officers killed and were killed in endless wars, while priests sang their praises. Only women knew the pain of all of that.

"Personally, I don't support the cruel measures that many people preach these days, filled with prejudices against the Turks," Tesla concluded. "The greatest victory the Balkan countries could ever achieve will be their ability to show that they are ready for the twentieth century and can start dealing equitably with everyone—both Turk and Christian."

Westinghouse looked at him with polite incomprehension. He did not know that this pacifist was assigned to a military unit by the very act of being born.

"The two of us are heading in the right direction." Tesla smiled at his old comrade in arms as they were about to part. "I work with the New York public school system. Our electricity has the potential to raise mankind's intelligence and cure mental retardation."

Two partners from the old times bade each other farewell.

Tesla hurried on, followed by the sound of his steps in the hall. He was late for his meeting with the pigeons. As usual, he whistled as soon as he stepped from Forty-Second Street into the park behind the library.

A few solitary pigeons fluttered down, struggling against the wind.

Two mounted policemen rode by along the path.

Tesla glanced at the wrought iron clock. It was 12:20 p.m.

Suddenly, an unknown woman sprang up in front of him, dark and tall—as if he had stepped on a rake.

The expression on her face was icy.

The treetop of Tesla's nerves caught on fire in response to the frequency of the constellations. Something spoke to him and he pushed the woman away. At that moment, something slammed into his shoulder.

A policeman jumped from his horse, tackled the madwoman, and wrenched her gun away.

"You're wounded," he warned Tesla.

In court, Miss Tara Tiernstein's piled-up hair made her look elongated.

How well she knew that the city was empty of living souls. They would not take pity on her. She held her hands against her breast like a corpse. In a hissing voice, she explained to the judge, "He cast electricity on me."

Tesla told newspaper reporters, "I feel sorry for the poor thing."

"I've suffered a lot," Tara Tiernstein said repeatedly to Judge Forster.

Judge Forster sent her to an asylum where they treated her with electricity.

CHAPTER 100

For the Souls!

*And there was a tremendous earthquake and all-consuming fire . . .
and only after the fire a soft voice was heard,
and the Lord was in it.*
Akathists, Kondak 6

And then the Serbian conspirator who suffered from tuberculosis fired a shot at the chest of the Austrian archduke who also suffered from tuberculosis. The archduke's last words were:

"It is nothing."

Enthusiastic crowds in Berlin, Moscow, and Paris rushed to the slaughterhouse as if they were going to a wedding. Just like Tesla, all the Europeans knew:

The laws are becoming more just.

The first victories of the war were Serbian. In the West, there came months and years in trenches. Cannon barrages mixed French mud with human clay, which God blew life into by mistake.

Between strings of barbed wires, heavy guns buried and unburied corpses. The soldiers still believed:

The laws are becoming more just and the rulers better.

Then came gigantic guns. Then came flamethrowers and suffocating smoke. In the era of industrial death, people poisoned other people like rats. The entire Serbian army retreated through the Albanian gorges. Serbian ghosts took with them some forty thousand Austrian ghosts. The conscripts sang:

So long summer, winter, fall,
We'll never come back at all.

The laws are becoming more just, the rulers better, music sweeter.

Turkish machine guns decimated New Zealanders at Gallipoli. Austrians and Italians slaughtered each other among the mountain crags as sharp as razor blades. Gunboats bellowed smoke in front of Jutland. The forks of seagulls' wings fluttered above the slanted sea.

The laws are becoming more just, the rulers better, music sweeter,
people wiser and happier, and the heart of an individual . . .

People asked themselves if the age of light was the age of enlightenment. Howitzers pummeled twelfth-century cathedrals that were erected by a rooster's crow. Austrians hanged Serbian peasant women in Mačva. Germans forced Belgian civilians to labor for them. The British fleet imposed a blockade on an increasingly starving Germany. German submarines sunk merchant ships.

. . . and the heart of individuals were becoming more just and more
tender.

Progress enhanced evil.
Uranus ate his own children.
A certain Edgar Bérillon distinguished himself with his claim that an average German produced more excrement than other members of the human race. Turks massacred Armenians. In the Royal Village, Rasputin killed birds with a glance. Like insects, Russian armored

trains quivered their gun barrels as they sped across the steppes. Stars fell like figs shaken off a tree. The drowned exited oceans wearing white dresses. The Serbs, the French, the Germans, the Romanians, the English, the Russians, the Italians—*all of them*—hated with a "healthy futuristic hatred." The fatal verses finally fell into their place:

We want to exalt movements of aggression, feverish sleeplessness, the double march, the perilous leap, the slap and the blow with the fist! We want to glorify war—the only cure for the world.

Up until then, Doctor Jekyll was sitting in Europe, while Mr. Hyde was sent away to the colonies. In *White Man's Burden*, Kipling sang praises to Hyde's achievements in the heart of darkness. Now Hyde was back from the Congo, and he rushed to the Somme.

Something whispered in the ear: the horror!

Something growled from the darkness: the horror!

Something screamed in the mind: the horror!

Tesla's foster son, Stevan Prostran—his "Serbian servant"—became a Serbian volunteer on the Salonica Front and sent him a postcard through the Red Cross.

British sculptors and German painters ran through the expressionist smoke and the pointillist world of shrapnel. Like Kemmler, soldiers sweated drops of blood. Bergson and Nietzsche shivered, enveloped in chlorine gas and mustard gas. The human form was raped and disassembled in the trenches.

"If people were able to harm the gods, would they do it?" Katharine Johnson asked.

Every day, in New York Nikola Tesla watched flocks of birds in flight spread apart and gather together above the library building. He whistled. Pigeons alighted on his hands and the brim of his hat. While the seeds flew from his hands and fell on the rock, in the thorns, on the fertile soil—as in Christ's parable—he thought about the dead automatons in Serbia, in Germany, in Belgium, in France.

"Is it possible to feel sorry for evil fools?" he asked himself and responded, "Yes, it is!"

He felt sorry for those dirty scum, for those soulless cheats. He felt sorry for people. He felt very sorry for the elderly. And the little children. Everything that lives.

"Birds should be fed for the souls of the drowned," his mother Djuka used to say.

"For the souls . . . birds should be fed," Tesla repeated. "For the souls . . ."

In order to wipe guilt away from mankind, our sentimental positivist wrote in his articles that people were machines made of flesh, whirled around by great powers. People did not have souls. They had backs that were unburdened from moral responsibility. Each human automaton was an unconscious cannonball. The planet carried it around the sun with considerable speed—nineteen miles a second. The velocity of each automaton's body was sixty times greater than the velocity of a projectile fired from the largest German gun ever made. If the planet screeched to a halt, each man would be catapulted into space with enough power to hurl a sixty-ton projectile twenty-eight miles.

We have all been catapulted—but where?

CHAPTER 101

East of the Sun, West of the Moon

He carefully examined the photographs of Roosevelt's family, and then the photographs of military units of various armies. The *New York Times* reported on the surrender of the city of Niš in Serbia. The wretches in uniforms marched in the gray afternoon heading . . .

. . . somewhere.

A waiter snuck up to him in his ballet shoes. He balanced a tray on the tips of his fingers.

"Put it there!"

A school of goldfish shimmered through his consciousness.

The appreciation in the waiter's eyes reached the level of insanity. A wave of sudden adoration poured over the scientist.

Once again, Tesla was in fashion.

People said that he was a collector of what Emerson called internal light. Tesla's internal light glared in shop windows and in the trains that fired out into the void of night from the Chicago railway hub—*clackity-clack!* Thanks to him, subway cars strobed through brightly lit stops in:

Boston

New York

Paris.

What would have happened if someone deprived people of the light that, like a golden visor, fell over the eyes of young Tesla?

Night would have swallowed up golden windows. America's shiny industrial carnival would have turned into a scene from an Edgar Allan Poe story.

The Knight of the Sad Countenance leafed backward through a war newspaper. As he moved toward the front page, the headings became sadder. He finally came upon the one that said, "Edison and Tesla Will Be Awarded Nobel Prize."

Did he really want to get a Nobel Prize *after* Marconi?

The golden school of fish shimmered through one more time.

And *with* Edison?

Manfred read his own statement:

> *He said that he still hasn't been officially notified. He believes that he won the award for his discovery of the wireless transfer of electricity. Mr. Edison is worthy of a dozen Nobel prizes. No, he has nothing to say about the discovery that made the Swedish officials select Mr. Edison to receive this great honor.*

Praises showered on him.

The school of fish shimmered.

Tesla coughed maliciously, swirled his pen above a sheet of paper, and wrote back to Robert:

Dear Luka,

> *Thank you for your congratulations. In a thousand years there will be many thousand recipients of the Nobel Prize.*

> *But I have no less than four dozen of my creations identified with my name in technical literature. These are honors real and permanent which are bestowed not by a few who are apt to err, but by the whole world which seldom makes a mistake, and for any of these I would give all the Nobel prizes that will be distributed during the next thousand years.*

Yours truly

Motherofgod! Even if he had sent a much more politely worded wire in which he lectured the esteemed members of the Nobel Committee—

the individuals who *were apt to err*—on the difference between a real inventor like himself and the various "makers of better mouse traps" . . .

That year, the Nobel Prize for Physics was not awarded.

"Lusitania!" the streets thundered.

For a full two years, Tesla lived in tense luxury, on the tide of Nobel glory. The flashes of inner light returned, but they were tepid, not golden like before. More platinum-like, resembling a silvery film. In these flashes, the inventor saw the dance of his new turbine.

In the course of those two years, American military officers danced the same waltzes that Mojo Medić once tried to master. They spun like high school teacher Martin Sekulić's silver ball. Within those incomprehensible dancing circles, animus and anima were joined together.

Our hero left the ceremony at which he was awarded the Edison Medal and wandered off to a nearby park. He threw hemp seeds to white and gray pigeons. They landed, making music with their wings and orchestrating their presence with cooing.

The organizers tactfully brought him back to the ceremony.

Tesla thanked them quietly. "I am deeply religious at heart, and give myself to the constant enjoyment in believing that the greatest mysteries of our being are still to be fathomed. In this way I manage to maintain an undisturbed piece of mind, to make myself proof against adversity, and to achieve contentment and happiness to a point of extracting some satisfaction even from the darker side of life."

Then the paperboys' palates—like triumphant gongs—announced that German submarines had started to attack American ships yet again.

Then enthusiastic columns of people wearing straw hats started to march along Broadway carrying flags. Preachers thundered about bleeding suns and heroism. People were made to believe that any personal experience was inferior to the great transformative idea that would lead them out of all experience.

"War! War!" the arrogant revelers chanted.

The laws are becoming more just . . .

In the middle of the Great Repulsive War, our hero initiated a legal suit against Marconi. And in the war—what an irony!—he had Telefunken on his side against Marconi's British connections.

Music is becoming sweeter . . .

In that other war, as we will see, it was not clear who would join what side.

Rulers more humane . . .

The Serbian oath breaker with three noses and two eyes—Professor Pupin—was pitted against Tesla. Pupin claimed it was he who invented wireless transmission, but that Marconi's genius had made it available to the world.

And the individual heart . . .

In America, the court ruling on the invention of the radio was halted by President Wilson's act suspending all suits concerning patents for the rest of the war.

At once more just and more gentle . . .

Tesla asked himself: who is the neighbor that I shalt love?

Newspapers railed against Germans. Cartoonists represented the "Huns" as gorillas. In America too, everyone started to hate "with healthy futuristic hatred."

The fatal verses fell into their place:

We want to exalt strong, healthy Injustice that will shine radiantly from young men's eyes.

Americans now imagined German submarines in Maine. Edison's cameras buzzed while merry children threw German books into bonfires.

"Come closer!" Newspapermen raised a shameless din in front of the circus tent of the world.

It was written everywhere that this was "a war between the West and the East."

"Between what?" Tesla asked and wrinkled his nose.

The alphabet, temples, sculpture, theater, and mathematics came to the Greeks from the East. Judaism and Christianity came from the East. Romans were proud of their Trojan origin. Medieval jousting horses and Arabic numbers came from India, the Gothic arc from Armenia, medical books from Egypt and Morocco, gunpowder from China, humanists from Constantinople.

The ditty about the clash between the Great Spirit of the East and the Evil Witch of the West, composed in the name of reason, did not speak to Tesla's ears. Nikola Tesla did not believe in the magical geography and did not know what war correspondents wrote about. The Balkans, where he was born, was the seam. It was an antenna. It was a cat's whisker. To be born in a bad place was to be born in a good place. A man from the border was familiar with the "prenatal darkness" of Serbian churches. He was familiar with Islamic adoration of light and water and with the Latin obsession with clocks and bells. No one had to explain Turkish and Russian cultures to him.

What West? What East?

CHAPTER 102

On the Too-Merry Carousel of the Merciless Sunset

"Curse God and die!" Job's wife said.

An old man had for months treaded through the Waldorf Astoria's plush carpets as if trying to stay invisible. The elevators in cages of iron, the marble, the orchids frightened him. The absurd Ming vases in hallways made him sad.

Do you worry about him, reader?

Our hero had completely forgotten that he owed nineteen thousand dollars to Mr. Bolt, the owner of the Astoria.

So what? Did not the world owe him something?

Is it true that he signed the Wardenclyffe Tower over to Bolt as collateral?

Tesla's tower was abandoned for years. Rust covered its shiny steel.

We have already pointed out that—in the years before the war— our dear disoriented hero had still sometimes boarded

The Night Train to Wardenclyffe

In the company of Edgar Allan Poe's shadow, Tesla headed for the slumbering colossal hall of Grand Central Station. At that late hour, the red hats of the porters were nowhere to be seen. He followed the echo of his steps and thoughts. He climbed up the marble stairs and stood over the deserted passenger arena. The four clocks on the orb in the middle pointed to midnight. Midnight. Midnight. Midnight. Midnight. Illuminated eggs hung suspended on bronze chains. Enormous windows were partitioned with supple wrought iron bars. Golden constellations of stars covered the cupola. The solitary man's footsteps resounded in the empty hall beneath the fate written in the stars.

He caught the night train to Wardenclyffe.

Like a moth, he peeped into other people's windows.

He lost himself in the *New York Sun* and traveled with Little Nemo. Drawn away. Drawn away.

He arrived at Wardenclyffe. The disinfecting hurricane of enormous voltage went through his still-childish heart. The heart that, ten years later, same as before, believed that priceless towers could not be torn down, regardless of what any legal contract might say.

They were drawn away, drawn away.

By the war. By time.

He was shocked that Bolt did not protect Wardenclyffe.

His neighbors from the surrounding farms—Mr. George Hageman, Mr. De Witt Bailey, and the nearsighted widow Jemima Randal—gathered to see the miracle of all miracles. Many a time, the light from this mystical place used to wake them up.

Smiley Steel Company was getting ready to pick the tower apart for less than a tenth of its value.

The storm was coming again. The clouds to the west became metallic. Desperate sunlight fell on Wardenclyffe. The tower was like a green fly. It took a ride on the too-merry carousel of the unforgiving sunset. Each steel girder of the one-hundred-and-eighty-foot erection glowed.

It thundered.

The spectators shook from the fall.

The landscape turned gray as if dusted with plaster dust.

The great razed eye of Wanderclyffe rolled in the saffron dust.

"This is the end of a dream," De Witt Bailey said in the ensuing silence.

CHAPTER 103

Millions of Screaming Windows

Tesla was in Chicago when they wired him.

The news made his tongue, in his dry mouth, drop like a whetstone into sand. *Perhaps a wise man is really no better than a fool*, he thought. *And a human is no better than an animal.* The tower stood, derelict, in the midst of the surrounding potato fields. Tesla's inner world did not look any different.

Wardenclyffe was his world's stage, his place of transformation, his sublime love, his cosmic crutch, a home he had never had.

Houdini could escape any trap. Tesla could not.

His laboratory had already burned down once. That was when he went deaf from horror. Soot snowed on his hair.

He turned down the suggestion of the cobbled street—to bow his head, kneel down, embrace it, and die. Until dawn, he aimlessly wandered through the city with millions of screaming lamps and a hanged man in every room.

"Curse God and die!" Job's wife whispered.

CHAPTER 104

Um-Pa-um-Pa!

When the news came, he was in the barber's chair. He threw away the newspaper. A wedge of golden light crossed the street. He crossed it too and felt the sun on his back. That was when he realized that he left the shop with shaving cream on his face.

"The war is over!" ruddy faces yelled.

Happiness and pleasant smiles splashed over him.

Tesla turned around to see mankind wholeheartedly dancing to the music of the universe. On the New York avenues, seductive machines smiled—full of heroic beer—charismatic machines delivered speeches, machines out of joint kissed each other and tap danced.

Everyone looked for someone to hug.

"It's over!" the revelers shouted.

Like petals of spring blossom, confetti showered on Fifth Avenue. *Um-Pa-um-Pa!*

From his fiery throat, Caruso sang a song of victory.

In the midst of the commotion, Tesla miraculously came across Johnson and the Spanish-American War hero Richmond Hobson. He wiped the lather off his face and threw away the bib. Then they embraced each other. Their eyes grew teary and sobs stole up on them from nowhere.

Infected with brotherhood, Tesla choked and celebrated with the smiling city.

In the lying world of newspapers, the sons of light defeated the sons of darkness.

"Ah," Tesla sighed. "It's time to put things back in their place."

But the gilded frame was broken, and nothing belonged to its place anymore.

As Tesla headed toward his hotel, two blocks away from Central Park, the jubilant crowd thinned. His face darkened. Once again, he became aware of the magnitude of the disaster. His sensitive eyebrow grew taut.

"In Paris, the victors will soon march through the Arc de Triomphe," the outstanding mathematician told Johnson.

"Do you know for how long? For two hours. Do you know how much time it would take only for the French dead to march through? Twenty-three hours!"

Flags streamed in the wind.

Holy rags streamed in the wind.

Brass bands passed each other at street intersections. Trucks carried bouquets of waving hands. Feet moved faster on their own. People kissed strangers, laughed through tears, tossed each other in the air, danced in the streets. They themselves could sense the rhythm of ebb and flow that pulsed within them. Everyone had rushed to war as if to a wedding. Now New York frantically celebrated the marriage to peace. There was no more artillery or blindness or food that reeked of corpses. Men with vacant eyes who lived through the abyss would come home. And Daddy would come home. Dear God, let him—if he could only come home. And the world would be free. And the world would be new.

Purple, red, and blue stars unlocked the heavens. The drummers advertised and advertised and advertised—the tragic miracle of life.

With teary eyes, through confetti, through silver sparks, people looked at each other—transfigured—all brothers and sisters. Ah, human yearning is the eternal sheep for shearing! They were deeply moved and their faces glowed. Emotional eyes radiated promises that no peace would ever fulfill.

CHAPTER 105

Lipstick

The only emperor is the emperor of ice-cream.
Wallace Stevens

The youth of Europe were dead.
  "That's boring!"
  "Let's dance!"

Hair and skirts became two feet shorter. The music of jangled pianos and pouty clarinets rang out. Young people leaped and threw their legs sideways. Beads bounced over women's breasts. Men cranked their gramophones and their cars. Everyone went crazy over airplanes. On the silver screen, people split their pants and threw pies at each other in jerky movements. Even the squirrels in Central Park moved in the strobe-like fashion of silent films.

This is how the poets sang:

  BRrrR!
  Dududum!
    dyNamo
    Dyn
    amO

That was how the poets sang.

Dadaism was the new realism.

Millions rushed home after work and turned the knob of the green prophetic eye. Voices boomed, overly tense in the magic of the radio plays.

The jellyfish lamps with hanging beads.

Gals with heart-shaped lips.

Lacquered art deco screens.

Faces verging on enigma, framed by hats.

Shimmering dresses.

Chromed grills with bug-eyed headlights and rounded fenders.

Figurines on the hoods of limousines gazing into the future.

"Burning kisses, hot lips," lounge singers repeated like sleepwalkers, with magnolia flowers behind their ears.

Liberated trumpets, previously muffled with hats, suddenly reached the clouds. Trumpeters blew, leaning back like yachtsmen as their golden pipes tore the sky apart and brought rain.

Distorted cities glided across the mirroring limousines.

People made bathtub gin.

Manic ads repeated: "There are three things people want—Lower prices! Lower prices! Lower prices!"

"Ha ha!"

"Ha ha ha!"

"Haha Haha!"

The world laughed.

The music was ragtime, except it was not. Girls' faces looked like people Tesla knew, except their laughter was like shrapnel. With its neon signs and the radio, the world resembled the Metropolis he and White had planned to build.

It was exactly like Tesla envisioned it.

Except it was unrecognizable.

There was a puff of cold breeze and all things declared:

Now we are alien.

When did it start?

Perhaps a year before the Great War started, about the time John

Jacob Astor IV perished in icy waves, together with the inlaid interior of the *Titanic*. That same year, Tesla attended J. P. Morgan's funeral.

The world was not the same without that colossal adversary. How was it to continue to spin without those tiny malicious eyes and that grotesque nose?

The following year, Westinghouse, the relentless fighter, passed away. The friend of nature, fragile and noble John Muir, went after him.

It is quite possible that those people did not seem real to Tesla even before they died.

Before the war, he himself was a strange but real person.

During the war, the government suspended the court's ruling concerning who was the inventor of the radio.

A lonely pianist played in the enormous lobby. Followed by the Buddhist smile of the headwaiter, Tesla quietly left the hotel in which he had spent twenty years. Each new phase of his life was a new expulsion from the Garden of Eden. A clear stream gurgled across the keyboard while he pushed the Astoria's revolving doors, for the last time, after two decades. He murmured, "We're life's apprentices forever!"

He looked at objects as if he could not remember what they were. He blankly gazed into other people's windows and other people's lives with an innocent smile, which approaching old age, made him look suspicious. Like a moth, he fed on light. The whole world appeared like a lit-up shop window, which our frozen loner now observed from the outside. The weirdest thing was that he was the one who lit up that window.

"Ha ha!"

"Ha ha ha!"

"Haha Haha!!"

The world laughed.

CHAPTER 106

The Nose and the Parted Hair

I keep attacking the malice of time,
which gnaws and devours everything.

Don Quixote

The nose and the parted hair, Tesla thought when he first saw him.

Hugo Gernsback sported polka-dot bow ties. He took Tesla to his electronics shop, under the tracks of the elevated train on Fulton Street.

"I'm lucky not to have a glass store," he shouted over the noise of the express train to Brooklyn. Gernsback's place was cramped. There was barely enough space for the six flies under the ceiling to perform their many-angled dance. Several cabinets were crammed in the small room. When observed more closely, they became radios. The radios crackled, tuned to various stations.

"Good Lord, what a mess!" the visitor exclaimed.

"Ideas are messy. The lack thereof is tidy," the nonchalant Gernsback responded.

"God, my dear God . . ." Tesla kept whispering.

The only object that brought peace in the chaotic environment was a lamp with a green shade.

Gernsback nudged his nearsighted assistant: "Introduce yourself."

"Anthony, sir!" the assistant said.

Next to his temple, a paper clip held his glasses together. Anthony did everything—he sold electrical equipment, received contributions for Gernsback's journal the *Electrical Experimenter*, quarreled with printers. He was prone to sudden outbursts.

"Who do you think I am?" He would yell at his boss, blowing up for no reason.

"You're an unusual character," Gernsback would say to calm him.

As we have already explained, the noble hero of this true story, Nikola Tesla, crossed over into another dimension after the war. With one foot, he descended into legend, with another one—into oblivion. He had once laid claims to superhuman status with shy modesty. Now, his bragging became more obvious.

"Would you be so kind as to explain to me why my ideas regarding the transfer of energy through the planet wouldn't be ranked on a par with the inventions of Archimedes and Copernicus?" he asked politely.

When the monumental Wardenclyffe project collapsed, he made Wagnerian noise in the newspapers to compensate for his lack of practical success. He guessed at what kind of life existed on Mars. Heroes and demigods were exiled from the earth into the intergalactic void.

Yes, Hector was there.

So was Achilles.

His old circle of friends was reduced to mostly widows and widowers, whose voices echoed through senile autobiographies.

At midnight, Hugo Gernsback and Tesla walked around the acoustic hall of Grand Central Station. Gernsback's oiled hair shone under the light of the brass chandeliers.

"Write!" Hugo Gernsback kept saying. "Write like the rest of them!"

"You know what I will call my autobiography?" Tesla asked.

"What?" Gernsback laughed out loud. "*Christ, Buddha, and I—The Hidden Differences?*"

"I'll call it *My Lives*," Tesla retorted.

O you forest nymphs, you dryads who dwell in mountain springs, you reveling selens help me to see once again the world of my childhood, which is twenty thousand dawns away from me.

The world of his childhood was like a temple from antiquity—overgrown with weeds, left to lizards and satyrs.

At first, his childhood memories were like deep-sea fish that explode due to inner pressure when fishermen bring them to the surface. Gradually, Tesla got used to seeing them.

"I remember everything as if it's there right before me: I can see the house, the church, the field, the stream by the church, and the woods above the church—right before my eyes. I could paint it if I were a painter."

The scent of the soil and the cow's udder returned him to ancient Lika. His world was inhabited once more by frogs with golden coins on their tongues and dogs with burning candles within their mouths. Steep-horned goats rushed uphill. Shepherds created music with tree leaves. Humans, gods, and animals lived together. Bogeymen and water sprites quarreled in the watermill. People spat; they were all under the spell.

Mother's eyes were at the center of his memories. Mother stirred something in a pot, and the world around her started to spin. Different lights flew within the whirlpool. One by one, the lights opened up for him and turned into images.

Mane threw quick glances with his chameleon eyes. With one hand, fearless Djuka tied a knot on her eyelash. Within a circle of pure light, the tomcat shook his paws. Father quarreled with himself behind the closed door and prayed in many voices.

"Jesus, my Savior, save me. Bright Jesus, with wounds of light, transform my unclean and dark life."

Father's friends looked huge and glorious like Menelaus and Agamemnon.

On the icon with his patron saint upon it, Saint George—oblivious to what he was doing—was killing the dragon.

Just like Cervantes, our hero started to write not with his "gray hairs, but with his heart that grew tender with years."

Once upon a time, in a far off country . . .

While he was putting together his own hagiography, he often came to the workshop on Fulton Street. Scientists might have stopped listening to him, but Hugo Gernsback—the father of the newly born science fiction—pricked up his ears. His friends did the same. They came to Fulton Street so that they could see "the greatest inventor of all time, greater than Archimedes, Faraday, Edison—the man whose mind was one of the seven wonders of the intellectual world."

In that store under the elevated train—the "El"—madmen and liars gathered. People with vertical laughs congregated there, men with frightening spectacles, enthusiasts who needed radio lamps, Gernsback's writers with pimpled faces and inflamed eyes.

"Don't you know that the Pre-Raphaelite Holman Hunt claimed he was able to see the rings of Saturn with his naked eyes?" one of them said.

"The wind on Saturn carries rocks like feathers," the other responded.

"The human body has the electrical potential of two billion volts," Tesla pontificated.

And was like an etiquette manual for shamans.

Above their strange words, a steam engine cooed like a diabolical dove.

In that store, which shook frequently, people believed that Tesla—rather than Edison or Steinmetz—deserved to be called the Creator of the Modern Age.

Odd characters flocked around the source of odd miracles.

Young writers and inventors listened to Tesla, amazed by the size of his ears.

He came from the stars. He *was* a star. He was Mephistopheles.

He did not exist. He was us.

Kindness and unnatural cunning fought within Tesla's eyes.

"Man is a puppet that stars move with invisible strings," he preached. "We all absorb thoughts from one source. In the future, we'll travel on the blue ray of energy. We'll force atoms to combine in accordance with previously determined designs—I will lift the ocean from its bed, move it through the air, and create blue lakes and noisy rivers as I please."

Gernsback, who had slicked-back hair, introduced a charmer with dancing eyebrows to Tesla: "This is my chief illustrator, Paul Bruno!"

Faced with a problem, Bruno would look *through* the person with whom he talked. Then his left eyebrow tried to escape from his forehead. Everything he heard, he immediately translated into the language he thought in—the language of images. The pictograms of Tesla's life streamed on a long strip before his eyes.

The echoes and shadows of the destroyed Wardenclyffe itched, ached, and awoke in Tesla's soul. The tower was like a green fly. Every single beam of the high edifice glowed again.

Bruno rebuilt the razed tower in his drawings.

In Tesla's stead, he finally completed the sensational project.

He filled the covers of the *Electrical Experimenter* with giant insects, flying saucers that circled around planets, laser guns that attacked wingless planes from a mushroom-like cupola, people who wore helmets that read thoughts.

"Do you know what's happened?" Hugo Gernsback asked Tesla one morning. Gernsback rubbed his frozen hands, while the steam engine puffed above their thoughts and shook the room.

"What?"

"Your *Inventions* has hit the one-hundred-thousand reader mark."

Tesla beamed and said:

"Excellent."

"Good," Gernsback concluded.

CHAPTER 107

Choose the Best Possible Life

President Wilson sent Robert Underwood Johnson as an ambassador to Rome. Our good Robert lived the way he had always wanted now that he existed at the uppermost level of official representation, with poets and aristocrats. His wife, with her thick silver-white hair, drew attention in spite of her age. As always around Katharine, people talked about things unknown to their hearts. Did not Edith Wharton say that diplomacy and journalism were two brotherly capitulations of personality?

Once again, Robert threatened to publish his guide to Tuscany restaurants. With Gabriel d'Annunzio, he quarreled about what food they served in Heaven. They talked about dancers who had live snakes in their hair, and about ancient tombs and theaters.

"Choose the best possible life, and habit will make it pleasant," D'Annunzio lectured.

Before, Katharine's laughter rang out like a dropped silver tray. Now she sat, bathed in light, under a glass jar. A paper bird swam in a cup of tea that grew cold. She learned how to do origami.

Her universe had become shrunk by conventions, like the bound feet of a Chinese woman. She let them purge everything that was interesting from the world. And whenever mystery is gone—life goes with it.

Katharine read a lot. She insisted that Proust was a good psychologist but a poor poet. She read Chekov and believed that his characters made a huge mistake by not living in America. After the war, just like Viereck and Freud, she came to a realization: rationality is a sham. Man exercises control only over those things for which he does not care.

In her childhood, she arranged funerals for dead squirrels. She loved to walk barefooted. She loved to get wet in the rain. As a maiden, they insisted that she wear a corset and advised her: be pretty if you can, be witty if you must, but be proper even if it kills you. However, she believed in the outbursts of emotions like in cloudbursts. The staple characters of Commedia dell'arte are lovers, old men, and clowns. Kate unified all three in herself.

"I don't understand how you can be indifferent toward so much devotion," she wrote to a familiar address, to the tenant of the Hotel Gerlach.

She quarreled with Tesla from afar.

"The truth without love!" she laughed as if she heard the funniest thing. "The truth without love! My dear, you comprehend through your spirit and believe that the heart is for animals. You will become a story that dragons in China will retell: come and listen to the legend of the man who wanted to exile love from his life! But you can understand only what you feel." She laughed a terrible laugh. "And you can't comprehend anything at all without the help of Amor, the awakener of slumbering minds."

When they traveled to Yugoslavia, Katharine described to Tesla the view from Kalemegdan of the confluence of the Sava and the Danube.

"I was sitting on the hill this afternoon and watched the blue waters and the sun behind them," she wrote. "And I wished I could lend you my eyes so you could have my vision and drink the beauty of the day with it. Your ears must have burned a lot because we talked about you, then about Rome, then about you, then about America, then about you."

CHAPTER 108

But People Never

*The world is full of ghosts. They drove me away from
hearth and home, from my child and my wife.*
The Cabinet of Dr. Caligari

In Chicago's barbershops, people raved about Jack Dempsey's style. In Boston's North End, crowds whispered about Sacco and Vanzetti. The busy Philadelphia streets were appalled by the schemes of the Great Ponzi.

"Where're you calling from?" Hugo Gernsback asked.

"From Worcester, Massachusetts." Tesla's voice was distorted by distance. "We're installing some machinery."

"He travels a lot," Hugo Gernsback explained to the enthusiasts at Fulton Street.

"Where're you calling from?" he asked on another occasion.

"From Buffalo. I'm testing a plane that lifts off vertically."

In the apartments of George Sylvester Viereck, Hugo Gernsback, or Kenneth Swezey, the phone sometimes rang after midnight.

Tesla laughed. He quoted Napoléon: "The rarest form of courage is three o'clock in the morning courage."

Tesla talked two hundred miles an hour. Tesla reached a conclusion. Tesla hung up.

"That's very interesting," Gernsback whispered into the dead receiver.

During the stock market rage, everyone grew rich except Tesla.

Once in a blue moon, Boston Waltham Watch required his speedometer patent, or Wisconsin Electric bought his film projector.

There was no reason for him to go back to New York, the site of his bankruptcy.

Yet he returned regularly.

With the agility of a young man, he leapt and dashed in between the onrushing cars. He claimed that he could still wrestle a twenty-five-year-old, that his hand was steadier than ever, that everyone grew older except him, and that he would not know how old he was unless he had a mirror.

He frequented movie theaters.

The lights went off, and a child's voice rang out in awe: "It's starting!"

In that mysterious twilight, madness was contagious. A sentimental piano envoked the passage of time. A young man and an old man opened their eyes widely while sitting on a bench.

Dr. Caligari, with his tortoiseshell eyeglasses, resembled an evil bug. He rang his bell in front of a circus tent: "Come! Cesare, who has been sleeping for twenty-five years, is about to wake up!" The black dot swallowed up the screen, coalescing over the images of the characters. The county-fair Mephistopheles and the head of the asylum were the same person. A madwoman played a nonexistent piano. The staircases and towers on the screen were askew, not because of the artistic stylization, but because of the recent war. A somnambulist walked through the distorted city, holding a sleeping girl in his arms.

While Tesla was inside the movie theater, an icy rain fell on top of the snow.

The streets became glassy.

Skewed buildings were falling over icy Broadway.

The city became secretive.

Many, many years before, Tesla had slipped on the glittering streets of Karlovac.

"One should walk next to the buildings," he reminded himself. "One should walk on one's toes."

At that moment, his heels flew up toward the stars.

"Cesare, who has been sleeping for twenty-five years, is about to wake up!" flashed through his mind.

The branching tree of his nerves fired, and Tesla surprised himself by sharply jerking his body, somersaulting, and then landing on his feet. He felt someone's fingers clutch his shoulder. A stranger's honest eyes examined him from up close. A frightened smile pulsed in the corner of the Good Samaritan's mouth. "Are you okay?"

"I think I am," Tesla answered softly, straightening his overcoat.

Then he recognized the man who steadied him:

"Giovanni! Out of prison? But of course . . ."

Twenty-five centuries of melancholy colored Giovanni Romanello's smile. "I paid my debt a long time ago," he said.

"I still haven't paid mine . . ."

Tesla looked like he was about to sneeze. This man, who used to tell him about Sicilian blood oranges and sweet lemons, did not recognize him! Tesla was not sure if he had heard him at all. Giovanni was preoccupied with something else.

"Excuse my asking, how old are you?" Giovanni asked in a suddenly muffled voice.

"A few short of seventy."

"Unbelievable," the visitor from the past whispered. "I've seen cats do that but people—never."

CHAPTER 109

Only Pains Hear, Only Needs See

Upon their return, the Johnsons found it difficult to make the mental somersault that the new times required. Speakeasies had replaced the blind tigers. The world rushed forward with the jerky, accelerated pace of silent movies.

The crowds seemed to whisper, "Our thoughts are blown by the winds! We are hypnotized by advertisements."

Yet another dog's life had passed. A puppy named Richard Higginson III now barked inside Johnson's apartment. The puppy was so little that it rolled to the side as it walked, and they had to pick it up and hold it whenever a larger dog was around.

The whole world became an invitation to a dance that Katharine did not know how to accept.

"I don't know why I feel so blue," she wrote. "I feel as if everything in my life has slipped away."

Once upon a time, enormous hats hovered above Katharine's aunts. The aunts believed that it was better to be adequate at what you were not interested in, than excellent in what thrills you. To them, everything interesting in life was a personal threat. Logic was a Cinderella in their house of rules learned by rote. Even in her dreams, it was impossible for Katharine to pick up a wrong fork. She lived like Alice in a "how dare you?" version of Wonderland, surrounded by cousins who bore false witness to their own lives. The aunts claimed that discretion was the mother of all virtues. It appeared to her that discretion and thinking did not go hand in hand.

"Discretion?" Katharine mused. "That's not our natural state. We'll become discreet when we die."

So what was the truth? Katharine Johnson, née McMahon, wondered like Pontius Pilate.

Whatever the truth about the prewar life was, it could not be compared with Katharine's present need for psychological security. She now missed the bygone world that used to be so boring to her. She missed all the irritating lady recitations that she had detested all her life.

> *It's unacceptable to criticize the piano no matter how out of tune it is. No one should clown around in the ballroom and dance by himself. Acquaintance made at balls can lead to lifelong misery. You can stifle a sneeze by pressing your upper lip with your finger. In the drafty ballroom, ladies who are too scantily dressed often catch a chill that they never recover from. While an obtrusive guest tells his last story in the doorway, the hostess often catches a cold and dies.*

"Mom! Get out of those dark, draped rooms," her handsome son, Owen, yelled. "Jazz will cure your tuberculosis!"

"Okay," Katharine agreed, without enthusiasm.

With a bright smile and suffering eyes, Owen dragged his mother and father to a party at East Egg on Long Island.

The Studebaker glided along the dusty tree-lined road.

The golden lions of summer roared during the day and purred at night.

Owen and his parents raced the moon on their way to East Egg.

Yes?

In the garden, men and girls came and went like moths, among the whispering, champagne, and stars.

Yes?

A Rolls-Royce kept bringing in guests until after midnight, when the second dinner was served. Bare calves flashed as ladies stepped out of the car in their sparkling dresses the color of the moon or in their outfits of peacock feathers. Many of the incoming guests did not even know Mr. Gatsby. In Katharine's time, a young gentleman was allowed to touch a lady's waist only with a glove or a handkerchief. It was only yesterday that no one could monkey around and dance alone. Now, after the Great War, they danced the shimmy and the Charleston, flailing their legs to the side in the swirling smoke.

Johnson, who looked more and more like a grieving lion, made a reconciliatory remark: "Now it's their turn to be young."

The pool's color was the essence of azure.

Drunken girls tried to walk on the water. They splashed the water with their arms, and people pulled them out sopping wet, amid a lot of squealing. The music was fast and then three times faster. Saxophone players leaned backward like yachtsmen. Our Katharine felt sick among these he-and-she loonies who danced alone.

"We're too old for all of that," Robert said when they returned home.

"The world had changed less from Plato to my elementary school days than since my elementary school days till now," Kate sighed.

The former beauty threw her jacket on the floor and went to her room. Owen's wife, Jenny, really got on her nerves. She could not stand that urban face and that body exuding erotic laziness. Out of "refinement," Jenny ate only oysters and fruit. The silly woman could not understand why people thought so hard to come up with something original instead of simply repeating what the rest of the world was saying. Her fancy girlfriends used to be equally devoted to sailing and interior design. Their beloved fashion was a thoughtless force. (As if previous fashions had been thoughtful!) This unimaginative younger generation was the same as the older one—it only snuck up behind Katharine's back.

Katharine did not understand the limitations of life. The grandmotherly role did not suit her. They say that women—when no one desires them anymore—gladly become grandmothers in order to receive a little tenderness from beings who have no other choice.

Yet she still felt hunger. She still felt shivers. Desire.

Tesla's cold-fire baths were not available to her. She drank opium tinctures.

And so . . .

So . . .

So . . . charmingly . . . she smiled at the floor.

"O world!" she murmured. "In you, only obsessions choose. Only weaknesses understand, only pains hear, only needs see."

O world!

CHAPTER 110

Did We Live the Same Life?

The pains that accompany old age were nothing compared to the pains of the soul. The old woman with wrinkled cheeks, propped up against three pillows, with a heavy heart, she thought about her life and could not remember anything good.

Robert did.

When they were young, Kate protected a perfect spiderweb on which drops of dew looked like jewels. "Don't brush it away. Look how it gleams in the sun."

Over and over again, he told the story of how a reporter caught their wedding bouquet.

When they undressed together for the first time, he kissed her left breast. "And now her little sister, so she doesn't feel neglected."

"Mmmmmmm," she murmured.

Like Szigety a long time ago, Robert loved that she walked around the room naked so he could see in her hips the same force that spun stars and planets.

She caressed the tree of life between his legs. Her moans sang in harmony with his in the bed.

With his lips on his wife's ear, Robert watched the streetlights on Lexington Avenue come on.

When she got pregnant, he kissed her stomach. When Agnes was born, Robert got up at night and tiptoed to the cradle to see if the baby was breathing.

"Do you remember?" he asked her.

She did not remember anything anymore.

Robert compared his memories to hers and spread his arms. "I wonder—did we live the same life?"

CHAPTER 111

I Didn't Know How . . .

"What's Katharine doing?" Tesla asked.

"Cultivating her moods." Robert grew darker. "But she's also ill."

"What's wrong with her?"

"Something in her chest."

After they came back from Rome, there was no more hiding.

Before, the wrinkles gathered around her eyes. But old age truly arrived when her cheeks wrinkled. Her once-clear blue eyes became clouds of milk in tea. Yes, they became cloudy and so did everything else. It was truly painful to look in the mirror. But even the suffering that accompanies old age was nothing compared to . . .

I dreamed that I was the servant and you the maid and that we spent the night in the ice palace, on a bed of ice.

The residue of one smile tore up her insides. She remembered the October afternoon of more than a quarter century before when squirrels swirled their tails and with ebullient leaps rushed through shimmering nature. She and he strolled through the yellow and auburn of Indian summer. Ducks slept afloat. The sun was in the corners of her lips and eyes. Heraclitus's invisible flame licked the world.

But the palace was made of ice. The blind statues were made of ice. Their wedding room was also made of ice.

She dreamed about whirlpools and geysers. She dreamed that she stroked unicorns who fed on fruit in Brazil. That she skied down a mountain of diamonds, that she gave water to hummingbirds and dragonflies from a thimble. She dreamed about *the other side of the air—uninhabited and uninhabitable.* She dreamed that the pianists tickled her.

"I believe that many different lives are owed to each and every person," Arthur Rimbaud wrote.

But . . .

The veins stood out on the hands folded in the lap. Katharine was not only reluctant to go out—she refused to come down to the living room for days.

He whose body warmed hers their entire life now got on her nerves. Robert's eyelids became swollen, and his eyes turned into slits. He chewed not only with his mouth but with every single wrinkle on his face. She always knew what he was going to say before he said it. His resemblance to a grieving lion repulsed her.

"If I brought her gold, she'd say it's too yellow," our good Robert complained to his son, Owen.

Katharine's aches came in duets and then turned into choruses.

"But everyone loves to be forgiven for something," Robert added.

She became anxious because of the inner horror of things.

The phone rang. She did not get up. She thought: *The phone will ring just like this, and I will be no more.*

She put off going to bed: will I wake up again?

The balustrades and chandeliers were made of ice.

Is this all? Kate thought.

The little French tables and tricorn armoires were made of ice.

What will I say to Saint Peter? Kate smiled a smile of spectral joy.

Her bed was made of ice. Her hair was full of icy powder.

"Ah," she finally sighed. "I'll tell him what everyone else says: I didn't know how to live any other way."

CHAPTER 112

Dear Tesla

October 15, 1925

During the last night of her life, Mrs. Johnson asked me to stay in touch with you. That's not easy, and it won't be my fault if I fail.

Yours faithfully,

Luka

CHAPTER 113

Whenever . . .

Whenever a button fell off his coat, whenever a shoelace broke—he remembered her.

CHAPTER 114

A Letter to the Dove

Soft one! Dear one! My own!

O full of light and cooing. O you gracious elusiveness! O whiteness! Cleanliness! Brightness! Spotless, fluffy dream. O you who rinse the world with the beauty of your wings, misty from speed. O mercy with which the blood of all beings throbs. O sorrow, realized through tears from an honest heart and forgiven. O you homeland of my soul. O my soul.

The gracious weakness that rules over strength!

O you who hovered above the waters before creation! You whom Noah first released from the ark after the flood!

I feed you by feeding myself and the whole world whose essence you are. When your flock, like confetti, grows silvery above the city, I fly with you. I know you right away by the beauty of your flight. By your whiteness.

Sacred pure soul, stay with me.

Anima! Amen!

As I hold you on my hand, your beak pecks at the corner of my lips. Radiance flows out of your eyes and from the center of the world. Light splashes over my feet and sloshes above my knees. The flood of inner light engulfs my thighs and reaches my hips, my heart, my forehead. My lips touch the rosy beak. Blinded by whiteness, sightless, I can finally utter the last words of Christ according to John:

"It is finished."

CHAPTER 115

And Then

The roulette of the twenties stopped on Black Tuesday. Brokers at the stock exchange rushed as the second hand of the clock whipped them along. In the drowning voices, the brokers announced that stocks and bonds were sinking. The mobs rattled the doors of closed banks. Above the entrance to Wall Street, they engraved Hobbes's words: "Man is a wolf to man."

In the west, farmers burned their crops. In New York, people fainted from hunger.

Impossible!

Women sold "Eden's apples" to avoid begging. In soup kitchens, they poured soup into the hats of the walking wounded.

Impossible!

For six meals a day, the hungry hallucinated in dancing marathons.

Impossible!

Then the widower Johnson came back from Paris. He sighed and complained, "Wherever I go, there I am."

He smiled and boasted: "When you travel all the time, you never become parochial."

"I don't think so," Tesla corrected him. "One's soul is either a provincial town or a metropolis, regardless of the place where one lives."

As a surprise, Robert brought Tesla a copy of the Serbian surrealist journal *L'Impossible*.

"Impossible," Tesla started to laugh. "That's the refrain of my life.

That's what they have been saying about each and every one of my ideas—from the very beginning."

"Have you ever seen a miracle?" Johnson inquired.

"Ever? All the time," Tesla snapped.

During the seventies, in Graz, women wore something that looked like a lacy bib. The passage of time turned that into a miracle.

Johnson told him how André Breton listened to "the Earth's geo-magnetic pulse" and how he loved the impossible.

"Impossible." Tesla laughed once more. "The refrain of my life! From the very beginning."

The next day, he was scratching his bowler hat.

"It's become too expensive," he said. "It's become impossible."

"What?"

"The laboratory."

Gernsback spread his arms in a gesture that expressed wonder and agreement at the same time. He watched over the move with Tesla.

Twenty trunks with correspondence, theoretical papers, and proto-types sank into the frightening storage room of the Hotel Pennsylvania.

CHAPTER 116

The Honoree

Birthday cards with best wishes from Albert Einstein, Lee de Forest, Jack Hammond, and Robert Millikan alighted in his room like white doves.

"Here's one, and another, and yet another," the maid said as she threw the envelopes on the desk.

With his palm, Tesla flattened the white envelopes. As he put them in a box, he felt a bit embarrassed for desiring to get more of what he despised.

With a drowsy, blank gaze—like a figurehead on the prow of a ship—he walked down to the hotel lobby at a quarter till noon. A bevy of reporters rushed in at noon.

The seventy-five-year-old was barely aware of talking to them, and yet, he talked about the day when women would be superior to men, when his awesome turbine would be vastly improved, and his electrical pump implanted into the human body. Then he elaborated on fasting and hard work.

"What do you mean?" inquired the journalists, resting their notepads on their knees.

The skinny old man raised his index finger.

"People simply shouldn't eat that much. I stopped eating fish. I switched to a diet of bread, milk, and 'factor actus'—a mixture of leek bulbs, cabbage and lettuce hearts, white turnips, and cauliflower. This will make me live for a hundred and forty years."

The skinny old man raised his index finger again and told them about his ancestors who owed their longevity to plum brandy, including the one who lived to see one hundred and twenty years.

"What was his name? Methuselah?"

"No, his name was Djuro."

The reporters' smiles stiffened and their chairs squeaked as they wrote in their notebooks.

"Don Quixote has turned into Sancho Panza," jotted the writers. "He's mocking his own wisdom."

"I regret not interviewing him back in the nineties, when he was among the Four Hundred and changed gloves like a magician," complained Mr. Benda of the *New York Sun* to the gorgeous Miss Jones. "People went to the Astoria just to catch a glimpse of him."

With his cigarette holder, Benda underlined the text of a yellowed article from the 1890s on his knee. It read: "The airless glass light bulbs that Mr. Tesla held looked like the bright Sword of Justice in an archangel's hand."

In her tweed suit, Miss Jones of the *Times* tried to imagine the crinolines from that time period. Her button nose was powdered. Her inconsistent smile was like a needle in a compass. She said she also regretted that "I did not meet him back then in Colorado, when he was creating thunderbolts!"

Ever since the horse-faced septuagenarian started celebrating his birthdays through the press, these two had always attended.

Tesla was changing before their eyes.

At first it seemed that he came from the pits of hell, with its traces of darkness all over him.

But for Miss Jones the man from hell soon disappeared and was replaced by a feeble old gentleman, with two youthful springs beneath his eyebrows.

Then that one vanished too and a prim, catlike man appeared, surrounded by an unearthly aura.

Whether reflected in mirrors or captured in photographs, his face was also changing. He himself did not know whom to expect whenever he looked in a mirror.

"Will anyone weep when this ghostly anachronistic futurist fades away?" whispered Mr. Benda.

Miss Jones took in the glowing horizons and gossamers in Tesla's dreamy eyes.

"He's cute," she whispered back. "I feel like hugging him. He seems to be cold. I feel deeply sorry for him."

The old man's emaciation fascinated both Mr. Benda and Miss Jones. His legs were crossed. They noticed his long, narrow, high laced shoes.

Among the many hats with press passes tucked in the bands, there were always two or three bonnets.

"Erect. Supple. Looks ageless," these ladies wrote in the notebooks resting on their knees. "Thin and compressed lips. Pointed chin."

"Prominent forehead. Classic Greek profile. Intellectual pursuits etched on his face. If you take the risk and look into his eyes—you'll disappear into space . . ." Miss Jones's pen danced on the paper.

She had to admit to herself that the smile of this interplanetary old man became a bit disconcerting. His charm came from old-fashioned mannerisms that occasionally radiated something irresistible. He changed the tone of his voice several times during the interview.

Tesla was bored by people and felt pity for them, but he knew how to hide it. These journalists resembled many he had met before—untidy, superficial, smart—almost brilliant but without true faith in themselves. (Each individual is as worthy as the things he takes seriously.) They were envious and condescending toward anyone with a real goal.

Miss Jones flashed her tango smile at Tesla.

"Will you tell us something that you haven't told anyone?" she asked him.

Don Quixote told a little tale from the "mauve" nineties that could be entitled:

Earthquake

Many years ago, in this very city, on South Fifth Street, Sicilian women with cracked faces arranged oysters on wooden boards covered with seaweed. Rotten cabbage heads rolled down the street. Live fish splashed in buckets. It smelled like smoke. In a side alley some boys played baseball under bedspreads hanging from clotheslines. They felt at home in chaos.

"Tonino! I'll kill you if the ball messes up the laundry!" shouted mothers from the windows.

Artists from Upper Manhattan used to come with their sketchbooks to this exotic part of the Lower East Side to draw street scenes from "Naples" or "Damascus." That day, on their way to "Damascus," the artists felt the ground shift under their feet.

The cobbled street started to shake. The glass panes on the Panetteria Italiana rattled. In the bake house, a chair first jumped up, and then, in two or three hops, limped to the side. Pots and pans started to shake. The head of a crystal chandelier swung sharply. Mysterious waves traveled through what Henry James would call "tiny vulgar streets."

"Earthquake!" announced an enlightened voice from a window.

Verily, verily I say unto thee, even birds in flight were shaken.

A young woman gave a shrill cry like glass being cut. In a maelstrom of shouts, the cursing of carriage drivers merged with the wailing of pedestrians. Carmine Roca hastily collected his wares. A large eggplant fell onto the cobbled street. The buckets tipped over. The fish flopped in the dust.

All of East Manhattan was shaking.

The conductor of the El stopped the train.

The voices went hoarse as they shouted, "Earthquake!"

Two policemen ran left and right, not knowing where to go first.

"Wait a minute!" said a man from Taormina. "This isn't an earthquake. An earthquake stops after the first shock, but this is getting stronger. It must be that crazy scientist."

Tesla chuckled at this point in the story.

"He's going to kill us all!"

"Let's kill him before he kills us!"

"Go upstairs, quick!" the people shouted.

The helmet fell over the policeman's eyes. Stumbling, he rushed up my staircase.

"Actually," said Nikola Tesla softly, *"that morning I fastened a small oscillator on the bearing wall of my laboratory on South Fifth Street. As new oscillations combined with existing oscillations, they amplified and traveled to the foundations of the build-*

ing. As the whole of Manhattan started to shake, my room was as quiet as the eye of a hurricane."

"Bam, bam, bam!"

The situation turned serious.

"Bam, bam, bam!" *The policemen were banging on my door.*

Tesla smiled slyly.

"I hit the oscillator with a hammer. I closed my eyes and sighed as everything quieted down completely."

On that day the entire Lower East Side was abuzz about the mysterious earthquake. There was a rumor that two women miscarried, that the El derailed, that construction workers jumped off scaffolding, that robbers fled from a bank, that a panicking woman threw her child out the window, that some man who happened to look up caught it, that a bearded Russian swept the silver coins off his eyes with the back of his hand, got up from his deathbed, and took off down the stairs.

With crossed legs, nearly shouting, Tesla concluded his story and hit the top of the desk with his stiff index finger: "I could produce vibrations so strong that the earth's crust would heave up for hundreds of meters, toss rivers from their riverbeds, shatter buildings, and practically destroy an entire civilization. I could illuminate the entire globe with a mild aurora borealis effect. I could send messages to any and all places in the world."

There was a *pianissimo* touch of madness in his words.

"Man reins in and tames Prometheus's fierce, destructive spark—the titanic power of a waterfall, wind, and tide," Tesla yelled. "He curbs Jupiter's thundering bolt and annihilates both time and space. He even turns the magnificent sun into his obedient, diligent slave."

"Even though he looked into the abyss of the Great War, Progress still has him inebriated," Mr. Benda whispered into Miss Jones's magnetic ear.

The honoree was so obsessed with Progress that even the sentimental Miss Jones wondered, *Could Progress be mad?*

At that moment, a flash of light momentarily blinded the honoree. On this photograph he looked like the ghost picture of the Swedish

Queen Astrid, taken by white light in Copenhagen, with the medium Einer Nielsen.

The old man's voice was tense. More than anyone else, he had the right to be called the father of the electric era.

"So why aren't you?" someone cut in.

"I'm not a crook," he proudly complained. "Money doesn't mean anything to me. Neither does fame."

Did Tesla's words make sense? Hmm . . . He might as well repeat the words of the self-proclaimed knight Don Quixote, who insisted that all he did "was in accordance with the rules of knighthood." Tesla did not believe in people anymore, but he still believed in Progress, just as his father believed in God—despite Voltaire.

Tesla was hesitant to take his leave.

The Angel waited for him in his hotel room: "Jacob, let's wrestle!"

"What was he like as a young man?" the beauty asked the fat, enamored Mr. Benda.

"Self-possessed and gullible about the world and its evils," answered Benda. "And he was always a step ahead of his time."

"Isn't it more fun to dance cheek to cheek with one's time?" asked Miss Jones, ever the coquette.

A denizen of the most exclusive hotel in the world, a member of the Four Hundred in New York society, a friend of Astor and Vanderbilt, of Twain and Dvořák, of Vivekananda, and so on, and so on . . .

Everything that was known about him was contradictory.

Hadn't that Tesla fellow won the Nobel Prize?

Hadn't he ripped up a million-dollar check?

Some wrote that his eyes were quite bright while others insisted that they were small and dark; some said he would not shake hands, while others remembered his firm grip.

He orchestrated galaxies of lightbulbs like a conductor.

Abhorred flies and earrings. Liked beggars and birds.

He caused the Tunguska catastrophe. Wanted to control climate on earth and turn it into a lightbulb. Hovered above while they applauded him. He was one of those who disturb the sleep of the world.

He was like the African deity who painted one half of his face blue and the other white, so those from his left side asked, Have you seen the blue god? while those from the right inquired, Have you seen the white god?

Surrounded by cowards, he was the only one who had the courage to let the hurricane blow through his body. He stood on the blue stage under the rain of sparks, as in a dream.

He was a Neoplatonist, inspired by a desire to enter the mind of God. Like Isaac Luria, he released "holy sparks" that were held captive in the physical world.

No! He's a madman and a crook! A homosexual Balkan mythomaniac! A friendless monomaniac.

No! He's a man with the mark of Cain.

He's the incomprehensible. The very attempt to define what he represents is offensive. If we deprived the modern world of his inventions . . .

"What would human solitude feed on without narcissism?" whispered Miss Jones to Mr. Benda of the *New York Sun*.

For years, Tesla lived in bliss. He was a flaring, impersonal force. He created earthquakes. He was the first human god of thunder on earth. He avoided women and germs. Satan caressed him with high voltage currents. But never a woman.

"Shush . . ."

"Hasn't he ever?"

CHAPTER 117

Forgotten

On one Monday . . .

In 1828 . . .

They found a strange boy in the town square of Nuremberg.

He was sixteen years old and had a note in his hand: "I want to be a cavalry man like my father."

He bore a striking resemblance to the Grand Dukes of Baden. Because he had spent his entire life in a dungeon, he could not speak. He only knew the jailer who gave him food. When they led him out, light struck him like a rock, and he fainted. He loved twilight. In the dark, he was able to read and to see colors. A wildcat that would attack everyone else grew calm next to him.

People educated him and wounded him.

People taught him his name: Kaspar Hauser.

Throughout Europe, he turned into a symbol of bottomless solitude.

How can one describe a rainy day in New York in the thirties?

The lapels of the coats were turned up. Hats pushed against hats on the streets. Prohibition was finally over. "No more thirst!" the winners celebrated. Inside quiet bars, martinis and cocktails glowed like yellow and red lamps. Ashtrays brimmed with rouged cigarette butts. Someone played the piano in a sly manner. The sounds dripped . . . Men and women finished their dinner and sighed, "Oh, God!" Sappy movies started to idealize the tenements. In the shadowy apartments in the former tenement buildings fingers turned knobs. The green eye came on. Roosevelt's aristocratic voice vibrated: "The only thing we have to fear is fear itself."

In his room, the gray-haired somnambulist read an old newspaper:

The Crowd Packed Times Square to See the Arrival of 1910. Theaters and Hotels Full! Woman Set on Fire in the Café Martin at the Stroke of Midnight! Revelers Panick. Morgan Pays a Visit to President Taft. Francolsa Mutarsolo and Emil Arthur Springer Issued a Wedding License. She Is Fifty-Seven Years Old, the Green Bridegroom Is Twenty-Three! Professor Percival Lowell Explains That They Build New Canals on Mars, Causing Disturbance of Dust on the Planet.

Tesla placed the newspaper back with the other yellowing papers and went out to take a walk.

The whole world was lit up like the World Exposition in Chicago once was.

Sometimes he had Hobson clearing his throat by his side, the Spanish-American War hero whose cheeks women flocked to kiss during the gay nineties. Sometimes it was the pug-nosed and persistent Kenneth Swezey. Sometimes the biographer John O'Neill took a walk with Tesla, and sometimes visitors from Yugoslavia. Dwarfed by Manhattan, they were happy to talk with one of their own. His countrymen threw furtive glances at him and compared his features with the drawings on cigarette papers from their childhood, under which it read, "Here's the feature of his face, whose works we all embrace."

On the radio, Rudy Vallee sang, "Brother, can you spare a dime?," the sad song of the Depression.

Workers ate their breakfast sitting on girders fifty stories above the city.

With its ever rising towers, New York rushed into the sky.

The Manhattan Company Building was the tallest building in the world.

William Van Alen's Chrysler Building overtook it.

For a few months, it wore a crown.

Then the Empire State Building outgrew it.

Tesla watched them on his walk through the city.

What's the point of obsession with the biggest? he wondered. *The earth isn't the largest planet, or the planet closest to the sun, but life exists only on it.*

He held Dane by his hand and carefully—as if he considered death to be some sort of disability—led him across the street.

He read *Magnetic Fields* by Philippe Soupault, ate his pathetic "factor actus," and praised his own subconscious plan for self-annihilation.

The angelic fragrance of a Chinese laundry wafted by him as he passed. A wooden Indian stared at him with its white eyes. The sound of guitars and irregular *terza* intervals came from a Cuban bar. (Jesus would have loved to have had a drink in such a place right after they took him down from his cross.) In an Italian café, a gigantic espresso machine with an eagle hissed like an airplane coming in for a landing.

Beneath the elevated train on Second and Third Avenues, Don Quixote stalked through an interplay of shadows that made him dizzy. He strolled by stone churches in the canyons between the buildings. Fire escapes and water tanks on the roofs rose above him. Time and again, he wondered at the trees planted on the terraces of the ziggurats. He looked up at the sky that was squeezed between the cliffs and his head spun. From Pennsylvania Station, trains rattled, fired out into the world.

Dreams, movies, and neon signs were mixed up with everyday life.

Tesla watched the movies Vermeer from Delft directed. Blonds stared at him through a veil of smoke. Shady characters dressed in tweed chased femme fatales down wet streets. Shadows were as deep as chasms. Fans turned slowly in bars. On the screen, the train wheels rattled in the smoke. Sheets of illuminated rain whipped the windowpanes while the hero and his fiancée left the station. Then Bela Lugosi focused his crazed and anguished eyes on Tesla from the screen.

"I love to go to the movies," our hero would say. "I look through the pictures like through glass. It's relaxing, and yet I can think."

Deaf from solitude, Tesla left the movie theater.

He blinked and fed on the city noise. All around him, the dangerous and enchanting New York screeched, growled, hummed, and screamed.

The only city on the planet made of villages. He listened to the barking of the elevated train as it curved.

It grew dark. Automobile headlights in the streets became something sacred. Seen from above, the liquid jewelry slowly crawled along the streets.

The view of New York was a drug.

Neon oracles on the roofs . . .

Pulse! Pulse!

. . . repeated the same things.

"Part of my laboratory has always been out in the streets," the hermit smiled.

The tireless stroller pushed through the throng of people in front of Broadway theaters. In front of the entrance, a lightly dressed girl hugged herself and shivered.

A newsboy with a flat cap practiced Tarzan's scream with a breaking voice.

"I need to apologize?" a scrawny man shouted at a woman. "I'm too skinny to apologize!"

Once again, like before, couples sniffed each other all around him. They rubbed against each other and squeezed each other—the couples. They were barely able to tear apart their honey-sweet lips in the movie theaters, the entrances, the alleys—the couples. In the hotel rooms—the couples.

Undulating roundness. Tightness. Possessing. Recoiling and submitting, dissolving in affluence and sensuality. The couples.

Each woman was a boundless promise.

Each young man wanted to be a bull, and a swan, and a shower of gold.

Lights hovered, and the city burned around our Kaspar Hauser. Around the wrestling ring in Harlem, the spectators howled. Faust and Job tossed each other on the mat. King Kong roared from the Empire State Building. In Caribbean restaurants, cooks softly prayed to Yemanja, the African goddess of the sea. In a bar in Greenwich Village, the Grand Inquisitor accused Jesus of giving people too much freedom.

Nikola Tesla entered the lobby of his hotel and nodded at the porter in livery.

An unread daily paper waited on the table.

In the paper, Roosevelt shook hands with a forgotten man.

"You remembered me," the Forgotten told him.

The Bride of Frankenstein

Three rows of neon signs rose above the movie theater. Tesla entered the Palace of Illusions on his own two feet, and left it on someone else's. Whenever he stepped into the lobby, freshness enveloped him.

The lobby was plastered with mysterious semi-profiles and sensuous smiles of movie stars.

The sweetshop offered candy and cigars. The lobby appeared to be a cross between a mosque, the Kremlin, and a Chinese restaurant. Ornamental wriggling lines created an illusion of movement. On the boxes, even ornaments were ornamented.

There was an abundance of special, exhilarating space inside. The fans blew freshness and the scent of perfume at the visitors. A war widow and a chubby man who slaved in his office for eight hours were finally able to wipe their foreheads with relief: "This is the life."

White rays streamed across the room.

The metallic voice in the background lent authority to the images of foreign and domestic news. Roosevelt kept signing on and on. A voice resounded in the back of Tesla's mind: *Come! Cesare, who has been sleeping for twenty-five years, is about to wake up!* Hitler introduced mandatory military service. Mussolini's shadow loomed over Ethiopia. In New York, they listened to "Lullaby of Broadway."

Tesla grinned.

The movie started with thunderbolts, darkness, and wind. In a warm boudoir on Lake Geneva, Byron, Percy Shelley, and his wife, Mary, laughed. Then the scene darkened, and the story about Frankenstein's monster began—or rather continued. To the spectators' utmost amazement, it turned out that the monster did not die. It surfaced from the underground tank beneath the burning mill.

Tesla's chiseled head stood triumphant above his suit, which grew crumpled and sank into itself.

After the murders and the ensuing mobs, Frankenstein's monster came across the hut of a blind hermit. The blind man never asked him a question.

"No one will hurt you here," the player of the sad violin told him.

He gave the monster bread, wine, and a cigar. He taught him words:

Bread good.

Wine good.

Friend good.

At that very moment, Doctor Pretorius appeared unannounced at Frankenstein's castle, followed by an enormous shadow.

"Let's create life from the dust of the dead together," Pretorius suggested.

Baron Frankenstein threw his hands up. "I'm fed up with that hellish course of action."

"Come," Pretorius said, luring Frankenstein. "After twenty years of secret scientific work I have also created life."

At that point, Tesla remembered his Prague days, Doctor Faust's house, and the Golem. He giggled.

The widow next to him turned her head in disapproval.

On the screen, Baron Frankenstein revealed a worrisome weakness of character. Curiosity overcame scruples, and he let himself be dragged into the laboratory. With his horse teeth, the demonic Pretorius somewhat resembled President Wilson. He clenched his face like a fist and toasted: "For the new world of gods and monsters!"

It turned out that Pretorius produced miniature people in his laboratory.

He lifted a piece of felt from some glass jars. He showed the cute homunculi to Frankenstein:

King

Queen

Bishop

Ballerina

Siren

The Mephistopheles-like Doctor Pretorius moved the tiny people around with tweezers. He was annoyed by his inability to achieve a larger size.

"That has never been a problem for me," Tesla giggled.

On the screen, Mephistopheles hissed at Baron Frankenstein: "Our mad dream has been realized only halfway. You created a man by yourself. Together, we'll create his female companion."

"You mean . . ." The baron did not dare to understand.

"Yes. A woman."

Finally, the heroes of the movie found themselves at the most exciting place in the world.

The spectators' eyes lit up.

That was an interstellar gate, the tower of alchemy, shrouded in silence. Its heart drilled into the heart of the earth. Its eye stared into the spheres of heaven.

It was Wardenclyffe!

Silently, our hero laughed so hard he choked.

The special effect expert Kenneth Strickfaden redesigned Tesla's magic coils for his own purpose. Blinding streaks whipped all around the tower and disappeared into the darkness.

Lo and behold—a female mummy with discs on her temples was already waiting, lying on the table. Lazy sparks surrounded her body. They became vibrant, started to caress her aggressively, and turned into frenetic fireworks.

Oh, do you still remember the walks in front of Dr. Faust's house?

Do you still remember the Golem?

Do you remember Prague, Nikola?

"The artificial brain is waiting for life to enter it," Pretorius announced in a funereal voice.

Do you remember the thunderbolts that resembled sea snakes you created in Colorado?

Do you remember the sparks that flew around your shoes?

A shout came from the screen: "This is going to be a tremendous storm!"

The assistant was Edison's Igor, who once winked at the bearded lady.

"The storm is coming!" Igor screamed. "Release the kites!"

At that very moment, the apparatuses were turned on and lit up their faces. The sparks boiled over. Thunderbolts started to rumble. The mummy ascended toward the opening in the Wardenclyffe Tower. Turbulent clouds could be seen through the opening. The kites danced in the night. A thunderbolt hit one of them with a blast. The bed with the female mummy started to descend from the roof.

"Did she receive life?" a shaky voice asked.

A Promethean spark brought the dead flesh to life.

"May I be cursed for meddling with the mysteries of life," Frankenstein wailed.

Yes, what has been said about Allah could be said about electricity: without shape or smell or sound, but nothing can resist it once it makes itself known!

The woman's hand moved.

"She's alive!" Pretorius screamed.

Frankenstein's bride stood upright before her creator, with stitches beneath her chin, looking insane. She had a most fascinating hairstyle: gray streaks shot up from her temples like thunderbolts.

"Look at her! She's beautiful!" Tesla could not tear his eyes away from the pure femininity that electricity created.

"He made me from the dust of the dead. I love the dead. I hate the living," the monster said.

The monster approached the woman.

"Friends? Friends?" he mumbled with shy hope.

The woman was perfectly grotesque. Attractive. Repulsive. With her hair standing on end.

The electric beauty saw the square head with electrodes from up close and hissed like a cat.

"She hate me," the monster stammered.

"The levers!" someone warned.

The desperate monster grabbed a lever.

416

People's screams did not prevent him from pulling it.

Wardenclyffe shuddered and once more collapsed into nothingness.

Tesla saw the movie five times, staring at his own thoughts through the moving pictures. Hermes Trismegistus whispered into his ear: "That which is Below corresponds to that which is Above, and that which is Above, corresponds to that which is Below, to accomplish the miracle of the One Thing."

In Mary Shelley's book, the monster was some kind of superman. In the movie, a solitary beast took his place. In popular speech, the name Frankenstein was used for both the monster and his creator. Thus the genius turned into a monster. And the other way around.

CHAPTER 119

Because There's No Money

"Eight decades. That's not something to joke about."

The Czechoslovakian ambassador awarded Tesla his country's decoration. Mr. Fotić, the Yugoslav ambassador, encouraged the guests to help themselves:

"Please, have some crummy caviar and some humble champagne."

Mr. Fotić pinned the White Eagle ribbon to Tesla's scrawny chest.

Many of the guests noticed that Tesla himself looked like an eagle. His shoulder blades lifted the back of his tailcoat like a tent. Tesla's nose protruded from his face, and his cheeks were sunken as if he had just taken a drag from a cigarette. His ears flared out, large and petrified. The part in his thinning hair was at the same place it had been fifty years before. His eyebrows stood up. His stare was fiery—a true Dinaric peasant who would draw an enthusiastic greeting from any child in Lika: "How are you, Grandpa?"

In the midst of the Great Depression, Prince Pavle gave Tesla a Yugoslavian royal pension of six hundred dollars a month.

"Here's some crummy caviar and some mediocre champagne," Fotić kept saying.

Skeletal in his tailcoat, Grandpa promised that the trend to spend more on war than on education would be reversed in the future, and that all the problems of the world would be solved by the essential substance *akasa*, the source of free energy.

"Gramps is harping again on his plans to contact other planets!" Consul Tošić whispered to Tesla's biographer O'Neill.

"For a long time, people have been scraping the aura off things," O'Neill frowned. "But we must be able to recognize the sacred even when it is in a profane disguise," he raised his voice. "He . . . only feels that we're suffocating. He feels that down here it gets so bad that— unless we contact some other life form, then really . . ."

After the ceremony, a priest approached Tesla. The priest had a large head, fat cheeks, and almost Chinese eyes.

"You know, they celebrate in Smiljan as well," the priest said.

"What do they celebrate?"

The priest continued to smile:

"Well—you! From the king to the last Lika peasant. The royal government issued a railway discount in your honor. They also issued a stamp with your image."

"And you are?" Tesla frowned in distrust.

"I'm Petar Stijačić. My relative, Father Matej Stijačić, is now the priest in Smiljan and lives in the parish house where you were born."

"And so?" Tesla was confused.

The fat priest almost melted into his smile. "They organized a local festival in your honor. As if with poppies, all the fields were strewn with Lika hats. The Zagreb Bishop Dositej officiated at the liturgy."

The priest tugged at a button on his jacket, benevolently reached for a drink that a passing waiter offered on a tray, and went on: "They put a nice plaque on your home. *Nikola Tesla was born in this house on July 10, 1856.*"

Father Stijačić looked at the saintly old man with emotion and added, "A committee was established in Smiljan with a goal to more permanently mark your anniversary. Some wanted to dig a well with good drinking water right beneath the church, so that any Lika man can quench his thirst and remember his great compatriot. Others suggested that a lighthouse be erected on the top of Velebit Mountain."

Tesla finally showed some interest.

"So, what's going to happen?"

"Nothing." The priest beamed with the same syrupy smile. "There's no money."

CHAPTER 120

The Ghost Taxi

New York's towers were wrapped in drapes of clouds. Wind whipped the puddles with rain. The March downpour was too much for the taxi's windshield wipers and water coursed down the windshield like oil. Blinded by the shower, Tesla was walking back to his hotel. The wind had turned his umbrella inside out, so he did not see the taxi and its driver did not see him. The taxi driver did not hear his own brakes as the muted tires slid over the water.

The impact threw the old man five yards away. His left shoe flew across the street and wound up in a planter. As soon as he opened the door, the driver was drenched.

"Even my butt was wet," he complained that evening, soaking his feet in hot water.

He saw the old man who was as white as if he was boiled, sitting in the puddle full of shimmering circles.

"Mamma mia!" he wailed in silent Tesla's stead.

Maria Ganz, the owner of the nearby jewelry store, lifted up the old man. The driver poured the water from the shoe and handed it to Tesla. With his eloquent hands, he explained that it was not his fault. Drenched passersby opened their umbrellas above them.

"Can you manage?" they asked.

"Let me go," the old man muttered in a muffled voice. "Let me go."

"Do you want to go to the hospital?" Miss Ganz whispered like an accomplice.

"Just take me to my hotel," Tesla mumbled.

The same driver who hit him took him to the hotel. With his small hands, the Italian clutched at his heart and at Tesla's shoulder. The injured man frowned as the taxi driver and the receptionist in a raincoat carried him in. In his spirit, he was trying to overcome the pain for two days.

"It's nothing," he said over and over again.

Utterly unpretentious and therefore much more serious, the hotel doctor disagreed. "Rib cage contusions," he passed the verdict. "Three broken ribs. Pneumonia!"

As he got older, Tesla could not stand people contradicting him. Couldn't he feel his own body? He had almost drowned twice, once he narrowly escaped being boiled alive, and once avoided dying in a fire. Doctors had given up on him three times.

"Noli me tangere!" he ordered.

He spent countless hours in the company of a solitary spider. The spider's legs were so thin it was as if it had spun them itself.

Fainting spells assailed him frequently.

The flashes in the sky competed with the flashes of the neon signs. It flashed in his ribs. Everything flashed.

The sky was marbled with streaks of light. Its color was repugnant. Thunderbolts undulated and tried to lick him. Nikola simultaneously wept and laughed with terrible laughter.

"So you wanted Promethean light? Here's your light," a voice spoke to him from the lightning.

He wept through the roaring guffaws. He was lonely—the loneliest man in the world. He was so lonely that he was glad when he discerned a terrifying silhouette in the sky, when the wings beat and a huge eagle fell on his sides.

"Hello, my only friend."

The eagle stabbed his liver with its talons.

Tesla howled roaringly.

A forked thunderbolt stuck out its tongue. Tesla bared his teeth, and it ricocheted as from a mirror. The Caucus Mountains shook.

"Let me go!" he whispered.

The eagle did not have the eyes of a bird—it had human eyes. It raised its bloody beak and blinked good-naturedly. Nikola screamed so that the entire sky lit up with lightning. Yes, those were human eyes, familiar eyes . . .

The eyes of his brother, Dane.

The phone rang through the lightning and dragged him back from the nightmare.

"How are you?" Gernsback asked him.

Tesla whispered painfully into the receiver: "The worst thing about sickness isn't our inability to meet our goals—it's that those goals seem meaningless."

To see the meaninglessness of the world added to his suffering.

"The *Hindenburg* burst into flames. So what!" the old man was annoyed as he remembered the *Titanic*. "They've discovered Pluto. They've split the atom. So what?"

The gray-haired Miss Skerritt, his former secretary, brought him books he did not read.

"Here's H. G. Wells's *The Shape of Things to Come*," she encouraged him. "Read it, please."

"Thank you," he responded in a vampire voice.

Miss Skerritt left. Tesla wandered away in his thoughts so much that maids could freely clean the room in his presence. Minutes or maybe hours went by as he daydreamed. A cat brushed his face with its tail, or did it just seem that way? Once again, a balloon lifted his sleepy head beyond the visible.

The bellboy, Kerrigan, materialized from the mist. Kerrigan spoke out of the corner of his mouth and squinted with his right eye. He reminded Tesla of Stevan Prostran so much that he almost expected him to ask, "Are you my father?"

The bellboy brought him a soiled envelope that came flying from the maelstrom of the Spanish Civil War. The volunteer Stevan Prostran sent his photograph from Barcelona. The fear of being alive and the joy of being photographed merged in it. Prostran put his hand on his hip in the company of the smiling anarchist Durruti and a dandy with sideburns and with a sailor's hat on his head. A cathedral that looked like a termite mound rose in the background.

"Is that all?"

The redheaded Kerrigan gave him Robert's letter. On a blue sheet of paper, in handwriting that no one used anymore, it said:

Oh, if only I could somehow help you in your sickness. Except for the Hobsons and us, you have few friends left who can look after you. Call Agnes to come and visit you because I can't.

The light-eyed Agnes came with fruit he did not eat and flowers they put on the windowsill. The erstwhile little girl was sixty-four years old. Her husband was French Holden, a bohemian and the grandson of a general. As a witty Englishman used to say, "All the time he was able to spare from being intoxicated with himself, he dedicated to neglecting his duties." Since their children moved out, Agnes could not stand him. She dragged an easel around, trying to paint stars "as seen through a dog's eyes." Her avant-garde endeavors turned out quite conventional.

"They're a bit unclear," Robert complained, looking at his daughter's paintings.

"Only the unclear brings us the sensation of eternity," Agnes responded.

Shivering with unswerving dedication, Agnes sat on the sickbed and remembered how the driver of Tesla's coach took them on a ride through the deep shadows of the park.

Clippity-clop!

"That was a more peaceful time," Robert's daughter sighed.

She never admitted to him that she feared his fiery eyes back then.

In addition to Tesla, Agnes waited on yet another sick man.

"My good Johnson," Tesla whispered. "How is he?"

Dad's back hurt. He groaned every time he got up or crossed his legs. He complained that arthritis and a cough were the worst combination because he did not dare move, and whooping cough made him jerk.

With fake serenity, Agnes mentioned that sometimes Dad could not remember the right word, and the man of belles lettres hesitated, humiliated with the forgetfulness of old age.

A few years before, he had had a minor heart attack. Afterward, he felt like he was made of glass. He would pause in the middle of the street, not daring to move forward or backward.

"I'm afraid I'll burst like a soap bubble," Robert whined.

CHAPTER 121

I'm Not Afraid Anymore

With the swirling leaves, the wind wandered down the cemetery paths. A few former members of high society walked through the swirls. They spoke ever softer and slower, like crickets in October.

Tesla recognized the sharp eyes and frog mouth of George Sylvester Viereck. Yes, Viereck stood there with a leering expression as if he were silently belching while attempting a sophisticated smile. From the few words they exchanged, Tesla realized that not even Hitler's madness had tempered the poet's love of all things German.

"Viereck embarrasses himself," sighed Sigmund Freud in resignation.

"I knew I was going to see you here!" Viereck said. With a ruthless glance, Viereck handed Tesla the first part of Musil's *The Man without Qualities*.

"Take a look at this!"

Viereck's mouth curved downward as he smiled. "We should get together more often."

Most of the mourners were Agnes's friends. Tesla expressed his condolences to Owen. The former boy was tinged with gray like his father was when Tesla first met him at the Chicago Expo.

"I feel the raindrops on my head," he admitted, which was his charming way of saying that he was going bald.

Even at the cemetery, Owen's wife walked harnessed to the idea of her own beauty. She hated even the dead Katharine. Her absentminded smile said, "They had their own time. We have ours."

The walls of smoke swirled on the paths. The monuments grew

bigger as they approached the center. Watching his every step, Tesla passed by columns and sarcophagi of pink granite. Venerable names were inscribed on small classic temples or pseudo-Byzantine chapels.

They walked behind the coffin covered with deathly garlands. "Flowers are the way the earth laughs," a poet said. *What does it laugh at?* Tesla wondered. He was dizzy. It seemed to him that the breeze of nonexistence—rather than the wind of this world—touched him. The pug-nosed Swezey supported him the whole time. Tesla did not like anyone to touch him, but he could not help it this time. His step, always so light, now barely made sufficient contact with the earth to hold him down.

You're not bound to your body, and one day you'll be able to observe your own skull with modest interest like an object on the table.

Madame Blavatsky told him that.

They passed through otherworldly luxury.

A square mausoleum resembled Morgan's library. It was inscribed: *Robert Underwood Johnson.*

In his mind Tesla saw the marble nose and the heavy mustache that flowed into the beard. He remembered Luka's passionate advice: There's no happiness outside the community of humans.

And his Katharine . . .

Breathless from a sudden burst of laughter, she squeezed her glowing cheeks between her palms. That laughter turned around the Electricity Pavilion once, and all the men attending took a ride on it. Her entire ear fit into Robert's mouth. Robert kissed her on her heart and her stomach when she was pregnant. She used to say that a man and a woman, embracing, created a fortress in the cold universe. She believed in outbursts of emotions like cloudbursts of rain.

There she lay in safety, surrounded by the urns of her four dogs.

Katharine was a sailboat with sails full of wind. Robert was an anchor.

They had what he never had. Because . . .

There's no happiness outside the community of human order!

Something else became clear to Tesla:

There is no happiness within it either . . .

Agnes squeezed his arm and said, "Both Mom and Dad are here.

I'm not afraid of death anymore because now I have some of my own over there."

A chest pain echoed those words. All of it was too much for him. From the outside, he looked as cold as an iguana. His soul—whose existence Buddhists deny—pained him relentlessly.

Birds alight on the same branch only to fly away in opposite directions. Clouds meet and part in the sky. That's the destiny of all earthly things . . .

Swezey gave him a ride to the New Yorker Hotel, which looked like a stocky ziggurat.

He almost carried him to his room.

Tesla forgot to close the door to Suite 3327. The draft slammed it.

The next day, the Do Not Disturb sign appeared on the door.

Dane visited him every night.

His fainting spells never stopped.

CHAPTER 122

The War of the Worlds

*Show to them ... the blinding thunderbolt and they will
never ask you for either the Beauty or the Good.*

La Brier

The musical theme of the Mercury Theatre rang above the clink of
silverware in Tesla's New Yorker Hotel. The announcer's voice said,
"Ladies and gentlemen, the director of the Mercury Theatre and star
of these broadcasts ..."

"We know now that in the early years of the twentieth century this
world was being watched closely by intelligences greater than man's
and yet as mortal as his own," Orson Welles intoned. "We know now
that as human beings busied themselves about their various concerns
they were scrutinized and studied, perhaps almost as narrowly as a
man with a microscope might scrutinize the transient creatures that
swarm and multiply in a drop of water."

Tesla started to show some signs of interest in the broadcast when
the announcer's voice became distinct from the fog: "We now take you
to the Meridian Room in the Hotel Park Plaza in downtown New York,
where you will be entertained by the music of Ramón Raquello and his
orchestra ..."

While Ramón Raquello tried to entertain him, Tesla was told that
there was a phone call waiting for him. Mr. Dučić and Petar Čubrić,
the consul from Gary, Indiana, called from there to tell him that the
news that he agreed to be the patron of the local church was received

with great joy. In raised voices, they read excerpts from the American Srbobran over the phone.

"*Our world-renowned patron greets our world-renowned Gary! This morning,* the Srbobran *received a historical wire from Gary which reads: A great honor has been bestowed on our famous city,*" the bull-like voice bellowed over the phone. "*Our great genius NIKOLA TESLA agreed to be the patron of our Gary temple, which will be consecrated on November 24.*"

"Thank you. Thank you." The patron acknowledged them in a muffled voice.

"But how about this?" Dučić shouted. "*In our opinion, there's no greater genius in the history of mankind, the one who has made the life of ordinary people easier, than Nikola Tesla.*"

To them, everything was crystal clear. Tesla was a Serb, born of a Serbian mother, a Serbian genius who drew his inspiration from his Serbdom, so great Serbian thoughts occurred to him—a Serb!

"Thank you."

"They say that at one point all the factories in America broke down, and you fixed them all. And they say that you spend every night in Lika."

"Thank you. Thank you."

"But how about this . . ."

Tesla went back to the dining hall. As soon as he drew up his chair, the announcer spoke: "Ladies and gentlemen, here is the latest bulletin from the Intercontinental Radio News. Toronto, Canada: Professor Morse . . . reports observing a total of three explosions on the planet Mars. . . . This confirms earlier reports received from American observatories. Now . . . comes a special announcement from Trenton, New Jersey, [where] a huge, flaming object, believed to be a meteorite, fell on a farm in the neighborhood of Grovers Mill.

"We have dispatched a special mobile unit to the scene, and will have our commentator, Carl Phillips, give you a word description as soon as he can reach there from Princeton."

The announcer shook off the burden of concern and sighed in relief: "In the meantime, we take you to the Hotel Martinet in Brooklyn, where Bobby Millette and his orchestra are offering a program of dance music."

The pouting clarinets played swing for only twenty seconds.

A light tenor blared above them: "We take you now to Grovers Mill, New Jersey."

Voices buzzed in the background, and police sirens screamed, as a voice out of breath joined in from New Jersey:

"Ladies and gentlemen, this is Carl Phillips again, at the Wilmuth farm, Grovers Mill, New Jersey. . . . Well, I . . . I hardly know where to begin. . . . Well, I just got here. I haven't had a chance to look around yet," Phillips said. "Yes, I guess that's the . . . thing, directly in front of me, half buried in a vast pit. Must have struck with terrific force. The ground is covered with splinters of a tree it must have struck on its way down. What I can see of the . . . object itself doesn't look very much like a meteor, at least not the meteors I've seen."

Tesla waved to the waiter: "Please, bring it."

The waiter smiled and brought him a silver mug of coffee that the old man sniffed with his eyes closed, but did not drink.

Carl Phillips continued: "Now, ladies and gentlemen, there's something I haven't mentioned in all this excitement, but now it's becoming more distinct. Perhaps you've caught it already on your radio. Listen . . . It's a curious scratching sound. The professor here thinks it comes from the unequal cooling of its surface. But no . . ."

Voices: "She's movin'! Look, the darn thing's unscrewing! . . . It's red hot, they'll burn to a cinder! . . . Keep those idiots back!"

On the radio, a piece of metal rang as it fell.

The competent and tragic voice of Carl Phillips announced: "Ladies and gentlemen, this is the most terrifying thing I have ever witnessed . . . Wait a minute! Someone's crawling out of the hollow top. Someone or . . . something. . . . It might be a face. It might be . . .

"Good heavens, something's wriggling out of the shadow like a gray snake. Now it's another one, and another. They look like tentacles to me. There, I can see the thing's body. It's large, large as a bear and it glistens like wet leather. But that face, it . . . Ladies and gentlemen, it's indescribable. I can hardly force myself to keep looking at it, it's so horrible . . . The crowd falls back now. They've seen plenty. This is the most extraordinary experience. I can't find words . . . I'll pull this microphone with me as I talk. I'll have to stop the description until I can take a new position. Hold on, will you please, I'll be right back in a minute."

The voice faded out into the sound of the piano.

Having been preoccupied with the broadcast, Tesla remembered himself. He smiled and turned around as if he wanted to say: What's going on?

Carl Phillips came back and reported: "A humped shape is rising out of the pit. I can make out a small beam of light against a mirror. There's a jet of flame springing from the mirror, and it leaps right at the advancing men. It strikes them head on! Good Lord, they're turning into flame!"

Screams and unearthly shrieks came from the loudspeaker.

"Now the whole field's caught fire," Carl Phillips wailed.

An explosion cut him short.

Several people shrieked in the dining hall. A woman at the next table covered her mouth with her hands. A man with a small mustache pulled a girl toward the exit.

The sudden silence was interrupted by the announcer: "Ladies and gentlemen, due to circumstances beyond our control, we are unable to continue the broadcast from Grovers Mill."

Tesla gave a slight smile. His infallible memory recognized the text. He smelled the coffee one more time and went to wash his face. He heard the maître d'hôtel whispering to two younger waiters: "One should keep a cool head."

A chubby man ran downstairs, leaving his wife and child behind.

"Gentlemen! Gentlemen!" pleaded the white-haired black receptionist.

There was an indescribable mess around the exit door.

Instead of going out into the street, Tesla returned to the dining hall just in time to hear the metallic voice of General Montgomery Smith.

"I have been requested by the governor of New Jersey to place the counties of Mercer and Middlesex as far west as Princeton, and east to Jamesburg, under martial law."

Fresh as a rose, the announcer cut in: "Ladies and gentlemen, I have a grave announcement to make. Incredible as it may seem, both the observations of science and the evidence of our eyes lead to the

431

inescapable assumption that those strange beings who landed in the Jersey farmlands tonight are the vanguard of an invading army from the planet Mars."

Tesla smiled darkly.

"The battle which took place at Grovers Mill ended in one of the most startling defeats ever suffered by any army in modern times; seven thousand men armed with rifles and machine guns pitted against a single fighting machine of the invaders from Mars. One hundred and twenty known survivors. The rest strewn over the battle area from Grovers Mill to Plainsboro, crushed and trampled to death under the metal feet of the monster, or burned to cinders by its heat ray."

The father of the laser gun laughed loudly at those words.

"The monster is now in control of the middle section of New Jersey and has effectively cut the state through its center. Communication lines are down from Pennsylvania to the Atlantic Ocean. Railroad tracks are torn and service from New York to Philadelphia discontinued. . . . Highways to the north, south, and west are clogged with frantic human traffic. . . .

"Langham Field, Virginia: Scouting planes report three Martian machines visible above treetops, moving north towards Somerville with population fleeing ahead of them. Heat ray not in use; although advancing at express-train speed, invaders pick their way carefully. They seem to be making conscious effort to avoid destruction of cities and countryside. However, they stop to uproot power lines, bridges, and railroad tracks. . . .

"Here is a bulletin from Basking Ridge, New Jersey: Coon hunters have stumbled on a second cylinder similar to the first embedded in the great swamp twenty miles south of Morristown."

Bells were ringing over the city, and then gradually diminished.

The announcer's voice reflected the gravity of the moment: "I'm speaking from the roof of the Broadcasting Building, New York City. The bells you hear are ringing to warn the people to evacuate the city as the Martians . . ."

Someone screamed in the hall. None of the hypnotized rose to their feet.

"Estimated in last two hours three million people have moved out along the roads to the north, Hutchison River Parkway still kept open for motor traffic. Avoid bridges to Long Island . . . hopelessly jammed. All communication with Jersey shore closed ten minutes ago. No more defenses. Our army wiped out . . . artillery, air force, everything wiped out. This may be the last broadcast. We'll stay here to the end."

Over the speakers, voices were singing hymns.

Pandemonium broke out in the streets. The radio kept adding fuel to the fire. "Five mighty Martian machines are outlined above the city," the announcer informed them in a steady voice. The sound of boat whistles was heard in the background.

"Now I look down the harbor. All manner of boats, overloaded with fleeing population, pulling out from docks!" the announcer exclaimed. "Streets are all jammed. Noise in crowds like New Year's Eve in city."

Tesla was soon able to see that all of this was actually happening. At the time when ideologues purposefully used all anomalies of perception, when Chamberlain—who has swallowed a broomstick—and Daladier—looking like a provincial waiter—were photographed in Munich, when the black shaman Hitler bellowed above torchlight parades, at the time when Himmler dreamed of projecting movies on clouds, crowds pulsated with their own rhythms. The same crowds that Ortega y Gasset and Gustave Le Bon wrote about clogged the streets of New York.

Shadows were broken. Faces were thrilled with terror. All the people were the visible pulsations of the invisible fire. People grinned with foxes' and wildcats' faces. The faces turned into masks. The lights of neon signs bounced off them like the lights of bonfires. Some simply lingered, gaping. Others ran with their heads thrown back, dragging children by the arms, and—from the depths of their throats—calling to someone who refused to answer.

It was too late to reassure them:

"This is Orson Welles, ladies and gentlemen, out of character to assure you that *The War of the Worlds* has no further significance than as the holiday offering it was intended to be. The Mercury Theatre's own radio version of dressing up in a sheet and jumping out of a bush and saying Boo! There were no Martians. It's Hallowe'en!"

But madness was contagious. The black dots blotted out the characters. Stuck in the world of fiction, people clogged roads, hid in basements, loaded guns, wrapped their heads with wet towels to protect themselves from the Martian poison gas. Ha! When Tesla talked about Martians, they called him crazy. The world became dark and hallucinatory . . . much more insane than he was.

On the other hand, everything that happened that evening could be found on the pages of Gernsback's *Amazing Stories*. At long last, our lonely hero was united with other people by the same illusion. A tiny excited smile lit up his face. He turned around in disbelief.

He walked on slowly through crippled shadows. That horrible other walked beside him. He did not know whether he heard the wind or police sirens.

In the midst of the carnival, he stumbled upon his bellboy Kerrigan, who grinned like a Cheshire cat.

"Mr. Tesla!" he shouted. "You finally got out of bed!"

CHAPTER 123

The Furies

Thou art holy, Our Lord, who decided that the sun, the moon, and the stars cease from shining and that the earth and everything on it be transformed with fire and that a new sky and a new earth on which justice shall rule appear in their stead . . .

Akathists, Ikos 9

Tesla was reading a play by Aeschylus.

Clytemnestra had just pounced on the slaughtered Agamemnon in order to bathe in his blood when the phone rang and Swezey exclaimed breathlessly, "Germany invaded Poland."

A force older than the gods broke loose, which was constantly at work without ever thinking about what had been done.

Those were not Eumenides.

No!

The Furies breathed down humanity's neck.

In the meantime, a sharp whistle echoed in the park behind the library every night and woke the pigeons up. When Tesla opened his vampire-like coat wide, the wings rustled melodiously. Cooing spilled along the park's paths. He poured seeds on the brim of his bowler hat. A couple of birds alighted on it. With the fluttering wings above his temples, the old man looked like a black Mercury.

So the Poles sent cavalry against tanks . . .

Since the taxi broke his body, the world had been fractured into details.

He did not know when that had begun. Everything was familiar to him. Every moment in time reflected his life.

In Budapest, he put rubber pads under his bed to avoid vibrations. He was a symbolist and a decadent long before Des Esseintes and Baron de Montesquieu. During the feverish two-day-long insomnia in his laboratory, lit with lightning, he was a futurist before Marinetti. The subway beneath the city and the neon signs on the roofs were his work. Orson Welles frightened people with his death ray.

France and England declared war on Germany.

The aged god of thunder promised that his defensive shield between nations—the invisible Maginot Line—would render wars obsolete because no country could be attacked successfully.

Hitler circumvented the Maginot Line and crushed France.

The Stukas howled. The fiery reflections swallowed the Thames and Parliament.

Our hero kept saying that, working in two secret and perhaps imaginary laboratories, he developed the death ray.

"We'll send destructive energy in a ray as thin as a thread, which can penetrate the thickest armor. We'll wipe out an army two hundred miles away."

Thus spoke the fragile old man, light as dandelion fluff, whom a careless passerby could kill with a sneeze.

He communicated with the chiefs of staff of the United States, England, Yugoslavia, and Czechoslovakia. The generals wistfully looked through the window and fidgeted, not knowing whether to take him seriously or not.

Tesla smiled with the thin smile of a mummified cat.

Through the soles of his feet, he felt the purring of the planet, which all creatures imitate.

He felt like a fashion model for the floating world. Chaplin's tramp
Charles resembled him from the time he once dug ditches. Fritz
Lang's Fredersen, the master of Metropolis, was—he. He was
also the mad scientist who used Tesla's coils in the movie about
Frankenstein. The elegance and manners of the impeccably dressed
aristocrat with a widow's peak, played by Bela Lugosi, were his.
Had not he, long before Breton, listened to the geomagnetic pulse of
the earth? Even Hitler sported his mustache.

Everybody and everything reminded him of himself.

Like lovers, the Furies breathed down humanity's neck.

Greece and Norway Fall, headlines screamed. *Denmark Too. Also Belgium.*

"What about Yugoslavia?" they asked him. "What's the situation there?"

Huge demonstrations overthrew the government in Belgrade, which signed a pact with Germany.

"The Yugoslav people found their soul today," Churchill said.

"Thanks so much," Tesla muttered to himself.

German airplanes roared above the burning roofs of Belgrade. Twenty thousand people perished in the flames.

Hitler squashed Yugoslavia.

Blood started flowing.

Each night, Dane came to put his hand on Nikola's head. At times, Nikola was composed. Other times, not so much.

People did and did not believe in the news concerning Jews.

And the news that came from Lika was . . .

. . . Was horrible.

And so, while human hearts were offered as sacrifices to the gods of Progress and Quetzalcoatl, while the divine scribe Thoth weighed hearts against feathers on the scale, while Charon navigated thousands of barges across the dark sky . . .

A local story he had always known was becoming universal. Up
until recently, lofty New York towers competed for the title of the

world's tallest building. In the First Serbian Uprising, the voivod
Stevan Sindjelić defiantly fired at the munitions dump. Thus he
killed all of his men in addition to many Turks. The future Grand
Vizier Hurshid Pasha ordered that the heads of the dead Serbs be
flayed and built into a tower full of gaping smiles. The necrophiliac
wonder, by the name of Ćele-kula, was erected in the vicinity of the
city of Niš in Serbia. In Tesla's never-ending dream, Jewish, Serbian,
Gypsy, Russian, Chinese skull towers rose above one another. Un-
countable bottomless smiles kept falling into the boiling sky.

"The Furies," the first human god of thunder whispered vengefully.
"The Furies!"

In the meantime, Patricia Donnelly from Michigan was Miss America. She wore the first nylon stockings. The movie *The Wizard of Oz* made Baum's boyish fascination with the Chicago World Expo come to life. The grieving lion from the movie looked like Robert Underwood Johnson. The shimmering TV screen showed Roll-Oh— the housekeeping robot.

Then the American fleet at Pearl Harbor was bombed.

"Good Lord, they're turning into flame," Orson Welles could have now reported truthfully.

CHAPTER 124

Continuity

"Uncle Nikola."

No one had called him that in a long time. The maelstrom of the war brought his nephew Sava Kosanović to New York as a member of the Yugoslav Mission. On the phone, he could barely breathe from excitement.

"Shall we see each other?"

"Of course."

The nephew showed up, somewhat redheaded, with glasses, a broad smile, and a blotch of spinach between his teeth. Tesla immediately and instinctively licked his soul. It was a silly soul —go this way, go that way, then go back to the beginning. But in its silliness, the soul was somehow content.

The uncle made up his mind: "Embrace and forget."

They smiled in silence. Tesla looked at him askance. "You look more and more like your late father."

Parakeets tweeted among the palms in the hotel dining room. In the lobby, ashen old men took out their cellos from the mummy boxes and prepared to play. Nikola raised his long finger to call a waiter.

Kosanović had brought several Belgrade newspapers.

"I don't know if you're interested."

"How has the war affected you?" Tesla asked worriedly as he leafed through the newspaper.

"I believe I've gone a little crazy," Kosanović smiled.

That evening, the uncle and the nephew went out together.

They took a walk the next day as well.

And the months that followed.

"I love noise," the uncle said. "That's creation."

The nephew had been to New York before. And yet, he was still not sure whether people in America were bound by gravitation or freely hovered above the streets like birds.

Blacks lit up the streets with their broad smiles. Bow-legged seamen put coins into bar jukeboxes. Ruth Lowe wept, "I'll never smile again." Latinos with dark glasses loitered at the corner barbershops. Music on the radio flowed by itself like falling rain. A blue flag stood in the window if someone from that flat was a soldier. A gold one—if someone had been killed. Wartime chocolate tasted like soap.

Tesla bought a newspaper and saw the sorry state of the one-time proud villas in Newport. Architectural vases fell off the famous Breakers Villa, which he used to visit with Stanford White. The current owner, Baroness László Széchényi, complained about the sad state of affairs. The garden grew wild. In that same newspaper, at the bottom of the page, the king of all Russian, Bulgarian, and Serbian Gypsies, Steve Koslov from the Bowery, stated, "I despise work."

The city was like Moses's burning bush. And everything in the world was interconnected the way insane people believe it is. The scream of neon signs sent messages from the advertising oracles. Hypnotized crowds floated in the squares. The walkers were parts of the larger soul, the *pneuma*. All individual features were rented like carnival masks. A small distortion transformed faces into masks. Love lent value to the masks. A man told a woman in Robert's voice, "You look gorgeous when you yawn."

People vibrated in between the vibrations of the world.

"You're the devil!" came from the crowd.

Another voice responded quickly as if hitting a tennis ball back: "You've listened to gossips."

Slow and draaa-ged ouuuuu-t, words flowed beneath the sounds of the world.

For the third time in his life, Tesla heard the fragments of the forgotten song from the age of the Great Migration of Peoples. In front of a Puerto Rican fruit and vegetable store, a fat man was finishing the old story about the truth: "So do you know what the old hag of Truth told the young man? When you go back to the people and when they ask about me, tell them that I'm young and beautiful."

Tesla remembered how Mr. Delmonico once asked him to play a game of billiards.

"I played billiards in Prague to support myself." He smiled at Kosanović. "Still, I approached the table as if I were seeing it for the first time. I examined the cue as if deliberating whether to smell it or bite it. Then I chalked it and bent over. A whip of hair fell across my eye. As soon as I broke the balls, I knew how to finish the game. Playing flawlessly, I finished it in five minutes without fanfare. Everyone was in awe. Delmonico asked me, How did you do that? I explained to him that mathematical calculations help the scientist solve problems in all life's situations."

Tesla laughed soundlessly and then remained motionless, with his mouth open.

The uncle and his nephew walked through nervous horns, terrified sirens, frightened locomotive whistles.

Thousands of lights shine all around, every color imaginable, stars, reflectors, and rays cross each other, the rumble of over-the-ground and under-the-ground streetcars muffles the noise of crowds so vast the eye can't take them in while I walk beside this great man as if in a dream. I can understand his melancholic, somewhat com-passionate smile which hovers around his mouth. I listen to his soft voice. Gentleness and a strange intensity radiate from him.

With gentleness and a strange intensity, Tesla murmured, "I feel continuity."

What continuity?

Where were the boxers who pummeled each other with their naked fists in fifty rounds? Where was the audience who applauded to gramo-phones? Where were the forgotten towns with tree-lined streets and a cat in each window? Where was the independent and melancholy Gibson Girl? Where were the two hundred feathers of Chief Standing Bear that trembled on the Ferris Wheel?

Where were the bowler hats filled with hemp fibers? Where were Lizzie the Dove and Tender Maggie? Where were the boulevard epics as dramatic as *The Odyssey*? Where were upturned bottles reflected in the stormy mirror of Chick Tricker's Flea Bag and McGurk's Suicide Hall? Where were the star-eyed Hudson Dusters? Where were the minstrels and the ventriloquists, the female opium smokers, the beeswax figures, the learned phrenologists, automatons, Lady Mephistopheles?

"I feel continuity," Tesla repeated, gazing with his wounded and mysterious eyes through the millions of visible shapes of the larvae-like world.

Kosanović did not understand what kind of continuity his uncle felt.

"Dear Sir," Mr. Weilage, the manager of Manhattan Storage, wrote to him. "This is our third warning. If you fail to pay your overdue storage fees, we will put the stored items up for public auction."

Some ten years before, his correspondence and prototypes left the Pennsylvania Hotel and moved to the Manhattan Storage warehouses. Everything was there. Since Tesla ignored the last warning, Weilage announced the sell-off in a local newspaper.

Under Tesla's eyelids, some lunar-infernal mists twirled.

His biographer O'Neill saw the ad by chance, and—for less than three hundred dollars—saved Tesla's entire legacy from perishing.

"Let it go," Tesla addressed humankind which, like a spectral choir, listened to what he would say in his solitude. "If you don't care, why should I?"

CHAPTER 125

The Bard

The spark in the soul that has never touched either time or place
rejects all created things.
Master Eckhart

Kosanović was somewhat annoyed because Tesla thought he knew better than the doctors.

"Well, it's all about me," the uncle explained.

The bewildered nephew wrote his uncle's political speeches.

They talked "about everything."

They often went to the movies together.

In the movie The Cat People, *the painter Irena Dubrovna obsessively sketched the black panther in the zoo. Fears of the supernatural and the unknown afflicted her. Her fiancé, Oliver, showed some interest in a sculpture of an equestrian piercing a cat which she had in her apartment.*

Each time Nikola went to bed at night, Doctor Dane came in and put his hand on his head. "When will you come to me, brother?" he asked with his face beaming. Blindly and lovingly, Tesla whispered back, "I know: you're a demon."

At those words, the room turned into an elevator and started to sink.

"That's King John of Serbia," Irena explained in the movie. *"In the Middle Ages, he used to kill witches who often assumed the shape of a cat. King John was a good king. He drove the Mamluks out of Serbia and liberated his people."*

Light started to rise from Tesla's toes. It splashed his feet, washed over his knees, but then turned abruptly green, like defective match heads. A flood of inner light reached his thighs. All of a sudden, it smelled like sulfur. The old golden sheen flashed beneath Tesla's eyelids, transformed into some kind of lunar-infernal mist.

"That's not a real cat," Irena continued. *"It represents the evil customs my village once practiced. You see, the Mamluks came to Serbia long ago and subjected the population. But, people were good at first and praised God in a truly Christian manner."*

Tesla inquired about his relatives in the old country. He remembered how his father and the Catholic priest Kostrenčić had held hands in front of the Gospić church.

"In Lika, we used to live with Croatian Catholics in complete harmony," he repeated. "There was no hatred whatsoever until high politics sowed it."

But, bit by bit—the people became corrupt. When King John drove the Mamluks out and came to our village, he unearthed horrible things. People bowed to Satan and sang a Mass for him. King John cut some of them down, yet others—the craftiest and the most evil ones—escaped into the mountains. Their curse still haunts the village where I was born . . .

The news that Kosanović brought from "frightful home" was terrifying. "Right now it's hell over there," he said.

Hundreds of thousands of Serbs had been killed in Croatia. Many of his relatives, priests, were slaughtered. The Croatian Nazis, the *ustaše*, burned the house in which he was born.

444

"That's not the Croatian people." Kosanović was holding Tesla's hand. "Those are the fascists—the traitors."

"Sure," Tesla whispered.

"Of course," Kosanović confirmed in a tense voice.

"Do you know where the biblical hell is located in which the souls of the damned burn eternally?" Tesla asked unexpectedly.

"Where?" Kosanović was surprised.

"On the sun. The distance makes it the source of life."

In the Bronze Armor

Kosanović wanted to surprise him.

He brought a real Homeric bard to suite 3321 of the New Yorker Hotel. The bard's face was deeply wrinkled. His eyebrows and Adam's apple stuck out. He introduced himself: "Petar Perunović. The folk *gusle* player."

Nikola explained to him why he lived on the thirteenth floor: "The higher up you live, the fresher and cleaner the air gets, there are no insects, and in the summer it's not as hot and humid as on the lower floors. The street noise and bustle don't bother me here."

They discussed the war. The folk *gusle* player said, "In this world, we're God's sheep. A ram is a ram. But—only one ram is in charge. He wears the bell."

The nephew reminded Tesla that Professor Milman Parry proved that the Homeric tradition was still alive in the Balkans and that he had brought "a ton of sound recordings" from Yugoslavia.

"He also interviewed me!" the mustached Perunović beamed.

From the thirteenth floor, the vista opened onto ziggurats, elevated trains, bridges, and the humming multitudes.

"Take a look at that!" Perunović murmured above New York.

The bard smiled. In the midst of the glass and steel of the 1940s, he did not look out of place. Not having a traditional tripod stool to sit on, he sat on Tesla's sickbed.

"Oooooo," Perunović drawled out through his nose as he tuned his one-string instrument, which ended with the figure of an eagle carved in wood.

"The *gusle* isn't an instrument—it's an anesthetic," Kosanović said in a whisper. "It numbs the doubting body and makes the soul fly to the realm of tales."

"So reality becomes irrelevant?" the aged Don Quixote asked.

"Oooooo," the bard repeated through his nose and outshouted the hum of New York with his monotonous string and trembling voice:

Almighty God, what a great event,
When Milić the standard bearer got married . . .
He couldn't find a girl to match his beauty
A great hero, he found a fault in each of the lasses
And he was about to forsake his marriage . . .

Nikola smiled with the smile of a sly lord in ancient Greece. He felt the bronze armor constrict him. Even his voice had suddenly turned bronze. While the bard sang, he saw what he had not seen in a very long time: The icicles on the roof of Father's house looked like a frozen waterfall. The diamond wind blew over sunlit snow. People's footprints glimmered. The traces of small animals zigzagged. A depression indicated that a field mouse burrowed under the snow, where it was warmer. A deer's hoof was imprinted onto the whiteness as clearly as a stamp.

Dark and forbidden, sacred tools hung in the barn. Fish in the spring stream were like female cousins, while people were the gods' younger brothers.

At one time, *gusle* epics celebrated one piece of bronze clashing with another. Now the whole world resounded with the steel of Midway Island and Stalingrad.

It seemed to Nikola that the same string that played at the world's beginning was still playing. Three thousand years since Homer's time and eight decades since the time of his childhood had not passed. Like Mojo Medić once said—time does not exist.

CHAPTER 126

Ghosts and Pigeons

Sometimes it seemed to Tesla that the New York sky was as dark as the Styx and that Charon's barges ferried thousands across it. At other times, it looked as if the gloomy ferryman did not ferry anyone—Tesla was only reading about it while sitting in Charon's barge in between life and death.

The wind blew away the beams of the spotlights on Times Square.

Naked lovers caressed in a room colored by the pulse of neon lights.

Death ticked in the clock.

Only one throb of the pulse separated him from the kiss of him whom they say is . . . Horrible—seen from afar. Beautiful—seen up close.

One single throb of the pulse.

If muscular tension relaxed for a brief moment, the hole within him would expand beyond his outline, and the creator would dissolve into his own creation. Nikola would vanish into the lights of New York.

Did not Saint Gregory Palamas say that he who participated in God's energy, partly, himself becomes light?

Ever whiter, ever more translucent. With the wind at his back, he felt like a paper kite. He went out for midnight walks.

Like a blind fish, he roamed around Broadway at the hour when one could hear footsteps.

The world was a thorn of light in a sleepless shopwindow.

He shimmered like a ray of light in the mass of trembling iron, glass, and stone.

Who's waiting for me at home? he wondered. *Who's waiting for me?*

Yet, they waited for him.

Old friends, mostly dead.

Ghosts and pigeons.

CHAPTER 127

Pain, Time, and the Importance of All Things Cease to Be

This world is . . . what?
What is the purpose of existence?
Milutin Tesla

When Tesla returned to the New Yorker Hotel from his midnight walk, Dane opened the door for him. "Welcome, brother!" he said.

A young woman curtsied in front of him. White thunderbolts streamed up from her temples. She stood before him, with stitches underneath her chin, straight and insane looking.

He addressed her with tenderness: "Katharine!"

Deaf from her death, Katharine only smiled.

In the newly created light, everything looked ecstatically clear. The world appeared starched and plated with silver. In the mirror, Tesla could see each and every wrinkle on his brow.

Fritz Lowenstein, Koloman Czitó, George Scherff—all his assistants as well as his two secretaries—came out grinning, accompanied by vaudeville music, lifting their knees high.

An emphatic, almost frightening cheerfulness reigned among those present. The small room turned into a fiery opera stage.

From the left and the right, Szigety with a lipstick blotch on his face and Stanford White with a hole in his forehead came to the center of the stage and bowed.

"Look at her! Look at her!" the invisible shouted.

With her breasts bared, holding snakes in her hands, Tara Tiernstein looked like a Cretan goddess.

"Whom do you love?" she asked him in a husky whisper.

The sting of lightning shivered. Just like in King David's psalms, the breath from God's nostrils laid bare the foundation of the world.

The light-footed John Muir and the fairy-eyed Vivekananda made such deep bows that they swept the floor with their hair.

Tesla smelled the fresh electrical air. The animated parquet started to sparkle.

"What's that?" he asked, upset.

"The end of the show," the invisible responded.

"Everyone loves to be forgiven for something," Szigety said, starting to sob.

But why?

A flashbulb went off. In its light, Tesla appeared as white as the ghost of the Swedish Queen Astrid.

With his canine mouth and dead hair, Edison raised his hand toward the uncatchable star and recited, "Pain ceases to be . . ."

A chatter of approval came from the invisible in the background.

Smiling Tannhäuser, Mojo Medić, and Kosta Kulišić materialized before Nikola. They bowed and pointed at each other.

As if in a circus ring, Stevan Prostran rode once around on the back of his hunchbacked father.

Marquis Marconi and his father, Gepetto, smiled in triumph.

The Four Hundred—who could all fit into Lady Astor's salon—flashed their tooth enamel and jewelry. All of those who used to go sailing and spent summers in the Newport castles were there, from Nikki Vanderbilt to John Jacob Astor IV with seaweed in his hair.

The orchestra of the blind started to play the tunes of John Philip Sousa with which the twentieth century commenced. Imperceptibly, their playing turned into a musical avalanche. That was an infernal cancan announcing death. Girls screamed and fell into splits. Scrappy clarinets and pouting trumpets reared up. And—quite inexplicably—an opera choir started to sing: "Celestial spirit, descend upon us, give us glory."

Nikola's skeletal face lit up. He sang with the chorus from *Aida*, like he once had sung with the thunder.

Robert Underwood Johnson and Westinghouse held hands. Knightly visors gleamed above their foreheads.

"Time ceases to be!" they shouted in unison.

"Make room for the boiling nose of John Pierpont Morgan!"

"Don't look at the nose!" wailed Tesla.

The nose looked like fireworks: dandelions made of hissing sparks, red and white stars, a propagation of bangs and smoke.

"It thunders. It will explode," a joyful voice from the studio of the Mercury Theatre was heard. "It turns into flame!"

"Encore! Encore!" the specters shouted.

The choir enthusiastically sang the songs of the ghosts that Mr. Jaubert, the municipal judge in Carcassonne, had collected.

Father Milutin had no legs. His black frock undulated like an octopus. In his moving bass voice he announced, "The importance of All Things ceases to be."

That was almost the end.

Mother's eyes were the center of the whirlpool. "My Niko," she whispered. "One needs to feed the birds for the souls of the dead."

Among the ghosts and pigeons, Tesla looked more fatigued, more exhausted than anyone else. The reader has been worried about him for a long time.

"Encore! Encore!" the invisible audience shouted.

"Take your mask off!"

"Everyone, take your masks off."

"What mask?" He was horrified.

"What do you mean—what mask?"

Like wine enveloping the palate, Szigety's merciful voice nested in his ear: "Everyone loves to be forgiven for something."

The midnight room was Nikola's Crystal, his universe, his cabaret with spirits. Everything became magical and frightfully profound. It also hurt terribly.

He was submerged into the unforgiving power of nature, he was married to a wonder as enormous as death.

That was when Dane touched his shoulder.

A lethargic smile made the brother's face much more beautiful. His hands were blue. His hair was full of icy powder. Mysterious with the mystery of youth, he eagerly asked:

"Do you know the story of the Siamese twins, brother? Their names were Chang and Eng," he explained confidentially. "Chang died first. Eng dragged along his conjoined brother's dead body. The brother's dead blood mixed with his live blood. The heart pumped it into both bodies. Eng dragged along the dead Chang and screamed as he went through the distorted world.

"Do you know the story of the Siamese twins, brother?"

Vladimir Pistalo was born in Sarajevo in 1960. He studied law in Belgrade and Sarajevo and received a PhD in American history from the University of New Hampshire. He is currently a professor of liberal arts at Becker College in Massachusetts where he teaches US and world history. Pistalo's first story came out in a literary magazine when he was eighteen, and his first book was published when he was twenty-one. Since that time, he has published eleven books of fiction, ranging from poetic prose to novels, and his stories have been included in major anthologies of Serbian and Bosnian prose. His novel *Millennium in Belgrade* has been translated into four languages and was a finalist for the Prix Femina, a prize for the best translated novel in France. *Tesla: A Portrait with Masks* won the NIN Literary Award, the most prestigious literary award in Serbia, for best novel in 2008, and has already appeared in ten languages. This is his first book to be translated into English.

The Lannan Translation Series

Funding the translation and publication of
exceptional literary works

The Scattered Papers of Penelope by Katerina Anghelaki-Rooke,
edited and translated from the Greek by Karen Van Dyck

The Last Brother by Nathacha Appanah, translated from the French
by Geoffrey Strachan

The Accordionist's Son by Bernardo Atxaga, translated from the
Spanish by Margaret Jull Costa

The Lovers of Algeria by Anouar Benmalek, translated from the
French by Joanna Kilmartin

The Star of Algiers by Aziz Chouaki, translated from the French
by Ros Schwartz and Lulu Norman

Before I Burn by Gaute Heivoll, translated from the Norwegian by
Don Bartlett

Child Wonder by Roy Jacobsen, translated from the Norwegian
by Don Bartlett with Don Shaw

A House at the Edge of Tears by Vénus Khoury-Ghata, translated
from the French by Marilyn Hacker

Nettles by Vénus Khoury-Ghata, translated from the French by
Marilyn Hacker

She Says by Vénus Khoury-Ghata, translated from the French by
Marilyn Hacker

A Wake for the Living by Radmila Lazic, translated from the Serbian
by Charles Simic

June Fourth Elegies by Liu Xiaobo, translated from the Chinese by Jeffrey Yang

No Shelter by Pura López-Colomé, translated from the Spanish by Forrest Gander

The Life of an Unknown Man by Andreï Makine, translated from the French by Geoffrey Strachan

New European Poets, edited by Wayne Miller and Kevin Prufer

Look There by Agi Mishol, translated from the Hebrew by Lisa Katz

Karate Chop by Dorthe Nors, translated from the Danish by Martin Aitken

I Curse the River of Time by Per Petterson, translated from the Norwegian by Charlotte Barslund with Per Petterson

Out Stealing Horses by Per Petterson, translated from the Norwegian by Anne Born

To Siberia by Per Petterson, translated from the Norwegian by Anne Born

In Times of Fading Light by Eugen Ruge, translated from the German by Anthea Bell

Shyness and Dignity by Dag Solstad, translated from the Norwegian by Sverre Lyngstad

Meanwhile Take My Hand by Kirmen Uribe, translated from the Basque by Elizabeth Macklin

Without an Alphabet, Without a Face by Saadi Youssef, translated from the Arabic by Khaled Mattawa

Book design by Rachel Holscher. Composition by BookMobile Design & Digital Publisher Services, Minneapolis, Minnesota. Manufactured by Edwards Brothers Malloy on acid-free paper.